CU01545389

Rousseau's Lost Children

Also by Gavin McCrea

Mrs Engels
The Sisters Mao
Cells

Rousseau's Lost Children

GAVIN McCREA

JOHN MURRAY

First published in Great Britain in 2026 by John Murray (Publishers)

1

Copyright © Gavin McCrea 2026

The right of Gavin McCrea to be identified as the Author of the Work has been asserted by him in accordance with the Copyright, Designs and Patents Act 1988.

All rights reserved. No part of this publication may be reproduced, stored in a retrieval system, or transmitted, in any form or by any means without the prior written permission of the publisher, nor be otherwise circulated in any form of binding or cover other than that in which it is published and without a similar condition being imposed on the subsequent purchaser.

Walking route maps drawn by Barking Dog Art
based on illustrations by Gavin McCrea.

A CIP catalogue record for this title is available from the British Library

Hardback ISBN 9781529370065
Trade Paperback ISBN 9781529370072
ebook ISBN 9781529370096

Typeset in Minion Pro by Palimpsest Book Production Ltd, Falkirk, Stirlingshire

Printed and bound in Great Britain by Clays Ltd, Elcograf S.p.A.

John Murray policy is to use papers that are natural, renewable and recyclable products and made from wood grown in sustainable forests. The logging and manufacturing processes are expected to conform to the environmental regulations of the country of origin.

Carmelite House
50 Victoria Embankment
London EC4Y 0DZ

www.johnmurraypress.co.uk

John Murray Press, part of Hodder & Stoughton Limited
An Hachette UK company

The authorised representative in the EEA is Hachette Ireland, 8 Castlecourt Centre, Dublin 15, D15 XTP3, Ireland (email: info@hbgi.ie)

For Alexey

Contents

List of Characters	ix
Boundaries – *Gratitude (I)*	1
First Walk – *Happiness*	31
Second Walk – *Indifference*	57
Third Walk – *Pity*	83
Fourth Walk – *Disgust*	103
Fifth Walk – *Fear*	131
Sixth Walk – *Shame*	157
Seventh Walk – *Anger*	191
Eighth Walk – *Guilt*	215
Ninth Walk – *Sorrow*	241
Tenth Walk – *Love*	273
Freedom – *Gratitude (II)*	299
Acknowledgements	321

List of Characters
(In order of appearance)

Walkers
Jean-Jacques Rousseau
Gavin Mulvany

Correspondents
Thérèse Levasseur, companion of Jean-Jacques, Paris
Pedro Souza, husband of Gavin, Dublin
Barbara Digby, agent of Gavin, London
Cyprien Abreo, former friend of Gavin, Paris
Olivia Hayes, editor of Gavin, London
Alan Keogh, colleague of Gavin, Bristol
Mathilde Goudichaud (formerly Abreo), ex-wife of Cyprien, Paris
Jeanne Cloutier and 237 others, scholars of eighteenth-century studies, Paris
Elizabeth Wawrzycka and 304 others, scholars of eighteenth-century studies, Paris
Zoé Chauvin, ex-lover of Cyprien, Paris
Céline Labille, contributor to *Libération*, Rennes
Esmé Ozanne, contributor to *Le Figaro*, Lyon
Anne-Laure Abreo-Goudichaud, daughter of Cyprien and Mathilde, Paris

BOUNDARIES

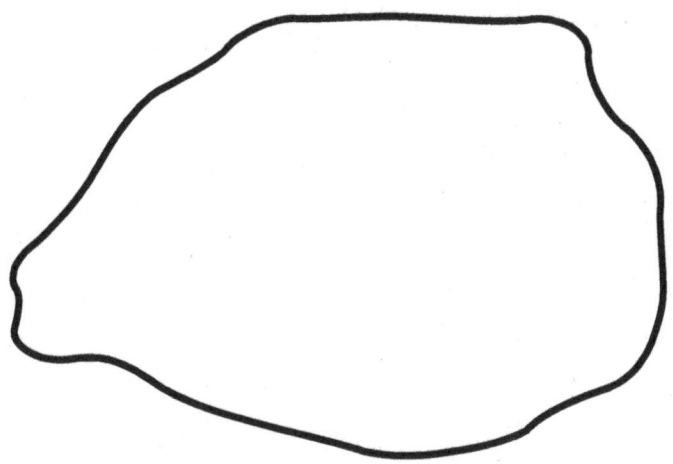

(*Le périphérique de Paris, walking clockwise: porte d'Orléans – porte de Sèvres – porte de Passy – porte de la Muette – porte Maillot – porte d'Asnières – porte de Clichy – porte de Saint-Ouen – porte de la Villette – porte de Bagnolet – porte de Vincennes – porte de Charenton – porte d'Italie – porte d'Orléans; 35 km: 8 hours, 35 minutes*)

Gratitude (1)

Letter 1: JEAN-JACQUES ROUSSEAU
to GAVIN MULVANY

Paris, 30 April 1777

I am extremely concerned, sir, for the disturbances that your proposal will create. I am writing to say that my initial reply to you, in which I agreed to this preposterousness, was a mistake, one which a man of my age ought to know to avoid, and I regret it. I expect to hear nothing more from you on this or any other matter.

Letter 1a: JEAN-JACQUES ROUSSEAU
to GAVIN MULVANY
[Marked 'Postscript']

Your forthrightness startles me. Have I got it right? You, a stranger to me, have begged that you should be allowed to accompany me on my daily walks? With the purpose – entirely without hidden motivations, you say – of observing me in my habitual mode and conversing with me there, getting to know me as I am, as opposed to the public's idea of me? Is this the proposition you dare to call 'not unreasonable'?

Letter 2: JEAN-JACQUES ROUSSEAU
to GAVIN MULVANY

Paris, 1 May 1777

I was still in bed this morning when I heard a loud knocking at my door, which I immediately ordered my housemaid to ignore, for I had a foreboding that the caller would be you. In our stillness, while we waited for the intruder to tire of his pounding and go away, I was struck by how witless I had been even to entertain your scheme. That, on top of that, I should have deigned to lift my pen and send you words, well, that was a step beyond; much more than witlessness, it showed signs of positive delirium, the source of which I discern in two well-intentioned but misleading sentiments. The first of these is the anxiety that I should please an incoming foreigner, be accommodating to him, display to him the better side of myself. The second, much more pernicious, is the hope that I should accidentally find what I have ceased to look for, which is *a man of justice and truth*.

Thus, sir, does the prospect of friendship prey upon the heart of the outcast and cause him such painful agitation.

Now let me set the matter straight. No one in the world knows me, or can know me, except me. Those who presume to interpret my actions and my conduct are in fact more ignorant on the subject than those who do not. I can guess who might have led you to me, and what false promises they made in my name, but there is no point dwelling on any of that; I have given up resisting the plots my enemies cook up for the torture of my sensitive soul. Suffice to inform you directly that I have placed myself in a solitary state, the only one in which man can live happily and well, since it is the most independent of all and devoid of the necessity of harming others. As to friendly attachment, I shall have no more of it with anybody.

Letter 3: JEAN-JACQUES ROUSSEAU to GAVIN MULVANY

Paris, 2 May 1777

I have been comparing your handwriting to that of my other correspondents and picking out the similarities between them. This has left me sceptical of your claim that you are an independent man of letters from the country of Ireland, entirely unconnected with our famous intellectuals here. The turning point, which has impelled me to contact you a final time, came just a moment ago. As I leaned forward to bring my eye nearer to the glass, the better to interrogate the dubious curve of your G, the face of none other than Voltaire reared up in my mind, along with some of the more poisonous missives he has addressed to me in the past, including certain vainglorious phrases that chime closely with yours. In that instant, I was persuaded that, contrary to your avowals, you do have dealings with our crowd of idle geniuses, that you intermingle with them – that indeed you might be Voltaire himself! 'Voltaire?' I said to my housemaid, and she agreed that this was not such an outlandish notion, given our Great Man's well-known penchant for hiding behind masks. The one doubt we had in this regard related to the quality of your prose. Even Voltaire would struggle to mangle the language so successfully.

Letter 4: JEAN-JACQUES ROUSSEAU to GAVIN MULVANY

Paris, 2 May 1777

I suspect, in any case, that what pulls you in this direction is not really me, or the prospect of knowing me, but Paris itself. Travellers always seek out the great cities, which provide a kind of homeland common to all. Perhaps you want to dun me for an introduction to some drawing room or other? Be apprised, sir, that I can facilitate no such immersions into society, and I would advise you to give such places a wide berth. Circles and clubs, what are they but manufacturers of false opinion, slaughterhouses of modesty and virtue, and the cause of a world of unhappiness for all who frequent them. Every year scores of naïve and ambitious men just like you climb over each other to get through their doors; they come to Paris expressly for this purpose, which leads to nothing but their intellectual and moral end. In your shoes, I would detach myself from this horde. Take another path. Stay away from Paris altogether. Better boredom and decency on the peripheries than stimulation and wickedness in civilisation. This is some wisdom I can give you.

Letter 5: GAVIN MULVANY to
JEAN-JACQUES ROUSSEAU

Paris, 3 May 2022

I've been in town for a couple of days and constantly on the go. It's a complicated business to find a place to stay, track down the people whose names I've been given and get stocked up with the necessities, all of which seem to require my attention simultaneously. This morning I moved to a Catholic seminary in the university quarter which lets out its empty rooms to Irish artists and writers for temporary stays. The previous hotel forwarded your letters. The concierge handed them to me in a bundle, together with a fresh bin liner and a little bar of soap which my room was lacking. As I took these things from him and tried to find a safe spot for them among the items in my shopping bags, for I had just returned from the market, laden and in quite a sweat, he mumbled something to me which at first I didn't catch, but which, when I thought about it for a second, sounded a lot like: 'Nothing like receiving a proper letter.'

The snout!

Evidently, on seeing your renowned signature below the seals, he had taken the liberty of peeking inside, perhaps even of perusing the entire contents. When I demanded an explanation, his manner turned predictably hostile. He was adamant – I mean, I had to tell him to keep his voice down – that the letters had arrived to him in this precise condition, with the wax already broken. (Not an entirely unlikely story, as the hotel I'd vacated was a dump, one staffed by a band of identically moue-faced adolescents who took against me the moment they laid eyes on me writing in my notebooks on the patio outside. You should've seen their faces when I asked them the simple favour of sending my post on to this address; it was as if I'd asked them to convey my body in a throne on their backs.) All the same, I wasn't minded to let this man off the hook. His innocence hadn't been proved. With a stern tone – 'There's a lot I could do right now that I'm not going to do' – I gave him to understand as much.

Which is all to say: you ain't wrong about Paris! Nothing, and no one, is to be trusted here. Everyone who comes learns this lesson sooner or later. For my part, I received my education quite some time ago, in my twenties, when, in pursuit of a special friendship – of the very kind you mention – I arrived with the intention of staying for the rest of my life. Instead, in no time, I found myself reduced to a sorry state. Chastened. Humbled. Let down. Lied to. Betrayed. I lasted a year.

I say this by way of reassurance to you. I'm not, nor could ever imagine being, a member of any Parisian club. The entire mass of intellectual life here is unknown to me, and I to it, and I've no wish to change this state of affairs. Truth be told, I haven't been back at all in the twenty years since that failed friendship. I've stayed away as a wounded man does from the site of his accident, for fear of what feelings it'll call up. And it's with great reluctance that I return now. Far from wanting to make a name for myself, or to have my presence felt in some literary scene, I've come with one simple aim in mind, which is to walk with you.

Letter 6: GAVIN MULVANY to THÉRÈSE LEVASSEUR

Paris, 4 May 2022

I've been trying to persuade your companion to come out with me. In my letters to him I've been unable to satisfy him that I am who I say I am. Which is simply an enthusiast who feels indebted to him for the many illuminations his writings have inspired in me, and who'd do anything to accompany him on one of his daily walks. I've heard he leaves at one o'clock each day and turns back only once he reaches the countryside. Taking into account the uneven roads, the design of shoe, his age, I estimate it takes him thirty minutes to cross the city limits in the north, ninety minutes in the east or the west, or two hours in the south. Is it too much to ask that I take from his solitude just a few minutes of this time?

Letter 7: GAVIN MULVANY to PEDRO SOUZA

Paris, 5 May 2022

The seminary smells like old priests: funny how the obvious things can be the most surprising. Initially they put me in a large room on the second floor, what in a proper hotel would be called a 'suite' because it has a separate living space. (Here no sofa, just dark wooden cupboards and a hard bench, in front of which it was easy to imagine a man kneeling, late at night, asking for forgiveness. Perfect for my yoga though. It was in child's pose, with my nose against the carpet, that I came to full cognisance of the odours.) The only problem was, that room gave onto the street, and I don't need to tell you what I'm like about my sleep; there were drunken students and scooters all night, so I asked to be moved.

After much humming and hawing, the administrator, not a priest but definitely embedded in the cult, reassigned me to a tiny room on the top floor. Way at the back, overlooking the courtyard. Much better, I thought. I'll be invisible here. Forgotten about. But, later that evening, on hearing voices outside, I went to the window and saw that directly beneath me was the communal kitchen, outside which was placed a large table where the resident artists and writers, the whole bunch, it seemed, were gathered. As you know, I must have an air current, I can't breathe otherwise, so all night I had to listen to the full volume of their talk, which I kept expecting to end, and then didn't; the most risible dirt, I thought I'd go insane. I've since learned it's a nightly thing. All encouraged to attend. Famous. There goes the peaceful oasis I was promised, I thought. But you can't have everything, isn't that what you say? Compromise etc?

Letter 8: PEDRO SOUZA to GAVIN MULVANY

Dublin, 5 May 2022

So you want to be in touch? You said you intended to use your time in Paris to be alone to think about things, no texts or emails. Have you changed your mind?

Letter 9: GAVIN MULVANY to PEDRO SOUZA

Paris, 5 May 2022

You're putting words in my mouth. Never said no emails. Rather I politely, and not unreasonably, requested that we put a specific subject of discussion, albeit your favourite one, i.e. *adopting children*, on ice until I've finished my research here and written a first draft. Hardly too much to ask?

Note by GAVIN MULVANY

Paris, 6 May 2022

Got in easily enough. Had to wait outside for a while, but then man came, neighbour, who held door. Flat is on either fourth or fifth floor, accounts differ. Neighbour disappeared on second. Climbed to third. Creak of hinges above, woman's face over banister: 'Sir, go no further, he can't receive you.'
   Stairwell dark, squinting to make out features.
   'Madame, does Mr Rousseau live here?'
   'Go away, sir.'
   'Might I speak with him?'
   'What do you want?'
   'To get a response to a letter I wrote to him some days ag –'
   Talking to air. Gone back inside.
   Continued up, found place. Didn't need to knock. Must've been peeping through the hole.

'Are you an author?' Without opening, shouting through.

'Of sorts.'

'He doesn't receive authors.'

'I come as a devotee really. Mr Rousseau is the true author. My own efforts don't –'

'What I mean to say, sir, is that he doesn't speak with people at all. My husband has renounced everything, he has given it all up. He would like nothing more than to help you, but at his age he needs his rest.'

No choice. Tail between legs. Came back fifteen minutes later though. Angry (not showing it). Don't take no this time.

'I've travelled a long away, and those stairs are lethal. Can I bother you for a glass of water at least?'

Inside, a sort of antechamber, kitchen utensils neatly arranged. Smell of soup. Didn't take my jacket. No glass of water. Put wine bottle on table.

Next room. Just two. Actually poor or just a show?

'Come in.' Bit late for that.

Instrument a bit like a piano (look it up – a spinet?). Two little beds, blue cotton covers. Wall hangings. Picture of a forest. Engraving. Chest of drawers. Table. Chairs, three. Desk. Man himself seated, busy. Writing? No, copying music. Didn't look up.

Woman went to chair by window, took up sewing. Linen, it looked like.

Yellow bird in a cage. Sudden burst of song.

'What is it?'

Don't know why. Obviously a canary. No response anyway.

Took a seat, wasn't offered. Potted plants. Didn't ask the type.

Working: glance, draw, glance, draw, glance. High concentration. Dark complexion. Slanting lines, descending. Sagging eyebrows. Recessed eyes. Sadness in the creases. Looked older than sixty-four.

Cleared throat, too loud. Stretched neck to try to see work. Far away but looked beautiful.

Breadcrumbs on the windowsills. Sparrow came to peck.

Shifted round. Thought he might say something. Didn't.

Furious. Could feel face red.

Saw a book, reached for it. Michel de Montaigne. *Essays*. Volume iii. 'On experience': *'No desire is more natural than the desire for knowledge. We assay all the means that can lead us to it. When reason fails us we –'*

'The Mister likes reading.'

That's it. Got up to leave.

Woman smirking. Sat there.

The man himself suddenly found some manners, insisted on bringing me out. Short, only came up to my shoulder. 'One has to behave like this towards people whom one doesn't know very well.'

Letter 10: GAVIN MULVANY to BARBARA DIGBY

Paris, 6 May 2022

Finding it hard to settle, unfort. No further progress on the MS. Having trouble gaining access to that author I need to talk to. His input is key, so hope he'll change his mind. Fear the book as currently envisaged won't be possible without him. Perhaps you might ping Olivia and prep her for changes? Still hoping to deliver soon, just need to start thinking about alternative approaches if things fall through. You also might ask her for another short extension. Sorry sorry sorry. Doing all I can.

Letter 11: JEAN-JACQUES ROUSSEAU to GAVIN MULVANY

Paris, 7 May 1777

Last week, indeed just a couple of days before I received your first letter, I was walking along the new boulevard on my way to study plants on the banks of the Bièvre round Gentilly. As I was approaching Porte d'Enfer, I made a detour to the right and cut through some fields, which brought me up to the Fontainebleau road that runs at a height, parallel to the river. The route was of no significance in itself – but it was not, I noticed, the most direct route to my destination. Why was I going this roundabout way? And why, without even realising it, had I chosen to do so several times in the preceding weeks?

As I walked, I searched myself for the cause of my mysterious actions, and soon hit upon the answer. In a corner of the boulevard, just by the Porte d'Enfer, a woman sets up a stall every day in the summer to sell fruit, rolls and tisane. This woman has a little boy who is very sweet, but a cripple, and he hobbles about on his crutches begging from passers-by. The boy's manner is by no means unpleasant, and over time I struck up a sort of acquaintance with the little fellow. Every time I went past, he came up to me without fail to make me a compliment. 'The sky today matches the colour of the Mister's frock coat,' or 'Where is the lady of such a fine arm?' – that sort of thing. He even took to calling me Mr Rousseau, not impertinently, mind – it was me who had shared my identity with him – but in a manner that caused me to feel much sympathy for him, as a father might.

The first few times I was delighted to see him and gave him a few coins willingly, and I continued doing so for some time with the same pleasure, usually even giving myself the added satisfaction of engaging him in conversation and listening to his chatter. However – and this is what I am writing to tell you – this pleasure gradually became routine. Then it somehow transformed into a duty, which I began to find irksome. What the boy ultimately wanted from our contact was money, and now I felt obliged to give it to him. I was, I could see, caught in a sort of ritual with this boy, a familiar trade, one from which I did not know how to extricate myself without hurting him, or without giving his watching mother an unfavourable picture of my character. For this reason, I felt less inclined to go that way, and in the end I unthinkingly adopted the habit of making a detour to avoid it.

As I walked along the river, thinking on the matter further, I determined that this was not an isolated case. While I know and feel that doing good is the truest happiness that a human heart can enjoy, I have often found my good deeds a burden because of the chain of duties they dragged behind them. Many acts of charity, which I performed with an overflowing heart, gave rise to a succession of continuing obligations which I did not foresee and which it was then impossible to shake off. In such cases, pleasure vanishes, and it becomes intolerable to me to keep giving the same assistance which at first delighted me. My initial favours are, in the eyes of the one who has received them, no more than a promise of more, and with that a freely chosen act of giving is metamorphosed into an indefinite right to anything he might subsequently need. In this way my dearest joys have been transmuted into heavy loads.

The weight of these obligations does not seem overwhelming as long as one lives obscurely, out of the general gaze. But once one has made a kind of name in the world, one becomes the universal provider for all the needy or those who claim to be, not to mention all the tricksters in search of a mug. I have lost count of the number of men who have used the pretext of the great influence they believe me to command to attempt in one way or another to take possession of me.

To be sure, you will say, and will earnestly believe, that you do not want anything from me that I cannot freely give you. But the real and basic motives of our actions are not as clear to us as we suppose. Your real intention, hidden even from yourself, is, I fear, to constrain me, such that any favour that might appear to emanate from my own desires would in fact be carried out in obedience to yours.

MS Extract: from *Rousseau's Lost Children* by GAVIN MULVANY

Last edited: 7 May 2022

In Rousseau's time, Porte d'Enfer was a stretch of road on the Left Bank, south of the Luxembourg Palace gardens, at the southern limits of the city. Previously a barrier in the fortifications surrounding Paris, it was demolished in 1670, along with the rest of the old walls, and replaced by a new boulevard. Just the name remained: 'Hell Gate'.

The demolition of the walls happened fifty years before Rousseau was born. New city fortifications would be built at the end of the eighteenth century, but that was years after Rousseau's death. For the entire span of his life, therefore, Paris remained an open city. When he entered for the first time, in 1731, aged eighteen, it was not by crossing a moat or passing under an arch, but simply by stepping from a field onto a path, or by crossing a road. Likewise, as an older resident fond of daily walks, he was not impeded by any visible barriers from moving into the countryside. At Porte d'Enfer, he went through not an actual but a figurative gate, and the hell that he experienced there – for what he describes in his story about the boy is a kind of hell – was a personal one, fabricated in his own imagination.

Unlike Paris, the Geneva in which Rousseau had been born and raised was enclosed by thick walls and wide moats. It looked and operated like a fortress, its gates locked and guarded every night. On Sundays, it was not uncommon for people, in part to escape the strict religious observances that were otherwise required, to walk into the countryside and stay there until the evening curfew. The adolescent Rousseau, who worked as an apprentice engraver, used to take such excursions with his friends. Twice, however, he failed to make it back before the gates were closed, for which he received beatings from his master. This made him determined to be punctual in the future, to obey the rules, but in the end his unhappiness with his job, his resentment towards his tyrannical boss and his staunch belief in his own specialness were the stronger forces; without his fully realising it, they were driving him to rebellion.

At the age of sixteen, returning from a day in the fields with two friends, he was locked out for the third time – on this occasion not because he was late but because the guard had taken it upon himself to shut the gate half an hour early. What villainy! What injustice! Within sight of the walls, Rousseau heard the horn and doubled his pace. Then the drum started up and he broke into a run. He arrived breathless and sweating, his heart pounding. In the distance he saw soldiers already at their posts. He ran towards them, shouting hoarsely. It was too late. At just twenty paces from the advance guard he saw the drawbridge go up.

Aggrieved, he flung himself down on the embankment and roared into the earth, while his companions laughed light-heartedly at their misfortune. The three of them spent the night outside, staying with farmers who had been kind to them in the past. His friends returned to Geneva in the morning – but Rousseau did not go with them. During the night, lying on straw in a barn, he had decided not to return to his master. In fact he had resolved not to go back through the re-opened gate at all. Instead he would turn around and walk the other way. Geneva had rejected him; now in his turn he was rejecting Geneva.

He wandered around outside the town for several days, staying with peasants he knew, all of whom welcomed him, lodged him and fed him without looking for credit. At any moment he could have returned to the city and begged to resume his half-finished apprenticeship, but his anger kept him away. In his mind, he had no choice but to be a man without a trade and to take his chances in the world. For the next two years he travelled on foot, from Annecy to Turin to Lyon to Lausanne to Neuchâtel, sheltered by wealthy benefactors or in seminaries, or paying his way as a music tutor. In Soleure, shortly before turning nineteen, he was offered a job as tutor to a young gentleman in Paris. He walked the entire way to the capital, all five hundred kilometres, politely declining whenever someone passing in a carriage offered him a lift. The journey took him two weeks.

He entered the city from the south, near Porte d'Enfer. Here the barrier he encountered was not a wall or a moat or a gate, but rather a warren of dirty little streets with ugly dark houses, an air of filth and poverty, and an advance guard of beggars, carters, menders of clothes and pedlars of tisanes and worn hats – people, that is, like the crippled boy and his mother from his story.

The memory of this first impression of Paris stayed with Rousseau. In his final years, lodged in the centre near the Palais-Royal, his awareness of the slums that formed the city's outer layer gave him a secret dislike of living in the capital. Never quite able to acclimatise to the splendour that surrounded him, he felt the need to get out as often as possible, to walk into the countryside, even though he knew that, to do so, he would have to pass through the squalid outskirts, where the memory of his disenchanting arrival would be relived and reinforced, making his return to the glorious centre that evening even more uncomfortable. After each trip, battling with these revivified images of poverty and failure, he would, as a counteractive measure, plan to take more trips into nature, and thus the cycle would continue.

After a while, however, he began to vary his routes. That is, he learned to avoid the places that caused him the most pain. In particular Porte d'Enfer, where a city gate had once stood, and where now, in the gate's place, a crippled boy always asked him to pay a charge, a fee, a tax. Rousseau felt deep sympathy for this boy, he adored him, went as far as fantasising about bringing him home, adopting him – but at the same time he hated the boy, for the sight of him, and especially his demands for money, evoked feelings that were difficult to name, and impossible to bear. Maybe if he could eradicate this boy from his mind – just this little boy! – he would be able to come and go from the city in peace?

But the boy would not leave him. With little effort, indeed without even being conscious of his actions, Rousseau could physically circumvent the boy, but he could not do the same with the pictures of him that were engraved on his mind. In Rousseau's thoughts, the boy would not stop asking him for money. Day and night. Over and over. 'Please, Mr Rousseau, please.' Rousseau gave and gave, made larger and larger offerings, in an effort to generate enough gratitude in the boy to shut him up and keep him away for good. But the boy kept coming back. He was insatiable, famished.

The title of this book, *Rousseau's Lost Children*, refers to the five children that Rousseau, as a young man, famously abandoned at birth. The book will argue that his decision to reject fatherhood and forsake his offspring is key to understanding both his personality and his philosophy. Rousseau's story of the boy at Porte d'Enfer is a case in point. The hard-line position on gratitude that Rousseau arrives at here, which in and of itself hints at an uneasy conscience, assumes its full significance only when we consider Rousseau's past treatment of his own infants. In this light, the boy no longer appears as just a boy. He stands in for the lost five, who, Rousseau implies, should not expect anything from their father. Rather they should wait to receive whatever he willingly chooses to give them. In fact, they should not even wait. They should have no expectations of him at all. Only then will they receive from him something that they can truly be grateful for. And in the meantime, they should be happy for all he has *not* given them, since withholding freely is always better, always kinder, than bestowing under duress.

Letter 12: GAVIN MULVANY to
JEAN-JACQUES ROUSSEAU

Paris, 8 May 2022

With your story about the boy at Porte d'Enfer, are you trying to tell me something about gratitude? As a younger man, I was brought into contact with a fellow, a Parisian, who gave me one or two lessons on this subject. Allow me, please, to relate these to you, before I leave you in peace.

At the time I met this man, whose name was Cyprien Abreo, I was training at the university in Dublin to become a professor in French literature, and was under considerable mental strain, as the deadline for my thesis was fast approaching. Although I'd done a considerable amount of reading related to my topic, I'd yet to convert this groundwork into anything substantial. In a few months' time the examination board was expecting to receive from me three hundred pages of polished argument, but thus far all I'd managed was a rough twenty. To make matters worse, the stipend I'd been awarded by my department at the beginning of my studies was about to run out, and, without a completed thesis, I was in no position to apply for a salaried position to replace it.

My supervisor at the university, a Professor Alan Keogh, was a brash and brilliant man, a bit of a celebrity in Irish academic circles because he had written a book about sexual relations among the religious orders of the *ancien régime* that had once got him onto a panel on Friday-night television. But Alan (as he insisted I call him) was also very busy, with a wife, at least one girlfriend, a lot of children and a social schedule to attend to. Moreover he didn't, by his own admission, feel any great affinity with my chosen area of study, which was Montaigne. (Specifically the essays on fatherhood. Which at first glance appeared an ill fit for me too, given that I had no children of my own.)

I don't mean to suggest that my supervisor was to blame for the poor progress I was making in my work. By any standards, Alan made an unusual amount of time for me, agreeing to meet with me more regularly than stipulated in the guidelines, allowing our meetings to run over the scheduled ninety minutes, and often inviting me to continue our conversation at the pub or over dinner in a restaurant, paid for by him. It must be said that, from time to time, Alan did allocate to me assignments which, strictly speaking, he had sole responsibility for and ought to have completed himself, and which he knew would interfere with my work plan. Out of a sense of loyalty to him, however, I never refused. To tell the truth, the closer my deadline, and the more tension I felt about this, the more willing I seemed to be to take on his extra tasks, and the more grateful he appeared when I agreed to do so.

On a midweek morning in November, Professor Cyprien Abreo arrived at the university to deliver a paper. Alan was available to show the Professor around the campus and take him to lunch, and to give the introductory address at the event itself, but an unspecified clash in his diary, something of great moment that could not be moved, meant he had to leave before the end. It fell to me, therefore, to take the questions from the audience, make the summing-up remarks (the gist of which Alan supplied to me in advance), host the drinks reception afterwards and, if Professor Abreo professed to be hungry, take him for a cheap bite.

Over the following weeks and months I was to form a tight bond with Professor Abreo and eventually move to Paris to be close to him. But that evening in the pizzeria he paid only scant attention to me. Some other students, women, had overheard me inviting him to eat and had hitched themselves to the cart, so to speak, insisting on doing so even when I told them they'd have to pay for themselves. None of them were pretty, though of course they were smart, and, by constantly exaggerating the magnitude of the matters they raised, and by toggling the volume of their own laughter to make it seem as though they were being unceasingly but varyingly funny, they managed to put Professor Abreo into a sort of trance, whereby he couldn't see further than their moving lips and flashing teeth, while I receded completely from his view. It was on account of my frustration about this unforeseen situation that, after the meal, having seen the women off to the night bus, I offered to accompany him on foot to his hotel, which was not far away.

On our solitary walk through the pedestrianised streets around the campus, I was able to talk to him properly at last. The night was quiet, and I was nervous. I didn't want him to find fault with my French, so I limited myself to asking questions, which he answered carefully and at length, without, thankfully, asking many in return. Somehow, I think aided by this imbalance, we managed to find common ground. And, at the door of his hotel, before saying goodnight, almost as an afterthought, he recommended your work to me as a possible alternative to that of Montaigne.

I was, it goes without saying, already aware of your writings and had read your major political discourses. But the Rousseau that Professor Abreo talked about, with considerable enthusiasm, was the Rousseau from the later autobiographical works and from the letters, who was quite different from the Rousseau I'd learned about in my undergraduate lectures, and who I liked the sound of much more. It was cold outside, so I can't imagine we stood talking for more than a couple of minutes, but in that short time Professor Abreo had all but convinced me that, if fatherhood was indeed a concept that absorbed me, I'd be advised to put Montaigne aside and to write about you instead.

It would be inaccurate to say that, after this, Professor Abreo took over as my supervisor. Alan continued to give me his guidance as I worked, with newly discovered vigour, to bring my thesis to completion. But it is undoubtedly true that without Professor Abreo's input, which from the outset was steady and thorough, I wouldn't have written the thesis I did, nor one that was anything like as good. The day after Professor Abreo left for Paris, I sent him a note asking him for some pointers about where to start in my investigation of your work. He responded immediately with a long letter that included a hand-drawn chart detailing various possible avenues of exploration, along with a lovely print of the first cover of your essay on inequality, rolled up in a hard tube. For a long time I looked at that tube without opening it; I just stood there holding it in my hands. Never had I felt so visible, so alive.

Once I had read and re-read your writings in the order that Professor Abreo suggested, I sent him some of the notes I had taken, and he replied with detailed comments. Soon after, I sent him sections of the new thesis itself, and, over the telephone, we went through them, adding, subtracting and amending material. In these exchanges we kept strictly to the subject at hand. Never did we veer into matters of an obvious personal nature. Yet in my perception your words enabled us to open up to each other as friends.

How to be sincere in relation to oneself and others? How to do away with the dead language of ordinary social life and replace it with total transparency? How to express the feeling of existence in its naked state? How to use phrases that illuminate what's hidden within? How to transmit emotions to one's eyes and face? How to choose an interlocutor sensitive enough to take it all in? These were the questions that Professor Abreo drew out of your philosophy and arranged in front of me, there to gleam under the blaze of his intelligence, and profoundly I could relate to them.

You see, the manners of the society in which I'd been raised, the typical modes of communication there, which ought to have been second nature to me, had always confounded me. As hard as I tried to conform to them, I was constantly being misinterpreted – seen as arrogant rather than forthcoming, critical rather than discerning – and as a result I struggled to form lasting bonds. In rebellion, I adopted manners of my own, which dispensed me from the need to fit in, but also accelerated my alienation. If I was separate and alone, I was constantly being told, I had only myself to blame. Yet now you were teaching me that there was nothing wrong with my way of being. According to you, it was worth the trouble to present myself sincerely at all times, and to brook no compromise in this, because even in a society with which I had broken relations, there may be someone – a visitor like Professor Abreo, for instance – capable of understanding me.

When I finished my thesis, much sooner than I could ever have hoped, just a couple of months after the initial deadline, I felt it was my duty to put Professor Abreo's name before Alan's in the acknowledgements, as a reflection of the relative weight of their contributions to the final argument. It wasn't correct, I'm aware of that. I don't know if Alan noticed; he certainly didn't mention it. But Professor Abreo did. In a note full of reproofs – but also heartfelt thanks. 'Falsehood,' he wrote, quoting you, '*is capable of an infinite variety of combinations; but the truth has only one manner of being.*'

I was, to say the least, overjoyed to have acquired this rare intellectual friendship. I couldn't believe my luck. In the face of enormous pressure to change, to be less myself, I'd stayed firm, and this was my reward: a man whom I would know, and who would know me, completely. Nothing less than the ideal. There was no question that I was going to move to Paris and live it out.

At the same time, I didn't fail to notice that I was the driving force in this new alliance. My trips to Paris, which began soon after I submitted the thesis and continued for more than year, until I eventually relocated – these trips didn't come about as a result of any invitations from Professor Abreo; rather they followed from petitions of mine. *Could I? Will he? Might I? Please?* I expected, and always got, a yes. In a letter: yes. On a postcard: yes. On the phone: yes. 'Of course, Gavin, you don't have to ask.' And with each yes, I felt enormous gratitude to this man, this relative stranger, who so easily, with such little fuss, gave me what I wanted.

Except on the rare occasions when I had come into some money, in which case we split the costs of a proper hotel room, I stayed in hostels near Professor Abreo's flat in the eighth arrondissement, booked by Professor Abreo himself. Then, in advance of my more permanent move, he found me a flatshare on a street parallel to his. As an interim solution, while I looked for teaching work at the universities, he sent me students who were willing to pay me for private English lessons.

As you might expect of two friends living in such proximity, we saw a lot of each other. In the evenings, or on my days off, I'd drop into his flat unannounced, which he appeared happy for me to do. We'd drink tea in his study, and play with the dog, and his wife would ask me to stay for dinner. To thank them for this generosity, I offered to give their daughter English lessons for free, so I was regularly there on Saturday mornings when he and his wife were in their dressing gowns and showing no compulsion to change on account of my presence. After these lessons, at my suggestion, Professor Abreo (whom by now I addressed informally using his first name, Cyprien) and I would often take long walks through the city, making sure to cut through one of the cemeteries – Montmartre, Montparnasse, Père Lachaise – where we pronounced the names carved into the stones and imagined alternative lives for ourselves in different eras. To be honest, though, I didn't care to have an alternative life. I was totally content with this one, which, after many long years of famine, had finally begun to share its abundance with me.

You say in your letter that for good deeds to be truly good, they must be free of all obligation. I suppose this is another way of saying that true gratitude can only be felt when a gift is received without the receiver having demanded it. But what Cyprien taught me, and what I'm trying to articulate here, is that there's another side to this question. On the one hand, I was truly grateful for every favour Cyprien granted me, every gift he bestowed. On the other hand, it is also true that, as our association matured, and as his favours and his gifts added up, the gratitude I felt gradually weakened. A person gets used to things. It's hard to admit it, but, at a certain point – probably around the time I started staying in his flat while he was away – I began to take Cyprien's largesse for granted. Bit by bit, my initial transports of appreciation, my gushing exclamations, transformed into dull smiles, which then became routine nods with little emotion attached, except sometimes resentment that I wasn't getting more. As shameful as it sounds, there even came the moment when I started to wonder why I should be the one receiving all the time: ought Cyprien not allow me the chance to give now and then? By simply asking something of me, he could have done this, but he so rarely did.

Which brings me to the core of what I want to say to you. To give a person something and receive ingratitude in return is unquestionably painful, and I understand why in such a situation you might choose to end your giving. But much worse – infinitely so, in my opinion – is to give so much that the receiver forgets how to live without such bounty and then one day, without warning or explanation, to cease this giving. To stop it dead.

This is what Cyprien did to me. On a Monday he was available; on the Tuesday, suddenly, he was hard to reach. Our regular teatime conversations were put on hold, then never resumed. Our walks became a thing of the past. As an excuse for cancelling my lessons to his daughter, he told me that the Irish accent wasn't the ideal one for her English. After that, my texts and calls to him went unanswered. The door of his building remained firmly closed when I buzzed.

So, helpless, like a child dropped off at an unknown gate, I found myself alone and friendless in Paris, trapped in an uncongenial flatshare and unable to find work equal to my qualifications. The hole that this opened up in my life was immense; I was swallowed by it. I couldn't believe that such blackness was possible. Nor did I have any idea about how to get clear of it. Leaving Paris wasn't enough. Getting older neither. Today, two decades later, I still have the mark inside.

Letter 13: GAVIN MULVANY to CYPRIEN ABREO

Paris, 9 May 2022

Online you can see images of the different fortifications that used to surround Paris. One that I've spent a particularly long time looking at superimposes outlines of all the once-existing city walls onto a modern map, so that they form concentric circles of ever-increasing diameter. The tiny Gallo-Roman wall at the centre. Around that, the medieval walls. Around those, the Charles V wall from the fourteenth century, later expanded by Louis XIII in the early seventeenth century, then destroyed by Louis XIV a few decades later, to be replaced by the great boulevards. Around that again, the Wall of the Farmers-General, constructed in the late eighteenth century, then torn down in 1860 and transformed into a second belt of boulevards. And finally, around that, the Thiers wall, built in the 1840s, demolished in the 1920s, making way for today's ring road, *le boulevard périphérique*, which was laid between 1956 and 1973.

Isn't it remarkable, Cyprien, that the various walls of Paris eventually metamorphosed into roads? That what one epoch experienced as a boundary, another experienced as a thoroughfare? But there's a difference, isn't there, between the boulevards that became part of the fabric of the city, and *le périph*, which continues to act as a fortification. *Le périph* performs its defensive function far more effectively, through its noise and its fumes and its speeding metal, than the Thiers wall ever could have with mere bricks and mortar. 'There's only one reason to cross *le périph*,' you said once, 'and that's to go to the airport.' Which I found to be a strange statement coming from a man who'd been born in the suburbs, in 'a place no one has ever heard of called Plaisir'.

Yesterday, from my current lodgings in the fifth arrondissement,

I walked down boulevard Saint-Michel to the fourteenth, and followed the connecting boulevards south, reaching *le périph* on avenue de la porte d'Orléans. The bridge over the ring road had a central island with its core cut out and railings surrounding the resulting void, which enabled me to lean over and look straight down at the cars passing below. The cars I could see through the hole appeared to be going much faster than those approaching the bridge on either side. This is the most interesting thing I can say about porte d'Orléans.

On an impulse I decided to cross the bridge and follow *le périph* on the outside, *extra-muros*, going west, that is clockwise, against the flow of traffic on the road's outer lanes. At porte de Vanves, then at porte de la Plaine, then at porte de Sèvres, I paused for a minute to take in the similarities. The simplicity and clarity of everything. Arrows on the roads. Branding on the buildings. All objects named, all movement directed. Life funnelled. Nothing left to chance. What a bizarre, hermetic little universe. I went to a Supermarché G20 to buy water and chocolate then, because I understood that I was going to walk the entire way round.

In 2004, a motorcyclist called 'Ghost Rider' completed a lap, completely illegally, in nine minutes and fifty-seven seconds. Driving at the upper speed limit of seventy km/h on a clear road, it would take half an hour. Going at the average speed of thirty-five, an hour or more. During congested periods, what, two or three hours? It took me over eight hours, from porte d'Orléans to porte d'Orléans, including stops. Eight hours gives you a lot of time to look. And there was a surprising amount to look at, actually. After a while I began to discern texture and variation in a landscape that at first appeared uniform. I saw wildlife in unlikely places. I crossed paths with other pedestrians at the most inhumane-looking intersections: caught eyes with them under overlapping overpasses, the traffic thundering overhead, and perceived our collective vulnerability. Quite something.

The best thing, though, was that I didn't feel obliged to be especially attentive to my surroundings. Because I was walking in a place that was really a sort of non-place, I felt free to let my thoughts wander. It turns out, Cyprien, that *le périph* is a perfect spot for reverie. Not that you'd ever go and find out for yourself. Definitely not your thing. But that is sort of my point: it felt as if I was doing the walk for you. Taking a step that you never would, so that I could tell you about it. Impress you. To be honest, for the entire expedition, I felt you there by my side. Criticising me, yes: you wouldn't be you if you weren't doing that. But also not; also being nice. When I got home last night, as tired as I was after all the exercise, I couldn't sleep, you were so present.

You don't have to worry. I'm not writing to – well, look, I'm writing to thank you. Do you remember the book on Rousseau that you said I should write? I've finally got round to making a proper start on it, and this time I think I'll actually get to the end.

You probably don't recall. In Paris, during one of our walks, you suggested that I use the material from my PhD as the basis for a book. At the time I dismissed the idea with a show of false modesty, but your words lodged themselves in my mind, there to take up the full expanse of my ambition. On my return to Dublin after my time in Paris, I got a non-specialist lectureship that required me to teach across the different periods of French literature and only allowed me to make cursory dips into Rousseau every now and then. As my academic career chugged along, I published bits and pieces here and there, in which I argued for the sake of arguing and tied myself in knots about questions that in truth didn't engage me, which caused me to feel near permanent dissatisfaction with myself. What saved me from descending into absolute despair was the thought that one day I'd act on your advice and write that Rousseau book.

Every so often, in the breaks between terms, a panic would grip me and I'd rush to a rented cottage in the countryside with a suitcase of tomes, where I'd rack my cranky inner machinery to come up with a book proposal of sufficient glister to wow the great publishers of London. Invariably, though, the results of my labour would fall short and end up in the bin. Pedro – my boyfriend then, today my husband – had a theory. He said what I was attached to was merely the idea of the book, its picture in my imagination, as planted there by you. My inability to write it was, in his analysis, a form of deep resistance whose purpose was to preserve something that existed only in your mind and in mine: my last remaining connection to you. Were I ever to make the book a reality, an object to hold in my hands, it would come home to me, once and for all, that I no longer possessed you as a friend. That no material thing could be an adequate substitute for what we once shared. That you were in the past, gone. And I couldn't admit that.

'What your whole attitude boils down to,' Pedro said to me, 'is fear of commitment.'

Out of pride I argued against this interpretation, but the evidence was stacked against me. I continually put off getting a mortgage because I feared the regular repayments would prevent me from taking unpaid leave in the future to write the book. For ages after it was legalised, I resisted getting married, in case the arrangements got in the way of my notional writing routine. And more recently, when Pedro began to talk about adopting children, I refused point-blank to consider the question until I'd finished a first draft. It came to a head about four years ago, when, one Sunday evening, he came to stand in front of my favourite television series, which at that moment I was enjoying, and served me an ultimatum. I was to make one last stab at writing a proposal. If I secured a publishing contract within six months, he'd hold off on the adoption papers until I'd produced a full manuscript. If not, and if I still refused to put my name on the dotted line, he'd leave me.

Having no reason to doubt his sincerity – he'd never made such a threat before – I journeyed into the countryside a final time and, with an ease that almost alarmed me, rustled something up. *Rousseau's Lost Children*, I called it. An inspection of Rousseau's life and thought through the lens of fatherhood. At base, a philosophical biography of the traditional sort, undaunting to a general audience. Its only claim to novelty: a promise (impossible to keep) to use hitherto unseen historical documents to reconstruct the likely fates of Rousseau's abandoned children.

That did the trick. With a book now under contract, I was riding high, triumphant. Until, that is, the time came to start writing, at which point I entered a new phase of agonising failure. As soon as I sat down at the desk, I found myself blocked. The words wouldn't come. I spent the days procrastinating. I lost faith in what I was doing. Either the proposal I'd sold was a lie, or I wasn't up to it.

The next four years I spent faking progress on the project. Submission dates came and went. The publishers sent increasingly stern emails to my agent. Happily the pandemic gave me a reprieve, but when the university reopened, I went back to skulking between the library and my study at home, painfully aware that I ought to be in Paris, trawling the archives. Many times I was on the verge of returning the advance and bowing out. Indeed, in bed just a few weeks ago, as I reached to turn out the light, I said to Pedro, 'I've had it. I'm not doing this any more. I'll sell all my possessions to pay back the advance.' To which he rolled over, whipped the adoption papers out of the bedside drawer and slapped them onto my chest, saying: 'Time?' I booked a flight on my phone then and there.

Now I'm kicking myself for not coming to Paris sooner. On the very first night in my lodgings here, I had a breakthrough. While unpacking and arranging my folders of notes, I found myself reviewing the draft introduction to *Rousseau's Lost Children*. As I did so, something you once said to me came back to my mind. At dinner at the Ethiopian place near your office – do you still go there? – you gave me a gift of an early edition of *Reveries of the Solitary Walker* and suggested that I should focus my future book on that. The *Reveries*, you said, was Rousseau's best work, his masterpiece. It contained in crystallised form everything of interest Rousseau had written elsewhere. And it was extremely beautiful, besides. What a crime that more people didn't know about it. It was time, you said, for a young scholar like me to open up its wonders to a new generation of readers. 'We need another who is willing to speak.'

On remembering this, something clicked. A boundary gave way to a thoroughfare. I opened my laptop and drew up a new plan for the book. One that I'm confident I can execute, since it accurately reproduces your original vision for it, which you passed on to me that evening, clear and fully formed.

Like the *Reveries*, each chapter will take the form of a walk in Paris. Ten walks, ten directions, ten destinations. I'll start each of these walks at Rousseau's old house and make my way out of the inner city to the countryside, just as Rousseau himself did. Each time I'll exit through a different gate of *le périph*, navigate through the vast expanse of 'the city on the other side' and won't stop until I have reached uninterrupted green – long hikes, of five, six, seven hours. Then, back at the desk, I'll write as accurate an account as possible of the thoughts I'd had while walking, putting these thoughts into dialogue with some of those that Rousseau had while he walked and that he recounts in the *Reveries*.

Do you approve?

The old title, *Rousseau's Lost Children*, I'll keep for the time being. I'll no longer pretend, however, that I can miraculously materialise the identities of Rousseau's abandoned children. Instead, during my walks with him, I'll find out from Rousseau himself what he thinks and how he feels about his abandonment of them, and demand from him some kind of recompense on their behalf. (An explanation? An apology? I don't know.) In this way, I'll be the abandoned one who reappears to confront his abandoner – and who must, in the process, face the question of what is compelling him to return to the source of his pain. Why go there? Will it make him any less lost?

Letter 14: OLIVIA HAYES to BARBARA DIGBY
[Forwarded to GAVIN MULVANY]

London, 10 May 2022

Sorry, just getting to this now. Can we please agree on a final-final deadline for *Rousseau's Lost Children*? Gavin has already missed several. Anything I need to know? As for new approaches, how new is 'new'?

Letter 15: PEDRO SOUZA to GAVIN MULVANY

Dublin, 10 May 2022

Have I ever put limits on you? From the beginning I've encouraged you to do what you love. No one wants you to finish this book more than me. If being in Paris helps you to get the thing over the line at last, I'm all for it.

But Gavin, look at the date. It's exactly twenty years since your last stay there and we both know how that ended. Do you expect me to believe this is a coincidence?

Be straight with me. Are you planning to meet up with that man?

You make your own decisions. I'm past telling you what you should and shouldn't do. All I ask is that before doing anything stupid you take a minute to remember the shocking state you came home in last time, thanks to him. Maybe you've blocked it out? I don't have that luxury because I was the one who nursed you back to health. (Not your family. Not your friends. Me.) Trust me when I say I won't do it again.

Letter 16: GAVIN MULVANY to PEDRO SOUZA

Paris, 10 May 2022

As I've told you a million times, we have 'that man' to thank for bringing us together. But you can relax. He wouldn't agree to see me even if I wanted to (and I don't).

Letter 17: JEAN-JACQUES ROUSSEAU to GAVIN MULVANY

Paris, 11 May 1777

We must meet after all. I feel obliged to return to you the bottle of wine you left at my house. Gifts already? Please retrieve any morning after eleven and before one. Then, once we are on even ground again, with no outstanding business between us, we can have the appropriate goodbye, and you need not darken my door again.

FIRST WALK

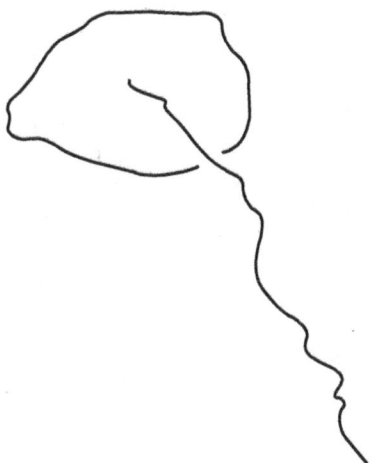

(*To bois de la Grange, walking southeast: rue J.-J. Rousseau – rue Saint-Honoré – quai de Gesvres – quai aux Fleurs – quai de la Tournelle – quai Saint-Bernard – boulevard Périphérique – Ivry-sur-Seine – Choisy-le-Roi – Villeneuve-Saint-Georges – bois de la Grange; 27 km: 6 hours, 20 minutes*)

Happiness

MS Extract: from *Rousseau's Lost Children* by GAVIN MULVANY

Last edited: 12 May 2022

When Rousseau first came to Paris as an eighteen-year-old in 1728, he did not end up staying long; his search for an occupation and an education took him off to other places. But in 1744, now in his thirties, he returned, determined to make a name for himself this time. Already he had lived in France, Switzerland, the duchy of Savoy and Italy, and had been an engraver's apprentice, domestic servant, seminarian, music teacher, interpreter, clerk, tutor and composer of music, all unsuccessfully. There was, frankly, only one profession left for an international wanderer of his background, and with his ambitions: that of philosopher.

In Paris, through a Swiss acquaintance, he was introduced to Denis Diderot, with whom he formed a close friendship. Diderot was a year younger than Rousseau, son of a small-town artisan, and similarly eager to leave a mark on history. Unlike Rousseau, however, Diderot had come to Paris at sixteen to pursue his studies, taking a master's degree at the Sorbonne, and had since transformed himself into an urbane sophisticate; he was now at the heart of the unusual intellectual ferment in the city, the Enlightenment.

Diderot treated his new friend like a younger brother or even a pupil, and at first Rousseau accepted this role. Rousseau attended weekly dinners with Diderot and other intellectuals, from which materialised the project of the *Encyclopédie*: a complete compendium of Enlightenment thought, to which Rousseau would eventually contribute hundreds of articles. Rousseau at this time was cautious, obliging, charming, trustful; everybody liked him. The other men of letters reproached him only for his timid politeness which seemed to them too provincial. However, there were things on Rousseau's mind that, as yet, he was not revealing to them: 'I am so disgusted with society and dealing with men that nothing but a sense of honour keeps me here, and if I were ever to attain the height of my desires, which is to owe nothing to anyone, I won't be seen in Paris twenty-four hours after.'

In 1749, following the publication of a subversive text, Diderot suffered a brief period of detention in the prison at Vincennes, and Rousseau went to see him almost daily. One day, tramping the eight kilometres of dusty road to the prison, Rousseau stopped under a tree to rest. Idly leafing through a copy of a literary magazine he happened to have in his pocket, he came across an announcement for an essay-writing prize, which induced in him an unexpected and overwhelming episode of revelation: 'Suddenly I felt my mind dazzled by a thousand lights. Crowds of vivid ideas presented themselves there with a force that threw me into inexpressible confusion.'

Those ideas which remained after the confusion had lifted, he scribbled down on the spot, before writing them up on his return to Paris. The resulting essay, *Discourse on the Sciences and Arts*, now known simply as his *First Discourse*, won the competition and earned him instant renown. Its central thesis was that the progress of the sciences and the arts in society had led to moral corruption. '[T]he arts, literature, and the sciences . . . stifle in men's breasts that sense of original liberty, for which they seem to have been born; cause them to love their own slavery, and so make of them what is called a civilised people.' Before society emerged, Rousseau argued, people had lived in 'a state of nature', in which they had enjoyed the advantage of being able to see through one another, read one another's emotions, understand one another's motives. This transparency, of which modern people no longer felt the value, had afforded humanity security and contentment, and prevented their having many vices. In the enlightened eighteenth century, by contrast, people did not dare to appear as they really were. They shaped their actions according to how others behaved and thus never knew with whom they were dealing. Truly felt emotions were masked by politeness. In this way, sincere friendship and real esteem were banished from their lives.

The work of all the mainstream Enlightenment thinkers, including Diderot, rested on the presumption that progress in the sciences and the arts had led, and would lead in the future, to more happiness for everyone. Rousseau attacked this view as a prejudice, a delusion, one that confused the cause of a sickness for its cure. Given that the advent of civilisation had robbed humankind of paradise, more civilisation could never be its route back. Whereas his colleagues saw in ever-advancing knowledge the promise of an escape from suffering, Rousseau saw in the same knowledge the very source of their suffering, to which they were blindly rushing. Thus, just as the *Encyclopédie* was about to appear, Rousseau was emerging as a potential traitor to the movement.

Note by JEAN-JACQUES ROUSSEAU
[Acquired by GAVIN MULVANY]

Paris, 13 May 1777

For now I was not going to think about my enemies or their amazing plot. I was going to enjoy my walk. To Ivry, I thought, for I had not been there in a while, and the clematis and the tamarisk would be plentiful there at this time of year. Lately I have been annoyed with myself and feeling not a little guilty for neglecting my herbariums. The justification I have been offering Thérèse, when she is kind enough to inquire, is that I am too tired to go and collect new samples, on account of the late hours I have been keeping since starting the new book, my *Reveries*. But in fact it is a sort of reluctance that has overcome me, for which I have no real excuse.

Carrying only my secateurs and my empty sack, I set off through this city which will forever be the abyss of the human species. On my route down to the river, there was hardly a corner that was not paralysed with rude and desperate people. Only by calling out and otherwise drawing attention to myself was I able to carve a path through the chaos. But I was sorry then, for my actions opened me up to everyone's excess of curiosity. Which, of course, was less curiosity than derision, since most of them had already seen me a hundred times on this road. They stopped to stare with a gaze that had little to do with French urbanity and took great care to point me out to their immediate neighbours, and with their sneering whispers placed me in a unique, almost unbelievable position: a man more alone on rue Saint-Honoré than Robinson on his island.

On the Pont-Neuf, which I reached almost running and damp with perspiration, I was able to steady myself. At my preferred spot, in the fourth bay on the left, behind the bookstall, whose owner, an admirer of mine, lets me squeeze by so that I am away from the bothersome pedlars, I could take a breath, look down at the quays where the children were playing in the water and give myself over to the pleasure of conversing with my soul, since this is the only pleasure that men cannot take away from me.

With whom did I come into contact then, as I parleyed with myself? With whom indeed but a man with no brother, neighbour or friend, nor any company left him but his own. A most sociable and loving man who has, with one accord, been cast out by all the rest.

From the bridge, the fastest way to Ivry is through the Faubourg Saint-Marcel, but I have found that following the banks of the Seine, thereby skirting the popular districts, is more agreeable, by reason of the fresh breeze that comes up the river, and the absence of the alleys and the enclosures into which a man of my age and reputation enters at his peril. Having unhesitatingly crossed to the Left Bank and gained the quai de la Tournelle, it began to sink in, however, that perhaps the healthful route was not, on this day, the safe one. For it left nothing hidden from the eyes of those who, quite suddenly, I felt were observing me.

A flash of something I had seen on the Pont-Neuf returned to me. On coming away from the bay and passing the statue of Henri IV, I had heard a commotion from the area in front of the tooth-puller's stand. Looking back over my shoulder, I had found it hard, with all the pushing and shoving, to make out what was going on, whether it was a brawl or some acrobats' game. I was glad to be well clear of it, though not before the scene had caused in me an outbreak of perturbation. Was that woman smirking at me? Was that man mouthing my name?

Recalling this, my feet stopped dead on the sands of the quay. I was urged by an inner force to check behind me again. After concealing myself behind the bow of a moored boat, I surveyed, this time thoroughly with my eyeglass, what lay in my wake. An instant, and I had picked out a man in the middle distance, at the corner of rue des Grands-Degrés, heading my way with an air of certainty. I had no doubt that this was the same man I had glimpsed through a gap in the mêlée on the bridge but of whom I had taken scant notice in the moment, precisely because, to my eyes, he stood out too much to be a spy.

Had I been wrong? Was this man the sort my enemies would send? An eccentric attire and ungainly gait. A disagreeable and elongated physiognomy. The type who lived alone in washerwomen's rooms on rue de Cordeliers. Pah! He did not frighten me. No beard, no weapon, he was clearly not a watchman or a sergeant. I was not going to run away. Let him follow me as far as Ivry, if that was his mission; I would not prevent it.

All the way through the Faubourg Saint-Victor, I kept my gaze fixed ahead, refusing even to turn my head sideways towards the widening river, or, in the other direction, towards the Royal Gardens and the farmland beyond, though I do own to feeling maddened by not knowing how close or how far behind me the man was. Thus restricted in my vision, and distracted from my usual reveries, I felt the length of my journey more keenly than normal and was quite exhausted by the time I reached the windmill just before the fork in the river, which has always been my marker to part from the bank and push into the meadows.

After a minute, when I was far enough into the green to get the measure of my solitude, I paused and listened for the sounds of the high grasses crunching under the man's shoe and brushing against his legs. In this way I estimated that he was no more than twenty paces behind.

One, two, three, four: here he came. I rotated half-round to confront him. His lips parted to speak. I made to interrupt him, but then, hearing him stumble over his words, I had a pang of agonised regret. For I recalled suddenly who he was. A devotee of mine. A recent caller to my home. A naïve immigrant from the fringes of Europe, unschooled in the ways of society. An ambitious sort but clearly out of his depth.

The hand he reached out to me was mottled and shivering from nerves. The red poppy which I had just picked and was now presenting to him, was, I pointed out, on the verge of losing one of its petals, and needed to be handled with some care. That knocked the strained smile off his face. For until this moment he would have been working on the supposition that I was so unhappy, so consumed with bitterness, as to be incapable of such gestures. I know just how to deal with men like him.

Letter 18: GAVIN MULVANY to JEAN-JACQUES ROUSSEAU

Paris, 14 May 2022

I knew it was you I saw yesterday, running away from me. It was you. I didn't tell you in advance that I was going to drop by, for I took your last letter to be an open invitation – '*Please retrieve your bottle of wine any morning after eleven and before one*' – and I made extra-sure to obey these instructions, timing my arrival for the dot of twelve. In fact, I was just coming up rue de Grenelle – with a bit of a hobble, I have to say, for I banjaxed my knee during an impromptu walk I took a few days ago around the circumference of the city, an expedition about which I'm eager to tell you more – when I caught sight of you leaving rue Plâtrière, then crossing rue Coquillière into rue Sartine. A fortuitous event, I thought. If I could catch up with you and persuade you to join me at the nearest café, you could buy me a glass of wine in return for the bottle, and I wouldn't have to climb all those stairs to your flat!

I cut into rue Mercier to try to meet you as you came round the Corn Exchange, but you were too fast for me; already you were disappearing down rue Varenne. I lost you then for a couple of minutes; even without this injury and in my modern boots, I've been struggling to cope with the mud and the streams of shit and the dead cats everywhere. On rue Saint-Honoré, I was further hindered by the people crammed together and the carriages driving on the wrong side of the road. I almost gave up.

But luck was on my side. Thanks to a parting in the throng caused by a pair of soldiers on horses, I caught sight of you up ahead, at the crossing before Les Halles. Apparently the state of the road there was particularly poor, for some industrious types had placed planks over the running waters and were charging people to cross. Up to this point, I'd been glad to see that your fellow Parisians didn't appear in thrall to your celebrity and were leaving you in peace. Now, witnessing these hucksters link arms to form a chain, then shepherd the crowd aside so that you could walk the plank undisturbed, and then refuse to accept any payment from you on the other side, I was, more than glad, overjoyed to see that you were receiving from them the honour you deserve.

After that you disappeared again, but I surmised, correctly as it turned out, that you'd take the Pont-Neuf across the river. I found you tucked away in one of the alcoves, turned away from the multitude, and arched forward so that you could peer right down over the edge. You had, in the extended moment during which I observed you, a smile on your face.

A natural, wide-open smile that made me smile in turn.

As tempted as I was to go to you and kneel at your feet, so that for a moment, however inadvertently, you'd be smiling down on me, I held back and kept my distance. I confess, however, that I couldn't contain my curiosity about what was making you so happy. So I went to the next alcove and, after checking I wouldn't be spotted by you, leaned over the low wall.

On the sands by the quays, small groups of children – boys, half-naked, fully naked, poor, very poor – were sunbathing. Other groups, wet from the water, were chasing each other around, playing hide-and-seek. And others again were in the dirty water, swimming and splashing around. I turned to look at you in the next alcove once more. The distance between us was too great to make out your eyes, but not to appreciate the full expression of your mouth, which had taken command, of not just your face but your entire form, and from which there emanated shimmering rays of melancholy.

It was Descartes who said: 'Often even a false joy is worth more than a sadness whose cause is true.' Watching you, it occurred to me that perhaps Descartes had got it wrong. It might be truer to say that a sadness whose cause is true, because it can summon from the depths the purest joy, is worth more than all the shallow delights combined.

Letter 19: JEAN-JACQUES ROUSSEAU to GAVIN MULVANY

Paris, 17 May 1777

It is an old saying that the same object seen at a different time, with the eye in a different state, makes a different impression on us. Quite involuntarily, I have been remembering the smile on *your* face as you approached me in the meadow. At that moment, hurried away by my passions, I conceived it as a deceitful grin. But now, as I look back on it, the same smile takes on another, more uncertain guise.

Never has a premeditated lie approached my mind. Never have I lied to my own advantage. But I have often done so out of timidity, to avoid embarrassment. When I am taken by surprise, or am under pressure to give an immediate answer, shame impels me to falseness. In this, do I speak for you also? Is it impertinence to suggest that your smile was a false gesture of this kind? A mask of cheerfulness worn over the trepidation that our encounter was arousing in you? And would it astonish you to learn that I, who should be too old for such feelings, felt the self-same trepidation? Or that your smile, in a rough and imperfect mirror, was that of a friend I had long ago and whom I miss with all my heart?

After you left, I continued to collect plants for a couple of hours, before going back to the riverside to rest. This spot, though it is not far from the city, is free of broad roads suitable for carriages and is little visited by travellers, and therefore fascinating for solitary dreamers who love to drink deeply of the beauty of nature and to meditate in a silence that is unbroken but for the occasional song of birds and the low hum of insects. Sitting on the rough ground, with my swollen feet steeped in the passing water, encircled by flowering shrubs, I began to contemplate, with the same pleasure, a picture of the simplicity that must have prevailed in the earliest times. Was this beating in my breast the sense of original liberty, for which man had been first created? Can you imagine that, once, at the beginning, we did not think to seem as anything other than what we really were? That when we smiled, it was out of happiness? That when other men saw us smile, they knew we were happy?

Letter 20: GAVIN MULVANY to CYPRIEN ABREO

Paris, 20 May 2022

I took my first walk with Jean-Jacques the other day. I accompanied him as far as Ivry, where I helped him to collect some plants. Attached is a photo of a red poppy I picked.

After saying goodbye to Jean-Jacques, I retraced my steps back to the Seine. I then turned right and followed its course south-eastwards, against the flow of water, to the place where it appears to split in two, but where, of course, it is actually being joined by the river Marne. From here, my journey would continue for five more hours. Along the river path, through extensive belts of monotonous port infrastructure. Across a bridge to the town of Villeneuve Saint-Georges, where the industrial landscape gave way to tree-lined streets of red-roofed chalets, and where large groups of people were gathered at the train station and bus stops awaiting passage to the centre. Then due east, past the nineteenth-century fort where the firefighters of Paris are trained. Finally reaching the bois de la Grange, where the green of the countryside begins. But in this letter to you, I want to linger on this spot, at the confluence of the two rivers, and describe the experience I had there – a most unusual occurrence that helped me to understand better some aspects of our relationship.

On the spur of land jutting into the merging waters, rearing out of the dreariness, were several buildings constructed in a kitsch orientalist style. Together these buildings formed, in fact, a simulacrum of the Chinese Imperial Palace in Beijing. At the centre was a red wall mimicking the one that surrounds the Forbidden City; all that was missing were some portraits of Mao. Positioned around this wall was a collection of large concrete structures, each one a pastiche of a wooden water pagoda, complete with stilts, green tiled roofs and gold-coloured eaves. Red letters on one of the roofs announced that this monstrous conglomeration was the 'Galerie Chinagora'.

As I was standing on the riverbank, staring across the water, trying to take in this improbable wonder, out of the blue I felt dazzled by sharp points of light, as though I was going to faint. It was not fear or apprehension overpowering me, but rather a sort of intolerable clarity. Unable to breathe, I crouched down, clutching the low wall for support. Having sprained my knee during my previous walk, and despite the brace I was wearing and the painkillers I'd taken, I was only able to sustain this position for a few seconds, after which I let myself fall to the ground, where I lay stretched out exactly where I'd landed. When I eventually sat up, more than half an hour later, and drew my forearm across my face, I noticed my skin was wet from my tears, without my having felt that I'd spilled any.

By now my heartbeat had slowed and my breathing evened out, but my mind continued to throb with activity, producing thoughts at a rate that was giddy-making. I leaned back against the wall and took a drink from my water bottle, and then, without asking myself what had just happened, or why, I took out my notepad and pencil and began to write. Oh, Cyprien, if I'd been able to capture a quarter of what I saw and felt at the Chinagora, with what ease I'd have written a whole book! The bits and pieces I was able to retain, I'll feebly scatter in my next few letters to you.

Letter 21: GAVIN MULVANY to CYPRIEN ABREO

Paris, 21 May 2022

<u>Smile 1</u>. 17 April 2002. A Wednesday. Six days after I'd moved to Paris permanently. Four days before the presidential election, do you remember?

That evening, we took our first walk. You came on foot to pick me up at my flatshare. You didn't come upstairs, preferring to wait on the street. I was running a bit late since I was making an extra effort with my hair. When I came down, a couple of minutes after the appointed time, I found you already in motion, walking away from the front door towards La Madeleine, thus requiring me to jog to catch up with you.

'Sorry,' I said, but I don't think you heard me; you were already quite deep into a description of the route you wanted our walk to follow.

I'd been expecting a hug from you, and had been hoping,

moreover, that we'd go for dinner and that you'd foot the bill, for I was working on the assumption that you'd want to mark my arrival in the proper manner, by raising a glass, and that you'd also take my tight budget into consideration. But I did my best not to show my disappointment at learning that you'd be stretching only as far as a promenade.

'That sounds great,' I said.

Coco was with you. You'd only just got her, and she wasn't yet used to her new name.

'Saved,' you said, 'from that lame-brain Éric in applied languages,' who'd recently 'and extremely unexpectedly' won an important fellowship and was moving to the United States for two years. 'I'll take her forever, I told him, or I won't take her at all.'

Coco was in that lovely phase just before entering adulthood, when her personality hadn't yet been disciplined out of existence. I thought she was divine. I scratched her ears and kissed her nose and asked a couple of questions about the arrangements at home – 'A big change,' I said – which you answered wearily, as though the practicalities of the matter (the hairs, the furniture, the doggy bags, the consistency of the shit) did not qualify for consideration by a mind as highly tuned as yours.

'My daughter chose the name,' you muttered. And then, sharply changing the subject: 'I thought we'd take a grand tour. To get you acquainted with the place. The Palais-Royal. The Tuileries. Île de la Cité. Finishing at the Panthéon. Then we can take the metro back. What do you say?'

I was young then, only twenty-five, but I'd been coming to Paris on visits for years. I had a good grasp of the location and history of most of the central monuments. Paradoxically, however, now that I was a permanent resident of the city, you treated me like a tourist on a short stay. As we went – stopping and starting according to Coco's inclinations, but otherwise ignoring her – you treated me to a near-constant commentary on the landmarks, the streets, the vistas. Except, of course, yours wasn't the ordinary sort of narration. You'd no intention of imparting the standard anecdotes about Paris, the ones peddled by Australians in cargo shorts and designed to amaze by revealing a hidden complexity that supposedly lies under the streets' homogenous surface. Your aim, rather, was to show just the reverse: that there was no depth to reveal, that everything was false, and that the falseness was plain for all to see.

'Truly,' you said as we headed southwards from my street, past La Madeleine, 'most of it's just a façade. Take a close look at these houses here. Sure, the front looks old and sort of fancy, but hidden behind are modern developments, built just ten or twenty years ago. They keep the front, like a stage set, and knock down everything else. If you took away the skin, what you'd see are blocks of flats no different from those in any city in Europe.'

Did I appear at that time to have illusions about Paris that needed to be stripped away? It was as though you'd forgotten who I was, how much I'd studied, not to mention what we'd accomplished together in my thesis, the rare intellectual partnership we'd established.

'Are you following the election?' I asked – stupidly, I admit, but I urgently needed to change the course of our conversation as my embarrassment about being seen as a tourist had become acute.

'Of course I'm following it,' you said with irritation in your voice.

'Who are you going to vote for?' I said.

You didn't answer, choosing instead to make a dash across the road, in a break between two fast-moving cars, hauling poor Coco after you.

Once I'd caught up with you, I didn't dare to repeat my question. I had returned to hoping that we'd be able to revive the subject later, over dinner, and thereby rekindle the enjoyable to-and-fro of our old bond. Much to my consternation, however, you didn't pick up on my prompts – not even my mournful backward glances at the terraces we passed by – that we should stop for a bite or a drink, as previously we would have done. Instead, passing a bistro full of people, one of the more touristy ones, you mumbled into my ear that I ought to take careful note of the food on the plates.

'You'd get a better meal at Quick,' you said.

Midway through the route, on the Pont-Neuf, we paused. After giving Coco some water and settling her obediently at your side, you leaned your thighs against the eastern wall of the bridge and pressed your scarf to your neck to protect it against the oncoming breeze. I copied both of your gestures, unconsciously – before becoming aware, a second later, of my having mimicked you, and I began to wonder then, while I waited for you to speak, whether you'd noticed. Perhaps sensing the responsibility I was placing on you, and wanting to oppose it, you persisted in saying nothing. The longer your silence, the more uncomfortable I felt. Finally I plucked up the courage to say that the golden light of the street lamps reflected on the water was nice. At which you <u>smiled</u>, and said, 'They might as well be riding the log flume in Disneyland!'

At first offended, then confused, I realised with some relief that you hadn't paid any attention to what I'd said. In reality you weren't sneering at me or my aesthetic judgement, but at the tourist barges that were passing beneath us.

'Poor sods,' you said, as though truly convinced that the people on the boats deserved pity. 'They actually believe they're photographing something old. Something real. Someone ought to tell them the truth.'

'Which would be . . . ?' I said.

'Which would be that not a single brick from the original Pont-Neuf remains. Bit by bit, over the centuries, all its material components have been renewed, more than once.'

The amplified voices of the tour guides on the boats were bouncing off the quay walls and reaching us as weird incantations. Suddenly, tilting your torso over the edge, you shouted down to the boats in English: 'It's new! Just as the name suggests! Totally new!' which greatly amused you, and mortified me, though I impelled myself to chuckle along.

At the end of our itinerary, we sat to rest on a step beneath the Panthéon.

'Feast your eyes on the Enlightenment's biggest sham,' you said, nudging me with your elbow.

On our walk, you'd reserved your fiercest criticism for the examples of neoclassical architecture that we came across – La Madeleine, the Hôtel de la Marine on Place de la Concorde, the east façade of the Louvre – and I recognised with an inner sigh that I was about to get more of the same. My focus was on Coco, whose belly I was strenuously and unremittingly rubbing. But you wanted me to look up, so I did.

'Not content with everything that Greece and Rome gave us the first time round,' you said, 'the Enlightenment chewed it all up and regurgitated it, pediments upon colonnades upon pediments upon colonnades, until they had this colossal eyesore. Everyone loves to laugh at Caesar's Palace in Las Vegas' – at that time, I wonder, did you know of the existence of the Chinagora in Ivry? – 'but the Panthéon is no better.'

The expensive watch on your wrist, at which I was glancing with increasing regularity, told me that I'd now had two hours of this truth-telling, this separating out of what was real and what was not, and I was desperate to make it stop. At last I plucked up the courage to suggest that we move to a small bar that I knew on a quiet street around the corner, where the proximity of other people in an interior space would, I hoped, snap you out of your caustic mood, and we could forget all about façades and falseness, and take up finally the true topic of ourselves. But you said you couldn't, you'd have to go home in a few minutes. 'School night.'

So, for the remainder of our time together, we stayed put, squinting up at the walls of the Panthéon. I couldn't help feeling I'd been tricked.

Letter 22: GAVIN MULVANY to CYPRIEN ABREO

Paris, 23 May 2022

<u>Smile 2</u>. After parting company with you, I began to doubt that I'd ever see you again. In bed that night, unable to sleep, puzzling over your conduct, I had the feeling – a nagging worry that over several restless hours swelled into dread – that I'd made an error in moving to Paris. I was here to start a new life. I'd said goodbye to the second-rate people I'd hung around with in Dublin, and had come to Paris to replace them for good. A second chance at happiness. Would that that moment in which I was racing towards you had lasted forever. For now that I'd reached you, I was beginning to think you weren't who I had thought. As I ran our walk over and over in my mind, the image that rose up most often, charging into my vision with violent force, was your smirk on the bridge: on each appearance it made me more and more furious.

I tossed and turned. I ground my teeth. I clenched my fists and drove them into the pillow. You were nothing but a phoney! A fraud!

The next day, despite the rage that pulsed through me still, I sent my first text to you, to say how much I had enjoyed our walk and meeting Coco, and to ask if you might be free for a coffee soon. Your response, which came promptly, was to invite me to your home the following Friday.

<<A-L AT SCHOOL. M AT WORK. PLACE TO OURSELVES>>

Heart pounding, I kept pressing the buttons on my phone to illuminate the screen and to move the text up and down. I typed in English: 'I look forward to seeing you :) :)', deleted it and rewrote it in French. Then I thought to myself, Eight days. Oh God, eight days? An eternity.

I didn't have any work yet, nor did I have any other friends with whom to fill the time. You said you'd pulled strings to get me into this flatshare, and I was grateful to you for it, though I did wonder if you hadn't designed it as an initiation test for me. One of my two flatmates, an employee of BNP Paribas, ate dinner alone at the same overpriced restaurant on the corner every evening and went to visit his girlfriend in Rennes every weekend. The other, who did marketing for Orange, ate instant noodles and played computer games and watched porn videos in his room at all hours; the explosions and the moans came through my wall in unpredictable, alternating patterns. When I was in the kitchen, making the pasta sauce with tinned tomatoes and tuna that I lived on, I saw them both pass by the open door in their suits, and then again in their tracksuits on the way to and from the gym, and we'd greet each other, but we didn't make much more of an effort than this. We all of us knew I wouldn't be hanging around for long. As soon as I had a salary, I'd be getting the hell out of there. An attic room in Belleville was what I fantasised about, with flea-market furniture and Moroccan cushions that would allow us to sit on the floor and drink tea and read together by the light of the window.

On top of the fridge was a small TV – I'm reminding you of this because you so rarely set foot inside – on which I watched the election coverage and poorly dubbed detective series while I ate. In the mornings, and again in the evenings after dinner, I went to the internet café to check my emails and browse the job listings. At eleven most evenings I got a second wind; my mind raced and my emotions boiled up, and I began arguing with you again in my mind.

'Don't lie here doing this,' I would say to myself. 'Go out. To a bar or a club. Meet someone. Have fun.' But I didn't budge.

On Sunday, election day, I turned on the TV as soon as I got up at midday. I watched the coverage until it ended in the early hours of Monday morning. In the run-up to the results announcement, they kept running a clip of Jean-Marie Le Pen in his campaign office, saying: 'Everyone's in for a big surprise. Just wait and see.' We were being primed by the TV people for what was about to happen:

// CHIRAC: 20% // LE PEN: 17% // JOSPIN: 16% //

'Oh shit!' I said aloud, and typed into my phone, 'Are you watching this?'

I waited in a state of high anxiety for your reply. Like a medieval torture, I switched my attention from the TV screen to my mobile screen, and when eventually the tension got too much, I put on my runners and went to your street. The road was narrow, but, when standing in front of the Chinese restaurant on the opposite side, I could just about see into your sitting room. The main lights were off. A small table lamp near the window gave the room a green hue, while the flickering colours on the visible section of white wall indicated that the TV was on. I walked around the block a few times, passing under your window on each lap, hoping you'd come out on to your balcony and catch sight of me and invite me up. I didn't dare to press your bell. All evening I just kept walking round and round. A demonstration against Le Pen was already taking place at Bastille, and there'd be many more in the days to come. For now, though, our neighbourhood was eerily quiet. If people were feeling anything, they were keeping it inside. At some point after midnight, I saw the lights in your flat were off, and I went home.

On the Friday morning, having received no reply from you, I considered not turning up for our appointment. Even when I was showering and getting ready, I was thinking, I'm not going to go. Even when I was buying éclairs to bring: No way, not a chance.

Your voice sounded on the intercom when I buzzed on the dot of eleven, but it was Mathilde who answered the door to the flat. I tried to hide my surprise.

'Ah, Mathilde,' I said, embracing her, 'you look great.'

I gave her the éclairs. There were only two in the box, so, thinking quickly, I told her they were for you and her. She thanked me and took them into the kitchen, and I followed her there.

'Terrible news, right?' I said.

'Fucking awful.'

On the kitchen table, a half-drunk cup of coffee. A bowl streaked with leftover yogurt. A laptop and two piles of papers. She put the éclairs on the counter and apologised for the mess. At breakfast there had been what she called 'a little crisis', which had delayed Anne-Laure leaving for school.

'I had to stay and sort it out,' Mathilde said, 'so I missed my first meetings. There was no point going in then, so I decided at the last minute to work from home.'

'Ah, I see,' I said, looking around for somewhere to put myself. 'It happens.'

She sat back down, put her glasses on, looked up at me through them. 'He's in the study.'

Crossing the sitting room, I could hear Coco scratching on the study door, then your voice shouting at her to stop. As I entered, she jumped up on me and I got down on the floor to play with her. You were sitting at the desk, a copy of *Libération* spread over your raised thigh.

'Are you going to go to the demo tomorrow?' I said.

'Sure,' you said.

'I might go too.'

'–'

'What went wrong, do you think?'

'Why are you asking me? Tell me what you think.'

I told him that when the vote on the left is so fragmented, all it takes is for the rightists to cohere momentarily behind an extremist, and that extremist will slip through. Often it has happened this way in history. Le Pen wouldn't win in the second round. But by having him as a candidate, a precedent would be set. He'd lose, but not before getting a vast amount of media attention, which would make it far less shocking when he got into the second round again next time.

'He'd never be voted in,' you said.

'Didn't you once tell me that only ignoramuses use the word "never"?'

'Ignoramuses overuse it. As you did in your thesis.'

At that, I turned away from you and dropped down onto my side, so I could get closer to Coco, and gave her my face for licking. I'd stay one more minute, I said to myself. Just long enough to put away my hurt – the most important thing was that you shouldn't detect it – and then I'd leave.

'What was her old name?' I said weakly.

'Hmm?'

'Coco. What was she called before?'

'Oh, Layla. The Arabic for "night". Because she's black, I suppose.'

'I think Layla is a beautiful name.'

'Well, Anne-Laure commands in this house, so the dog responds to Coco now.'

From what looked like an old-fashioned book of matches, you extracted a toothpick and jabbed it into a gap between the bottom lateral incisor and the canine. The effect this produced was a menacing smile.

'Is everything okay with Anne-Laure?' I asked.

You extracted the pick, 'Difficult age,' then resumed, at a different spot on the right side.

You had large teeth, whiter than the average, certainly more so than a coffee-drinker and smoker like you had any right to.

I stood up and brushed the dog hairs off my jumper and jeans.

'Are you going?' he said.

'I probably should.'

'Oh.'

You took a cotton handkerchief from your trouser pocket, unfolded it onto the surface of the desk, then ceremoniously laid the used toothpick on top of it.

I'd planned a speech: *The other night, you were being disingenuous. Your criticisms of Paris are a liberty you take as someone who's completely devoted to the city, who adores it, in all of its artificiality. Who would you be without the falseness of Paris?* But in the moment I ditched all of that, and instead said, quietly, conspiratorially, 'I miss our talks.'

'Your thesis is finished, Dr Mulvany.'

'Ha ha, yes. Thank you. I mean, it's just, the other night, I was annoyed with you –'

'You were?'

'– and I'm sorry about that.'

'Pfft! No need to be. I didn't –'

'I think I misunderstood what you were trying to say.'

'I don't really remember what I was –'

'I thought, well, I thought you were patronising me. But now I see that you were probably just picking up the threads of our conversations about Rousseau. We used to talk a lot about Rousseau's attitude to Paris. About how disgusted he was by the behaviour of people in society here.'

'Sure, but I don't think I was saying anything about Rousseau. Maybe unconsciously.'

'Anyway, sorry again if I came across –'

Coco, who was lying at my feet, raised her head and looked towards the door a few seconds before it opened.

Mathilde now swung in. 'Cyprien, can you do me a favour?'

She put her glasses onto her head and leaned on the door handle while you summoned yourself up and followed her out, closing the door behind you. From the snippets I could hear, I gathered she wanted you to drop off a key at the gallery she worked at. If you did this for her, she would, in return, make lunch and walk the dog.

I took three strides away from the door in preparation for your return.

'I've been called up for a mission,' you said. 'Coming?'

Letter 23: GAVIN MULVANY to CYPRIEN ABREO

Paris, 25 May 2022

<u>Smile 3</u>. At the front door, as we were putting on our coats, Mathilde came out again and gave you a letter – 'Sorry, darling, can you post this as well?' – which you put into an inside pocket.

We took the metro to the gallery, which was in the Marais. Once you'd handed in the key, we had a quick look around. I'd been there before and the collection on view remained largely unchanged, so there was no reason to linger. From there, we walked to the Sorbonne because you said you wanted to pick up a book from your office, and there was something you wanted to show me. The walk took half an hour, during which, much to my pleasure, you engaged me in a conversation about my career. You warned me – in the same breath as encouraging me, as you'd done many times previously – about the difficulties I'd face in finding a teaching position in Paris. But I didn't share your pessimism. I was confident that, with you speaking in my favour on the inside, I'd be given the requisite foot-up, after which I'd do everything in my power to make myself indispensable.

At the department building, you told me to wait downstairs while you grabbed your things. A homemade poster stuck on the wall outside the main door said: 'I'M ASHAMED OF BEING FRENCH.' A minute, and you were back with your satchel slung over your shoulder. I'd already guessed where you were taking me.

'The Museum of the History of Medicine?' I asked.

'Have you been?'

'No. But you have often said we should go together.'

'Ah! Well, here I am, following through on my word.'

You stayed talking to the woman selling the tickets for a while, so I began browsing the exhibits alone. You caught up with me in the eighteenth century, where I was wincing over some cauteries that looked like hammers. At once you drew my attention away from these to an iron speculum used to keep the mouth open for oral surgeries. Histrionically, as a mock-demonstration of how this speculum worked in reality, you used both hands to prise open your mouth as far as it would go, a gesture that exposed your back teeth and your throat to me, and which made your mandibles bulge, allowing me to appreciate, really for the first time, the full size and the apparent strength of your lower jaw. I laughed, and made a similar face, adding a mime of a pair of tongs slowly pulling my tongue out. Which made you laugh in turn.

This, then, was our dance as we made our way around. I'd point and grimace at something horrible, and you'd laugh and point at something that you thought was even more gruesome, and we'd both pull faces at each other and exclaim loudly and then laugh. I went for the obvious things like drills for boring holes in the skull or pincers for extracting kidney stones through the male urinary tract, while you tended to pick out the smaller and less flashy objects

– little bullet removers or forceps or hooks – and you made a special fuss, I noticed, over anything involving the mouth.

Towards the end of our visit, when we'd tired ourselves out and become inured to the brutality of the objects on display, you stood in silence for quite some time in front of a case full of porcelain dentures. I was tempted to make a crude joke about Madame de Pompadour and blowjobs, but, perceiving a new solemnity in your bearing, I thought better of it.

How often, Cyprien, did we find ourselves in this arrangement: shoulder to shoulder, looking out on the world and judging it? Too many times to count. Our reflection in the glass of the display case was attestation of the odd couple we made. Your large nose, stubble, square jawline, thick black hair standing up. My round face, smooth cheeks, snub nose, fine fair hair falling forward.

'Did I ever tell you about my mouth?' you said.

What you said next was, up to that point in my life, the most intimate thing anyone had ever revealed to me.

'I was born with an underbite. Do you know what that means? My bottom teeth used to jut out from under my top ones. Like this.' You tried to show me, but you couldn't move your lower jaw that far forward any more, so you made a moving model with your hands. 'It's not something I tell many people. I had a terrible time at school on account of it. The other boys – oh God, I won't bore you with that. It was bad, that's all I'll say. As soon as I stopped growing at seventeen, I got surgery.'

'Oh?' I said.

'Basically,' you said, 'they split my upper jaw in half and pushed it forward.'

'Yikes, fuck.'

'Yeah, and still my top teeth don't quite reach over the bottom. They rest on top, do you see, so my mouth is never fully closed?'

You widened your lips to a grinning <u>smile</u> and opened and closed your lower jaw, as though biting the air between us. Then you clamped your jaws together to show how your upper incisors sat on top of your lower ones. To my eyes, the whole effect wasn't bad-looking; the unusual angles and volumes saved you from ugliness.

'Didn't you notice?' you said.

I shook my head. 'Only now that you're pointing it out.'

'I demanded the money from my parents for the surgery. A private clinic, you know? Cosmetic. The state would have covered it, it was serious enough. But it was my face, you know, I wanted the best. Of course, my father exploded when I asked him for the money. "You little twerp! The best surgeons work in the public hospitals! Only crazy millionaires go to private quacks!" Today I know he was right, but back then I wasn't having it. We had many terrible fights. But in the end, would you believe, he gave in, but only as a loan.' You knocked on the glass with the knuckle of your index finger, as though to get the attention of the dentures inside; as though to stop them grinning at you. 'He made me take part-time jobs all through university to pay him back.'

I was at a loss about how to react to all of this, except to say, 'I'm sorry.'

To which, again, you bared your teeth. 'What on earth are you sorry for?'

Letter 24: GAVIN MULVANY to CYPRIEN ABREO

Paris, 26 May 2022

<u>Smile 4.</u> Back at the flat, Mathilde had moved her work things onto the sideboard and set the table for lunch: a shop-bought quiche, salad and bread.

'You took your time,' she said.

'We went to the Museum of Medicine,' you said.

'Oh, I hate that place.'

She hadn't waited. A slice was missing from the quiche and only two settings remained. She left the room, only to come back a minute later with her runners on and Coco's lead around her neck.

'All good at the gallery?'

Your mouth was full of food. 'Uh-huh.'

'Did you post that letter?'

You took a gulp of water and swallowed. Then you said, without a flinch or the hint of a smirk, despite those teeth of yours which I now perceived to be permanently bursting out, 'Gavin posted it when I was up in the office. Did you get a receipt, Gavin?'

For a second I concentrated hard on my food, feeling deeply the shame that had seemed to pass you by. Then I lifted my eyes and met yours, which appeared dead in the water, not even a shimmer on their surface.

'I sent it normal post, Mathilde,' I said, turning to her with hot cheeks and possibly the sincerest tone I'd ever mustered. 'So no receipt. They said it would arrive on Monday. Tuesday at the latest.'

By rights, I should have been feeling the thrill of complicity. The pride at having been chosen to enter your secret society. Such acceptance was exactly what I'd desired from you. But for this? It was just a letter. The post office was still open. You could easily have said you forgot. You could have gone and posted it then.

I ate quickly, stood up before you were finished and put my plate in the sink. I wanted to be gone before Mathilde got back from walking Coco.

You saw me out. As I was fumbling with the lock on the door, you went to the cupboard to retrieve the letter from your coat. Now, it seemed, you were going to make me responsible for the untruths I'd created solely to hide yours; now you were going to try to make me believe that all I had to do to soften your heart, all I had to do to make you happy, was to lie for you.

At last I figured out the latch and rushed out. I pressed the button for the lift three or four times. You came out as the doors were opening and I was getting in. Standing in the way of the sensor, which caused the doors to keep shuddering in and out of their cavities, you folded the letter and pushed it into the front pocket of my jeans, reaching your fingers right down so that they glanced off my penis. Then you stepped back, allowing the doors to close. My only consolation, as I watched the closing doors wipe your smile out of existence, was that you, looking back, couldn't see the sick, animal excitement I was feeling. As far as I could tell, you weren't even looking at me but at the mirror behind me, practising your deception on yourself.

SECOND WALK

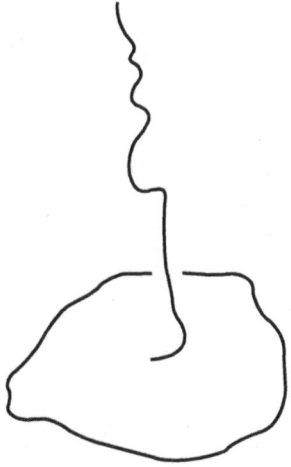

(*To Montmorency, walking north: rue J.-J. Rousseau – rue du Faubourg-Poissonnière – boulevard Ornano – boulevard Périphérique – Saint-Ouen – Saint-Denis – Épinay-sur-Seine – Montmorency; 17 km: 4 hours, 25 minutes*)

Indifference

Letter 25: GAVIN MULVANY to PEDRO SOUZA

Paris, 1 June 2022

My circadian clock is all over the place. In the evenings after my long walks, I go to bed while it's still light outside and sleep ten or twelve hours straight. But on the other days, which I spend tied to my little desk, fighting off wave after wave of tiredness, I end up working late into the night to make up for my lack of productivity. To make matters worse, the dinner parties in the courtyard are increasingly raucous, as the residents get better acquainted and lose their misgivings about getting drunk in front of each other.

This evening, the war came up. And would have dropped away again, in happy consensus, had not a man, a musician I'd bumped into a couple times around the place – a fiddle player of all things, his voice box turned to gravel from the smokes – expressed a late opinion on the question of sending arms: he was firmly opposed. Thus revived, the debate went on for another half an hour, the volume gradually rising, until someone lost their temper and accused the fiddle player of being uncaring. Something like: 'You call it pacifism, but really it's indifference!'

I was struck by this because I'd been interrogating myself, as I listened, about why I was showing so much interest in what the people in the courtyard were saying. What was stopping me from putting on my headphones and getting on with my work? For what reason was I plugging in to these strangers' feelings about the war? And why did their feelings about the war seem to carry more weight in my mind than the war itself, which I'd stopped reading about weeks ago?

Irate, and with no sign of the party outside winding down, I gathered up my papers, my laptop and the table lamp, and took them to my secret retreat-within-a-retreat: a little kitchen that I've located across the courtyard, on the other side of the chapel, through the back door – visible only to those in great need – of an admin building. I'm writing to you from there now. It's a bit spooky, I have to say. While there's every indication that the room is cleaned on a regular basis, I've never seen anyone else use it. The watchman drops in at around three and tells me, sweetly, not to stay here for much longer and to take all my belongings with me when I leave. I look forward to his appearance. The softness of his manner gives me a warm feeling in my chest. I picture his wife serving him his breakfast when he gets in from his shift, and him taking it without feeling the need to thank her, for he knows that she knows that he's grateful. Then at seven the guy who takes over from him, the regular concierge, comes in and gruffly orders me back to my own kitchen. He says that the security code on the door will be changed that day – which is a lie; the code always stays the same. Yesterday when he came, I decided to challenge him on this by saying that the code on this door is the same as the code on all the internal doors, and that I hope it *is* changed because it wouldn't take a genius to figure out 1789#.

Which seemed to amuse him, for a split second.

So I followed that up with, 'Are you from Paris?'

'Saint-Denis.'

'Oh, that's a coincidence' – I was, I admit, trying to butter him up, for I wanted to be able to continue to come here – 'I'm planning a walk that'll take me right through Saint-Denis.'

'You can catch the RER.'

'Well, it's for a project, you see. The point is that I walk.'

'Saint-Denis is just a place people live. What're you expecting to find there?'

'I don't know, you tell me. Is there anything I should look out for?'

'There's the basilica.'

'I meant something I wouldn't have heard of.'

'Hmm.' He kept up a deep hum while he ran the back of his index finger under his nose several times. 'Have you heard of poor people?'

MS Extract: from *Rousseau's Lost Children* by GAVIN MULVANY

Last edited: 1 June 2022

The poverty in eighteenth-century Paris was appalling and omnipresent. Of a population of approximately six hundred thousand, one third was regarded as poor by the standards of the time, but this proportion could rise sharply in times of dearth. A member of the popular classes needed a daily job with a sufficient salary in order to stay out of dire straits. Those intermittently unemployed, not to mention those incapacitated by age, illness, accident or family failure, could expect to live in penury or close to it. Many had to scrounge to survive.

Begging was punished in the severest manner, even though official efforts to provide alternative modes of assistance were virtually nil. Statutory decrees exhorted workers, merchants and servants not to offer the poor protection of any kind. The Hôtel-Dieu, the main hospital of Paris that functioned de facto as a poorhouse, was in a scandalous state, with each of its filthy beds shared by several bodies, often both dead and alive. Those unfortunate enough to be confined to its wards did not expect to come back out.

The presence of an increasing multitude of homeless drifters, while grudgingly accepted under normal conditions, became intolerable to many Parisians during periods of shortage. At these times, the sight of desperate figures congregating in squares and on the embankments provoked widespread anxiety and disapproval. Since the Middle Ages an impressive arsenal of repressive measures to deal with the poor had been at the authorities' disposal. In the eighteenth century, new powers were added to these, which allowed the police to clear the offending people from the streets by charging and imprisoning them, putting them to compulsory work or even transporting them to the American colonies.

In 1747–8, there was a famine in some of the grain-growing areas of France and a resultant influx into the capital of famished immigrants, sparking rumours of imminent scarcity in the city too. The perception among Parisians was one of mounting insecurity. In 1749 the crown issued an edict commanding that 'all beggars and vagrants found in the streets of Paris, be they in churches or at church doors, in the countryside or surrounding districts of the capital, of whatever age or sex, be arrested and taken to prison, there to be detained for as long as shall be deemed necessary'. The lieutenant of police would pay his constables by the number of arrests they made.

This period, the 1740s, was when the immigrant Rousseau properly established himself in Paris. In 1742, soon after grain shortages, he had come hoping for a career as a musician. On his return a year later, with anxiety about scarcity in the capital growing, he gained entry into the circle of Enlightenment intellectuals. In 1747, with famine striking in the countryside, he was composing an operatic ballet. In 1749, when the police were rounding up vagrants en masse, he was writing articles on music for the *Encyclopédie*, and the following year he published the *First Discourse*.

In view of his upbringing, there was every possibility that Rousseau himself could have ended up as one of Paris's poor. If it is not right to call his family failed, it is undeniable that it underwent a slow dissolution. First his mother died. Then his father got into hot water with the law and fled Geneva without his two sons. Rousseau's elder brother, François, instead of offering Jean-Jacques fraternal protection, chose a life of libertinage, was admitted to a house of correction and then disappeared altogether. This gradual decomposition of familial bonds impelled the young Rousseau to move further and further from the fold, towards ever-greater insecurity, and to seek, at a still-tender age, a separate system of support for himself elsewhere.

The circle of the Parisian Enlightenment that received Rousseau was in principle open to fresh talent from any background. In practice, the career of philosopher required significant capital to launch and sustain. A man of letters could not hope to strike it rich with a bestseller, because the publishers did not pay royalties and the scale of piracy precluded significant earnings from sales. Instead he had printed a certain number of copies of the book, which he peddled around town, hoping to gain admirers, build some prestige and catch the eye of a patron.

Most of Rousseau's circle were, like him, 'stateless men'. Hacks who drifted from job to job. Floaters in the intellectual trades of journalism, tutoring, playwriting and library administration. These men relied for their current or future success on the income from a sinecure procured for them by a protector. Getting a protector required knowing the right people. Then getting a sinecure involved the protector pulling the right strings on your behalf. More than anything, it meant writing a lot of letters. Here a hint. Here a plea. Here an account of the writer's rising reputation. Here a well-timed reminder of the secondary immortality that would be bestowed upon anyone whose name was linked with his. It was, in other words, a very polite, very private form of begging.

Some Enlightenment philosophers coped better than others with this constant, unremitting quest for protection. 'I have seen so many men of letters who are poor and held in contempt, but I long ago decided I ought not to increase their number.' Thus spoke Voltaire, who accordingly developed a peculiar expertise in seeking out and profiting from men and women of high rank. Frederick of Prussia and Madame de Pompadour were only the most exalted of his protectors. A host of marquises, dukes and duchesses, viscounts and marshals showered him with gifts and pensions, which he received without compunction, and with which he made canny investments on the stock market that amassed him an unbelievable fortune.

Rousseau, by contrast, had a characteristically ambivalent attitude to the system. On the one hand, he accepted lodgings from numerous wealthy admirers. He was, at various points, the contented occupier of castles, country mansions and lakeside cottages. He regarded these arrangements as relatively impersonal and usually insisted on paying rent of some kind, however nominal. On the other hand, he was fanatical about refusing gifts that in his eyes were traps set against his independence. For instance, when a noblewoman called Louise d'Épinay invited him to live in one of her country homes north of Paris, which she renovated especially for him, he was flattered and welcomed the opportunity to leave the city. But when she subsequently offered him a pension of a thousand livres, he was insulted: 'How badly you understand your own interest in wanting to turn a friend into a valet!'

It is perhaps no surprise then that Rousseau, in his follow-up to his *First Discourse*, took on the subject of inequality, nor that there is in this text a marked ambivalence to poverty and wealth, freedom and servitude. *Discourse on Inequality* (or the *Second Discourse*), published in 1755, does not offer observations of any kind on the living conditions of the popular classes, or indeed the affluent, in contemporary France. The *Discourse* has nothing to say about the specific social structures that underpinned the disparities of fortune in that time and place, and fails to give any suggestions as to what might be done to mitigate them. Instead the text sets out to describe the deep psychological changes that must have taken place in primitive man to cause all subsequent inequality in human societies. To this end, it travels back to the very beginning of history, to a time when fixed human communities did not yet exist. Living in a putative 'state of nature', man was both devoid of civilisation and entirely happy, since his body was healthy and his heart at peace. He was neither warlike nor sociable, but solitary, self-sufficient. Lacking self-consciousness, he lived in the immediate, was at one with the rest of nature, and was unable to compare himself to others. Equality reigned without his even knowing what equality was.

At some point, however, self-awareness appeared, and man began to perceive the differences between things. He discovered that he was separate from other men and soon wanted to be superior to them. To achieve this, he believed he had to be selfish, to accumulate possessions. Indifferent to his true inner needs, he invented new desires that he was unable to satisfy immediately, on his own. Thus he was obliged to take an interest in other men as a means of providing for himself. Both the opinion and the labour of others became indispensable: 'Man must now, therefore, have been perpetually employed in getting others to interest themselves in his lot.'

Over time, this process permanently implanted relations of domination and servitude into society. But, according to the *Second Discourse*, those occupying high social positions are no less enslaved than their servants, since they too depend on others to meet their own needs. 'All ran headlong for their chains in the belief that they were securing their liberty.' The *Discourse* is unwilling to grant that, either morally or emotionally, the rich are any better off, or suffer any less, than the poor. In civilisation, everyone, from top to bottom, finds themselves living in equality – an equality of oppression and non-existence.

Such a thesis was radical for its time. Other Enlightenment

thinkers who tackled the same subject tended to find justification for social inequality in the natural order or in providence. Rousseau was upending common sense by telling the rich that they were also victims in an unjust regime, and the poor that their subordinate position was not God-given. Yet, in reality, when given the chance to choose between being a famous man of means and an obscure pauper, Rousseau was not indifferent; he had a preference. The *Second Discourse* represented an attempt on his part to stand out and apart from the crowd. Likewise, it was an effort to escape material precarity in a highly inequitable society. And on both counts it succeeded. Although not a sensation like the *First Discourse*, it confirmed Rousseau's originality as a thinker among the literati. His passage to pre-eminence was assured. Now a wealthy protector would be easy to come by. Although still trapped in an oppressive system, he would no longer be a beggar.

Letter 26: GAVIN MULVANY to PEDRO SOUZA

Paris, 3 June 2022

I've just been going over some of my research. I keep a folder dedicated to the subject of the emotions, into which I've been throwing anything relevant that I come across. Journal articles. Conference papers. Book chapters. Whole books. Psychology. Biology. Neuroscience. Social science. In a word, the sciences. Most of which don't come across as particularly scientific to me. The cohorts used are small, the parameters wonky, the methods dubious. Both the starting points and the conclusions seem to rest on an edifice of unquestioned assumptions. All the same, I do find the larger ideas that the authors are tinkering with – like, can we ever hope to identify and express accurately our own emotions? and how can we truly know what other people are feeling? – to be useful in some way I can't quite grasp yet.

Predictably, the scientists have divided themselves into two camps. On one side there are those who adhere to the view that emotions are built-in from birth. This crowd conceives of emotions as distinct, recognisable phenomena inside us. Emotions, they say, come on quickly and automatically in response to things that happen in the world and are broadcast outwards from our body by way of characteristic expressions and gestures. Our voices, our bodies and especially our faces hold the key to assessing emotions objectively and accurately. Each emotion is displayed as a particular pattern of movements. When we are happy, we smile; when we are angry, we furrow our brow. For scientists in this camp, it should be possible, in normal circumstances, to be able to tell from a person's facial movements, bodily gestures and verbal expressions their true emotional state. To prove this, they visit tribes in remote villages and ask them to identify the specific emotions being expressed in different images of human faces and bodies. When the tribespeople successfully match, say, a smiling face to the feeling of happiness, this is taken as evidence that emotions are universal, that is to say, that people of every age, in every culture, in every part of the world experience the same emotions in roughly the same way.

In the other camp are the sceptics. Instead of heading to the rainforests, these scientists attach electrodes to people's faces and measure how the muscles move during the experience of different emotions. And what they find is enormous variety, not uniformity. On the basis of this evidence, they argue that muscle movements don't reliably indicate when someone is feeling a particular way. They contend that an emotion like happiness doesn't have a single expression but rather has a diverse constellation of expressions that varies from one situation to the other. In their view, an emotion such as happiness takes no single physical form. On different occasions, in different contexts, within the same individual and across different individuals, happiness manifests itself as different bodily actions. So-called universal expressions are stereotypes, conventions, which our culture created and which we duly learned. We perceive others as happy by applying these conventions to their movements and their voices. We do this with such speed that it seems to us as if emotions are being transmitted to us, from others, simply and clearly, when in fact we are making simulations and predictions of their emotions in our own minds. Any time we think we know how someone else feels, our confidence has nothing to do with knowledge; in fact the emotions we perceive are guesses.

While reading these, I made lots of notes. As I go over them now,

I'm frankly touched to see how personal many of my responses have been. In the margin of one particular article ('Reading Emotion from Faces in Two Indigenous Societies' from a recent edition of the *Journal of Experimental Psychology*), there is a comment box containing an unusually large amount of text (which I forget writing) describing a memory that is most painful to recall. The night of my suicide attempt on 3 January 2003. I talk about the note I wrote to Cyprien. And the pills. And the blackness. I talk about waking up in the French hospital. The other patients. The doctors. The nurses. My mother coming the next day to bring me back to Ireland. The week I spent in her house in Dublin while waiting for a hospital bed. Then my admission, and more patients, more doctors, more nurses. Including you.

Actually I talk a lot about your face. Because – I don't think I've ever told you this – I couldn't read it at the time. I couldn't figure out from your expressions what you, my assigned carer, were feeling. Or indeed what I was feeling. Was it indifference on your part? On mine?

Because in the days immediately after admission, I was so dazed I couldn't differentiate you from the washes of burgundy – how you hated the colour of that uniform! – that spread through the atmosphere around my bed. It took me a week or two even to absorb the fact that I was on a ward. That I'd failed. And that five other failed men were there with me. At night I could hear these men moan and fart and call out. Then during the day I could see them doing these things, except now they were wandering about at the same time, mixing with other figures, not all of whom were male. From time to time these not-all-male figures approached me and went away from me.

It wasn't until late into the second week that your voice properly registered with me for the first time. It was after lights-out, and you were in the corridor outside, talking on your mobile in a strange language. Much later I'd learn that you were having a disagreement with your then boyfriend. But at the time I wasn't able to make that out from your tone. If truth be told, in that moment I didn't care about what you were saying. I didn't care about you or anybody else in that place. But this feeling of not-caring evidently had its own spectrum, because when you passed by the open door holding your phone to your ear, I paid enough attention to your appearance to speculate that you were Arabic. And to form the additional thought that it was probably against the rules for nurses to use their phones on the ward, and not a little insensitive besides, given that my own phone was taken away from me every evening to be locked in an office elsewhere (since I couldn't be trusted with the battery wire).

For the first week or two, remember, my mother and my sister visited every evening. A nurse had to meet them in the foyer downstairs, accompany them up in the lift, unlock the ward door for them and bring them to that jumble of mismatched sofas and armchairs in the open-plan part of the corridor, where visits took place. 'The fishbowl,' I called it, because everyone coming in or out of the surrounding rooms could see who was sitting there, and they always seemed to slow down and have a good gawp. The people sitting there, meanwhile, could see into the rooms, the doors of which were kept open, and whose occupants appeared at ease under the gaze of those for whom they felt such apathy.

At some point, you were given the task of retrieving my family. And from then on – this was my impression anyway – you did it whenever you were on duty at visiting time. From my place in bed, if I planted my elbow and leaned left, I had a sightline that cut right across the corridor into the fishbowl. So I was able to spy on you coming round the corner, two steps in front of my mother and my sister but twisting at the waist so that you could turn back to speak to them. You hovered by them then, while they settled into the seats, and I sat back on my pillow and looked away in preparation for your arrival. I knew that you knew I'd been watching. You didn't seem bothered that I didn't get out of bed of my own volition and instead waited for your summons.

'Your family are here, Gavin,' you said briskly, before going off to do other things.

You didn't accompany me to them – you drew a line there.

After each visit, I'd return to bed and draw the curtain round, so that, although I still had to listen to the TV, I didn't have to see it. Today I can see that in hiding myself so visibly I was asking for attention: yours. I wasn't unduly conscious of it then, but I remember a feeling of relief when, thirty minutes or an hour later, your feet would appear in the gap between the curtain and the floor.

On learning of this drill, a doctor said, 'How about we take a break from the family visits?'

And I said, 'All right.'

Two weeks was the period agreed upon, during which my family wasn't to come to the hospital or otherwise contact me, and I was to keep a journal of my changing emotional states. If I became irritated or despondent, or indeed excited or elated, I was to write down as accurately as possible where in the body those feelings were occurring. You came and went as before, only now the curtain wasn't closed, and you weren't as rushed. You stayed for longer periods to keep me company. And you were softer with me, I felt. Whereas before you'd been stern in your orders to swallow my pills and wanted to check under my tongue in case I was hiding them, now you said, 'That's it,' and, 'Good man,' and touched me gently on the shoulder. You even helped guide my feet into my slippers, and carried my toiletries to the bathroom, and made sure the water wasn't too hot – which, for reasons I don't particularly wish to analyse right now, I found tender and sort of sexy.

You recall all of this, right? I'm not making it up.

One day, on seeing my journal untouched on my bedside locker, you asked why I wasn't writing into it as the doctor recommended.

'Have you even tried?'

I'd been looking at the TV while you buzzed about the vicinity; now I turned away from the screen and found your eyes. 'Can you pull the curtain?'

When you'd done so, you came to stand at my right side. 'You okay?'

'Pedro?'

'Yes.'

'From Brazil.'

'Uh-huh.'

'Have you ever been rich and then lost everything?'

You shook your head. 'No.'

'I phrased that badly. I'm not talking about money. I'm talking about the feeling of being enriched. Protected. At the centre of things. And then suddenly one day finding yourself poor and out in the cold.'

You gave me one of your impenetrable frowns.

'I'm losing you. Let me put it another way. Have you ever cared about something?'

'Something or someone?'

'Someone.'

'Of course.'

'I mean really, really cared.'

'Yes.'

'Did that someone disappoint you?'

'It's normal to feel disappointed in others from time to time.'

'You see, I've been thinking about what we're supposed to do when the person who disappoints us is someone who means the world to us. I know we're told it's not wise to think the world of anyone. Better to keep a sense of proportion in these matters. But what happens when, through no choice of our own – call it sensitivity or whatever you like – we do think the world of someone, and that someone lets us down? Surely we have no choice but to expect less from the world? To reduce our relations to everything to a lower level?'

'Well, maybe the lower level is the right level. Maybe things are more real there.'

'I could never live there.'

'Of course you could.'

'I'm telling you, I couldn't.'

'You probably live there already, and always have done, and now you're just realising it.'

I shouldn't have opened my mouth; that's what I was thinking now.

'Sometimes when we're hurt,' you went on, 'we prefer to give the impression that we're not fighting for anything any more. But honestly, I've never met someone who isn't fighting for something, deep down. Even if it's just fighting to get out of bed in the morning.' You took the journal from the table, laid it on your thigh, opened it to the first page, then turned it around and put it on my lap. 'Lots of us have a hard time telling the difference between our emotions, which can create confusion in our mind, and a feeling that everything is out of control. Take worry and sadness. I used to use these words interchangeably to describe periods of stress in my life. I'd say I was worried when I was actually sad, and vice versa. I thought it didn't matter what I called my feelings. I was feeling shit and that was the end of it. But in my training, I learned that the names I put on my emotions do matter. Because what we call our emotions can actually determine what we feel, and for how long.'

'What do you mean?' I said. 'Are you saying I'm making my feelings up?'

'Not at all,' you said. 'When I took a proper look, I saw that worry and sadness, which I used to mix up, aren't even close to one another. They leave my body in opposite physical states. When I'm worried, I'm worked up and tense and thinking that something bad will happen. When I'm sad, I'm quiet and unenergetic, which isn't always unpleasant. I've learned to tell the two experiences apart. So that when they come up I'll know what to call them, and I can then make friends with them.'

Now, nearly twenty years later, the recollection of this overpowers me. I feel love, or at least something that bears down like love. Back then, the feeling didn't come so freely. A nurse? A child of the favelas, for all I knew. What species of 'training' had you had? Could it even properly be called an education? And how old were you anyway? Younger, by an important margin, than anyone wise. A Mass-goer too: I saw your chain. Or a born-again, one of those nuts. In this way my thoughts conspired to detach my affections – that is, those vague, fleeting sensations that passed for such – from you, until once again I felt nothing but cold indifference.

But early the next morning – after waking up from a dream in which I was on the metro in Paris and kept missing my stop because Cyprien, who was sitting beside me, kept saying, 'It's not this one, it's the next' – I did write something in the journal.

Letter 27: PEDRO SOUZA to GAVIN MULVANY

Dublin, 3 June 2022

You couldn't concentrate with the TV on, which it was all day every day, so you took it to the chapel to write in. Stayed there for hours at a time. Scribbling away. That earned you a name, did you know? People had heard about your PhD and wanted to bring you down a peg or two. 'Is he finished his grand opus yet?' And to be honest, the parts you gave me to read did intimidate me. Your friendship with Cyprien, which you described in detail, went over my head. You felt so much for him that my feelings for my own boyfriend seemed small in comparison. I was unsure what I was dealing with and told myself to step back.

Reading your emails now gives me déjà vu.

Letter 28: GAVIN MULVANY to CYPRIEN ABREO

Paris, 9 June 2022

Do we still have any interests in common, you and I? Your continued silence makes me doubtful. I went to knock on your door. Not to cause you discomfort or make a scene. I just wanted to clear up some of the misunderstandings that inevitably arise as soon as two people are parted. But of course it's been a long time. People move. You used to say you'd like to get a bigger place. With separate offices for you and Mathilde. Space for a proper desk in Anne-Laure's room. And a yard for Coco to shit in. The dog must be dead by now. Presumably Anne-Laure has moved out. But has the rest come your way?

I asked the woman who answered the door, hoping that she might be an acquaintance of yours, if she knew where the previous tenant had moved to. But she couldn't help me.

A yard for Coco: I never took this to mean that you wanted to move to the suburbs. But maybe this was short-sighted of me. Maybe the burbs were where you were headed all along. Back to Plaisir?

I checked the university term dates. The repeat exams finished last week, and the final juries were today. The last push. Getting the stragglers over the line. Then afterwards to Zig-Zag for burgers and beer: some traditions never die.

Your colleagues took a table, but you stayed at the bar and let people come to you. You said you weren't staying long. You hung around for an hour before saying your goodbyes. 'Have a great holiday.' Kiss-kiss.

You've kept your hair. Grey but still thick. You're one of those men who so irritate women by looking better in middle-age than ever before.

Now where? Towards Maubert–Mutualité metro station. But today you didn't go down the stairs into the metro like you used to. You went right past. Then up Saint-Germain towards the river, then onwards to boulevard Voltaire, where you entered a door on the left. I ran across the street to see. There was nothing for a minute. Then a light at the top. Two windows, one open, which you now closed. An attic? One room? Where was the extra office for Mathilde? In fact, where was Mathilde? It was too high to see in. But I didn't need to. In my mind's eye I saw exactly what it was. The refuge of a lonely and unhappy man, isolated from everything that's dear to him.

Even while I consider myself free from blame, I'm not free from regret when I see where you – where we – have ended up.

You must take pity on me. Agree to see me, no matter how.

Letter 29: GAVIN MULVANY to CYPRIEN ABREO

Paris, 10 June 2022

Are your lectures on the Marquis de Sade as famous today as they once were? I supervised a student recently whose thesis argued that the figure of the libertine in Sade, like the child who is being beaten, desires violence as proof that God isn't indifferent to him. The thesis was well written. The student defended it eloquently before the jury. We passed it without corrections; it would have been unreasonable of us not to. Yet as I was sitting there listening to the arguments and the counterarguments, the familiar forward and back, I distinctly remember thinking, What's the fucking point of this? Smart people that we were, couldn't we be expending our energy in more useful ways?

At work on the book this morning, I found myself trying to come to grips with a minor point that Rousseau makes in one of his little-read letters. I went online to see if anyone had published anything that might shine some light on the matter. Naturally I felt impelled to check the news while I was there. And I came across an article in the *Irish Times* about a gang of youths in Dublin who rove the streets attacking food-delivery riders. The gangs are white adolescents from areas of the city that have been neglected for decades, while their victims are Afghans and Bolivians and Brazilians and Nigerians – migrants, in short, many of them earning as little as a euro per delivery. Reading about this, I felt that what was being revealed to me was nothing less than the nub of all our social ills. Surely, if intelligent, educated people like us set our minds to understanding this single phenomenon, rather than the esoteric writings of long-dead men, that would be a far better use of our time?

After that, I found myself googling the demonstrations that took place in Paris following the first round of the 2002 presidential elections. I think I wanted to remember a time when I cared enough about external events to take to the streets in protest; a time when I saw it as my duty to be seen to be taking a stand. I quickly became immersed in the footage of the protest against Le Pen on 1 May. How surreal it was to think that I was there on that day with you and your family. I half-expected our faces to flash up on the screen.

You'll remember that the demo was enormous and, because the trains were rammed, we took a roundabout route there, with a couple of changes, and got out a stop or two early. You and Mathilde were dressed casually but smartly, as though you were going to the cinema. Not knowing which idea of myself to project, I'd got changed a few times before settling on old jeans and trainers. It was up to Anne-Laure to bear the heavy load for us. She was wearing a white T-shirt that said 'no', had an EU flag tied around her neck so it fell down her back and was holding a homemade placard on which was written, in her own hand, 'Le Pen = Little Pétain'.

At Nation it was difficult to move. We stayed together by holding onto each other's sleeves. It wasn't until much later in the afternoon, when the crowd had begun to thin out, that we finally made contact with your students. A plan was made to regroup at a bar a few streets away, which as expected was heaving, but the atmosphere was good, so we stayed. Mathilde was joined by some of her friends; she and Anne-Laure stayed with them at a quieter table at the back, near the toilet. Your students, on the other hand, congregated on the terrace outside, where there was space enough for you to introduce me properly. You described me as a 'brilliant ex-student' of yours, gave them a précis of my PhD thesis and told them of my plan to join one of the literature faculties in Paris. I was on the cusp of an exciting career, you said, and you spoke of the choices I'd made in getting this far as ones which might sensibly be emulated.

I was over the moon. After the incident with the letter at our previous meeting, I'd feared I'd have some work to do to regain your esteem. It transpired that the reverse was true: you'd expected to be faced with animosity from me, and you were now endeavouring to win me back. It was clear you believed you'd accomplished this task when, an hour or so later, you accepted a joint from one of your students, drew on it and handed it on to me with a wink.

The hash and the wine disrupted my ability to follow the precise course of the group's conversation, so I can't remember exactly how the subject came up. But at some point – I think you might have speculated aloud about what Le Pen would say when he saw the TV images of so many people demonstrating against him – I mentioned that I'd been at the National Front rally at Opéra that morning.

'You attended the Le Pen rally?' You sounded shocked.

The line of perplexed faces confirmed that I'd said something wrong.

'I didn't attend it,' I said. 'I went to see what it was like.'

Your eyes searched my face. 'Why on earth would you do that?'

'As you know, Cyprien, Opéra is quite near my flat, so I went to have a look.'

'But, but' – I could hear how cross you were with me for showing you up in this way – 'why?'

'I just wanted to see for myself what kinds of people would be there.' It was dizzying how quickly the convivial atmosphere had transformed itself into that of a criminal trial. 'I was curious to know what they'd look like and how they'd behave. History this big doesn't happen in Ireland, so I wanted to be a witness to it. Obviously I wasn't there as a supporter. I'd never vote for Le Pen.'

What a fatal mistake to state the obvious like this. Even to me it sounded suspicious.

'You shouldn't have gone,' one of the students said.

'The best thing,' another said, 'is to starve them of attention. They want us to look their way, but we mustn't give them the satisfaction. They need to be ignored out of existence.'

I should've stayed quiet. I should've just agreed with the shared sentiment of outrage and changed the subject. But now I really did have something to defend: a fundamental principle. 'I disagree,' I said. 'I think we should be looking very closely at what people like the National Front are saying and doing. If anything, we should analyse them out of existence. If we want to learn about fascism, we need to learn about fascists, no? What makes them tick?'

'What did you expect to learn at the march?' you said.

'I don't know.'

'What did you find there then?'

I described a few of the things I'd seen. The men in aviator glasses holding baguettes under their arms. The nationalist songs. The signs saying, 'FRANCE FOR THE FRENCH.' The young girl shouting, 'Against the dictatorship of the media!'

'Did you listen to Le Pen's speech?' a student asked.

'It went on for hours,' I said, 'I just stayed for the first bit. It was the usual soundbites. He was the only candidate who opposed the system . . . The existing powers had ruined France and were now joining forces to mount a hysterical campaign of insults against him . . .'

'Were you surprised by anything you saw?'

'It was all predictable enough.'

'So if you weren't learning anything new, what were you doing there?' How I hated this condescending tone of yours, which you adopted whenever you feared you were being undermined by a more rational, less emotional view. 'You're a scholar of the eighteenth century, Gavin, so you'll know that, in that period, the glorious reigns of Louis XV and Louis XVI, the authorities dealt with the immigrants and the poor by rounding them up and imprisoning them in the most appalling conditions. You'll also know that this authoritarianism is exactly what Le Pen wants to bring back.'

'I couldn't agree more. But only by listening –'

'No. To analyse Le Pen properly, we must keep a healthy distance from him.'

'Are you saying there's nothing to learn from witnessing an event with your own eyes. Empirical reasoning? The Enlightenment's principal gift to us?'

'This particular event? Best not to get too close, I think. Was there any moment when you thought, "Well, that's not so extreme"?'

You had me there; rightly you took my defensive shrug as an admission of guilt.

'A day like today,' you said, 'is about choosing sides. A person who decides to go to both demonstrations, even just out of curiosity, is someone who isn't really fighting. It's someone who claims to want objectivity, but who'll be found on closer inspection to occupy a very subjective position. That of apathy.'

'Making the effort to go to the Le Pen rally,' I insisted, 'and to learn from it, is the opposite of apathy.'

At this point, another group of your students, who had happened to catch sight of their friends as they walked by, burst onto the terrace. I was instantly forgotten as everyone laughed and hugged and said, 'What a crowd! Two million!' A chant then kicked off, in which you participated for a few seconds before slipping away. I went inside after you. You were at the back table, talking in an animated fashion to Mathilde. Mathilde was listening to you with a serious expression on her face, one she didn't break as she glanced at the moving figures around her. Over your shoulder, she caught a glimpse of me approaching and tapped you on the arm. You turned to face me. Then you stopped what you were saying, mid-sentence.

'What are your plans?' you said with admirable speed.

'I don't know. What were you thinking?'

'I think we're going to go home. Anne-Laure is tired.'

Anne-Laure had stretched her arm across the table and was resting her ear on her bicep, and from this angle was observing the throng with marked insouciance; she was at that age.

'All right,' I said brightly, though I was desperate for you not to leave.

'Stay and have a good time,' said Mathilde. 'Make some friends.'

'Oh, I will,' I said, embracing her. 'Thank you.'

In the toilet, I took a cubicle and stood inside it for a few minutes. Unable to console myself for what had just happened, I left, avoiding your students on the way out, and walked home on my own.

Letter 30: GAVIN MULVANY to PEDRO SOUZA

Paris, 12 June 2022

Today I walked northwards through Saint-Denis to Montmorency. I set off from rue Jean-Jacques Rousseau. Took in rue Montorgueil, rue des Petits Carreaux, rue de Cléry, rue Poissonnière, rue du Faubourg Poissonnière: street after identical street. The same sand-grey stone. The tribes of inhabitants, the tribes of tourists: the modern crowd. To walk among them was to search for a fracture through which volatility could erupt. And then, as I approached the city boundaries – boulevard Barbès and boulevard Ornano – the white faces turned to brown and black, and the shops split open and their contents spilled onto the path.

The visible form of hardship changed from intermittent filth and derangement to a population of tired eyes, plodding gaits, distant gazes. There were so many people on the pavements, so many barely getting by, that I had to walk behind the market stalls to make headway in reasonable time. When I turned my head right, I had the privileged view of the street sellers. The world framed by their wares. Horizons shrunk to the length of their tables. Passers-by existing only for the couple of seconds it took them to enter and exit their view. It was loud. People were shouting. Horns were honking. Which disturbed me, for I hadn't merged with the multitude, hadn't established myself among them. I wasn't buying from them, wasn't selling to them. Wasn't hanging around the doorways and the corners with them. From where I looked, they appeared to be having a different version of human experience, and I therefore assumed hostility on their part towards me.

Le périph appears on the map as a thick line, but my consciousness of the border began well before I reached it. Several hundred metres in advance, in fact, with the gradual dissolution of the city street and the emergence of large blocks of flats set at a distance from each other and separated from the pavement by railings. And in the immediate approach to the city gate, a market filled with knock-off designer bags, sold like weapons that the traveller would require in the wastelands beyond.

Crossing the line – walking under the overpass – was only an instant.

On the other side, the borderland went on: it took in the entirety of avenue Michelet, whose warehouses, ramshackle shops, train depots and tower blocks would together have marked a clear end to the city, had they not been forced to contend with residual segments of Parisian streetscape poking out of the surrounding lowlands like invasive weeds.

I lingered for a minute on the eastern edge of place Pleyel, marvelling at Pleyel Tower, a 1972 skyscraper whose outer skin had been stripped away and innards extracted, leaving a rust-coloured skeleton that resembled dried bones. The boarding surrounding this carcass declared that the latter was being transformed into a 'business resort'. Which sounded like a contradiction to me. As soon as I saw the ploy, I knew I'd left the city behind.

Passing underneath a motorway overpass, which vibrated deeply under the roll of its traffic, I penetrated Saint-Denis. After a short while, I heard live music. African drums and singing. It was coming from a dilapidated building that might once have been a factory or a school. I searched the windows, many of which were broken, for movement or light, but I could see nothing. I inquired of a group of men congregated outside.

'Is it a church?' I asked, for it was Sunday, and these were songs of praise.

The men studied me for a long moment before answering. 'Yes.'

I hesitated. I wanted to go in.

'Thank you,' I said, walking away, and as I did so, I was thinking, 'You're going to regret this. What's stopping you?' It was the poverty. That was the problem. These people were poor immigrants. Or the children of poor immigrants. They had their good shirts on for the celebration. But they also had plastic slippers as shoes, and old trousers, and weathered faces. And a little further up the road, in an open yard, Roma children were playing in a shopping trolley. Nobody was telling me to go away. Nobody was making me feel unwelcome. I was doing that to myself and blaming the poverty I saw.

Walking west from Saint-Denis, I crossed the river to Villeneuve-la-Garenne and turned north. On the banks, Arab families of several generations, groups of twenty to thirty people, were picnicking.

'I'm a popstar, not a doctor,' three teenagers rapped in unison in English.

I crossed the river again to Épinay-sur-Seine, where a boy at a busy crossroads was holding up a sign saying 'SYRIAN FAMILY' and was running to the open windows of the stopped cars to collect coins: a refugee from the war there. Further north, in Deuil-la-Barre, I ate my packed lunch in a park surrounded by members of a boxing club, male and female, black and white, punching the air that divided them.

After this, entering Montmorency was a jolt. Streets of large period homes, each with decorative patterns in its brickwork and an expensive car parked on the street outside. Climbing up a steep hill with lovely stone walls, lots of trees and views over Saint-Denis and the city beyond, I reached the Rousseau Museum a few minutes after four in the afternoon. The museum is housed in a villa once rented by Rousseau (after he had fallen out with his protectress, Louise d'Épinay, and was forced to move out of her house). Here he wrote some of the letters that would estrange him from the other Enlightenment philosophers and the sentimental novel that would earn him fame in Europe rivalling that of Voltaire.

At the reception desk I asked for a ticket, but was told that I'd missed the last tour. People could only visit as part of a tour; that was the rule.

'What time do you close?'

'Five.'

'Well, could I just have a quick look then?'

'As I say, you've missed the tour.'

'I've walked all the way from central Paris.'

'I imagine that's why you're late.'

'You don't close for another hour. I'll just take a quick peep round.'

'Not without a guide.'

I left the museum. At the gate, I paused and looked up the hill. For Rousseau walking was, above all, an emotional venture. As he walked, he tried to make sense of his feelings about things that had happened or that he imagined were about to happen. As oblivious to the world as he appeared to be during his walks,

Rousseau, in attempting to convey the current state of his emotions so accurately, was battling against the indifference he saw everywhere outside.

    I pushed on with my journey to where the open countryside begins.

THIRD WALK

(*To Versailles, walking southwest: rue J.-J. Rousseau – quai Malaquais – rue du Cherche-Midi – boulevard Périphérique – Issy-les-Moulineaux – Meudon – Sèvres – Chaville – Porchefontaine – Versailles; 19 km: 5 hours, 5 minutes*)

Pity

MS Extract: from *Rousseau's Lost Children* by GAVIN MULVANY

Last edited: 15 June 2022

Rousseau's primitive man, as described in the *Second Discourse*, seems at first blush to have lived in a state of indifference to his surroundings. Nature's spectacle was so familiar to him that it evoked no wonder. He lacked the intellect to be curious about how the world worked. His imagination portrayed nothing. Beyond his instinct for food, a mate, rest, his heart was empty of desire. Jealousy and hatred were therefore inconceivable to him. As was death. The only states he feared were those he had memory of experiencing directly: pain and hunger.

In fact, however, natural man was not devoid of all feeling. Rousseau was careful to attribute to him the fundamentals of an emotional existence. Two basic sentiments animated his being. One was self-preservation. The other was pity.

Both self-preservation and pity preceded any kind of reflection. The former was a rudimentary form of self-love that drove him to defend and nourish himself, and to reproduce. The latter moderated this self-love and sent him to the aid of those he saw suffering, thereby contributing to the mutual preservation of the whole species. It was pity that in the state of nature took the place of laws, moral habits and virtues.

When natural man became social man, his new faculty of reason bred vanity, turned him inward and separated him from everything that troubled him and caused him to feel pity. His rationality isolated him and prompted him secretly to say at the sight of another person suffering: Perish if you will, but I am safe.

Despite this, pity has not disappeared entirely. 'Such is the force of natural pity . . . that the most vicious immorality still struggles to overcome it.' In modern times, according to Rousseau, when we express generosity, mercy, humaneness, we are in fact activating the primal emotion of pity. Kindliness, and even friendship, correctly understood, is the outcome of an enduring pity for a particular object. Because we are far removed from our natural forebears, it is not easy to find this deep-seated pity within ourselves and to call it up. Yet: 'it is to this natural feeling, rather than to any subtle arguments, that we must look for the cause of the aversion that every man feels to doing evil.'

Letter 31: GAVIN MULVANY to THÉRÈSE LEVASSEUR

Paris, 17 June 2022

I write to give my side of this morning's events. It's true that I came to the house with some sheets of music for Mr Rousseau to copy. I was desirous of acquiring a souvenir of his hand, which has a reputation for having a rare exactitude, to take home to my country. It's simply false to suggest, as Mr Rousseau so vigorously did, that I had a whole other aim in being there.

I admit to feeling uneasy at joining the mass of waiting bodies. It's difficult to think of oneself as being merely one more petitioner. After waiting an hour, I began to fear that I wouldn't even get past the door. So, yes, I did offer the people standing in front of me on the stairs some small sums in return for letting me skip ahead.

In the chamber, several men, as many as nine or ten, were distributed around, leaving no piece of furniture unoccupied. I lingered by the entrance, hoping to be noticed by Mr Rousseau and to be called to him before the others. At that moment he was busy with a client.

'Look how clean it is,' he was saying as he handed the man some sheets of finished work. 'Try to find a person who copies music as well as I do. I doubt that a page of notation would leave the printing press as beautiful and as precise as it leaves my house.'

The man looked through the sheets by transferring them, one by one, from a pile on the left of the desk to a pile on the right. This done, he thanked Mr Rousseau fulsomely and plonked down a purse whose dimensions were, it was obvious to everyone looking, greater than they strictly ought to have been. Quite rightly your husband did not object to this; nor did anyone watching blink an eye. We all of us are on your husband's side and want only munificence to come his way.

The mistake the man made, which started the whole ugly business, was this. Once in possession of his copies, instead of taking himself off, as rightly he should have done, he dawdled with his coat. Then hummed and hawed with his stick. Which gave him the time to protest to Mr Rousseau, in well-meant but ill-conceived phrases, that a man of his genius ought to be focusing his energies on writing philosophy. This – and nothing I said or did – was what set Mr Rousseau off.

'You complain to me because I spend my time copying? You think I would be better off writing books for people who do not know how to read? Or, worse, for cruel journalists? You're wrong. I love music passionately. The originals I copy are, as you yourself have attested, excellent. This gives me a reason to live. It amuses me and is enough for me.'

The man was understandably shattered. I intervened out of pity for him.

'Please, Mr Rousseau,' I simply said, 'the man here is cognisant of all that you've done for society with your writings and merely looks forward to what you might yet still do.'

At this, Mr Rousseau came out from behind his desk to claim the most commanding position from which to speak. Instantly I knew that I'd been misunderstood.

'By working for myself,' Mr Rousseau said, 'I do all that I can for society. If I do little for her, I demand even less.' With large strides he made a circle of the room, proudly eyeing every object it contained. 'All of these things are my own. For a long time I'd been in debt to the upholsterer for them. It's only yesterday that I completely paid him off. Using money that I earned honestly by copying music.' Abruptly he pointed at me. 'You.'

'Yes?' I said.

'Society, you said? I'm on such good terms with society that I could henceforth rest completely and live for myself alone without scruple. And you?'

'Yes?'

'I know you. A writer, no?'

'A man struggling to write his first book, that is all.'

'Too bad for you,' he said, taking a step towards me. 'What are you holding there? Is that a score you want copied?'

I handed the sheets to him. 'I also hoped,' I said while he examined the first page, 'that when I return to collect it, I'd be allowed to accompany you on a walk. Or, if you have time today, I intend to go on foot to Versailles and would be honoured if you would be my companion, if not for the entire journey, then as far as you can manage.'

'Your money,' he said.

'Ah, let me see.' I rooted through my pockets and gave him everything I had, from which he extracted three livres.

'As you've wasted fifteen minutes of my time, I'll hold this back.' Then he slapped my music sheets into my chest, by way of returning them to me, and physically pushed me out of the room, calling, 'Thérèse, Thérèse,' until you came and took responsibility for putting me onto the stairs outside and for handing me the bunch of wilting flowers that I'd given you on my way in, through the half-closed door.

Letter 32: GAVIN MULVANY to JEAN-JACQUES ROUSSEAU

Paris, 18 June 2022

On leaving your flat – after you chucked me out – I walked west. As long as I'm near you, I'm in the Paris that you know; that's how it works. So on rue Plâtrière, and crossing rue Montmartre, and heading into rue Tiquetonne, I was still on the wet and stinking ground of your city. The medieval city. The unsegregated city. In which rich and poor live side by side, and above and below each other. Whose luxury flats flank arcades offering sideshows and cheap sex. Whose very palace has a slum built into it. I gave the flowers to a beggar from the palace slum, who, without blushing, dropped them under the hoofs of a passing horse, before scuttling away with the coin I'd covertly slipped to her as well.

In Les Halles, as I moved out of your sphere of influence, the scene gradually shifted. The warren of crevices and angular lanes, and the damp and claustrophobic courts, in which human life is densely packed and public order is never guaranteed, became blurred and soon disappeared. To be replaced by shorter houses on wider roads. Ordered avenues filled with light and air and commerce and reason. In which the people were comparatively well behaved. Out of which the poor had been pushed.

Once I found myself on the other side of the city boundary, in Issy-les-Moulineaux, I came by chance upon a rue Jean-Jacques Rousseau. Much of the street was under construction. Helpfully printed on the boarding surrounding the building sites were colourful depictions of what the finished buildings would look like. In one section there's going to be 'a trilogy' of apartment blocks: 1) Ecoverde, 2) Ecopolitan, and 3) Ecozen. 'THE CITY'S NEW NATURE', read the headline. '*An innovative eco-neighbourhood. A unique fusion of the city and nature. Promoting biodiversity. Shared outdoor spaces. Cascade terraces. Winter gardens. Bold architecture with curved wooden lines and rice terraces. Bright and clear.*' In good truth, sir, all you need to picture is this: in the second decade of the twenty-first century, on a street bearing your name, there'll be people living in concrete buildings masquerading as trees.

Leaving Issy-les-Moulineaux with the rain now coming down, I went through the village-like streets of Meudon, climbed the steep hill to Sèvres, then cut through the forest to Chaville. I rested under an old arch at the forest's exit. In Porchefontaine, I joined avenue de Paris, a thoroughfare of impressive width, designed to announce the imminent appearance of Versailles long before its actual appearance on the horizon. Walking under the canopy created by the seemingly endless lines of plane trees, I noticed that my pace increased out of a desire to behold the golden treasure at the end of the road. I was stopped in my tracks, however, about a kilometre away – the palace had just risen up in the distance – by the façade of a prison on my left.

There was no date inscribed on the prison wall, but I guessed (correctly, it transpired) that the building dated from the mid-eighteenth century – the precise period in which you were composing your essay on inequality – and that it had once been a seminary or a boarding school. I paused outside for only a few seconds. There wasn't much to see apart from the green-painted wooden bars in one of the windows, from which a dirty towel hung, the three sad-looking national flags above the gate and the large mirrored window by the pedestrian door, in which my drenched figure, like an emissary from the tropical rainforests, was reflected.

Versailles. The epicentre of royal power. But at a great distance from Paris. Five hours on foot. Or three hours by carriage. The most magnificent theatre of ritual and ceremony in the country, perhaps in the world, yet completely cut off from the people. Louis XV, until recently your king, who emulated the ostentatious courtly practices of his great-grandfather, was loath to venture outside it. His visits to Paris became progressively less frequent; after 1744 he never again spent a night there. And the man you have now, Louis XVI, doesn't stray far either. He has, you'll have heard, a preference for a homely ethos in his family quarters, and Marie-Antoinette too seeks her pleasure within the ambit of a restricted audience of courtiers and intimates; except for some favourites, designated by whim or intrigue, everyone is excluded. The outer gates remain open for the public to come and go, all sorts of unsavoury characters prowl the corridors and gardens, but the king and queen remain locked away in their private salons, ever more committed to their separateness.

On the terrace behind the palace, I positioned myself at the top of the staircase and tried to find the exact centre point – now shifting to the left a little, now to the right – so that I'd have a symmetrical view of the lower terraces, the green lawn, the Apollo Basin and the Grand Canal. Once I'd achieved this, more or less, I tried to visualise a horizontal line precisely at the place where the royal gardens stopped and the countryside began. The palace, although it felt infinite, had boundaries. Wherever those lay – I could just about make them out – was where royal imprisonment ended.

You say in your essay on inequality that ordinary people, once accustomed to their masters, become incapable of doing without them. That in society the common people are like prisoners, utterly at the mercy of the employer, the warden, the policeman, the judge, the king. You also say that the masters are equally enslaved, by their need of the services of others. In an unequal society, we're all in chains. No exceptions. This is your argument.

Upon reflection, I find that I don't feel much pity for 'the common man'. To him, I can be generous. I can give him any number of absolutions for the bad behaviour he might display or indeed the crimes he might commit. Perhaps he was born into deprivation. Perhaps he had negligent parents. No education. Perhaps undertaking unlawful deeds is, given his circumstances, the most rational way for him to make ends meet. Perhaps one day he'll catch a break. Get ahead. Be the exception. Within his imprisoned condition I can discern the potential for self-reliance, for pride in his employments, even for pleasure in being of service to others. And I understand also that he might just want to drop out. Admit defeat. Sit on the road and beg. I allow the common man this leeway. Which makes me mean in my pity for him.

The greater part of my pity – which I felt well up in me as I cast my eyes over the vast green expanse of Versailles – is reserved for the king. For he has been a captive of this hellish opulence since birth. As a matter of course, by force of tradition, he was neglected by his parents. Given a dreadful education founded on false ideas. Trained for a career in bloodthirsty murdering and international crime. And, the worst part, forbidden from ever leaving. Unlike the common man, he, the absolute ruler, possesses absolutely no means of turning his life around. His lot is his lot. No second chances. No escape routes.

People like you and me, Mr Rousseau, we claim to prefer the most tempestuous freedom in the wilds of our solitude to the most tranquil subservience in society. Yet in reality, whether in nature or in the city, alone or in the crowd, we feel pity for our masters. Our mercy and kindliness go to the ones at the top. Why this persistence in our affections for the people who hold our happiness – indeed our very survival – in their hands? For those one-time friends who turned on us at our feeblest moments and caused us the lion's share of our sufferings? They are our rulers, and we hate them. We hate their greatness. We hate their harshness, their prejudices, their pettiness, and their vices. But we'd hate them much more – indeed we'd be able to hate them with absolute purity – if we pitied them less.

Letter 33: GAVIN MULVANY to CYPRIEN ABREO

Paris, 23 June 2022

Although it's twenty years ago, I haven't forgotten the precise dates. I didn't hear from you between the anti-Le Pen demonstration and the second round of the election, that is between the first and the fifth of May. Five whole days, which I spent in a state of high anxiety, as I questioned myself suspiciously about the feelings I inspired in you. I tried to numb this tension, which was threatening to culminate in panic and then spiral downwards, by gluing myself to the election coverage on TV. Election day itself I spent in my pyjamas in the kitchen, eating toast and flicking between the national channels. After the results were announced at eight in the evening, I texted you:

<<CHOLERA 1. PLAGUE 0.>>

No response. The next morning, after a sleepless night, I called, but you didn't answer. So, after an hour or two of pacing around and getting worked up, I went to the computer shop on boulevard Malesherbes, bought a USB stick, loaded it with files, then took the metro to your office, timing my arrival for the dot of two o'clock, which was when your weekly class, 'Economies of Medical Discourse from 1600 to 1800', ended.

'Sorry,' I said. 'But you did offer.'

'Yes, all right,' you said, inserting the stick into the beige box of your computer, then searching through the files on the screen for my cv. 'How many copies?'

'Ten?'

'Uh-huh.'

You started skimming the document.

'There are a couple of things here. Should I . . . ?'

'Oh, please, yes, yes.'

You started by fixing little errors. Adding an accent. Formatting a line. Then, spontaneously, you started to embellish: building up, appending, downright lying. Watching you, I felt sick with yearning. Now, *now*, you'd make good on the promises you had made to me.

I pulled my chair, which was on wheels, closer so that my knees almost touched your thigh. Our bodies were now aligned in such a way that I could pretend to be looking at the screen while actually looking at you. The troughs under your eyes were deeper than usual, the rims of your eyes tinged red. You looked tired. You hadn't shaved in two or three days, though your skin gave off a citrus smell like aftershave. Two triangles of black hair on the back of your neck reached down into your collar. The table lamp illuminated the thick veins in your hands and the thin white arcs at the tip of your nails.

You clicked 'print' and the machine started to whir.

I pushed back my chair, crossed my leg over. 'Lifesaver.'

'It's nothing,' you said, half yawning.

'What about the election?'

You sighed defensively and rubbed your eyes. 'The outcome was as expected, I suppose. Chirac was never going to lose.'

'One in five citizens of the Republic voting for Le Pen?'

'Chirac is in,' you said. 'We did our duty. The worst has been avoided.'

'For now, yes. But what about next time? Or do you think the country has been vaccinated against the far right?'

'Vaccinated? I don't know.'

'You don't appear too worried.'

'I just can't seem to get as het up about Le Pen as everyone else. All I can muster for the man is pity.'

I shifted round in my chair. 'Pity?'

You turned from the window and well-nigh spat the word back at me. 'Pity. Yes, pity.'

I knew what you were doing. You were affixing the label 'pity' to your anger and disgust and shame because it sounded kinder, and because it seemed not to demand the same expenditure of energy. Pity, unlike outrage, arrived in your world cleansed of any duty to justify itself.

'Don't you remember what Rousseau said about pity?' You didn't seem to, so I conscientiously, thoroughly, gave an account. 'I don't think Rousseau would consider what you feel for Le Pen to be pity. You call it pity because that sounds sympathetic. Humane. It makes you appear more disinterested than you are. You use the mask of pity to conceal the real nature of your feelings.'

'Which would be . . . ?'

'Contempt. Odium.'

'I certainly can't deny that there's the potential in me to feel odium for Le Pen. But I'm afraid I have more important things on my mind.'

You were smiling. Apparently amused by my intellectual arm-twisting. And a part of me was glad that I'd goaded you into an expression of some kind. But the other, angry part understood that your aspect – your whole posture, from the sideways tilt of your head to the scuffed pointed tips of your green leather loafers – remained a dissemblance.

'To pity a person on Rousseau's terms' – I pushed on – 'is to wish that person not to suffer, which is nothing less than to wish them to be happy. Pity for Rousseau is genuine compassion. Genuine because it comes not from the reasoning mind but from the heart, the gut. If you really pitied Le Pen, you'd want him to be happy, and this desire would arise in you by instinct, without any feelings of resistance to it, which I don't believe to be the case.'

You picked up a pen and toggled it between two fingers. You could have terminated this conversation directly; you could have sent me out and ordered me to stay away forever. The only reason you didn't, I suspected, was that you pitied me too. That emotionally speaking, I was, as a friend to you, the equivalent of Jean-Marie Le Pen.

'But isn't Rousseau making the point,' you said, 'that civilised people can't recapture the feelings of natural man? That natural pity is no longer available to us? That we left it behind in the remote past? I'm not suggesting my pity is pure or natural. I fully admit that mine is a base sort of pity. Yet I still insist it's pity. It's the form of pity that we in today's society are capable of feeling and understanding.'

'Actually,' I said, 'Rousseau's point is that, although we can't go backwards in time and revert to being natural man, deep in our spirit we hold memories of our primitive feelings, which we can get in touch with by learning to see through the false ones that society has imposed on us.'

'In my pity for Le Pen, maybe I'm getting in touch with those natural feelings? Le Pen is a human being after all.'

'You've changed your tune. Just last week you were berating me for saying something similar.'

'As I recall, you were saying that we should all go to Le Pen rallies.'

'Trust me, if you'd come with me to the rally, if you'd witnessed it with your own eyes, you wouldn't be feeling any pity for Le Pen right now. All of your emotional concern would be reserved for those he was attacking in his speech.'

'What are you implying?'

'I'm not implying anything. I'm telling you straight, Cyprien. The social system has perverted your emotions in such a way that the natural pity you ought to be feeling for the victims of oppression is overwhelmed by the hatred you feel for the oppressor. And because this hatred for the oppressor is taboo, or too difficult to do anything about, you try to censor or contain it by calling it pity.' I had become infuriated by your disingenuousness and could no longer hide it. 'Who do you feel compassion for? Who would you like to see happy? If you were feeling natural pity, the answer couldn't possibly be Le Pen.'

'But don't you see there's a paradox there. As soon as you wish happiness for someone else, let's say an immigrant that Le Pen wants to deport, you're presuming they're unhappy. In fact, you're bringing unhappiness into the world, where perhaps it hadn't been before. If you look closely, Rousseau's pity isn't as pure as he'd like it to –'

Your office phone had been ringing through the last portion of this exchange: a computerised trill whose volume you'd fixed at the lowest setting, barely a whisper, but which nevertheless required us to raise our voices to be heard over it and to summon considerable strength of mind not to be diverted by the red light flashing in the corner of our vision.

'Yes?' you said into the receiver, audibly irritated at having given in.

Mathilde was on the line, speaking from a busy street: 'Can you hear me?' You rapidly pressed and re-pressed a button on the panel to reduce the incoming volume. 'I can hear you,' you said – and so could I. Not every word. But enough to build a picture of the enfolding crisis in your home. Mathilde had been trying to call you on your mobile, but you'd turned it off for your class and, no doubt because of my interruption, had forgotten to turn it back on. From what I could gather, there'd been some kind of altercation involving Anne-Laure at her school, for which she was being sent home. Your reaction to this news mustn't have been adequately scandalised because Mathilde felt the need to repeat the word 'expelled' until you said, 'All right, all right, I get it.'

'One of us,' said Mathilde, 'will have to go home and deal with this,' by which she meant Cyprien, for she was on a visit to an artist's studio in Romainville and had important meetings all afternoon. 'You'll have to go. Anne-Laure shouldn't be left alone. You know what she's like.'

'We have our annual meeting to set the exam questions in twenty minutes,' you said feebly.

'Skip it. One of us needs to be with her. And you're closer.'

You put down the receiver and stood up in the same motion. Then switched off the lamp and checked around to see if you were forgetting anything.

'Wait, Cyprien,' I said. 'Don't miss your meeting. I can go and make sure Anne-Laure is okay.'

'Of course not,' you said, though too late not to suggest you'd considered it.

'I'm serious. I want to help.'

'Are you out of your fucking mind?'

Forty minutes later I was at the door of your flat with a bag of food from the delicatessen at Galeries Lafayette, on which I'd spent my budget for an entire week, and which I wasn't sure you were going to reimburse. I rang the bell and after a while Anne-Laure unlocked the door and left it ajar.

'Anne-Laure?'

I pushed it open to see, briefly, her wild black hair flaring out, before she disappeared left, into her room, slamming the door behind her. I took a step into the resonance being produced by Depeche Mode at top volume on her stereo.

I put the bag of food down on the sideboard and paused, less in thought than in suspended emotion: somewhere between excitement and fear. Then I picked the food back up and went in, and further in, and further, to her door and knocked.

'Anne-Laure, it's Gavin. Your dad asked me to drop some food off. I won't stay long. Are you okay?'

Over the music, I heard Coco whimper and scratch.

'Shall I take the dog around the block?'

The bell on Coco's collar tinkled as, I imagined, Anne-Laure pulled her back.

I brought the food through to the kitchen, removed everything from its wrapping and laid it on the table, with good cloth table mats and wine glasses and napkins and a candle at the centre. I handled all of these things expertly, as though I'd trained my entire life for this single task. Then I went back to Anne-Laure's room.

'I'm sorry to hear about what happened at school,' I said through the door, even though I didn't know what had happened and wasn't feeling sorry at all. 'I know how hard it can be. School can be really shit. I'll be in the study if you need me, okay? Your dad said he'll be home very soon. Though who knows how soon "soon" is, right?'

I stood in the middle of your study for what felt like an age, looking out of the window into the flats on the other side of the street and listening: Depeche Mode switched to Pearl Jam switched to Radiohead. Then, without really being conscious of the change, I found myself examining the things on your desk. Semi-hidden behind a pile of books there was a small silver box that opened without a key. Inside, sunk into a black velvet bed, were the utensils necessary for preparing wax seals. A candle. A spoon. Three bars of wax in different colours. And a stamp with a wooden handle. The engraving on the latter was an elaborate C, which I followed with my finger before popping the stamp into my pocket. Fearful that it showed through my trousers, I immediately transferred it to my bag.

I was perusing the bookshelf when you came back. Or rather, when I heard the front door bang. I jumped out of the desk chair and dashed across to the shelves and took down a book, any book – a biography of Jean Genet, it turned out – and opened it. The music cut off. I went to the study door to listen. Nothing. Then, out of nowhere, shouting. You. Her. Both. Screaming now, really screaming. The bedroom door opened. Her voice wailed. Then the door slammed shut again. You were saying, 'We've given you everything you wanted, everything, everything, everything, everything – when was the last time you heard the word no from us? – and you just throw it back in our faces. You're an ungrateful sow, do you hear me? That's what you are. How many warnings have we given you? How many?'

My heart was in my throat. Up to this point, I'd lazily assumed that Anne-Laure had been the victim of whatever incident had occurred at her school. Now it was dawning on me that she was in fact the perpetrator. More, a serial bully. The oppressor. Which is to say, Cyprien, that I went from having no feelings either way about your daughter to suddenly being against her.

At the same time, I was alarmed by your remonstrances. The terrifying sound of them. Which Anne-Laure had had years to learn how to fight against and outdo, but which I, in her place, would undoubtedly have crumbled before without daring to struggle. If such submission amounts to love, then I was in love. But this, I was wise enough to realise, wasn't the time or the place to demonstrate this to you. So I went – half sneaking, half not; both wanting to be free and wanting to be caught – out the way I came.

I didn't hear from you in the days immediately after this, and I thought it wiser not to disturb you. To my surprise, however, in the late afternoon the following Saturday, you came to the flat unannounced, carrying a bottle of wine wrapped in gold paper.

'What's this for?' I said suspiciously.

'To say thanks,' you said with convenient inexactness.

I stepped aside to invite you in.

'No, let's go for a walk,' you said.

We went up to parc Monceau, where we did two laps against the flow of the joggers who seemed, like salmon, to be toiling in unison towards their deaths. Your exercise, you said, was walking the city, it got no more strenuous than that; for this, your modest reward was a pair of skinny legs and only a small paunch, which you now slapped and rubbed comically. With this kind of banal chatter you put off the moment when you'd have to confide in me and, in doing so, admit we were equal in our desire to be close. I tried unsuccessfully to think that your slow pace in acknowledging your desire for my friendship was something to be savoured. At several junctures I was on the verge of begging you to stop abusing your power and just spit it out.

'Mathilde has taken Anne-Laure to spend the weekend with her dad.'

'I noticed *Andrei Rublev* in your DVD collection. We could watch that?'

You projected the film on a screen that descended in front of the bookcase in your study. I sat on the small couch alone, you on the desk chair to one side. Using a licence that you seemed to think the re-watching of an old black-and-white film afforded you, you talked through the whole thing: titbits, analyses of character and scene, clarifications of historical detail, an account of a trip you once took to Moscow, as well as generalities unrelated to the film, such as food, likes and dislikes, gossipy tales from the university.

'So she goes to a private school?' I asked after you mentioned, as though by accident, the expense of Anne-Laure's education.

'I'm ashamed to say she does,' you said.

'I did think it was odd that she wore a uniform,' I said.

The decision hadn't been yours, you said. If it had been up to you alone, she'd never have darkened the door of a school that charged fees.

'Who's to blame then?' I said.

Anne-Laure had excelled at primary school, you explained. The top of her class. During her final year, however, she'd started to get into trouble and the quality of her schoolwork had deteriorated. You thought it was just a phase. The problems would resolve themselves once she started secondary school. But there the problems persisted, got worse. Upon investigation – that is, after a fractious series of meetings with the school administration – you'd concluded that Anne-Laure was, on account of her precocious intellectual development, simply bored. The lessons weren't moving fast enough, weren't delving deep enough. So, with financial assistance from Mathilde's father, a transfer was arranged to a private school with an English name on Place des Vosges, Living House, which offered advanced classes, a bilingual environment and a high degree of individual attention.

'Did I resist? Of course I did! You must understand, Gavin, that I'm totally against inequality in education. I argue for equal access to learning for all.'

As it turned out, Anne-Laure settled in quickly. Her grades improved. And she made a new group of friends, from all over the world, who came regularly to your flat to eat and watch films and sleep over.

'When I passed her bedroom door, I'd hear them speaking English to each other, with a fluency I've never had, nor ever will have, and

I'd think, wow, they're doing something right in that place. Sure, I still had misgivings about buying in to an elitist institution, but at the end of the day, this was my daughter, right?'

But towards the end of Anne-Laure's second year at Living House, things went wrong again. She started to behave outrageously to impress her friends. She got into spats with her teachers. She stopped studying altogether.

'Almost like a protest. I asked her what point she was trying to make. And she said, cool as you please, "Call me a nihilist, but since when has there ever been a point?"'

Now she'd been accused of orchestrating a campaign of taunting and ostracism against one of her classmates: a pretty girl, a champion chess player, who formerly had been quite popular, but who'd been born, it was one day revealed, in the north suburbs, in Stains near Saint-Denis, the daughter of Belarusian immigrants, and who was, mortally, a scholarship recipient.

'Anne-Laure picked her out and went in for the kill,' you said. 'And it wasn't the first time. There were other girls. Other incidents. But we hadn't believed it before. How could we? It was too awful even to contemplate. But this time there was proof. Notes. Whole letters. Awful! Anne-Laure had used her friends as shields. She'd built an edifice of protection around herself. And one day, inevitably, it collapsed. Her bodyguards turned against her. Began telling the truth about her to the teachers. And it was over.'

The film had ended. You turned off the projector and turned on the main light.

'I have two consolations that help me sleep at night,' you said, bringing the dirty plates back to the kitchen and expecting me to follow. 'The first is the knowledge that the girl, the Belarusian, is white. If she'd been Indian or black, oh God, that would've been too much to handle. And the second is the knowledge that Anne-Laure didn't pick up these attitudes from me. My wife can sometimes be, well, she isn't always careful with her choice of words. But I don't totally blame Mathilde either. It's her fucking family. Spouting their right-wing bullshit from morning to night. They have a lot to answer for, no doubt about it.'

'So what happens now?' I said, putting my glass in the dishwasher. 'A new school?'

'Yeah. But not till September. We're taking some time out.'

'Are you going to leave Anne-Laure alone at home when you're at work?'

'She's fifteen now. She doesn't need babysitting.'

I watched you rearrange the items in the dishwasher, including my glass, so that they were more tightly packed.

'To be honest,' you said, straightening up and wiping your fingers on a tea towel, 'I was in two minds about telling you. I thought maybe you'd had a bad time at school. That this was a sore point for you.'

'What gave you that impression?'

'Nothing in particular. A hunch. I hope I haven't –'

'Weren't you bullied?'

'Me?'

'For your underbite.'

'Did I tell you that?'

'Yes, and I was glad you did.'

'Look, Gavin, don't be annoyed.'

'I'm not annoyed. I'm just pointing out that from direct experience you know how awful bullying is. What an impact it has.'

'I'm her father. It's my duty to try to see things from her side. In these situations, it's not just the victim that needs our understanding.'

I fiddled with a fridge magnet so I wouldn't have to look at you. 'You don't have to justify yourself to me, Cyprien. Of course you want to take care of your daughter.'

'I hope you won't hate her.'

I sighed and moved to the window, so that my back was to you.

'What she did was terrible,' you said, 'but she needs our support.'

I turned back to the room, though I was still unable to meet your eyes. 'I get it. You can count on me.'

Distractedly, you moved the bottles of oil beside the cooker around until they were all in a straight line, flush with the back tiles.

'Fundamentally,' you said, 'the problem is that she's been burdened with a very powerful mind. And she can be quickly overwhelmed by her emotions. These are her strengths, but too often they get the better of her. She hasn't yet learned to turn them to good account. It's pity for her I feel really.'

And there it was again. The pity. Saving you from having to

acknowledge your antipathy. And who'd blame you? What father wants to feel that for his own daughter?

'Is the dishwasher full now?' I said, pitying you in turn, and for this reason comprehending that we were now bound to each other, animus uniting with animus, such that ours could never be anything but a permanent friendship. 'Shall we put it on?'

FOURTH WALK

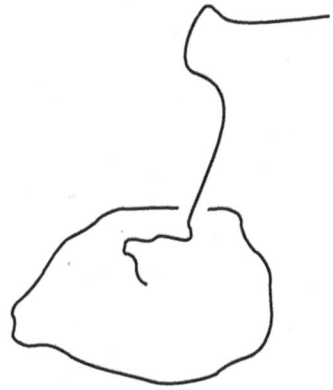

(*To Gonesse, walking northeast: rue J.-J. Rousseau – gare Saint-Lazare – rue de Rome – boulevard des Batignolles – boulevard de la Chapelle – rue d'Aubervilliers – porte d'Aubervilliers – boulevard Périphérique – Aubervilliers – Stains – Sarcelles – Arnouville – Gonesse; 28 km: 7 hours, 35 minutes*)

Disgust

Letter 34: GAVIN MULVANY to
JEAN-JACQUES ROUSSEAU

Paris, 1 July 2022

A few weeks after moving to Paris, I visited the Louvre with Cyprien. Our arrangement was two o'clock at the Pyramid. Arriving early, predicting chaos – it was the worst place, at the worst time of the day, on the worst day of the week, a Monday – I felt my heart sinking within me nonetheless. Ahead of me – and, before I knew it, all around me – the greater part of the city's tourist contingent was gravitating to the same nucleus.

'Oh, it's unbearable, I feel positively nauseous.' Coming into sight, Cyprien hooked his elbow onto mine and steered me through the milling bodies towards the northern wing of the museum, and I can attest that there's no faster-working antidote to the feeling of estrangement from the general masses than yielding to the iron will of a man whose unfitness for social life is in total accord with one's own. 'Did I say the Pyramid? My mistake. Let me get you out of here. Come this way. Honestly it's my fault. I should have told you the right place.'

He rushed us through a small door in passage Richelieu reserved for those in possession of a permanent pass. Then, upstairs on the first floor, he conducted us left to Decorative Arts, separating us from the main flow that was coursing in the other direction towards Italian Painting. Once inside the rooms, as we relaxed and eased into the stillness and the quiet, we separated from each other too. I went this way to look at one thing, Cyprien that way to look at another. I crossed his path, then he mine. I lost sight of him, or he of me, and, although our sense of togetherness didn't cease during these brief disappearances, when we saw each other again our gaze met and we briefly smiled to re-establish our shared status as men who took in the world and had time to reflect on it.

In the more stately rooms containing the royal furniture, we didn't say much to each other, each of us preferring simply to notice where the other's attention was landing – a writing desk, a commode, a bed, a tapestry – and to make a decision for himself about whether to afford it his own attention. Off the main corridor, however, in the windowless alcoves containing cases of smaller objects under strong artificial lights – here, yes, we began to share with each other our observations.

After a couple of hours, having traversed the length of the Richelieu Wing, I began to feel fatigued, which caused me to lose focus and move more quickly past the exhibits. Soon realising that I'd drifted far ahead of Cyprien, I retraced my steps to rejoin him. I found him alone in a dark recess, standing in contrapposto in front of a large pane of glass, behind which a few pieces of furniture were arranged as in a small sitting room. Approaching him from behind, slowly so as not to startle him, I placed a hand high on his back, just below the nape, anticipating with a rush that he'd turn to me and that I'd kiss him at last.

'Feast your eyes on that,' he said, defeating my hope by remaining immobile, transfixed by the display.

I withdrew my hand in order to step into position at his left flank and to bring my face closer to the glass. A quick survey of the exhibited items told me that Cyprien was probably referring to the child's straight-backed chair, a sort of mini-throne, carved – I checked the label to learn – out of golden walnut, with silk cushions embroidered in silver.

'The infant's chair?' I said.

'Is it just an ornament?' he said. 'Because functionally speaking, it seems like a waste.'

'I imagine its primary function was to show the world that you could afford a luxury that your child was quickly going to outgrow.'

'Presuming your child survived at all.' Cyprien took a turn examining the label. 'It's dated 1760. Which, as you know, was a time when infant mortality carried off one child in every four. Even among the noble classes, children had only a fifty per cent chance of attaining puberty. If you owned this chair' – uncharacteristically, Cyprien pressed his index fingertip against the glass, long enough to leave a mark – 'you were evidently concerned with more than just showing off your money. You were also anxious to hide certain things you didn't want to see. Namely, the uncivilised parts of your child. The animal parts. By sitting your beloved Quentin or sweet little Annabel in this chair, you were actively repressing the disgust you felt about the fact that your child was a creature that shat and pissed and vomited, and that might at any time flare up with the pox. A mortal animal. Stalked by death.'

'Ah, now all I can think about is baby diarrhoea seeping into the embroidery!'

'Flesh festering on the silk!'

Laughing softly, privately, then sighing with contentment – that had been fun – we came away from the alcove and into the light of a corridor. At one of the tall windows we delayed for a minute to look out onto the square, where the people were taking photos of each other under their parasols.

'On some level though,' Cyprien said, 'disgust must have its uses.'

'Helping us to avoid contamination?' I said. 'Nowadays the sell-by dates that appear on everything we consume probably render that form of disgust obsolete.'

'Obsolete? I'm not so sure. As a toddler Anne-Laure showed no aversion to her own excrement. She joyfully put her hand into her potty and played in it. We had to teach her that it was unhealthy, that it could make her sick. The memory of how exactly we did this escapes me, but I suppose we transmitted disgust in some way. Probably by pulling faces and saying, "Eugh!" a lot.'

The mention of Anne-Laure made my heart sink a little. Until then we'd been like two bugs in a jar, sealed off from our ordinary lives. 'I tend to think,' I said, 'that some of the aversions imposed on us by our parents are detrimental to our psychological well-being.'

Cyprien raised his eyebrows. 'Such as aversion to shit?'

'Even that. Especially that.'

'I'm all ears.'

'Well, as you say, disgust works as a kind of defensive illusion. It wants to protect us from existential terror. To draw a veil over our inevitable demise. To have us believe that both we and our loved ones are immaculate and immortal. In this sense, it appears to want the best for us. Ostensibly it works for our benefit. The drawback is that it ends up putting us at odds with our own physical bodies.

It demands that we perceive our own bodies as abject, that we set our faces against the very material that makes us what we are. It impels us to shun our own humanity.'

'But isn't there a case to be made in favour of disgust? Take the infant chair. There's no doubt I felt disgust while viewing it. My disgust, however, wasn't caused by the aesthetic qualities of the object itself. Or by any worry that it was infested by mites that I could contract, since there was a wall of glass separating me from it. Rather I was disgusted by what the chair represented. Economic inequality. Which is to say, my disgust was moral in nature. Rather than shielding me from ugliness or decay or death, disgust opened my eyes to the violations of justice that underpin the existence of the chair itself.'

'Are you arguing that there can be wisdom in repugnance?'

'I haven't given it a huge amount of thought, but, yeah, at first glance it seems to me that disgust, like any emotion, is an expression of something which, if interpreted properly, can reveal truths.'

A group of American tourists trundled towards us. Cyprien waited for them to pass before going on.

'You could go further and say that, in this age in which terrorists plan media spectacles, and in which the Yanks, with our assent, terrorise the rest of the world with their war on terror, disgust could be a voice that speaks up to defend humaneness.'

I had turned away from Cyprien to watch the passers-by and had kept my gaze averted while listening to the rest of his words. Now, guided by feelings I was as yet unable to name, I began to follow the tourist group up the corridor. On reaching the landing, where people were streaming out of various doors and going down the stairs, I halted, suddenly aware of my own strangeness, my own rudeness.

Cyprien, who had come after me, looked worried. 'Are you all right? Did I say something to offend you?'

'Sorry,' I said. 'I was feeling a bit faint.'

'Let's get you some water.'

At a café off the main atrium, we shared a half-litre bottle of Vittel and agreed that ordinarily neither of us would be seen dead in a place like this.

'Now are you going to tell me what's on your mind?' he said.

'You're my mentor, Cyprien. I have a lot of respect for you. I don't like to disagree with you.'

'Oh, now! Snap out of that and tell me.'

'It's not that important, really. I just don't believe disgust is relevant to deciding what's right or wrong, that's all.'

'And you could be right about that. You shouldn't be afraid to speak your mind with me.'

He was sitting in an awkward position with his elbow on the table and his fingertips gripping the lip of his glass and turning it around and around. My own right hand was resting too far forward to look natural; if I'd had the courage to turn this hand onto its back, he could, with little effort, have laid his palm onto mine.

'You used the example of 9/11,' I said. 'Like most people, I watched the images of the towers coming down. The people jumping. If I was really disgusted by what I saw, I'd have looked away, but I didn't.'

'You sound upset.'

'I'm just expressing my scepticism that disgust is a trustworthy guide to moral judgements or that there is any deep wisdom in it. Don't al-Qaeda use their supposed feelings of revulsion for the western liberal order to justify their atrocities?'

'They certainly do.'

'Likewise, if the majority of a given population is disgusted by something, should the government legislate against that thing, even if it is in reality causing nobody any harm?'

'I was right. You were bullied in school.'

I was stunned. 'What? How is that relevant?'

'I've been teaching for a while. I've had hundreds of students. By now I can pick out the ones that had difficult experiences at school. Like you, they have what you might call a sensitivity to rules that, as you put it, aim to instil moral probity rather than prevent harm.'

Cyprien had been bullied as well, apparently with similar ferocity. Yet it wasn't until much later in our friendship, when we'd become more intimate, that he let me in on the precise details of his own experience. That day in the Louvre he allowed me to talk, he inquired further, he listened, but he refrained from stepping in and taking his turn.

'Criminal,' he said. 'I'd reinstate the death penalty purely for those assholes.'

'When I passed them in the corridor, the other boys, and sometimes the girls too, would pretend to vomit. They'd put their hands to their bellies and cover their mouths and make retching sounds. They'd recoil. Make space around me, you know? As though avoiding some invisible material, a bad essence, that might be transferred through contact.'

'As though you were disgusting.'

'As though, together, they were the moral arbiters whose job it was to inform me that I was disgusting.'

This was the only coming-out I ever performed with Cyprien. Not once did I ever say to him, 'I'm gay,' or, 'I like men actually,' even though these expressions had hitherto come easily to me. In Dublin I'd been irrepressibly 'out'. As a form of defence, I'd gone on the offensive. Adopted a posture of fearlessness that I must have believed would save me from more pain.

He tossed back the remaining water in his glass and said, 'Let's get out of this hellhole. Have you eaten?'

Letter 35: JEAN-JACQUES ROUSSEAU to GAVIN MULVANY

Paris, 2 July 1777

Of all my writings, those on the science of teaching children have been the most misunderstood. My enemies have used them to attribute to me feelings that are so wicked they would never arise within the human heart. By purposely misreading my words and taking them out of context, it is simple for them to present me as contrary to nature and to make of me a monster such as may not even exist.

After reading your letter, I jotted down a few thoughts derived from it. New reflections have occurred to me on the subject. I have reduced the whole into a sort of system that I will send you once I have worked it out better, so that you may examine it in turn. In the meantime, we should arrange to meet in person, as I do not wish you to spend one more day in possession of wrong ideas about me. Stay where you are, do not move. I will come to the address written on your envelope and take you out for a walk. Then might I wake from this bad dream to find myself again in the company of a real friend?

MS Extract: from *Rousseau's Lost Children* by GAVIN MULVANY

Last edited: 2 July 2022

Together the *First* and *Second Discourses* made Rousseau's name in the intellectual scene in Paris. Rousseau was, however, irritated by homage and indignant at his celebrity. To receive the public attention which he had so doggedly sought, was undoubtedly thrilling – 'What can be most unfavourable to me is to be half known' – but, in the event, it also unnerved him, for he was by now a middle-aged man who had, during the wanderings of his twenties and thirties, fastened himself to the ideal of solitude. Moreover, he was beginning to understand that he could never be a Parisian, and got out of the city whenever he could.

His disgust with Paris reflected his deepening disaffection with the intellectuals of the Enlightenment, whose atheism and scepticism made him uneasy, whose moral complacency he found intolerable and whose sociability ran contrary to his impulse to free himself from society's influence. He quarrelled with Diderot and fell out publicly with other important figures, such as Voltaire and d'Alembert. He attacked the ethical legitimacy of the *Encyclopédie* and questioned the integrity of those dedicated to it. In short, he made a break for it. 'I despise my century and my contemporaries. I consider the peasants of Montmorency more useful members of society than the heaps of idlers paid with the fat of the people to go six times a week to gossip in an academy.'

A noblewoman named Louise d'Épinay became aware of his depressed state and invited him to live at a house known as the Hermitage at the edge of the forest of Montmorency, sixteen kilometres north of Paris and in walking distance of her château. Rousseau gladly accepted. As a sign of the respect she had for him, d'Épinay completely renovated the Hermitage in advance of his arrival in 1756. At his new retreat, released from the social obligations of the city and – thanks to financial support from d'Épinay – from the need to earn a living, Rousseau once again found himself with great tracts of time to himself. Between long walks in the woods, he composed several works which, on publication, were read far and wide and made him not only one of the most prominent thinkers of the period, but one of the most famous men in all Europe.

One of these works was *Émile*, a philosophical treatise thinly disguised as a novel about the unusual education of a young boy. How to overcome dependence on others and achieve self-reliance? In *Émile*, Rousseau maps out a programme of edification which has as its aim the liberation of the boy from the tyranny of adult expectations, so that his faculties may develop unfettered, each in its good time. The boy is separated from his parents and entrusted to a single tutor, with whom he lives in isolation in the countryside. The tutor does not aim to prepare the boy for any profession or other niche in society, but rather works to develop his unique temperament in the most rewarding way. To this end, the tutor gives his lessons in the outdoors, where he uses the phenomena of nature, rather than books, to foster in the boy the fundamental skills of self-preservation. He nurtures the boy's emotions, while refusing to reason with him or demand that he use reason himself. Instead of commanding the boy, he draws his attention to the limits that nature places upon him. Indeed he refrains from giving verbal lessons of any kind, since he believes the boy can learn better from his own experience.

With *Émile*, Rousseau was reacting against mainstream Enlightenment thought, which argued that men of a certain class ought to be trained in empirical reasoning and inculcated with 'sensibility' (that is, a capacity to be moved morally, spiritually and emotionally for the purposes of further civilising society). But that was not the whole story. In advancing a radical new mode of education, Rousseau was also grappling with his own upbringing, in which a formal education had played no part. As far as book knowledge was concerned, Rousseau was at a disadvantage compared to his conventionally educated peers. Feeling this handicap keenly, and determined to overcome it, he reasoned that there must be another way of looking at it. Was this gap in systematic instruction in fact the key to his ability for independent thought?

One might expect the young Rousseau, having lost his mother as a baby, and with his artisan father busy in the workshop all day, to have had more freedom than the average Genevan child of his time. In fact, under the care of his nursemaid and his aunt, who were kindly but attentive to his father's orders, Rousseau was kept in, fussed over, lavished with affection, idolised and by every other zealous means prevented from roaming the streets with the other children of the neighbourhood. After supper, and sometimes through the night until morning, he and his father took turns reading aloud from the books in the house library: world histories and the lives of famous men, but also romances left behind by his mother. Later, these books were moved into his father's atelier, where young Jean-Jacques was made to sit and read to his father while he worked. 'By this dangerous method, I acquired an understanding, unique in one of my years, of the passions.'

Rousseau was not sent to school. At the age of ten, however, after his father got into a quarrel and had to leave Geneva permanently to avoid arrest, Jean-Jacques was packed off, along with his cousin Bernard, to board with a pastor in the village of Bossey. The pastor did not neglect Rousseau's education, but nor did he overburden him with lessons. Instead, the boy who in Geneva had had no labour imposed upon him, was made to work around the house and grounds. What this gave him was a new appreciation for the activities that served as relaxation. His favourite of these was walking in the countryside, accompanied by Bernard, with whom he had formed a close attachment. 'This simple country life bestowed on me a gift beyond price by opening up my heart to friendship.' The spoilt and sheltered Rousseau had been in desperate need of a friend, but, now that he finally had one, he came to see that the possession of friendship had two faces. On the one side was happy companionship, on the other fear of loss and loneliness. To be separated from Bernard was, for Rousseau, nothing less than 'to be annihilated'. For this reason Bernard had to be held close, and, more critically, had to be kept away from the other children, who might steal him.

Thus Rousseau's early idea of friendship – which quickly transmuted into an ideal that he would cling to for the rest of his life – was one that required intentional disconnection from both blood and social ties. For Rousseau, from the beginning, friendship was a kind of solitary love-bond, one that was no less emotion-soaked for being chaste, and one that needed to be vigilantly guarded against attacks by the hostile crowd. As they walked alone together, Rousseau and Bernard – the odd couple of Bossey, the former short, the latter tall – could not help drawing attention to themselves. The village children mocked them as a pair.

After a couple of years at the pastor's, Rousseau returned to Geneva to take up his apprenticeship. Overseen by a cruel master, he developed an aversion to arbitrary authority and force as methods of ruling over others. He duly ditched his training after three years in favour of the open road. In 1728, at the age of sixteen, he found himself in the village of Annecy, where he was taken in by a baroness, Françoise-Louise de Warens: 'Ah, my child, you are too young to be wandering around the country; really it's a shame.' Immediately, Rousseau held Warens in awe and submitted himself to her charge. She, aged twenty-nine, became his protectress and educator; he became her 'work'.

Warens's first act was to send Rousseau off to a hospice in Turin to become a Catholic. Rousseau, eager to comply, and desirous of future favours from Warens, walked more than two hundred kilometres to get there. In the seminary, while allowing himself time 'to become accustomed to the idea of being a Catholic' (without ever, he said, really becoming one), he was propositioned and molested by one of the other male residents, an experience which engendered in him a lifelong disgust of homosexuality.

Returning to Annecy, aged seventeen, he now became Warens's lover and at around the same time began to call her 'Mummy'. Less in love than in the grip of youthful infatuation, Rousseau believed he had already found the ideal life he had been seeking, and had no wish to change it; but Warens did. Her plan was to find a profession suitable to Rousseau's talents and push him out into the world. She also had another lover, her servant Claude, and was keen to have time away from her demanding 'child'. So she sent Rousseau to live with a neighbour for music instruction.

There, Rousseau was merely an average student. He liked his master but did not feel particularly drawn to him. One night, however, a caller came to the door, who announced himself as Venture de Villeneuve, a French musician, with whom Rousseau would become instantly captivated. Venture claimed to know all the men and women of rank in Paris, and explained that his own poor financial circumstances forced him to make his way in the world by working as a substitute. It seemed improbable that this bluffer actually knew any music, but he offered to sing, and to everyone's surprise he performed superbly. He was invited to stay, much to Rousseau's delight. In Venture, Rousseau believed he had found a model to be emulated, but he was not the only one to fall under the newcomer's spell. Venture was soon being fêted throughout Annecy and being fought over by women. Jealously, Rousseau suggested that he share Venture's lodgings; Venture agreed.

Now Rousseau was able to watch Venture at close quarters. Listen to him without interruption. Soak up his every remark. When Venture went off to pay social calls, Rousseau would go out for walks on his own and muse on the Frenchman's merits, envying his rare talent and cursing his own limitations. Whenever his feelings for Venture got too much, or threatened to overstep the mark, his trick was to conjure up his 'Mummy', whose image acted as a 'powerful preventive against any excess of this sort'.

On his return to Annecy six months later, Rousseau found Warens had gone to Paris with her servant-lover, so he took to the road on his own again – Fribourg, Lausanne, Neuchâtel, Berne, Soleure – seeking, and mostly failing, to gain employment as a tutor. He would, in the not-too-distant future, be reunited with Warens and undergo a further period of study and self-improvement. But at this point, post-Venture, his childhood education, such as it was, was over. With the scant knowledge he had accrued, he was daring to make the switch to becoming an educator himself.

Thirty years later, when he came to write *Émile*, it was the characters and motifs from this unconventional early formation, rather than from any period of structured learning, that he used to populate the text. The relationship to which he gave most importance in the novel – far outweighing that of the boy with his parents, his siblings or his future bride – was that between the boy and his tutor. How might a tutor guide his pupil to independence without oppressing him? And, conversely, how might a pupil submit to his tutor without losing his autonomy? Rousseau thought he had hit on the answer.

Letter 36: GAVIN MULVANY to CYPRIEN ABREO

Paris, 4 July 2022

Jean-Jacques came to the seminary today, would you believe? In our dealings thus far he and I haven't seen eye to eye, our most recent run-in deteriorated into discourtesy, so I was startled when I came out of the main door to find him loitering there. From scrutinising the plaque on the wall, he took two steps back and flourished his walking stick at the freshly scrubbed outer façade.

'Who are you sharing with?' he said, diving straight in, no explanations sought or offered.

'Students mostly,' I said. 'Some artists.'

'Is it the religion in which you were born, or are you turning?'

'The former, most certainly.'

'I suspect that won't save you from hours spent in petty disputation and quibbling.'

'I tend to keep to myself.'

'Remain watchful for anyone who becomes free in his manner towards you or makes strange suggestions. Don't let your guard down.'

He loudly ejected the contents of his throat onto the ground. Then swung round, took my arm and led me up the street.

'For your own safety, I'm going to spell it out,' he said. 'When I was sixteen and still searching for my place in the world, I stayed in a seminary in Turin. One of the other lodgers, a bandit who claimed to be a Moor, took a liking to me. He stayed close by me, did me little favours and bestowed frequent kisses on me. In spite of the natural alarm I felt at his swarthy countenance and his fervent gaze, more furious than tender, I endured his attention, for I felt it'd be unkind to rebuff him. Then one day when we were alone together in the assembly room, he began his usual caresses, but with such violence in his movements that I began to feel afraid of him. He tried by degrees to move to the vilest of intimacies and, by directing my hand, to force me to do the same. I recoiled, flinging myself from him in disgust. As his convulsive movements began to subside, I saw something spurt towards the fireplace and fall on the floor, something sticky and white, which turned my stomach further.'

'Did you manage to get away unharmed?'

'My body remained unviolated. But in my mind I was left with the image of the man's terrible face inflamed by the most brutal lust. I've never seen another man in such a state, but if this is how we appear in our transports with women, they must indeed be bewitched if they can look upon us without horror.'

At the end of the street we entered the square where the Church of Sainte-Geneviève (i.e. your favourite place, the Panthéon) was still under construction and causing a lot of dust and noise. From his pocket Jean-Jacques whipped a handkerchief which, during the breaks in his speech, he put over his nose and mouth.

'Now, foreigner,' he said, 'out of the goodness of my heart I've come. Do we have a destination? Be our helmsman, for crying out loud.'

Unwinding my arm from his, I laid it across his shoulders where it was more comfortable, a gesture that belied the insecurity I was feeling about finally getting what I wanted from him. What now did he expect from me in return? Where was I supposed to be taking him? I couldn't say I was in control. While he didn't resist my steering, he did continue to set the pace, ensuring his footsteps landed ahead of mine, which caused my efforts to lead to appear absurd.

'Then again,' he said, 'Turin is nothing compared to Lyon! Lyon, of all European cities, is the one I regard to be most given over to corruption. There, when I was eighteen and trying to make my way as a tutor, an abbot saw me sleeping on place Bellecour and offered me lodgings for the night. When I got to his house, I discovered he had only one room and that in fact what he was offering was a share of his bed. I accepted the offer, hoping that here was a friend who might prove useful. It turned out, however, that this man of the church had the same proclivities as the Moor, though he displayed them less urgently. Rather than declaring them openly, he tried to win me over without alarming me. Better informed than on the previous occasion, I soon saw what he was about and, speaking with all the gentleness and firmness I could command, indicated to him that I was irked by his caresses and determined not to allow them to proceed.'

'Did it work? Were you able to make an escape?'

'Well, after that, we spent the rest of the night peacefully. Indeed he said a number of worthy and sensible things, and was clearly not devoid of all merit, in spite of being such a vile wretch.'

I removed my arm from Jean-Jacques's shoulder so that I could turn at the waist and look him in the face more fully. 'I'm glad you've chosen to speak to me about this. Your disclosures contain some knotty points that, unless you have any objections, I'd like to tease out with you.'

He gave a non-committal shrug.

'The Moor you talked about was a bandit, correct? By this I understand that he was an unemployed vagrant, a criminal, who was pretending to convert to Catholicism so that he could avail himself of the free food and lodgings in the seminary.'

'And what a fine performance he put on! A week after accosting me, he was baptised with great ceremony, dressed from head to foot in white to symbolise the purity of his regenerated soul.'

'From your description I gather he was an ugly figure. That he had poor hygiene.'

'The miserable fellow was so dirty and stank so badly of chewed tobacco that he filled me with revulsion.'

'Would I be right in assuming he was uneducated? Maybe even illiterate? Unused to polite company? Unschooled in chivalry or charm?'

'Barbarous. And I don't use that word lightly.'

'So you'd agree, then, that the Moor was a man who'd never learned the vocabulary of seduction, and that as a result his advances were rough, lacking in pretence. His desire for you, far from something possessing a loftiness of purpose, was, in his experience, a primal, grasping force, which he didn't have the wherewithal to conceal from you.'

'I'll concede that there is no soul so base that it is not capable of some sort of attachment. But I won't sanction a vindication of the Moor's misbehaviour, if that's what you're proposing.'

'On the contrary, I've no doubt that what the Moor did to you was wrong. At sixteen, you'd have had your own methods of seeing, thinking, feeling, touching. In trying to substitute adult methods for these, the Moor was denying your right to be a child before you're a man. I condemn his actions unequivocally. What I'm trying to comprehend, simply, is the nature of the disgust you felt for him.'

'The memory of what the Moor did, and especially what I saw him do, is so powerfully imprinted on my mind that my stomach still turns when I think of it. That's how complete my disgust for him was and remains.'

'Do you think it might be possible to identify the precise cause of your disgust? Were you worried that being touched by such a filthy man might give you a disease? Did you believe that being intimate with a low-class criminal would draw you into crime too? Or, on the contrary, was your disgust more moral in character? Was your disgust at the Moor's behaviour so extravagant because sexual relations between men goes against what you believe the natural order to be? Did you feel an ethical obligation to respond with disgust, so as not to be seen to be condoning sinful conduct?'

'I'm puzzled by your questions. Before my encounter with the Moor, I was ignorant of the existence of such relations between men. On being enlightened on this point, I felt profound disgust, which was a moral feeling in the sense that it sprang from my innate instinct of what is natural and good.'

'What confuses me about this is that you felt disgust for the Moor, but not for the abbot. Why?'

Starting behind his ear, Jean-Jacques wormed a finger under his wig to scratch a spot there.

'Isn't it the abbot,' I said, 'who truly merits disgust? He enticed you to his home under false pretences and abused his authority to gain sexual favours from you. In your own writings, you warn us against such deceitful and cunning men. "Let's be wary of perfect people" – those are your words. Placed beside the sneaky abbot, what is the Moor but a desperate man who hasn't learned to hide his misshapen features behind masks?'

Jean-Jacques removed his finger and peered at the flecks of dry skin on his long nail. 'Truth to tell,' he said, 'since learning of their depravity, I can't help feeling revulsion for all men on this earth.' He flicked the skin away, before setting his gaze squarely on mine. 'Women, on the other hand, have gained greatly in my eyes. I feel I owe them the tenderest regard, the homage of my whole person, in reparation for the offences of my sex.'

By now we had turned right onto rue Saint-Jacques and come to a halt in front of the arched entranceway of Collège des Jésuites (as Lycée Louis-le-Grand was then known). Despite this being the quiet period of the academic year, there were plenty of carriages on the road. Taking advantage of a brief gap in the traffic, I stepped out so that I could read the inscription above the school gate: COLLEGIUM MAGNI LUDO.

Jean-Jacques followed my gaze. 'You have a sense of humour, I'll give you that.'

'A favour to me. We don't have to stay long.'

'These days everything I do is a favour.'

He pounded a fist on one of the gate's lower panels, then called out his own name in such a way as to suggest that it was synonymous with the apex of the age and made him everywhere welcome.

'There's a bell here,' I said.

'To hell with the bell.'

Through the gaps of the wrought iron, I peered into the internal courtyard. 'Don't you envy Voltaire and Diderot even a little for having gone here?'

A Jesuit priest came to the gate and asked us our business. After much pressing from Jean-Jacques – 'This foreigner is on a mission for knowledge, and he seems to think he'll find it here' – the Jesuit agreed to accompany us on a tour of the central courtyard. After bringing us swiftly through the entrance arch, the Jesuit made to go clockwise around the neat garden in the middle of the yard, but Jean-Jacques split off the other way, and I went with him, leaving the priest to return to the entrance and wait for us there.

'"SCHOOL IS A BIG GAME,"' Jean-Jacques said. 'Isn't it marvellous that in undertaking to educate children, no other means of guiding them should have been devised than games of perversion?'

'If you had a child of your own' – was I speaking hypothetically or casting subtle reproach? I myself couldn't tell – 'if you had a child, a son, and you had the money, would you send him to such a school?'

'To a place like this?' With his stick he drew a circle in the air around his head to direct my attention to the lines of windows, all the little cells. 'Never. Or at least not until the child has learned elsewhere how to grow up.'

'So you'd educate the child yourself, at home?'

'Oh, I wouldn't presume to educate my own child. A child must be guided, not by his father, but by someone he considers to be a friend.'

'A tutor of some kind?'

'Someone who, before daring to undertake the formation of another being, has made himself a man. This is the only qualification I'd require.'

'Say I was a child. And you, a young man unrelated to me, were assigned to be my tutor. Would you remove me completely from my parents' influence?'

'The blind tenderness of your mother would be disastrous for you. Your father's tyranny a hundred times more so. I'd take you off their hands before they started tormenting you for your own good.'

'Where would you take me?'

'To a modest house in the countryside, where you'd be in direct contact with nature without the intermixture of opinion.'

'You'd raise me there alone?'

'You make it sound like a fearful prospect!'

'It'd be a big responsibility for you.'

'One I'm not unimpressed by. But my method would be simple at base. In the cottage, I'd live as I'd want you to live, that is to say, plainly and in harmony with nature. I'd show you that this manner of existing is the foundation of my happiness, and I'd thereby become a model for you.'

'Imitation would be your method? You'd impel me to copy you?'

'In no wise would I force you to do anything. I'd merely embody certain virtues in my everyday life with you, in our games, in our adventures, in our experiments, in our work, which, in time, you'd only see benefit in emulating.'

'I don't wish to be contrary, Jean-Jacques, but wouldn't it be difficult to sustain being a paragon at all times? It sounds quite stressful to me. I can't see how, even with your best efforts, you could avoid setting some bad examples.'

'I said nothing about being a paragon. I wouldn't waste a moment affecting magisterial dignity or trying to pass for an ideal man in your mind. How easy it is for the perfect teacher to combat passions he doesn't feel! On the contrary, I'd show you my weaknesses, so that I might help you to cure your own. I'd want you to see that I undergo the same struggles that you experience.'

'What if I wasn't able to emulate you? Or didn't want to? Wouldn't you be forced then to impose some discipline on me?'

'I wouldn't constrain you to stay anywhere when you wish to go away, or to go away when you wish to stay. You'd be at liberty to leap, to run, to shout, whenever you will.'

'When in fact I'd be tasked with constantly figuring out your unspoken rules.'

'There's no subjection so perfect as that which keeps the appearance of freedom.'

We'd arrived back at the entrance, where the Jesuit had extended an arm to direct us out. From a nearby arch, another priest, apparently of a superior rank, was reprimanding the Jesuit *magna voce*. Jean-Jacques got between them and gave to each a bow of thanks, which I then mimicked, possibly hamming the gesture up a bit too much, for the two men's expressions bespoke offence.

After the silence of the courtyard, it took a moment to adjust to the noise of the street.

'And now?' said Jean-Jacques.

We cut north across the Tuileries into place Louis-le-Grand (aka Vendôme), took a right on rue des Capucines, a left onto rue de Louis-le-Grand, crossed the tree-lined city boundary into the hamlet of Porcherons and were soon in open fields. Jean-Jacques broke away in search of specimens, while I sat on a knoll and watched the rotations of a nearby windmill. A few minutes later he was back with four different flowers which he didn't name, and whose various parts he pointed out without identifying or explaining their function. Then he sat down beside me and we looked west to the unobstructed horizon.

'At the end of the day,' he said, 'to know good and evil, and to sense the reason for man's duties, wouldn't be your affair. I'd keep you ignorant of these things for as long as possible. Rather I'd leave you alone to be amazed at what you see around you.' He pointed to a spot on the horizon. 'The sun will go down somewhere there.' He twisted round and threw an arm out in the other direction. 'But it came up over there. How can that be so? Isn't it a breathtaking wonder?'

'Based solely on my observations, without any book knowledge to direct my empirical reasoning, I'd probably say it's because the sun revolves around the earth.'

'Correct.'

'But it's false! I'd need diagrams, would I not, and globes and maps, and the explanations of a conventional teacher, to learn the truth?'

'Only deceptions that distort moral perceptions and judgements are, strictly speaking, falsehoods. What would matter, more than facts, is discovering what's really useful to you.'

'You'd allow me to walk around believing a patent untruth?'

'In school you learned to take something for granted because someone said it's so. You were ruled by opinion. Under my guidance, nothing would be true but what you saw to be true.'

'No, that's not how it would be. As your pupil, I'd recognise your superior wisdom and beg you to be generous with it. I'd want you to give me the truth.' Suddenly my face was in my hands. On freeing it a moment later, I found my vision blurred. 'I can't stand it! What you're saying –'

'What's so wrong with it?'

'– is a torture! When would it stop? Your tutorship, when would it end?'

'When you'd no longer have need of any guide other than yourself.'

'Who'd decide when that moment had arrived?'

'You.'

'Me?'

'Once you'd learned how to distinguish your real wants, the wants of nature, from those which arise from fancy. Once you'd begun to desire only what is. At that point you'd have no more use for me, and I'd let you go.'

'You're lying. Long before any of that, you'd give up.' I snapped my fingers in his face. 'Like that, no warning, you'd stop being my friend. You'd love me, you'd delight in me, then you'd abandon me.'

'Mine would be a healing education that would ultimately return you to yourself. There would come a time when my continued guidance would be detrimental to your burgeoning manhood and you'd have to strike out on your own.'

'You mean, a time when you'd grow weary of me. When I'd become useless to you.'

He reached out abruptly and cupped my jaw. Rubbed his thumb across my cheek. Both the roughness of his skin and its strong odour repulsed me, though I didn't pull away. 'Tears, of all the body products, are the one that doesn't elicit disgust. Isn't that queer?'

'You'd get bored with me and drop me. And in doing so, you'd cause me more misery than any good you'd have done me.'

Removing his hand, he peered at his thumb and forefinger as he rubbed the wetness between them. 'I imagine because they're seen as uniquely human. What animal cries?'

Letter 37: GAVIN MULVANY to PEDRO SOUZA

Paris, 5 July 2022

I took a walk with a friend yesterday. An author who agreed to share with me his expertise on a subject of some importance to my book. We parted ways on rue de Rome, near the junction with rue Bernoulli. Dazed after the rigours of our dialogue, I sat for a while on a ledge with my back resting against the railings that overlook the tracks of gare Saint-Lazare. On the other side of the road, looming over me, was a nineteenth-century fortress, with a chimney poking out of its central courtyard, iron bars on its windows and video cameras pointed onto the heads of the passing pedestrians: Lycée Chaptal, where Nicolas Sarkozy was schooled.

I slouched up the road, with the vague intention of finishing my walk in the countryside in the northwest. It wasn't until I found myself in Pigalle that I realised I'd taken a wrong turn. Loath to turn back, I went on as far as gare du Nord, and, consulting a map there, changed my final destination to Gonesse in the northeast.

In Aubervilliers, among the towers of low-income housing, I came across a vocational college named after the eighteenth-century thinker d'Alembert: '*Teach men to doubt and wait.*' I pressed ahead, arriving twenty minutes later at the Cité des 4000, the famous project built in the 1950s and 1960s. In 2005, after an eleven-year-old boy was killed by a stray bullet in front of a block of flats here, Sarkozy (picture Louis XIV in his high heels) visited the area and spoke with the locals on the street: 'I'm going to clean the Cité des 4000 with a high-pressure hose!' To which a young man responded, 'We're not animals!' Since the 1980s a programme of redevelopment has been underway, as part of which some of the more monumental towers have been demolished and replaced by four- and five-storey buildings arranged on gridded streets punctuated by green spaces. The insistent uniformity of this ever-transitioning world I found dizzying, and quickly became lost. Several times I passed and re-passed a vocational school named after Jacques Brel: *'Let me become / The shadow of your shadow / The shadow of your hand / The shadow of your dog / But / Don't leave me.'*

'How do I leave here?' I asked a woman at a bus stop, who helped me to locate a way-out, through parc Georges-Valbon.

In Stains, I took a road on to Sarcelles. By now the afternoon had become evening, the sky was darkening and I had a nervous feeling that I was on a wild goose chase. I simply wanted to cross from suburb into green space, so that I'd feel that I'd done at least the bare minimum. I scouted the eastern edge of a tableland of bungalows for a path east that would take me to Gonesse, still over seven kilometres way. This turned out to be a felicitous route. For I came upon a rue Jean-Jacques Rousseau.

On one side of the road was a row of modern suburban houses of varying shapes and sizes; on the other side, a tall, white metal fence, behind which sat none other than Lycée Jean-Jacques Rousseau. I went along the length of the fence, trying to get a proper view of the grounds. I counted four glass-fronted blocks of three and four storeys, as well as an athletics track and a basketball court. I gripped the bars of the entrance gate and leaned my weight forward: Lycée Rousseau was an almost identical copy of the secondary school I'd attended in Dublin.

I don't need to describe Saint Joseph's Community School to you, because we went there together once. On our second anniversary as a couple, if memory serves. We'd booked into a hotel in Wicklow for the weekend, and on the drive down, quite without warning, you turned off the main road and cut into my old neighbourhood.

'After everything you've told me,' you said, 'I want to see it for myself.'

'Is this your present to me?' I said.

'Just a minute to look.'

We crept past my childhood home, now renovated and occupied by strangers. Then I showed you a few spots where little events took place. But this wasn't enough to humour you. You wanted to see the school.

'All right, but we're not fucking getting out.'

We parked near the entrance. As at Lycée Rousseau, the grounds were bordered on one side by shrubs and trees.

'There,' I said, pointing.

'There?' you said.

We were both pointing then.

'Stop pointing,' I said.

Then we drove off again. But that was never going to be the end of it. At our nice dinner that evening, you said, 'Make use of me.'

'What use can you be?' I said. 'Were you ever dragged into the bushes by a group of boys and made to grope the breasts of a female classmate, as a cure for your homosexuality?'

'I was lucky, I admit. I was spared that.'

'Then you're of no use.'

'That hurts.'

'You stopped being my psych nurse precisely two years ago, Pedro. You're off the hook. Let's just eat.'

In the room afterwards, getting into our pyjamas, you were still quiet, so I said, 'You're worried, aren't you?'

'About what?'

'That my being bullied has turned me into a bully. That the cycle goes on, and you're the next victim.'

'You do scare me sometimes. Your temper.'

'Don't give me that. You give as good as you get.'

'You're still not over what happened.'

'Oh God. What would being "over it" even look like?'

On being released I had dashed away across the school grounds, regularly glancing back to check if I was being pursued. No one came out of the shrubbery after me. They stayed in there. Four boys and one girl. Dark pictures of what was taking place, or about to take place, flooded my mind, and along with these a distinct feeling of obligation. I had a duty to inform someone. But I didn't. In the following days, weeks, years, I was given plenty of opportunities to speak out about what had happened, the part I'd played, and to make amends to the girl. But I didn't take advantage of these. In the event I always plumped for secretiveness, for suppression. I kept it locked inside.

'It's obvious you blame yourself.'

'Who wouldn't? The groping happened under duress, I can give myself a pass on that. But afterwards, what did I do? Fuck all. I'm as disgusting as those bullies. Worse.'

'You were a child. You have to let that burden go. It's never too late.'

'Why should I let it go? Is a life without disgust a better life? Would I be a better person?'

'It comes out in your relationships.'

'By making me more empathetic.'

'When people don't do exactly what you want, when they don't meet your standards in everything, when they're anything less than perfect, they disgust you.'

'"People" meaning "you".'

'Not only me. I'm talking about everyone in your life right now –'

'Just worry about yourself, Pedro.'

'– and also about some who haven't come into your life yet.'

'Yeah? Like who?'

'Like the children we might have together one day.'

Letter 38: GAVIN MULVANY to JEAN-JACQUES ROUSSEAU

Paris, 6 July 2022

After the Louvre, Cyprien and I had dinner in a restaurant in our local area.

'These prices are too high for me,' I told him as soon as we'd received the menus, which he answered with an impatient, 'Get whatever you want.'

I watched him taste the wine. He took an unpardonably long time to give his approval to the waiter. His power over me was unimaginable. He controlled my feelings absolutely.

'Before I forget,' he said after taking a gulp from his now-filled glass, 'I was talking to the head of the Nanterre faculty. He might be open to meeting you for an informal chat.'

'Oh, thanks a lot.'

'Nice guy. But honestly, Gavin, I can't see why you'd want to get into this line of work.'

'Bad week?'

'You come to the academy thinking you'll be surrounded by brilliant people. Thinkers full of lively and new ideas. The shock comes with discovering that they're a bunch of overbearing dogmatists who can't endure that anyone should think differently from them on any subject whatsoever.'

'Is this about Anne-Laure? Did your colleagues find out what happened?'

'I should have kept my trap shut about it.'

'I guess, for people whose lives revolve around the university, being expelled from the system, for the reason Anne-Laure was, must be equivalent to being a suicide bomber or something.'

'The fact is, most of them don't have any real gift for their profession. They know only what they've studied, if even that, and lack any spark of imagination. As soon as they have to leave the beaten track, they're as lost as schoolchildren.'

'It can't be true that Anne-Laure has already blown her chances of getting into university. Surely if she knuckles down now –'

'What's this madness for university anyway? All branches of my family have it. Law is what everyone seems to have settled on. They want Anne-Laure to be a lawyer, can you imagine? No life is so barren, so monotonous, that they wouldn't want it for someone else.'

'She mightn't get into one of the elite lycées now. But there are other routes she can take. She's smart enough. If she wants to be a lawyer, she'll get there, somehow.'

'Why must my child go to a Big School, and have all those special frills? Let her go to work.'

'Also an option.'

'How much better it is to do good, to be really useful and beneficial to others.' He downed a glass of water, then filled it up again with wine and slurped from it. 'Do you think I'm critical? Too critical?'

'No.'

'A colleague has helpfully informed me that psychological parental control may play a key role in the genesis of bullying during adolescence.'

'It can also just be sensation-seeking. Or any number of other things.'

Anne-Laure was refusing to speak about what happened. But from the teachers' reports, Cyprien had gathered that she'd been spending time with a popular boy from the class, who suddenly turned his attentions to the newly arrived Belarusian girl. When Anne-Laure found out that the boy and the Belarusian were seeing each other, that they had in fact become a publicly declared item, she enlisted her classmates in a subtle campaign of ostracism, followed by a not-so-subtle operation of surveillance, taunting, threats, and eventually violence.

'Have you found a new school for her?'

'She's on the list for the local place, starting in September.'

'How is she adjusting to this new reality?'

Cyprien shrugged. 'She stays at home. We have tutors coming every morning. French. Geography.'

'English?'

'Also.'

'Oh.' I put down my glass, which I'd been posing with more than drinking from. 'Cyprien, you mustn't keep hiding from me what you wish me to do.'

'I don't wish you to do anything.'

'You know I'd do whatever it takes to help. And I wouldn't charge.'

'Don't sacrifice your strength to children.'

'It wouldn't be just any child, it'd be yours!'

'Ah, this new generation! What should we do with them?'

'I'd be the perfect fit.'

'When dealing with others, they think only of themselves. In understanding themselves, they think only of others. And who must we blame for that? Their parents, their teachers. Us.'

The waiter came with two starters that weren't ours. Cyprien offered to take them anyway, even though neither of them was something I was keen on, but the waiter quickly figured out that they belonged to the couple at the next table.

'All right,' Cyprien said, 'now that you mention it, I suppose she would benefit from someone taking an interest in her. Not in her education per se. But in her person.'

'You're talking about a mentor?'

'Diderot said that making people better was at least as important as making them less ignorant.'

'I'm trying to picture how it might work.'

'It couldn't be a formal lesson. She already resists the ones she has.'

'How about a couple of hours every afternoon. I could come on the pretence of offering English conversation, but then try to, I don't know –'

'She's headstrong. The other day, it was: "I can't learn. I don't want to learn. Stop fucking teaching me. It won't work."'

'My job wouldn't be to teach her.'

'Or condemn her. She's had quite enough of that.'

'Rather it would be –'

'To recognise her.'

'– to set a sort of example for her.'

'No rules, no tests. No standards.'

'Just two mates hanging out, losing time. The art of doing everything by doing nothing.'

'What are we saying?' He waved a dismissive hand. 'We must drop this whole crazy idea. It would compromise me in her eyes.'

'The advantages would outweigh the risks. For one, if she let slip any information about what happened with, you know –'

'The Belarusian.'

'– I'd be able to –'

Our correct starters arrived. He unfolded his napkin onto his lap. Picked up his fork. Shook his head. 'It's out of the question.'

On my side, I was perfectly still. Head cocked slightly. Napkin still rolled in its holder. Fork lying straight on the linen. Two fingers pinching the stem of the glass. At this table, before I put a morsel into my mouth, the future was going to be decided. Be humane, I thought. *Let me become / The shadow of your shadow / The shadow of your hand / The shadow of your dog / But:* don't deny me this.

FIFTH WALK

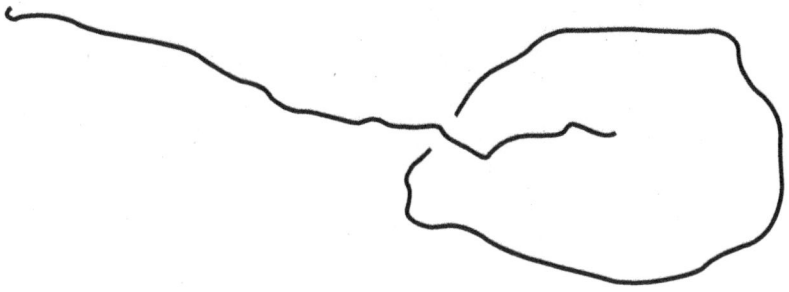

(To Saint-Germain-en-Laye, walking west: rue J.-J. Rousseau – quai Jacques Chirac – rue du Ranelagh – boulevard Périphérique – bois de Boulogne – Suresnes – Rueil-Malmaison – Chatou – Le Vésinet – Saint-Germain-en-Laye; 23 km: 6 hours, 10 minutes)

Fear

Letter 39: ALAN KEOGH to GAVIN MULVANY

Bristol, 10 July 2022

It's been a while. I hope you understand why and don't hold it against me too much. You can rest assured that I've been keeping an eye on your career from afar. I was happy to bump into you at those conferences in Oxford and Sofia, and to see you were in a much better place.

I should say that I did receive those messages you wrote from the hospital all those years ago. I wanted to reply but was torn between my sympathy for you and my loyalty to Cyprien, and frankly didn't know how I could help. Besides, at that stage I'd already accepted a job in the UK, which created a sort of clean break in my relationship to the matter. In the end I thought it best just to let you, both of you, figure things out, without my interference.

That being said, I doubt my reaching out to you now will come as a surprise. Cyprien has been in touch. He said you'd been spotted at the Sorbonne. There could've been a hundred reasons for you to be there, I told him. But then he let me in on the letters you've been sending him. He wanted to forward them to me but I insisted they were none of my business. While making no claim to be offering you advice, Gavin, I'll give you my frank opinion. Write your book, don't give up on that, it's your livelihood, but leave Cyprien in the past where he belongs.

Also, I take it you haven't seen the accusations against Cyprien that Mathilde put online a few weeks ago? The posts were only up a short time before she deleted them, but by then they had done the job. A tempest unleashed in French lit circles. Screengrabs flying around. People taking sides. I'm trying to stay neutral. Mathilde's split from Cyprien was so acrimonious, it's hard to know if her grievance is genuine or merely the product of bad feeling, designed to get back at him. Either way, Cyprien is absolutely wretched. I wouldn't go near him. Whatever you do, don't stoke those flames again.

Yours most philosophically and with sincere esteem.

Letter 40: GAVIN MULVANY to CYPRIEN ABREO

Paris, 10 July 2022

I've been so wrapped up in my research, the drama completely passed me by. Have searched online but don't see anything. Alan gave me the lowdown. There seems no need for further letters when we can meet freely. Saturday at 11, Brasserie de la Bourse.

Letter 41: GAVIN MULVANY to CYPRIEN ABREO

Paris, 16 July 2022

All day I waited, in a ferment of anxiety. Just this once couldn't you have saved me from playing this role? Couldn't you have been in the café, with your coffee and glass of water already ordered and neatly placed in front of you? I tried to arrive late. I added extra tasks to my morning. Washed strangers' dirty dishes. Took a detour through the Palais-Royal. And still I found myself there, punctual, even ahead of time.

I chose a table near the back where we'd have more privacy. Over bad tea, I read the same line of my book countless times. Didn't you get my message? Was there a misunderstanding as to the time, the place? I googled Mathilde and once again came up with nothing. You knew perfectly well I'd sit here and do this. You were aware of the torture this would be for me.

Descartes says that all desire looks forward. This goes not only for our desire to acquire or avoid something in the future, but also for our desire to stay in our present state: we can't wait to remain in situ. Live in the moment, I thought as I ate my soup (starter portion, €8.50), in anticipation of the moment in which I'd be living fully, finally, now. 'If he walked in at this instant' – this was the calibre of thought going through my fevered brain – 'would I be able to enjoy the spectacle of his arrival, instead of demanding that it immediately turn into something else: an approach, an embrace, an emotional reunion? Would I be able to look across the distance between us without wanting to close it up? Could I cherish my longing in the same way that I cherish the beauty of an object that can't be possessed?'

Around me, the lunch plates were being cleared away. I ordered an infusion and took it to a table by the window. I scrutinised the face and physique of every person outside and thought of you. I just closed my eyes – not even for long, a blink – and saw you straight away. I remembered what you looked like and seemed to hear your voice. Even with the racket in the café, I was able to concentrate on conjuring you up. It was agony and it was wonderful. I pictured you barging in, looking a fright, which gave me the chance to say, 'You're not dressed well, Cyprien. What's the matter, is it a hard time?'

Then, for a flash, I saw you killing me. You whipped a steak knife from a neighbouring table and thrust it into my neck. Why should I wish to fear you in this way? What's the appeal? Perhaps it's the pleasure of attaining anxiety in the pure state. Kill me so that I can be with you, the killer, as you loom over my body, internally seething, on the brink of an explosion of grief – that is, the guilt and sorrow by which you would be bound to me for the rest of your life. This, surely, is the worst thing that could happen. And yet, as Edgar in King Lear says: '*The worst is not / So long as we can say "This is the worst."*'

For the worst, I can assure you, is the uncertainty. I'm afraid you'll arrive because I both want you to arrive and don't want you to arrive, and I'm neither certain that you will nor certain that you won't. Nothing seems to depend on me. It's out of my hands whether my desires are fulfilled, and even what desires I have in the first place; I can't be sure that what appears to be good – your arrival – won't harm me, and vice versa. In such an oppressive regime, what I fear, most certainly, can't be death. Not even a violent and untimely one, such as a knife in the neck. For death, no matter what form it takes, is always certain. What I fear rather is the loss of fear. To lose my fear of you would be to lose my desire for you, and this would be more terrifying than my end.

Letter 42: GAVIN MULVANY to
JEAN-JACQUES ROUSSEAU

Paris, 17 July 2022

I became tutor to Cyprien's daughter not quite knowing what I was going to be tutoring her in, and also conscious that that was more or less the point, meaning I'd be obliged to surrender at the door that part of my dignity that refused to make myself absurd. I arrived at our first session carrying a pathetic-looking English grammar book. Anne-Laure came in to the study dressed in boot-cut jeans and a grey sweatshirt with YALE stamped on the front and a thin gold chain hanging outside the collar. Her hair, thick and dark, was loose to her shoulders, and frizzy on one side as though she'd just come from lying down. On her feet, thick pink socks, grannyish, with anti-slip grips on the bottom. She dropped heavily onto the chair opposite me, then got straight back up, let Coco in, and plonked herself down again.

'How long is this going to take?'

I spoke to her in English, reminding her of our schedule of appointments, then asking her general questions about her day, to which she responded reluctantly in French. Taking her cue, I switched language.

'How old are you supposed to be?' she said, scrunching up her nose. 'You talk like a senior citizen.'

So I switched back, and she stuck with French.

'I'm tired,' she said. 'Can we just get this over with?'

I was to come four times a week, Monday to Thursday, at four in the afternoon, and stay for two hours. Anne-Laure's first tutor, of French, came at nine daily. Then at eleven, another tutor, of English or geography or physics or chemistry, depending on the day, would take over. At around this time Cyprien's mother, whose name was Léna, would also arrive, having travelled all the way from Plaisir, and prepare lunch, which she served in the kitchen at one sharp. After eating with her grandmother, Anne-Laure was responsible for clearing the dishes but was then free to relax in her room until my arrival.

'Homeschooling,' I said to Anne-Laure, 'how are you coping with it?'

Throwing her eyes to heaven, then sighing, she left the table. Turned on the TV. Attached a cable to the projector. Lowered the screen. Found MTV, which was running a repeat of *The Osbournes*. Then she stretched out on the couch and, breaking the house rule, let Coco jump up beside her.

'Make a bit of dark, can you?' she said.

I couldn't take my eyes off the screen for the entire process of crossing the room and bringing the shutter down.

'You've never seen this before, have you?' she said.

'Heard of it, never watched it.'

'Oh my fucking God.'

She was robust, well fed but not fat. Sultry. With unblemished sallow skin, over which she was wearing no make-up, and fierce eyes better described as deep than large. Fifteen, but at least two years older-looking. I could, without any effort, picture her immature male contemporaries being frightened by her, and for this reason wanting to capture her, like a wild thing. When *The Osbournes* ended, instead of leaving the credits to run into the next programme, or flicking through the channels in search of a replacement, as I expected her to do – we had another ninety minutes to waste – she abruptly switched off the TV, an emphatic jab of her thumb on the button, and said, 'Come to think of it, there's something you could help me with.'

From her room she fetched a small stack of CDs. Selected one of them, Smashing Pumpkins' *Siamese Dream*, put it into the player and skipped to track six, 'Disarm'. Opened the booklet on the relevant page and handed it to me. The lyrics appeared as a handwritten scrawl in silver ink across a blurred monochrome photo.

'I understand the individual words,' she said, 'but I'm not sure of the overall meaning.'

First she played the song in its entirety. Then she put it on again, this time pausing it after every couple of phrases to hear my explanations. She listened carefully to what I said, demanded clarifications, picked at my interpretations without expressing either agreement or disagreement with them. Once satisfied, she put on Joni Mitchell's 'River', and we did the same. After that, Fleetwood Mac's 'Landslide'. And finally, Pearl Jam's 'Oceans'. Songs that revealed the weight of her parents' influence. Songs, also, of great melancholy. Songs I adored.

'It's about separation,' I said, referring to 'Oceans'. 'The longing for reunion. The singer is addressing a definite "you", but the desire he's expressing is also a sort of effervescence, an ardour without an object. Or, if you like, an ardour that takes itself as its object. The desire to feel desire.'

With her head cocked, acutely attentive, she watched what I did best, which was to orate on the meanings of things. She took in my every word, while straining not to be impressed by any of them. Hers was the false nonchalance of an adolescent frantically constructing a persona to confront the world. An achievement that was, I judged, depriving her of the openness that would reveal to herself and others what she wanted and needed, what her motives were.

'The song celebrates desire,' I said, 'as a sensation on its own terms.'

'Do you mean,' she said, 'that the singer doesn't really know what he's desiring?'

'He knows, and he also knows that he doesn't know. Which is what makes the song so sad. Well, actually it's as blissful as it is sad, don't you think? Blissfully sad.'

'How does it manage to be both?'

'By acknowledging that it's from your suffering that this gorgeous feeling of longing stems. The song understands that the fear of not getting what you want, and the desire to prolong your pleasurable yearning, are two sides of the same coin.'

While I was talking, someone had come into the flat, which had set Coco barking and obliged Anne-Laure to let her out of the study. When our session ended a quarter of an hour later, Anne-Laure said thank you politely, gathered her CDs and went to the kitchen, where I heard her exchange some fast words with her mother, then return to her room. How to classify what had just taken place? Trivial incident or important event: in either case it had been intolerable on account of how much I'd enjoyed it.

Quickly then, for I wanted to be away, I packed up my things and popped my head into the kitchen to say bye to Mathilde. But she'd already poured me a glass of wine, so I felt duty-bound to stay. We offered each other commonplaces. I tried to be especially pleasant to her. She believed she could afford to be magnanimous to me. Yet the intensity was high between us. She asked the same questions two or three times, sometimes translating for me unnecessarily, and she repeated my answers half to herself. After about twenty minutes of this, Cyprien came home. On hearing the front door open, Mathilde took a sharp breath, as though about to plunge into something before her husband reached us. The time it took him to cross the sitting room to the kitchen, Mathilde spent clearing a space at the table and getting a third glass from the cupboard, while I, from my seat, examined the Ernst Haeckel prints on the wall.

With Cyprien there, Mathilde loosened up. They began to talk about the refurbishment of a downstairs flat that was soon to begin. They discussed slowly, in detail, how this would impinge upon their lives, the possible disruptions it would cause, sounding in every respect like the people of a small town. Then they spoke about their forthcoming summer holidays, which as usual they were going to spend at the second home of Mathilde's family on île d'Oléron. They made provisional dates for departure and return in August. I hoped Mathilde would leave after finishing her wine but she didn't. She offered me another glass, which I refused, then poured herself one.

I made my excuses. Only when I was on my feet and checking I had everything, did I give in and mention my meeting with Anne-Laure. They hadn't inquired about it, which had suited me initially, but then, after the whole number about dates for île d'Oléron, I decided their reticence was weird. 'We didn't want to pry,' they said, but became instantly alert to what I was about to tell them. Which wasn't much. A word about Anne-Laure's evident intelligence. And another about her defensiveness, which I saw to be natural, and which I hoped to get past with time. They expressed gratitude for my having thrown them these crumbs, and said something along the lines of 'step by step'.

This, then, became the routine for the next four months, until Anne-Laure started at her new lycée in September. I came to the flat at four to take over from Léna. In the study Anne-Laure and I watched TV. Then, usually at my insistence, we listened to music and talked about it. When Cyprien and Mathilde came home, I had a chat with them, anything from a minute to a couple of hours, ostensibly with no why or wherefore, just a straightforward social ritual, but during which I sometimes – without ever being asked to – made observations about their daughter, or gave them information about her that I'd picked up and reasoned they ought to have.

For the first few weeks, before I'd built up enough trust with Anne-Laure that I could comfortably ask her about her life, before I'd learned to see through her techniques of camouflage and concealment to make proper sense of her answers, I was powerless to provide Cyprien and Mathilde with anything more than scraps of the most general nature. My breakthrough came around six weeks into the experiment. A Monday in early July. When, at the beginning of our session, even before turning on the TV, Anne-Laure, looking sheepish, produced *The Marshall Mathers LP* by Eminem, and put on the song 'Stan'.

'Until now we've listened to rock and folk,' I told Mathilde and Cyprien afterwards. 'Eminem is a radical departure.'

'*L'Obs* did a thing on him,' said Mathilde. 'He talks about beating women.'

'Killing them,' said Cyprien.

There was a lot to explain. In 'Stan', I told them, Eminem pretends to be one of his fans, named Stan, who's in the process of writing a letter to his favourite rapper, Eminem. Layered underneath Stan's voice is the sound of a pen nib scratching paper, which gives the rather quaint impression that the spoken words are, in the instant of their utterance, appearing as words on a page. The song is nearly seven minutes long, with four extended verses, during which the degree of Stan's obsession with Eminem is gradually disclosed, becomes increasingly disturbed and finally culminates in Stan murdering his pregnant wife and committing suicide, apparently out of anger at Eminem's failure to reply to his correspondence.

'There we have it,' said Mathilde. 'What on earth has got into that child?'

'He's white, right?' said Cyprien.

We were speaking in hushed tones, with the door closed. Mathilde told us to stay quiet while she went into the sitting room to get something. She came back with a folder of photos, which she rifled through until she came upon a posed line of young teenagers, casually but neatly dressed, arms around each other's waists, gazes straight ahead.

'From Anne-Laure's birthday last year,' she said, showing me the picture. 'We had a party here at the flat.'

She tapped her fingernail on a boy wearing a baggy white T-shirt and low-slung jeans. Pale skin. Spots around the mouth. Peroxide-blond hair combed forward. Far too Gallic, too soft-edged, to be an analogue of Eminem. But Mathilde wasn't wrong either: there was something, the pout, the attitude, that wasn't a million miles away.

'Milo. From her class. The one who's caused all this trouble.'

With Anne-Laure I'd spent a whole session deciphering 'Stan'. Then over the next couple of days we'd listened to the rest of the album and dug into 'Kill You' and 'Who Knew' and 'The Way I Am'. The problem for Eminem, I said, was that to sustain his identity, he requires everyone – the whole world, but mainly men – to recognise him and want to emulate him. Without this male adoration, he'd return to being a nobody. Which is a fearful position to be in.

'Personally I don't buy it,' I had said.

'Why doesn't that surprise me?' she said.

To feel like a man, I told her, Eminem desires the admiration of men. But such admiration can't be controlled. At any time it can spill over into something he doesn't want, like sexual desire or stalking. Which is why Eminem feels obliged to rap about hating faggots all the time. Stan is Eminem's greatest fear made flesh: the devoted man who doesn't obey the rules of devotion as laid down by Eminem. Stan oversteps the line. For this he can't be allowed to live. He must be got rid of.

Anne-Laure made a face declaring contempt. 'If only it was that easy.'

'What do you mean?'

'Nothing.'

'Tell me.'

'Oh, just a guy at my old school.'

'You'd like to see him die?'

'I wouldn't mind.'

'Which guy?'

'It doesn't matter which guy. The point is, he's an asshole. A wannabe like Stan. He used to go around rapping Eminem. Badly. His English was shit. He would mumble through the lines until he got to *faggot* or *slut* or *bitch*, then suddenly he'd start yelling and have a perfect accent.'

'I know the type.'

A slightly upturned corner of the mouth was enough to change Anne-Laure's entire demeanour from solemn to sardonic. 'Have you noticed how Eminem puts on women's voices?'

'And those little screams, as if he were a woman on the receiving end of his violence?'

'What's that about?'

She took the CD out of the player and wiped it on the end of her sleeve.

I gave her back the booklet, which, instead of lyrics, contained a grid of childhood snapshots of Eminem. 'Did the guy, the wannabe, give you this CD?'

She struggled to get the booklet back into the case. 'Fuck no, I bought it myself.'

'Did he ever call you names?'

She shrugged.

'Was he ever violent towards you?'

A pained expression made her momentarily ugly. 'What are you talking about? I'm going to tell my parents you asked me that.'

'What I understand,' I reported to Cyprien and Mathilde, 'is that Anne-Laure and this boy, Milo, had been an item for a while. That they'd been the class sweethearts. The good-looking ones, you know? The obvious match. But then Milo underwent a rapid transformation. He bleached his hair, changed how he dressed, swapped Nirvana for rap. Modelling himself on his new idol, Eminem, he began to speak in an aggressive, derogatory way about women and gays. His own mother even. This made him popular with some, unpopular with others, and left Anne-Laure with a difficult choice: was she going to go along with Milo's new persona or not?'

'You're going to say that she did,' said Mathilde. 'That she decided to go along with it.'

'She started to defend him. Even mimic him.'

'That doesn't sound right. The Anne-Laure I know has a stronger will than that.'

'At first it was just a game for her. Testing the water. Having a bit of fun. A phase. Some of her friends even joined in. Those who didn't, stayed quiet. The real problems for her began with the arrival of Sonia, the girl from Belarus. Sonia wasn't shy. She objected immediately and vocally to Milo and Anne-Laure's behaviour, going so far as to report it to a teacher. Anne-Laure, who'd got used to being unchallenged, and had so far avoided getting into trouble, was naturally furious about this. Her place in the pecking order was being threatened by this newcomer. What's more, she was jealous that Sonia had been brave enough to take the path she'd rejected, the one that went against Milo.'

'But didn't Sonia end up with Milo?'

'That's the painful irony. Only a few weeks after her arrival, and after displaying nothing but disdain for him, Sonia started going out with Milo. Milo didn't bother telling Anne-Laure about this. He just stopped contacting her. Kept his distance from her. Anne-Laure found out after someone saw Milo and Sonia kissing on the street and told her. Which must've been really tough for Anne-Laure. Not only had Sonia publicly stood up to Milo, but she'd also stolen him from Anne-Laure. Unbelievable, really. Anne-Laure must've felt she had no choice but to return fire and try to take Sonia down.'

'And your evidence for this?' said Mathilde.

'I'm going on what Anne-Laure has told me.'

'She told you all of these facts, exactly as you've laid them out here?'

'I've only shared what I'm certain of.'

Mathilde roughly pushed back her chair, went to the sink, wiped some water from the counter, threw the tea towel down, leaned against the stove.

'Anne-Laure needs our support,' she said. 'She's strong-willed in many respects, but, as these events have shown, she can also be susceptible.'

'We're all susceptible to some extent,' Cyprien said, sounding defensive. 'Given over to outside forces. Families, institutions, beliefs, environments.'

'If you don't mind, Cyprien,' she said, 'we're talking here about our daughter, not the entire world.'

'I'm just pointing out,' Cyprien said, 'that our fear for Anne-Laure is the same fear we all have for ourselves: that our susceptibility will be exploited. Which happens, and we should try to protect ourselves from it. But remember that without susceptibility there can be no passionate attachment or falling in love.'

Letter 43: JEAN-JACQUES ROUSSEAU to GAVIN MULVANY

Paris, 18 July 1777

Ah, so your pupil was a girl? You should have said. I never recall my young pupils, the girls, without being filled with pleasure. If only, by repeating the names of the most agreeable of them, I could restore them, and myself with them, to their former selves and to the happy age that was ours! Let's walk again, sir, and I can tell you more.

MS Extract: from *Rousseau's Lost Children* by GAVIN MULVANY

Last edited: 20 July 2022

In *Émile*, the final lesson the boy receives, at the age of fifteen, is on the meaning of his longings. At last the tutor reveals sex to the boy. But, in doing so, he skirts around the mechanics of the biological act and focuses instead on its spiritual qualities. The peak of sexual desire, he explains, is a man's love of God mediated by the love of a woman. The desire the boy feels is carnal, but its object, his beloved, contains virtue and beauty without which she would not be attractive to him, without which she would be repulsive in fact. For the boy, attaining bodily satisfaction depends on his beloved's excellence of character; in possessing her, he must be careful not to sully or destroy this. He must raise up his sexual energy so that he never stops admiring her during intercourse. Only by purifying and exalting his lust can he hope to form a real relationship with her.

The woman, for her part, must participate in the idea that the boy has of her. She must be formed in such a way that he will recognise his own highest aspirations in her. She must learn to be his ideal without frightening him away.

To accomplish this, she is given a separate education of her own. In her case, there is no need for a dedicated tutor. No isolation in the countryside. No communing with nature. No lessons in self-preservation. Instead she is kept at home under the care of her mother, who works to eliminate her most dangerous defects: idleness and disobedience. From an early age she is constrained, so that, when the time comes, it will not cost her anything to submit to the will of her husband. At the same time, she learns that it is she who rules the man when she submits to his will. It is her job to find out how to make him demand what she needs to submit to. Her own violence is in her charms. By these she constrains him in turn. She animates his strength by resisting him. In this way, she triumphs in the victory that she has made him win.

By the end of her schooling, the woman knows how to limit herself to things within her competence and to judge well. As she must obey a being who is imperfect, full of vices, she has learned how to endure injustice and to bear her husband's wrongs without complaint. This docility is her greatest skill in life, since she will never cease to be subjected to the judgements of her husband, or indeed of all men, and will never be permitted to put herself above these judgements. Feelings of bitterness and stubbornness will only increase the bad behaviour of her husband, whereas gentleness will bring him round and triumph over him sooner or later.

Even by the standards of the time, Rousseau's proposal for the ideal education of women was strikingly old-fashioned. Strains of rationalism and egalitarianism in Enlightenment thinking were questioning the same assumptions of sexual difference that Rousseau was reaffirming in *Émile*. The fear that Rousseau had, frequently expressed in the text, was that man and woman, husband and wife, parent and child would become mere roles, the result of play-acting and therefore liable to change. What was to stop one role from being assimilated into another? From man becoming docile like a woman, or a woman becoming vigorous like a man? In such a scenario, the family, which Rousseau saw as the only basis for a healthy society, would decay. The only reason a man cares for his children is out of love for his wife, who cares for them naturally. Were this distinction to break down, children would become burdens and not fulfilments, and the duty to raise them, to educate them, would dissolve.

Letter 44: GAVIN MULVANY to THÉRÈSE LEVASSEUR

Paris, 21 July 2022

Within the space of one short letter I don't know how to speak about everything that happened during my walk with your husband today. On meeting at your house, I suggested as our destination the fôret de Rouvray in the west, and he agreed. He put forward a route that would take us through the Tuileries, along the river, then across Passy to the forest. I was pleased about this, as I'd wanted us to make a social call in Passy – one which I couldn't have mentioned in advance because he'd never have gone along with it, but which now I'd be able to spring on him impromptu (a bad idea, you'll tell me, and you wouldn't be wrong).

We strolled down to the river and turned right onto the quays. In an effort to animate Mr Rousseau, who was uncommunicative and appeared gloomy, I asked him to expand on his memories of being a tutor to girls as a young man. This brightened him up. With rapturous intensity, he unloaded himself. There was a Miss de Menthon, who had a scar on her bosom by a scald from boiling water, which he used to find extremely distracting; and a beautiful grocer's daughter named Miss Lard, whose mother would flirt openly with him, even kiss him on the lips, in front of her husband; and a Miss Mellarède, who would have her entire lesson in *déshabille* – but here he broke off, his mood darkened again and he said, 'I think it best to let this subject fall into oblivion.'

'You don't have to be embarrassed,' I said.

'Do you see an embarrassed person?'

'You might have felt foolish, but I doubt that's how your pupils perceived you.'

'The truth is, I never laid a finger on any of them. I doubt any man had a more chaste youth than mine.'

'But you wanted to? Lay a finger on them, I mean.'

'I wanted to, and I didn't want to.'

'Are both possible at the same time?'

'It certainly felt that way. I sensed myself to be simultaneously enslaved by my passions and freed from them by my reason.'

I considered this for a minute. 'I don't understand how that can be.'

'It's afterwards that you see it. My worst torment, whenever I do succumb, is to sense that I could have resisted. That I could have heeded my reason's warnings. With my pupils, mercifully, I always managed to.'

'What's wrong with your desire that it needs to be constantly controlled like this?'

'Are you a libertine? Would you have had me ravish my pupils?'

'Not at all. I'm speaking now about women who aren't in your care. Grown women.'

'In the presence of all women, I like to be seen as a man who has morals and is in command of his nature. I don't want to be mistaken for one of the hundred thousand debauchees that inhabit Paris.'

'You make your desire sound criminal.'

'No, never criminal. Since it's not within my control to have or not to have passions, I consider all passions to be good, so long as I remain their master and can dominate them. My passions turn bad only when I let myself be subject to them.'

'I wonder did someone in your life, your father perhaps, or the aunt who raised you, make your passions frightening to you?'

'My father was a man of sound probity. My aunt was as good and gentle a woman as ever set foot on the earth. Their lessons taught me that men who have morals are the true worshippers of women.'

(Let me ask you, Thérèse, are you, or would you like to be, the woman worshipped? The woman adored from a distance? The woman who elevates men's lust to the level of prayers? The woman of virtue, who, after being possessed, fills men with remorse and at whose feet they fall down and weep?)

We went through the Tuileries, which was packed with the midday crowds. At the western end, near the Swiss Guards' booth at pont Tournant, a girl of fourteen or fifteen, shabbily dressed and carrying a ribbon of the sort a sympathetic lady might have conferred on her, made a signal to us – a flash of green silk – and dashed behind a wall.

Your husband shook his head. 'Girls in Paris are charming until the age of seven or eight. After that they become familiar with the ways of the world and the city's problems.' He made an arcing gesture in front of his belly to suggest a pregnancy. 'Did you see? She's already let the cat get at the cheese.'

We crossed place Louis XV diagonally to meet the river at port aux Pierres. I stopped to admire the boats on the water, whose masts collectively created a kind of ballet, and beyond them, in the distance on the other bank, the gold dome of the Hôtel des Invalides. Mr Rousseau was, in the meantime, drawing closer to the river's edge, where it looked as if a couple of women were being harassed by a group of fashionable men of rank. On closer inspection, however, the latter turned out to be what your husband called 'men-women, of the kind you might find at Chez Coulon', which is to say homosexuals, with whom the women, maybe actresses, were on friendly terms and sharing a joke.

'They can forget about finding matches as long as they keep that company.'

We continued along the river, following its southward curve past the Champs-Élysées and the île des Cygnes. Rarely on my walks out of Paris have I failed to be impressed by the city's capacity to devour its surroundings, to convert fields and marshes into spanking new streets. Now, as we rounded the river's bend and the southern horizon opened up, I voiced relief that the stone terraces were at last giving way to the wooden huts and shanties of the vegetable gardeners, and to the timber from the depots floating downstream, for it was proof that even apparently unstoppable forces had their rims and ends. Mr Rousseau didn't seem to hear me. He was busy mumbling to himself a monologue of which I only caught a snippet: '. . . their accursed chiffon has always sealed the doom of men and their families . . .'

(You, Thérèse, won't be familiar with your husband's writings, but I can't imagine that the following passage, from his book on education, will stump you: '*It makes a great difference for the good state of a marriage whether the man makes an alliance above or below himself. When he makes an alliance in the lower rank, he does not descend, he raises up his wife. On the other hand, by taking a woman above him, he lowers her without raising himself. Moreover, it is part of the order of nature that the woman obey the man. Therefore, when he takes her from a lower rank, the natural and civil order agree and everything goes well.'*)

Your husband had turned his head towards the river, where the strength of the light reflecting off the water was such that he was forced to shield his eyes.

'What about Thérèse?' I asked him. 'What drew you to her?'

'Thérèse was a housemaid to a landlady of mine. From a good family that were down on their luck. A simple and unaffected girl with whom I first looked simply for amusement. I soon saw that I had done more than this and had found a companion.'

'In winning her over, did you let yourself go a bit? Show her some of those bound-up desires?'

'At that time, the full tumult of my passions was reserved for an accomplished, dazzling woman, whose condition was superior to my own and who could in some sense decide my fate. In Thérèse I discovered the substitute I needed. For my part, I was rescuing her from misery. She depended on me for her subsistence.'

'And for her education too?'

'Well, I did my best in that regard. But it was a waste of time. She's as nature made her. Care and cultivation are unavailing.'

'She seems like a person of good sense to me.'

'I'll give you that. Limited as she is and, if you like, stupid, she does give excellent advice in difficult situations. She has often, when some catastrophe has overtaken me, seen something I didn't see myself and rescued me from dangers into which I was rushing blindly.'

We had reached the walls of the park at château de Boulainvilliers. Coming off the river path, we climbed the hill. The park walls were too high to see in, but we caught glimpses of the tips of the fountain jets and could hear the rushing water. On rue Basse, from the coach house of the Hôtel de Valentinois, coaches were emerging, as many as six or seven, raising dust and forcing us to move aside so as not to get run over.

At the main gate I registered our arrival with a porter.

'What's our business here?' said Mr Rousseau. 'What's this about?'

'I've arranged for us to see the villa gardens. Lots of exotic species, apparently. A surprise for you.'

The porter accompanied us across the courtyard towards the larger southern wing, on the threshold of which Mr Rousseau appeared to get a fright, causing him to go back down the steps and pull me after him. The porter, who'd opened the door, was left standing uncertainly, with one foot in and one out, his gaze cast back over his shoulder.

Your husband got very close to my ear. 'You've got the wrong pig by the ear, my boy! In all your life you'll never make a greater mistake than this!' The idea had entered his head that I'd led him to a *petite maison* – not an entirely unreasonable inference, given that Passy is home to many such establishments, but wide of the mark nonetheless. I reassured him that we, neither of us, were here for erotic encounters.

'Why then? Who receives us here? Spit it out!'

'Benjamin Franklin, sir.'

His face fell from a height. 'The electricity man?'

'The ladies' man.'

With an admonishing rap of his stick on the side of my foot your husband climbed the steps ahead of me and went through the door first. In an antechamber across the hall, where the porter left us alone for a minute, he rasped at me, 'Evidently the permission I've granted you to accompany me on my walks has led you to believe that my desire to be away from society is merely a posture! You want to turn me into another Voltaire and bury me alive among the living!'

Before I could answer a pair of doors opened to reveal a richly furnished drawing room, into which your husband went with startling resolution. After accepting Mr Franklin's hand (in the Puritan style), he bowed to the two women present: on a sofa, a lady in her forties, whom Mr Franklin introduced as his 'dear landlady, Mrs Le Ray de Chaumont'; and a girl of fifteen or sixteen, sitting at a chessboard, who was Mrs Chaumont's daughter, Polly. Then your husband took the armchair Mr Franklin gestured to, from where he watched me, as if he were already an old fixture in this place, as I was directed to a cushioned upright on his left side.

Once sure everyone was comfortable, Mr Franklin reinstalled himself opposite Polly. He was playing black, she was white and, judging from the relative number of taken pieces, dominant. The room was bright and hot, thanks to large south-facing windows.

Mr Franklin made the strategic choice of addressing me, the insignificant party, first. 'Ireland?' he said. 'A fine country. And Dublin a magnificent city. But the appearance of general extreme poverty among the lower people amazed me. In regard to the comforts of life, the poorest of our New England farmers are princes compared to them.'

Your husband, on whom the idea had never dawned that my homeland was a place that a person might physically journey to and stand on, stared at me with an expression of profound perplexity.

'But before we go any further' – Mr Franklin hadn't moved his eyes from me – 'I must ask, are you here to solicit a position for yourself in the American war?'

'Not me, Mr Franklin. I ain't one for the guns.'

'That's a relief.' Now he turned, with firm purpose, to Mr Rousseau. 'You can't imagine, sir, how I'm harassed. Not a day passes in which I haven't a legion of young men pleading to be sent over. Many of them are genuinely imbued with the ideas of the American cause, but the majority, I'm sad to say, are motivated only by boredom and a thirst for adventure.'

Mr Franklin was dressed plainly in a brown jacket and sported neither a wig nor the fur cap he's known for. From time to time, as he spoke, he scratched his bald pate using the fingers of his right hand. 'I'm afraid to accept an invitation to dine away from home' – his gaze made a seamless line across the room to Mrs Chaumont – 'being almost sure of meeting with some chancer who, as soon as I'm put in a good humour with a glass of champagne, begins his attack on me!'

Polly made a move on the board. 'Papa!' she said, in order to draw Mr Franklin, who was not her father, back into the game. 'Papa! Come on!'

For a while we were spectators to Mr Franklin and Polly's game, obeying an unspoken rule not to hurry the players nor disturb their focus. It came to Mr Franklin's notice that your husband was paying deep attention to the action on the chessboard. 'Would you like to take over?' he said.

He didn't need to be asked twice. Polly went to join her mother on the sofa and I pulled my chair round so that I was sitting perpendicular to the board, exactly between the two men – your husband on white to my left, Mr Franklin on black to my right: the fearless Hectors, the world conquerors, the great educators of womankind, facing off.

'On our walk here today,' I said to Mr Franklin while he waited for your husband to make a move, 'Mr Rousseau and I were discussing the education of women. You also have a special interest in this subject, am I right?'

(This, Thérèse, was my trap.)

Mr Franklin replied that this was indeed a consequential topic, and explained that, as it happened, he was giving private lessons to Polly on some of the subjects that excite him: barometers, electricity, the moon and, most recently, how the tides affect the flow of water at the mouth of a river.

'Not a day passes in which I don't think of "my little wife",' he said, blowing Polly a kiss.

'He writes to my daughter more often than to his own family in America,' said Mrs Chaumont.

'At the same time' – Mr Franklin had reddened – 'I'm concerned that Polly might take her studies too seriously. There's a prudent moderation to be used in a girl's education. There's no knowledge of equal dignity and importance to that of being a good wife and mother.'

Mr Rousseau, who hadn't seemed to be listening, finally moved a piece on the board and, as he sat back into the chair, said, 'The aim is to make a decent woman of the child. She ought to learn many things, of course. But only those that are suitable for her to know as a wife and mother.'

Mr Franklin nodded thoughtfully. 'Accounting, for instance, is likely to be of more use than either music or dancing.'

'I can think of many things that I wouldn't want my Polly to know,' said Mrs Chaumont. 'But must it be gaiety that's sacrificed?'

'Quite,' I said. 'Is a life without joy really what you both want for your own daughters?'

The men, in synchrony, peered at me sideways.

'May I ask,' I said, 'how the education of your own daughters is going? Have you prepared them well for marriage? I mean, would your own marriages, the specific arrangements between yourselves and your wives, be the sort you'd recommend to them? Would you want for them what your Thérèse and your Deborah got with you?'

Mr Franklin used the arm of his chair as a lever to twist his torso to face me, and to swing an arm round in an arc. 'The man has just raised the name of my late wife!' He unfurled a finger in my direction. 'Keep my wife's name out of your mouth!'

Your husband, who, to his credit, has a clearer picture of the world's acquaintance with his affairs, because it's virtually total, was cool as custard. He urged Mr Franklin to relax. All of this was much ado about nothing.

'The marriage arrangements of individual men,' he said, 'such as mine or Mr Franklin's, is neither here nor there. The fundamental principle applies across the board. Family is the basis of society. And there's no family if women aren't primarily wives and mothers. The symbol of humankind in its most natural state is a mother feeding her offspring from her own breast within a home.'

'But women don't always marry,' Mrs Chaumont said.

'Extreme ugliness,' your husband said, 'of the kind that produces disgust is the only excuse for a woman to remain out of wedlock.'

'Nor do all women produce children,' I pointed out.

'No,' your husband said, 'but that is their only proper purpose.'

(Of the five, Thérèse, how many were girls? If you'd been able, or allowed, to keep one, just one, what lessons would you have passed on to her?)

Following a single knock, a young man came into the room, bowed to everyone present and informed Mr Franklin of the arrival of a document that needed his attention. Mr Franklin introduced the man as his grandson, Temple, but didn't give him an immediate answer, obliging him to wait by the door and be a witness.

'These questions of yours,' he said then, overlooking the chess game to address me, 'intrude upon personal matters that no man should be obliged to speak on in public.'

'Now, now, Mr Franklin,' said Mrs Chaumont, 'we're all friends here, and moreover friends of the truth. The Irishman is asking a philosophical question that touches us all.'

'Forgive me,' I said. 'I merely wished to tease out a contradiction in your position. You want women to believe that marriage is a place of safety for them, while at the same time you demand that they live in fear of their husbands. Likewise you sell motherhood to women as a safeguard against a lonely, meaningless life, without considering that getting pregnant opens the lid on a whole new category of fear. Will she, the mother, survive childbirth? How many of her children will make it to their first birthday?'

Leaning over the chessboard, Mr Franklin appealed to your husband: 'Mr Rousseau, sir, you'll be on my side, won't you? It's up to the sex that nature has charged with the bearing of children to be responsible for them, which is bound to bring up some worry, I admit. But it's the sex that provides for and educates those children that fears most for them. Fathers pave the path for their children to walk on, so naturally it's fathers that most fear the prospect of their veering off it. The most dreadful sight in nature is not that of a dead child, but that of the father who must bury him.'

Mr Rousseau, presuming that Mr Franklin was making a veiled comment on his past, or perhaps because he really had just achieved checkmate, reached out and, with the tip of his finger, ever so lightly, tipped the black king over.

Letter 45: GAVIN MULVANY to PEDRO SOUZA

Paris, 22 July 2022

Yesterday I walked west. From rue Jean-Jacques Rousseau, I crossed the river to the Left Bank, then followed the quays as far as pont de Bir-Hakeim just south of the Eiffel Tower. Here I crossed back over the river to the sixteenth arrondissement, went through the bois de Boulogne, then the suburbs of Suresnes, Rueil-Malmaison, Chatou and Le Vésinet. My destination was the forêt domaniale de Saint-Germain-en-Laye, which lies beyond the château there. To get there, I crossed the snaking course of the Seine a total of five times.

Towards the end of my walk, as I was climbing the hill to the château, I found myself on a steep flight of steps. Feeling an ache in my legs, I paused halfway up and turned around. Although aware that I'd been walking uphill for some time, I hadn't realised that I'd achieved such elevation. The whole of Paris, it seemed, was stretched out at my feet. The wide river in the foreground. La Défense on the horizon. The top third of the Eiffel Tower peeping out from behind a hill. The pale stone of the streets carpeting the sloping ground in all directions. The city appeared at once far away and close enough to brush it away, like a layer of old dust, with my hand. Observing it, I felt a longing for something I thought I'd made my own but now showed itself to be external to me. First came joy at having escaped engulfment, then came a craving to be re-engulfed.

Being in Cyprien's company used to evoke a similar feeling. When he was in my sight, he appeared complete. From my vantage point – looking down on him, even though I believed him to be above me in every way – I could see all of him, head to foot, front and back. More of him than he'd ever be able to see of himself. He was there, wholly there, yet also far beyond me. Such a vast distance away that any approach I could imagine making would be, I knew in advance, a terrifying journey across unmapped terrain.

With you, it was the opposite. During your comings and goings on the hospital ward, rather than seeing all of you, I caught snippets – your moustache, your wrist tattoo, your ugly white clogs, your ordinary remarks – which satisfied me that the rest of you was there too. With a glimpse, I had enough. I didn't need to pay any more attention to you to know that it was you. Which, in a sense, made you more real to me. More dependably there. After Cyprien, I'd come to believe that I'd never again be capable of getting close to another man. Yet, with you, I had the sense that closeness was already factored in. Which I realise now is the experience of fear's absence.

One day, maybe four years into our relationship – you won't remember, because it was nothing really – we were waiting to board a flight, and I was watching, without properly seeing, a man with his children. Three girls and a boy. Ages, I don't know, maybe five to fourteen. I must've been staring because you said to me, 'Your future.'

'Is that really what you want for me?'

'Would it be so bad?'

'To create and then proceed to ruin the lives of other human beings?'

You were folding your boarding pass so that it fitted perfectly into your passport. 'I plan to have lots of kids.'

'A recipe for fear and loathing, if you ask me.'

'At least three. Two girls and a boy.'

This conversation wasn't arousing paternal sensations in me, if that was its intended purpose, but quite the reverse, was making me feel murderous. 'Why stop at three? The sky's the limit.'

From my headphones, which were hanging around my neck, emanated a tinny voice. To change the subject, you asked me what I was listening to. I showed you the face of my iPod.

'Eminem?' you said. 'You like him?'

SIXTH WALK

(*To Croissy-Beaubourg, walking east: rue J.-J. Rousseau – place de la Bastille – place de la Nation – château de Vincennes – Nogent-sur-Marne – le Perreux-sur-Marne – Bry-sur-Marne – Villiers-sur-Marne – Les Yvris Noisy-le-Grand – Croissy-Beaubourg; 28 km: 7 hours, 40 minutes*)

Shame

Letter 46: CYPRIEN ABREO to GAVIN MULVANY

Paris, 28 July 2022

First I'm told that security has caught you trying to get into the library without a card – I don't believe them. Then a couple of weeks later, I catch sight of you from my window hanging around outside my house. I refuse to accept it's you, even if it explains why the bell has been ringing at strange hours of the day and night. Door-to-door sales? Pranks? Your letters have destroyed the last bit of innocence left in me.

It should go without saying, but I fear I must say it anyway: if I appear in your book, in any guise – I mean if I'm mentioned at all, for any reason whatsoever, even in passing – you'll hear from my lawyers.

Would you like to hear Alan's assessment? He says it can't be the business of literature alone that's motivating you. You have grievances which you believe originate from me. Whatever it is you're up to, no one will be able to put a stop to it, I know, since by nature you're so unreasonably obstinate. For all that, I'm now wondering whether this same quality of yours, this infernal force of mind, wouldn't be of some help to me. (It should tell you the depth of my desperation that I'm even contemplating this.) If it's truly the case that you're pursuing a grudge, I urge you to look at the situation I find myself in now (screenshots attached in case you're the only one unaware) and reflect, please, on what I once did for you and how much you actually owe me.

Attachment: Online posts by MATHILDE GOUDICHAUD

Posted: 7 June 2022

Very fitting that **@academie_fr** has awarded the Prix de la Critique to **@cyabreo** for his book on Sade. Abreo is a known pervert who for years has been using coercion and violence to compensate for his own dysfunction. Worst-kept secret in the Sorbonne.

Posted: 7 June 2022

Complete disclosure: I was married to him for 27 years. Only learned about his depravity after divorce in 2014. I was spared the worst. Same can't be said for his daughter or his students. Far from lionising the man, we should be locking him up.

Letter 47: CYPRIEN ABREO to GAVIN MULVANY

Plaisir, 28 July 2022

There's a process underway, so you'll understand I must be careful about what I put in writing. I'll say this, however: any escalation of this matter would be bad news for you too. Your hands aren't exactly spotless.

I've been taking cover in Plaisir, but will be back in the city tomorrow. Saturday at 11, Père Lachaise, the old spot. Can I count on you to be there?

Note by GAVIN MULVANY

Paris, 30 July 2022

Early. Wandered over to Jim M. Grown man on knees. Reciting the poems. 'TRUE TO HIS OWN DEMON.' Back to H. and A. at fifteen minutes past. 'THE REMAINS OF HÉLOÏSE AND ABÉLARD ARE REUNITED IN THIS TOMB.' My demon pacing in front of railings.

Head hanging. Sunglasses. Caught sight of me. Turned away. Pushed hands into pockets. Saying something to himself? Turned back. Smile. Hug? No. Me: calm, attentive. Scrutinising his body. Unruly hairs in eyebrows. Nipples protruding through summer shirt. Narrowed eyes behind shades. Adjusted hair before speaking.

'Walk?'

Recollection of time we stayed up all night exchanging ideas for a doc film we both knew would never be made.

'It's painful to be here with you. I've wanted this meeting for so long, imagined it so often, now it hurts to have it.'

Says nothing to that. ROTHSCHILD. PISSARRO. COLETTE. ROSSINI. Glances. Searching hard for marks of corruption. Skin a shade darker. Few wrinkles. Preserved. Anyone ever injured by him would feel outrage to see how well he looked.

'Congratulations.'

'For what?'

'The prize.'

'Pah! Do you know how many prizes the Academy gives out every year? It's beyond me how Mathilde even heard. The ceremony was last November.'

'Maybe she was saving it up.'

'For the week before my election as dean of faculty? If so, exquisite timing.'

Promotion on pause. Talk of enforced sabbatical till voices die down. Accusations vague. No victim named. Crime left to reader to imagine. Me: no ordinary reader. Accessory to. Arrestable offence. Him nine parts guilty, me one part. Still: guilty.

'A storm in a teacup? Chances are the fuss will fade away.'

'I only heard about the posts a couple of days after. Thought it was a joke at first. Not like her. Completely out of character. Then I got a call from the university. Two other people had come forward in the meantime.'

'Who?'

'Ex-students. Bad ones.'

'Zoé Chauvin?'

'She's one of them.'

Knew it, knew it. 'I knew this wasn't over. That it would come back to bite us. Have you been charged?'

'With what? They've nothing on me.'
'Have you tried speaking to Mathilde?'
'Terrible idea.'
'How about Zoé herself?'
'That's what I wanted to bring up with you.'
'You want me to contact her.'
'Ask her what she wants. What her price is.'
'Shouldn't you leave everything to your lawyers?'
'You were there, in the middle. You could help her see sense. Get her memory of events straightened out.'
'She'd never agree to meet me. She'd know you sent me.'
'Worth a bloody try. Don't you see the opportunity this is for you too? To settle the matter once and for all.'
'Frankly, I see only risk. Why would she listen to me?'
'I don't know, I don't know. It's all I've got.'
Crunch of stones underfoot. HAUSSMANN. DAVID.
'How is Anne-Laure?'
'Working in a bank. Making shitloads of money like her mother.'
'I mean, how is she coping with all of this?'
Shrugs.
'You aren't in touch?'
'It's been a while.'
GÉRICAULT. BERNHARDT. Japanese women sheltering from sun under silver parasols.
'If I help you, Cyprien, it's not because I believe I owe you anything. You're the one in debt to me. I cleaned up your mess back then –'
'Our mess.'
'– and what did I get in return? Less than nothing. For twenty years I've been forgotten by you. Not a word. I don't think you can fathom how much I lost when you sent me away.'
Twenty years with Pedro. People call me faithful. Consider my monogamy virtuous. Give me praise simply for staying out of other beds. Friends ask for the secret. Nothing to it: just live whole other life in past!
PROUST. WILDE. STEIN. ABREO. MULVANY.
Was too happy once. Suspicious of all other happiness now.

Letter 48: GAVIN MULVANY to CYPRIEN ABREO

Paris, 1 August 2022

Since our meeting, I keep tracing back to the time I stayed in your flat looking after Coco while you were on île d'Oléron. What that dog needed, above all things, was a good run on the beach. But someone, probably Mathilde's father, raised objections to her being in the holiday house – 'Maybe next year,' Anne-Laure was told when she raged against this clear injustice – so for the entire month of August the poor animal was left in the baking eighth arrondissement with me. 'Woof!' you wrote on a postcard that arrived at the end of the second week.

I had, on your prompting, packed my bags and moved in. There'd been some slightly unpleasant fretting about which bedroom I should sleep in, yours or Anne-Laure's, and in the end you left it up to me. I tried both, then went between them, one being cooler, the other containing a drawer of your folded underwear that I liked to open and look into but not disturb. (From here on in, Cyprien, it's the facts or nada.)

Halfway through the third week, Mathilde was called back to Paris for a few days by reason of a crisis at the gallery. Of course I offered to move back to the flatshare for the time she'd be in town, but she insisted I stay on: 'I won't have a minute for the dog – you'd be doing me a favour.'

One evening – to my recollection, her last before her return to the island – she said, 'Are you in love with my husband?'

I don't recall much lead-in. I said I failed to grasp what she meant.

'Let me put it another way. Would you still want him if I wasn't here, preventing it? Is the existence of an obstacle what's turning you on?'

I'd cooked a meal, the sophistication of which she was surprised by (just veg and rice, for crying out loud). It was the first time Mathilde and I had ever been alone without the sensation of waiting for you to come in. The fact of our relative strangeness to each other deserved to be acknowledged and respected. I told her she was being outrageous. Being gay, I said, didn't render me incapable of maintaining a platonic friendship with another man.

'Is Cyprien just another man to you?'

'In the way you're suggesting, Mathilde, he is. I'll have you know that I have my choice of lovers. I'm far from desperate in that department. What Cyprien and I give to each other is something quite other.'

We were at the dining-room table, which I'd set with place mats and candles. The lights were dimmed. Mahler was on. I was ignoring the wine she'd poured for me. Honestly, I was ready for bed.

'Does he swing?' she said. 'Do you think he might?'

'I don't know. Do you think so?'

'Hmm, what do I think?' She kept a fingertip pressed against her temple while she drank from her glass. 'I think my husband is surrounded with people who worship him and whom he cherishes in return for that. The university is like a mill into which hundreds of susceptible souls are fed every year. To them, Cyprien doesn't appear as the tired civil servant that he is in reality, but as a priest at his lectern, a soothsayer. He's made for this kind of love on a gross scale. Nature has created him for general consumption. Rid yourself therefore of the hope, if you ever entertained it, of finding individual happiness with him.'

'Cyprien is a wonderful teacher,' I said, 'with a rare gift for kindling enthusiasm in his pupils. But I don't think it's true that he mistakes the esteem underlying his professional relationships for love.'

'Forced to decide between love and esteem, he'd choose the latter, I'm certain.'

'That's an artificial choice that no one is forced to make.'

'Forced at gunpoint, of course not. But we all make our choices. Cyprien, for his part, tries always to have a girl or two on the go. Do you think you can keep up?'

'What you're saying doesn't startle me, if that's what you're trying to do. I know plenty of people in relationships like yours. The point is, you stick together, right? That whatever happens in the outside world, you can count on one another.'

'Cyprien and I' – she turned her face to the breeze coming through the open window and took a breath, almost a gasp – 'we see each other as we are. The sentiment that connects us isn't passion per se. At least not any more. Ours is the attachment of two honest and reasonable people who, as much out of a sense of responsibility for our daughter as contentment with our lot, have committed to spending their lives together.'

'To my ears, what you're describing sounds a lot like love.'

'Of course if he'd never wanted me – physically, I mean – we'd get along badly. We've just settled into a situation in which each of us is exactly what the other requires.'

Most educated people, after their first encounter with her, would stop waiting for something shrewd or original from Mathilde. Even when she laughed, she didn't look as though she had a sense of humour. All hats off to you, however, for nodding along to her stale stories as if you hadn't heard them before.

'It sounds as if you and Cyprien have found a nice balance,' I said.

'If I was reincarnated, in a heartbeat I'd choose him again. The things I like, he appreciates. He keeps himself entertained with his books, and I don't bother him. To me, he owes his peace of mind, which is no small thing.'

There's a kind of shame, isn't there, in being the half that loves more? I was ashamed on Mathilde's behalf, on account of being able to see this shame in her.

'If I cut you out,' she said, 'forbade you from returning here, would you obey?'

'You mustn't do that.'

'Admit your feelings for Cyprien, and I mightn't have to.'

'All right.' My tone was defiant. 'What you asked before. The answer is yes, I think I do.'

The next morning, I found on the table next to her breakfast dishes, which it seemed she expected me to clean away, a note informing me that she'd booked an appointment for me with her GP – a Dr Lesnes, who was going to do me the favour of seeing me during the August break as a matter of urgency. I called Mathilde immediately. She was on the train.

'A full check-up. Tests.'

'Mathilde, you've completely misunderstood.'

'I'm taking precautions anyway. Not for him. For me. For Anne-Laure. He can be naïve. Which isn't merely my own opinion, it's everyone's.'

'I have to say, I'm a bit taken aback.'

'Hold on.' Snippets of conversations as she moved down the

carriage. Then the sound of a toilet door locking. 'Listen to me. This isn't toleration I'm showing. I don't have a tolerant bone in my body. I'm simply giving my husband the same that I expect from him.'

'I don't think I –'

'I trust you'll be discreet with our daughter. I reserve the right to alert you to anything that bothers me.'

'I'm not entirely –'

'Look, I have to go. I'll leave you with two bits of advice. The first, my husband is one of those men whom people think they truly insult by saying they feel nothing. He takes it as a compliment! The second, you must understand that the bond between Cyprien and me is solid. It's so because Cyprien has become accustomed to a standard of living that he wouldn't be able to sustain alone. And because he is the father of a child for whom I'd give my life.'

Letter 49: GAVIN MULVANY to CYPRIEN ABREO

Paris, 2 August 2022

In your flat that August, while waiting for your return from île d'Oléron, I took up letter writing. Email was taking off at that time. People talked about the end of physical correspondence. The analogue era was coming to a close. A development to which I'd no fervent objections. That month, however, armed with a stack of white wove sheets, and using your Montblanc fountain pen and your ink (Midnight Blue), I composed scores of letters by hand. To my mother. To my sister. To the university friends I'd kept and to those I'd distanced myself from. To relations. To neighbours. To the Irish newspapers. Even a couple to my father in Spain. An eighteenth-century level of production. A portion of which I even dared to post. In handcrafted envelopes sealed – the final statement – with a red wax seal stamped 'G' (purchased at the same luxury stationery boutique on boulevard Malesherbes that had sold you your 'C').

I'd just finished writing one of these letters when you came home unexpectedly. The dining room was in darkness apart from a single reading lamp. Eminem was blaring from the speakers. At the table, I had melted the wax onto the envelope and stamped it, and now – distracted, singing along with the music – I was dripping more wax onto my fingers and appraising the sensation, which approached but never exceeded the limit of what I could bear. When the main light came on, the shock made me drop the ladle, causing the liquid wax to splash over the envelope and the table surface. I pushed the chair back, quite roughly, and stood up to prevent my bare thighs from being burned, then surveyed the mess I'd just made. To my recollection, this was the first time you'd seen me out of my clothes. I adjusted the elastic of my underwear so that it sat higher on my hip, then tugged the back hem down, so that it fully covered my bottom. 'I thought you weren't back till Saturday.'

You went over to the stereo system and turned down the music. 'Relax. You don't have to be jumpy. You're not doing anything wrong.'

'You should've told me to expect you.'

'What are you, my mother?'

'It's just good manners.'

You laughed. You had, you said, some meetings to attend before the start of term. 'Writing letters?'

'To some people at home.'

'Lucky them.'

'Not at all. Just anecdotes.'

Leaving the table as it was, I brushed past you on the way to Anne-Laure's room to get dressed. When I came back out, you were already in the shower. I stood outside the bathroom door and listened for a minute, furiously, before calling through, 'Shall I fix you some supper?'

You were obliged to shout over the noise of the running water: 'Already ate!'

I lay down on the bed in Anne-Laure's room. Listened to you blow-drying your hair. Then pissing. Then brushing your teeth. On hearing the bathroom door unlocking, I quickly stripped down to my underwear again. Stretched my torso and my limbs out. Let my feet fall over the end of the bed frame. Tilted my pelvis a little towards the door. Placed one hand under my head to reveal my armpit. Closed my eyes. A second and I dashed over to turn off the main light, then positioned the bedside lamp so that it shone down the length of the bed. I reassumed my pose with one alteration: now I held a book in my free hand.

You knocked, opened the door a little way, stepped in. You were wearing a grey T-shirt and tartan boxer shorts. Bare feet. Your face bright and red.

I closed the book over my thumb and let it rest on the mattress.

'What time are you up tomorrow?' you said.

'You want me to do Coco in the morning?'

'Would you mind? I'll be at the faculty all day.'

I rolled onto my side. 'No problem.'

As if to spite my nakedness, your gaze didn't leave mine. 'I'll be home at six or seven. Will you be here?'

'I don't know.'

I scratched the hairs on my breastplate.

You nodded. 'All right, well –'

Using the same scratching hand, I slid my fingers under my underwear elastic and pulled it down as far as my upper thighs. My pubic hair sprang out – I'm picturing now what you must have seen – and my penis and testicles flopped over to hang down towards the mattress.

Your eyes went there.

The only proof I had that I was conscious was a thudding in my left temple.

You receded. The door closed after you.

I fell onto my back. Turned off the lamp. Pressed my fingertips into my eye sockets. Prepared myself for a sleepless night.

In the morning I waited until you were gone before emerging. After taking Coco out, I packed my bags and put them by the front door. All day I intended to leave but didn't manage to. You didn't show till after 8 p.m., at which point I'd been sitting on the long chair in the vestibule with my laces undone for close to an hour.

'Are you leaving?' you said.

'Shouldn't I?'

'There's no rush.'

'You know, I was concerned.'

You'd brought home food from the nearby Vietnamese restaurant, which you carried through to the kitchen. 'About what?'

I followed you, talking to the back of your head: 'You didn't text or call me at all while you were away. If I hadn't made the effort, I wouldn't have had any contact with you.'

'Don't be ridiculous. I was on a family holiday.'

'A text every now and then. A quick call. The least you could've done. I was looking after your dog, your plants, your home.'

'I presumed you had everything under control. Was I wrong about that?'

You put two plates out.

'Not for me,' I said. 'I can't eat right now.'

'You're whippet thin.' You took the lids off the various takeaway boxes, dug spoons into their contents and spread them out on the table. 'You should have something.'

I left the kitchen and went to the front door. Put my rucksack on my back.

'If this is about last night,' you said, re-crossing the sitting room with a large serving spoon in your right hand, 'there's nothing to be embarrassed about. You mustn't beat yourself up.'

I hooked my thumbs under the rucksack straps to alleviate some of the weight. 'How long is this going to go on for?'

'What do you mean?'

'This! This!'

'What's *this*?'

Feeling weak in the legs, I shrugged the bag off my shoulders again, dropped it on the floor.

'When Mathilde came to Paris for her meetings, I didn't go back to the flatshare. I stayed here. It's what she wanted.'

'She told me you'd talked, yes. There'd been some awkwardness between the two of you.'

Desperately, I wanted you to know that I didn't want to show my feelings. I wanted to be both pitiable and impressive. I wanted to be simultaneously a child and an adult. I darted down the corridor and into your bedroom.

'Where are you going?'

I was making a scene. One whose object I'd lost sight of. In the narrow space between the end of the bed and the dresser, I waited for you. I trusted you'd come and know what to do.

'Calm down,' you said when you appeared. 'You're in a spin.'

'This has to stop,' I said.

'What has to stop?'

I threw myself face first onto the bed. Moaned into the mattress.

No touch, just your voice: 'What the hell is wrong with you?'

Talking? We'd already done far too much of that. Reasoning? None is so complete as to leave you without more to say.

I sensed you standing over me. 'You're right, it's time you left.'

Now shaking me.

'Stop moaning like that. That's enough! Enough!'

I swung round and, with all my strength, pulled you down on top of me. The thud of the spoon falling onto the rug. Your weight on my ribs. My lips against yours for a short moment. Then a violent push and you were free. Standing over me once more. Your hand slicing the air: the lawmaker.

'That can't happen, Gavin!'

'But Mathilde said it's okay.'

'Well, I'm glad you two came to a deal. Now do I get a fucking say?'

I rolled away from you to escape confusion, only to meet shame.

You pounded out of the room.

I waited, curled up, until I understood you weren't coming back.

'Sorry,' I said from the kitchen doorway.

You were eating at the table. You'd set a place for me, to which I wasn't sure I was still welcome.

'Don't give me *sorry*,' you said. 'Just sit down.'

After a faltering start, we spent the evening talking. Kept mostly to the subject of work. Your research, you said, had been stuck for some time. You'd been running on the spot, not getting anywhere. But meeting me, working on my thesis, seeing the results, had unlocked your creative flow. You had new plans for articles, maybe even a book on Sade, to follow your previous one on Diderot.

'For me too, it's books or nothing,' I said, 'I have no plan B.'

'Those who succeed rarely do,' you said. 'But the same can be said of those who fail. Don't forget that with the sort of life you've chosen, sheer intelligence isn't enough. One false step and you'll be condemned without reprieve.'

At some point, despite your objections, I apologised in full for my behaviour. You cited my upbringing as a possible explanation. When a father leaves, you said, there's always a big impact. I thought I might cry but successfully didn't.

'It won't happen again,' I said.

'Can you live with just a friendship?'

'I can, if a real friendship is what this is.'

I told you a bit about my previous life, in the bars and clubs of Dublin. The difficulties I'd had bonding with other men. You said socialising with men hadn't always been easy for you either. Early on you learned to turn to women to get what men seemed incapable of providing.

'Are you saying,' I said, 'that you also approach women as potential friends? That your intentions are sometimes non-sexual?'

'Sure. The essential thing is, I'm upfront from the beginning. No one is going behind anyone else's back. The lines are clearly drawn. Sometimes sex happens, sometimes it doesn't. And when it doesn't, that's okay with me.'

'There are bound to be misunderstandings, even if you try always to be clear.'

'Of course. This is planet earth. Some people will end up resenting you no matter how you handle these things.'

'For what it's worth, I think your method is admirable.'

The child, post-tantrum, on realising the destruction he has caused, can't be certain that as punishment he won't be cast out. He believes that the magnitude of the shame he now feels precisely matches that of the hurt he has inflicted, which makes him a monster in his own eyes, unforgivable. There is some measure of elation, therefore, in the discovery that he can be pardoned, that he is allowed to stay after all.

'In all seriousness,' I said, 'this is probably what I've been looking for all this time. A clean connection, you know? Sex only muddies things.'

Letter 50: GAVIN MULVANY to CYPRIEN ABREO

Paris, 3 August 2022

Notwithstanding this, it was now your move. If you wanted to see me again, if we were going to pursue this mad concern, a pure friendship, you'd have to make the call. Which, in fairness to you, and kudos to me, not least for surviving twenty-one torturous days of silence, you did. On the morning of a Friday in mid-September. Two weeks into Anne-Laure's first term at her new school. The end of the first teaching week at the faculty. Your research day.

'I need some fresh air. Are you free? I thought Père Lachaise. Héloïse and Abélard's tomb at eleven?'

To answer your call I'd had to interrupt a private lesson I was giving to a businessman in my kitchen. As soon as I hung up, I cancelled my next lesson by text, citing sudden illness. You were disappointed, I think, that our paths crossed by chance at the cemetery entrance on boulevard de Ménilmontant, and that you then had to accept my help in consulting the map for the way to your chosen starting point. You counteracted this discomfiture by kissing my cheeks, quite naturally, after we'd already hugged in greeting.

We did two rounds of the grounds, sticking mostly to the outer paths near the walls and not straying in our conversation beyond the mundane or the practical, before making our way back to the metro station. As we approached the cemetery gate, you said this had been nice and asked me if I was free the following week. I said I was. On the train, you sat opposite me rather than on the empty seat to my right, and looked out of the window into the darkness without saying another word. From Saint-Lazare, you insisted on accompanying me to my address.

'I have a lesson at two,' I said at my door. 'But you could come up for an hour?'

'I should get back. See you next week.'

Upstairs, I went straight to my room and masturbated while looking at myself – the person that you saw – in the mirror.

The following Friday was the same: twice around Père Lachaise cemetery, then home for a solitary wank. The Friday after that it was Montmartre (two back-to-back). And after that, Montparnasse (in the shower). By which point these cemetery walks had become something of a tradition, an unspoken commitment between us, to which I looked forward every week. Already on the Thursday evening I began to get the jitters. Then on the day itself, as I went through the cemetery gates, I felt as I had as a child coming into the sitting room on Christmas morning, nauseous with the anticipation of receiving a substantial gift – back then it was a toy or a bike, nowadays the simple perception of your body moving through space next to mine.

One Friday in late October, at the northern point of Montmartre cemetery, somewhere between the graves of Offenbach and Delibes, we passed two men, loudly fashionable, hairdresser types, almost certainly an item. We all four of us nodded knowingly at each other. An innocent gesture of mutual recognition. Which you recognised as such only belatedly. Your own slowness made you clutch your chest and guffaw.

'You must spill the beans,' you said after you'd recovered. 'What do you like to do in bed?'

This was long before the advent of phone apps. As yet the assimilation of preferred sexual positions into gay men's social identity ('top', 'bottom', and so on) wasn't commonplace. I thus felt free to paint an idealised picture in which two men negotiated an end to the hostility they'd been educated to feel for one another, before searching together for their own unique path to intimacy. You were rightly sceptical.

'Come on. Have you really found such a spirit of equality in your relationships with men?'

'Flashes of it here and there.'

'Maybe that's as good as it gets for any of us.'

The following week, as we were coming round the southeastern corner of Père Lachaise, we overtook a group of German tourists, whose fascination with us you decided to indulge by veering towards me, pressing your upper arm against mine, synchronising the rhythm of our footfalls, so that we'd be unmistakably merged.

Emboldened by this, I went in with, 'So it's my turn to ask you. What do you get up to during your encounters?'

'Me? I'm a known expert on Sade, the most famous *débauché* in literary history. Moreover, my non-traditional marriage arrangements aren't exactly a state secret. It's unavoidable that I have a certain reputation. You must trust me, though, when I say that between the sheets I'm as conventional as the next man.'

'Are you and Mathilde still active?'

'A relationship as long as ours has many phases.'

You were first introduced to her through a friend, you said, who believed you needed someone who'd settle you down. You'd recently been awarded your doctorate. You were going out a lot. Drinking. Fucking around. Pretending not to care about the future. But it was the eighties. Inwardly, you were weighing up your prospects.

'So not love at first sight?'

'Don't get me wrong – Mathilde and I hit it off straight away. I knew the people, she knew the places, we had a crazy time. If anyone lived love's young dream, it was us. But with a woman like her, coming from where she does, you know there's a wake-up call coming. "Where is this heading? Do you foresee us having a family?" Mathilde was never going to let the party drag on too long.'

'She demanded that you make a choice, her or the wild life?'

'More like she understood that, at the end of the day, stability was what I really needed, especially for my career. How was I going to study and write books without some tranquillity, a routine? Anyway, then I got her pregnant, and that decided it.'

Mathilde's penchant nowadays was for wide-framed 'architect' glasses and abstract jewellery. She exuded the cold glamour of a world that only in exceptional circumstances admitted outsiders. I remembered she once said to me when you'd left the room: '*You know, when I met him, Cyprien needed a lot of support.*'

'Aren't you playing with fire?' I said. 'Isn't it inevitable that sooner or later one of your dalliances will cause a rift between you and Mathilde? That you'll lose everything you've got?'

'Mathilde controls the tap. She knows she can turn it off at any time. And it's hardly a one-way thing. As you'd expect, she has a private life of her own. Not as varied as mine, perhaps. But only because she's busier. She'll never leave me. There's no way.'

At the end of our circuit we found the area around the tomb of Héloïse and Abélard deserted. Spikes on top of the railings prevented people from jumping over and lying on the prone stone figures, as a pair of cats were so tantalisingly doing.

'Let's find a spot to sit down,' you said.

You led me onto a narrow track between two rows of graves. On a patch of weeds between two high altars, you spread out your jacket and sat on it. I hovered nearby, unsure: we'd never done this before.

'Are you uncomfortable?' you said.

Shaking my head, no, I plonked myself down cross-legged beside you. I had a view down a long, thin passage formed by closely packed blocks of stone scattered with fallen leaves.

'How many of your students have you slept with?' I said.

'Ah, *the million-dollar question*,' you said in English. 'The code of conduct is silent on the matter. But I have a personal rule. Work is for work. Play happens elsewhere.'

'*Don't shit on your own doorstep.*'

'–'

'It means –'

'I know what it means.'

'You've never been tempted?'

'That's a different question.'

'So you've just never acted on your urges.'

'As long as someone is registered in the faculty, they're off-limits.'

'What about after they've left?'

'Hmm, once or twice I've reconnected with people, yes. Also, students from other universities. Conferences abroad. Nothing stopping me there.'

We jumped when a couple of kids playing hide-and-seek, possibly earwigging, burst into our sanctum, made a circle around us, giggled, then ran away. You, then I, smiled at the sweetness of this.

'All right,' you said, 'if you absolutely promise to keep it to yourself?'

(I was in: the back room, influence, fringe benefits.)

'One of our current doctoral students. Not my supervisee. Another area.'

'Which area?'

'Modern. Twentieth century.'

Already she gave off a bad feeling.

'Did her undergrad elsewhere,' you said. 'Only joined us this term. Nothing has happened between us yet. But . . .'

'Something is going to happen.'

'I don't tend to be wrong in my forecasts.'

Letter 51: GAVIN MULVANY to PEDRO SOUZA

Paris, 5 August 2022

We have different theories to account for the bumpy beginnings of our sex life. I stand by mine. While nursing me in the hospital, you'd adopted the role of nurturer, which by definition is also one of subtle control. You instructed me to do things and praised me when I obeyed, chastised me when I didn't. Because you were accustomed to docility on my part, you were then unprepared for the requests I made of you in the bedroom, and intimidated by their urgency; you were unwilling to relinquish your position of command.

'Aren't you curious about what these are?' I said in bed one day while pointing to the scars on my chest, then turning over to show you the ones on my back. Not once in over six months of lovemaking had you remarked on them.

'I presumed they were birthmarks,' you said.

'They're burns, you dope. Hot metal.'

'Fuck. What happened?'

You asked the question before remembering you'd been afraid to know. Then, once I'd begun to explain, you felt obliged to hear me out, even though you were visibly itching to get up, get dressed, get away. You hated when I brought up Cyprien. For you he represented a deviation from healthy norms. A past experiment that had gone wrong and that now needed to be consigned to oblivion. But a person can't simply decide to forget things.

'Didn't you report the bastard?' you said.

'Pedro,' I said, 'you're not listening. I let him do it.'

What Cyprien did, and for what reason, was a cinch to explain. To the question of why I gave him permission, on the other hand, I could provide no coherent answer.

'Don't drive yourself mad,' you said. 'Sometimes we do things and don't know why. Put it behind you.'

The right advice for the moment, probably. And it worked, I swear, for a while.

Letter 52: PEDRO SOUZA to GAVIN MULVANY

Dublin, 6 August 2022

Take a breath. Before you start shooting your mouth off, get on a Zoom with Gráinne. (It's gone time you went back to her.) She'll help you figure out what's best to keep to yourself and what you might share with the world without upsetting your balance. Do you want to throw away all the progress you've made?

MS Extract: from *Rousseau's Lost Children* by GAVIN MULVANY

Last edited: 10 August 2022

While living in the countryside outside Paris under the protection of Louise d'Épinay, Rousseau had more than just the education of children on his mind. During his solitary wanderings, he brooded on the past, in particular the great love story he had never experienced. Exercised by this perceived lack, he began to plan a novel. A romance whose characters would live in rural obscurity. A tearjerker in which the lovers' passions would be founded, not on malice, competition or subjugation, as the sentimental games of urban sophisticates were, but on integrity.

He completed the novel in 1758 and published it three years later under the title *Julie, or the New Héloïse*. In common with several well-known eighteenth-century novels, *The New Héloïse* is told entirely in letters, and is a story of illicit desire. A young tutor, Saint-Preux, falls in love with his aristocratic pupil, Julie, but Julie's father has other plans for her. For reasons of class, but also, it seems, out of fear of honest and open sentiment, Julie's father intends to give her away to a substitute of himself: an older man, a friend who once saved his life, called Wolmar. Helped along by a religious crisis, Julie agrees to marry the man and has two children with him.

The married life of Wolmar and Julie is marked by extreme moderation. Wolmar has married Julie not out of passion, but out of an inclination to save her from disgracing herself with other, more passionate men. Julie bows to Wolmar's authority as her husband and professes to love him. Unwilling to keep any secrets from him, she reveals to him the history of her past relationship with Saint-Preux. Wolmar's response is consistent with his imperturbability: he writes to Saint-Preux to assure him of his friendship, and to invite him to come and live with them as a tutor to their children.

Together now in an ideal rural cottage, attended by well-treated servants, Wolmar, Julie, and Saint-Preux live frugally in peace and happiness. They do not behave like lovers with one another; no one is actively seducing anyone else. But nor do they deny the existence of a multi-directional chain that links them together. Julie and Saint-Preux are united in a chaste bond. Steered by Wolmar, their feelings for each other ascend to a higher plane.

Curiously, this threesome arrangement is not a source of emotional tension, as one might expect in a novel of this era, but a solution to that tension. In Rousseau's fictional world, where feelings constantly threaten to overwhelm people and drive them to committing outrages, the ménage à trois is the gate to virtue and serenity. This is at once a reflection and a reversal of Rousseau's own lived experience. The two most ardent relationships of Rousseau's life were triangular, that is with women who each already had a second male lover. On the one hand, these threesomes suited Rousseau, as they allowed him to express longing abstractly (that is, through beautiful phrases or masturbation) without having to face the shame that physical intimacy with women evoked in him. In this sense, they put an idealised veneer on what was a sexual dysfunction on his part. On the other hand, by creating conditions in which his own feelings of inadequacy and failure could prosper, they caused him to feel the very shame he was seeking to avoid.

The first of these relationships was with the noblewoman who took the sixteen-year-old Rousseau in off the streets, Françoise-Louise de Warens. With Warens, Rousseau behaved like someone in the grip of amorous obsession. He needed to be with her constantly and had tantrums whenever she received visitors. Rousseau would not actually sleep with Warens until a couple of years after first meeting her, but even then, on becoming her lover, he continued to stand in awe of her, as though she were an imperious mistress, and he her servant whose role was to obey her orders and beg her pardon. This homage was flattering to Warens, who was not above stimulating it flirtatiously and then mocking Rousseau when he burst into jealous rages. But it did complicate their lovemaking. He remained too inhibited to satisfy her, while she found his histrionics tiresome. At no point did she consider giving up her affairs with other men to dedicate herself to him.

Throughout their relations, Rousseau's attitude to Warens remained erotic to the point of fetishism. He would, for instance, kiss furniture that she had touched with her hand, or physically prostrate himself on ground he believed she had walked on. His agitation grew to the point where he sought out dark alleyways and exposed himself to female passers-by. Although while doing this he was sexually excited, erect, it was not his penis he revealed. According to his own account, he did not even think of doing that. Rather he exposed his bottom, 'the ridiculous thing': his shame on show.

Warens was attended by a young man named Claude, officially a servant, but secretly her lover. Initially Rousseau failed to grasp that Claude and Warens were sharing a bed. He fell into regarding Claude, six years his senior, as an older brother or even a father. Claude, for his part, was suspicious of Rousseau and kept him under constant surveillance. Not long after Rousseau arrived, Warens and Claude had a quarrel, after which the latter swallowed enough laudanum to kill himself. Warens found out in time to make him vomit it up, but in the hurry to revive him, she confessed to Rousseau the true nature of the relationship. Dumbfounded, Rousseau failed to see any connection between Claude's suicide attempt and his own arrival.

Eventually Warens outlined to Rousseau the conditions under which she would give herself to him. In essence what she offered him was entrance into a love triangle with her and Claude. Rousseau agreed to Warens's conditions, but he was far from unconflicted about the new physical dimension of their relationship. 'For the first time I saw myself in the arms of a woman, and a woman I adored. Was I happy? No. I tasted pleasure, but I know not what invincible sadness poisoned its charm. I felt as if I had committed incest.'

Three years after Rousseau's arrival, Claude died, probably by suicide. By then, Rousseau's infatuation with Warens had abated. She could not rid herself of the habit of treating him coolly, while he remained blocked by his apprehensions. Nevertheless, Rousseau remained in Warens's home, completing his self-education, for over a decade.

Twenty years later, in Louise d'Épinay's house, this pattern was repeated. While writing *The New Héloïse*, he fell in love again. The object of his affections this time was d'Épinay's cousin, Countess d'Houdetot – Élisabeth-Sophie-Françoise Lalive de Bellegarde, or to Rousseau simply Sophie – who was renting a house a few kilometres away. So intoxicated was Rousseau by Sophie that when he walked over the hills to her home, his knees would tremble and his body crumple. Unable to distract himself and think of anything else, he would ejaculate onto the ground, thereby purging himself of his erotic fantasies, only to be aroused again on arrival by the mere sight of her.

Mercifully, Sophie did not reciprocate his feelings. She was – with the approval of her husband, who had a mistress of his own – amorously attached to Jean-François de Saint-Lambert, a career army officer. Rousseau's courting of Sophie was thus always accompanied by a third presence. On the long walks in the forest that he took with her, Rousseau made a special point of feeling guilty for invading the rights, not of her husband, but of Saint-Lambert, who was also his friend. In actuality, however, the arrangement was one he found some comfort in. Their threesome protected him from the awkwardness and probable disappointment of intercourse – 'Both of us were intoxicated with love, she for her lover and I for her, so that our sighs and tears mingled deliciously' – while also allowing him to wallow in and overcome the embarrassment inherent in his position as an unlucky suitor, an interloper. It was enough that the lovers appeared to need him in order to have each other. Happy was he to be neither the lover nor the beloved but the point of contact between the two.

For Rousseau, this masochistic self-denial mixed with vicarious or mimetic desire – that is, the desire for something because it is desired by another, or the desire for the desire felt by others for one another – signified love. 'This time it was love, and love in all its force and all its fury.' He made no secret of the intimacy he shared with Sophie. To his mind, his feelings for her were pure and therefore nothing he needed to hide. Preoccupied with proving his own virtuous intentions to himself – did not his feelings of shame insure him against acting shamefully? – he failed to notice that he had become the talk of the local households and their visitors. Saint-Lambert heard rumours about the nature of their friendship and got angry. Louise d'Épinay, consumed by jealousy, tried to get her hands on Rousseau's letters to Sophie. Perplexed by these overreactions, Rousseau took the extraordinary step of complaining about them to Saint-Lambert himself. There were quarrels, tears, imperfect reconciliations, accumulated grievances. Sophie got a grip on herself and walked away. Rousseau moved out of the Hermitage and into a rented house called Montlouis (today a small Rousseau museum) in the village of Montmorency.

Letter 53: GAVIN MULVANY to CYPRIEN ABREO

Paris, 10 August 2022

Today I walked with Jean-Jacques to Vincennes prison to visit the Marquis de Sade. At his house, where we'd agreed to meet, I found Jean-Jacques in an open-handed mood, having just received payment for a new high-quality edition of *The New Héloïse*. On his insistence, before heading towards the prison, we went to the Palais-Royal pastry shop for meringues and lemon cakes, to a grocer on rue d'Antin for a speciality marmalade from Provence and then to a boutique on rue Saint-Honoré for stockings.

Every time I see Jean-Jacques he appears frailer. Today he coughed a lot and complained of burning in his urinary tract. Otherwise he was unforthcoming. I didn't mind. My own thoughts were keeping me busy. We passed through Les Halles. Our pace was slow. I waited until we stopped to rest under some trees beyond the Bastille walls to press him.

'The man we're visiting,' I said, 'this Sade, is a self-professed libertine. He's been put away for freely indulging in sensual pleasures without regard to moral principles. His crime is shamelessness.'

While considering this, Jean-Jacques hacked out globs of phlegm onto the ground. 'I appreciate the warning. But it's a basic law that lack of shame eventually turns to shame. Every imprisoned man comes to know this. I can give this Sade man my charity, secure in the knowledge that, if he was shameless once, he's faced shame in his solitude every day since.'

He extended an arm, which I used to help him to his feet, and we set off again. He appeared to breathe more easily now that we were in the fields of Faubourg Saint-Antoine. Sometimes, carried along by my reveries, I found myself a few strides ahead and had to stop and wait for him to catch up. On noticing halfway down rue de Charenton that I couldn't hear his breathing any more, I turned to see him leaning against a high stone at the edge of a meadow. Going to him, I took his arm and led him to a nearby tree, which gave more shade.

'Better?'

He wiped his face and nodded. Took a swig from the bottle I gave him. I offered him one of the lemon cakes we'd bought, but he refused, saying, 'Those are for the prisoner.'

I stood with the sun on my crown, looking at the city in the distance, while waiting for his wheezing to subside.

'For anyone trying to understand shame,' he said finally, 'the Bible really should be the first port of call,' and proceeded to give me an exegesis of the story of Eden. The first lesson Adam and Eve learn from the tree of knowledge, he said, their first shock, isn't that they're naked but that their nakedness was known by God long before it was revealed to them.

We continued on the road, and the Vincennes fortress soon skulked into view. Behind us on the horizon, the blocks and spires of Paris oscillated in a haze.

'Don't look behind you,' Jean-Jacques said quite seriously. 'Flee for your life.'

'I can't help it,' I said. 'Like Lot's wife, shame compels me to look back.'

'You're attached to Sodom. What have you done that shame would find so captivating?'

I told him about my life before meeting you, Cyprien. The conquests I'd undertaken as a single man in Dublin. The murky settings in which those had taken place. The lying and the cheating and the taking advantage I'd done to get what I wanted. The lack of remorse I'd felt for all this. Then I told him about my life in Paris with you. Specifically about the cemetery walks we used to take. About the refuge we found in them. About the affection we shared on them, without ever getting physical. How chaste everything was. And how much shame I felt, apparently for this very reason.

'This man Cyprien,' Jean-Jacques said, 'you loved him?'

'More than any man I've known.'

'And he you?'

'With a species of love he'd only been able to experience with me.'

'Then you're mixing up two kinds of love. On the one hand, the esteem two men of feeling have for one another. And on the other hand, the love-bond between man and woman, which is the basis of the family. No one relationship can have both.'

'Perhaps you're right. But with Cyprien, I dared to hope.'

Jean-Jacques took his time to digest this. I was prepared for the possibility that he wouldn't tolerate it, that he'd reject me on account of it, that he'd disappear for good.

'When I was walking with Cyprien in the cemeteries,' I said, 'I often thought about your relationship with Sophie. And also about Julie and Saint-Preux from your novel. Why would two people in love choose to enter a restrictive arrangement, in which they commit to seeing each other regularly, to sharing everything with each other, while at the same time refusing to become lovers proper? All the elements for happiness are in place, yet they opt for an inferior substitute, even though it causes them distress – why?'

'By distress you mean shame?'

'With Cyprien, before any happiness I felt, or after it, and sometimes even with it, shame inevitably arrived.'

'A chaste arrangement causes the lover shame only if he fails to be firm in his commitment to it. Were you merely pretending to be chaste, while inwardly you had other ideas?'

'My commitment to our agreement was iron-clad. I obeyed the rules fully in his presence. I tried to do everything right. I kept my hands to myself. I never lost sight of the reverence I owed, not only to Cyprien, but also to his wife. I was a regular Saint-Preux! And still there was shame.'

'Of course, the matter is complicated in your case by the fact of the authority being a woman, the wife. The shame you felt then and now undoubtedly derives from this violation of a fundamental moral law.'

'Once' – I brought this up as a counter-argument, though I fear I was really agreeing with him – 'Cyprien and I were sitting on the ground side by side in Père Lachaise. Telling stories. A perfect picture. Quite unexpectedly, two young boys came upon us. Such beautiful boys. They didn't stick around long. A few seconds. But for that time, they were our children, playing in our walled garden. And the world was complete. But then, later at home, with the space to reflect, I was able to see how we must really have looked in those children's eyes, and I winced. In an instant what I'd experienced as happiness turned to shame.'

A rattle in Jean-Jacques's throat gave warning: 'Those children were God. They were the eternal eye that sees all. That reads the depths of your heart. They were witnesses to the engagement you'd entered and to your faithfulness in observing it. And they saw you came up wanting.'

We'd arrived at the gate of Vincennes. Jean-Jacques leaned on my shoulder to rest while I peered around for someone who might let us in. A minute later, a head poked out of a window of the entrance tower and cried, 'Who goes there?'

'By order of the king!' I replied, and waved the official sealed letter (obtained from the lieutenant general of police, a major hassle – don't ask).

A warning bell was sounded, and the drawbridge descended. We crossed over the deep moat. After the letter was inspected, we were taken through three iron-reinforced doors, each requiring a separate key from the sentry outside and the guard within. Accompanied by two guards, we traversed the baked ground of the compound to the council room, where our meeting was to take place. The ceilings were high and vaulted, but the windows extremely narrow. The guard hung the lamp on the wall. Lit a second lamp on the table, opened a ledger and sat in front of it, quill in hand, ready to record what was said. Two more guards took up position on either side of the door. We were ordered to sit at the darker end of the table and to wait.

A good twenty minutes – distant banging and screaming – and the prisoner was brought in. Hard to make out, until he rushed to the light at the table, around which we'd arranged the gifts. He rifled through them, examined them intently, as we did him. Unlike us, he'd put in some effort for the occasion. An elegant grey coat. Deep-orange silk breeches. A feather in his hat. A cane. A bit younger than me, not yet forty, and still handsome, full-faced. But also – reaching us now – a terrible stench coming through his clothes. And scabs on his face and hands. And black nails. And now with his hat removed, long strands of greasy hair.

'Good, I'm absolutely out of these.' He had his hand in a stocking and was checking the heel for ladders. Once satisfied, he let the silk drop, soundless, onto the table. Then turned his attention to us. 'Are these things from my wife? Do you think, just once in her life, she could get everything on my list right?' He pulled at the hems of the expensive clothes he was wearing as though to reveal them for the rags they really were. 'It's boiling and I've nothing to wear except the winter clothes in which I was arrested. And what can she expect me to do without the books? One must be surrounded by books in order to work, otherwise one can concoct nothing but fairy tales, and I've no talent for that.' He came around the table to be closer to us. His eyes were visible now, wet and shining. 'And what about the big quills from Griffon's, which cost only a penny. Griffon's does an excellent job of sharpening the points, so where are they? And the sealing wax I asked for centuries ago, I don't see that here either. I shan't forgive her.' Suddenly remembering our presence, he froze for a moment, then fell to his knees at our feet. 'You didn't hear that. My dear friends, disregard what I just said. My wife is all that remains to me on the earth. My pet. My turtledove. You must help her to obtain permission to visit! It's been far too long! Please, I implore you!'

Sade was about to snake his arms around Jean-Jacques's shins, to embrace them – and Jean-Jacques, I foresaw, to kick him away – when a guard took hold of Sade's collar and wrenched him back. 'You know the rules, Number Eleven! No touching!'

Having landed on his backside, Sade remained there. 'You see? You see how these beasts treat me!' He planted his feet, leaned forward and folded his arms over his knees. 'I've no allies on the outside, except for my wife. If I lose her, I have nothing.' He got to his feet. Wiped his hands on his breeches. Picked his cane up from the floor, where it had fallen. Sat heavily in the empty chair. Lay the cane across his thighs. 'She has sent you in her place, hasn't she? I beseech you to pass on to her what I've just said.'

'My man,' Jean-Jacques said, 'I'm afraid we don't –'

I silenced him with a touch on the arm. 'We'll be sure to give your wife your message, Mr Sade.'

'Also, for the love of all that's holy,' Sade said, 'you must find out how long these bastards intend to hold me for. I've implored their mercy, their humanity, their pity, yet they refuse to give me a date of release.'

'Can I ask,' I said, 'what you are accused of? We've heard stories. But we're dispassionate people. We don't rely on public voices to make our minds up.'

'I'm guilty –'

'No whispering!' said the scribbling guard.

'– only of youthful indiscretions. Such as not showing proper regard for a whore's backside.'

'Remember yourself, Mr Sade,' said Jean-Jacques.

'Do you have a sister, Mr Rousseau?' said Sade. 'A niece? A daughter?'

'You can direct your revolting questions elsewhere.'

'If you do, advise her to become a whore. How can a girl be better off than in a situation where, in addition to a luxurious and easy life, plus the constant intoxication of debauchery, she also has all the support, influence and protection of the French state. What an enlightened age we live in!'

'The rumour I heard,' I said, 'is that you cut a woman's skin with a knife and poured hot sealing wax into the wounds.'

'Pah! I'm a libertine, that I admit. I've conceived everything possible in that area, but I certainly haven't practised everything I've imagined and never shall.'

'Are you an abuser of women?'

'I'm neither a criminal nor a murderer. I've been shut up like a madman in a cage of iron over a mere party involving some girls, exactly like any one of the eighty others that take place every day in Paris.'

'The *débauchés* of Paris that you mention,' said Jean-Jacques, 'every one of them, should be rounded up too, if they're found to have injured the virtue of a single woman.'

'The numbers of arrests would be so high,' said Sade, 'that to get them all, you'd have to turn the whole city into a jail. Or burn it down like Sodom.'

'Then so be it,' said Jean-Jacques. 'Those without shame ought to be made to have it.'

Sade planted his cane and used it to come to his feet. Unsteadily at first, he paced in and out of the darkness. 'You think the people of Sodom had no shame? That it was shamelessness that brought God's anger down upon them? Oh, you have it all wrong, Mr Rousseau. To live without shame is to be incapable of seeing how one's actions, good or bad, might appear to others. It is, in other words, a kind of innocence and God's highest blessing.'

'You two' – Rousseau used a fingertip in the air to draw a line connecting Sade and me – 'are birds of a feather.'

'The Sodomites' shame,' Sade went on, 'was a signal to God that they knew they were doing something worthy of punishment. The mistake they made was to accept that damnation was their inevitable end. What they should have done, and what would have saved them from the fires, was to defy God. Rise up against Him. Say: "Take your shame back. We have no use for it!"'

'I won't listen to any more of this blasphemous filth,' said Jean-Jacques, shutting his eyes and turning his head away.

'Naturally,' Sade said, 'if I were God, I'd have dealt with Sodom very differently.'

'Oh, yes,' said Jean-Jacques under his breath, 'now we're hearing the morals of our times.' At the table, he returned the gifts to their packages and tied the ribbons messily. He was taking them back.

Sade appeared bemused. 'Can there be anything sillier than imagining that a man deserves to be burnt alive because he prefers coming up an arse to coming in a cunt?'

Jean-Jacques, his arms full of parcels, appeared poised to launch them at the speaker of such filth. 'Unlock that door, guard, we won't be staying another instant in the presence of this heretic.'

Sade blocked his path to the door. 'Is it for you, Mr Rousseau, to say what is good and what is evil? You want the whole universe to be virtuous, but you fail to see that everything would perish in an instant if there were nothing but virtues on earth.'

'I shudder that people who have carried out adultery in the depths of their hearts dare speak of virtue! Now move out of the way, man!'

'There's no evil from which good does not come.'

'Is everyone listening? Are you taking careful notes over there? This is how the pedlars of the Enlightenment try to sell us false virtue that undermines the real.'

'I wouldn't be so quick to condemn either me or my way of life, Mr Rousseau. Yes, I'm a libertine, but I've never compromised the health of my wife, whom I love. I'm a libertine, but I adore my children, those poor little creatures, more than you can believe.'

By accident, while skirting round Sade to get to the door, Jean-Jacques dropped the box of meringues onto the floor. Sade picked the box up by the ribbon and carefully placed it back on top of the pile in Jean-Jacques's arms. 'And you, Mr Rousseau,' he said, 'what are you? A virtuous man who treats his wife like a servant, which is well known. A virtuous man who, rather than raising his children himself, and instilling his beloved virtue in them, put them in the lock-up and left them to perish.'

At this, Rousseau kicked the door with great force, and all three guards jumped to the task of chasing Sade around the cell, then lifting him off the floor, where he'd lain in protest, and putting his chains back on. Sade was calling out now, in order to be heard over the metal's scrape and the guards' yells: 'Understand, Mr Rousseau, that infanticide in itself is an imaginary crime. There's no greater certainty on earth than a mother's right over her children. That right is given in nature. It's incontestable. Even when her baby has already seen the light of day, a mother still has the right to destroy it. What you should ask yourself, Mr Rousseau, is whether it truly was your wife's decision to get rid of your children, or whether you did it against her will, which is another matter entirely, and one over which a man will unavoidably suffer undying shame.'

Letter 54: GAVIN MULVANY to JEAN-JACQUES ROUSSEAU

Paris, 11 August 2022

On leaving the prison, I was happy to help you distribute Sade's gifts to the beggars at the gate. But I preferred not to join you in picking flowers in Saint-Antoine. You looked dazed. Organising in your mind what had just taken place. Better to have a civil parting now, I thought, and to leave you to your own rationalisations, than to bother you with mine.

I went south, through bois de Vincennes to the Hôpital Esquirol, which you know as the Royal House of Charenton, the lunatic asylum where Sade, quite sane, would spend his final years. The gate under the stone arch was open, but I didn't go in, lingering long enough only to lament lives constrained unjustly, while others guilty of far greater crimes keep their freedom. It was Cyprien, my friend, who once told me – in reference to Sade, but speaking also in general terms – that if you want to find the truly crazy people, look not at who ends up in the asylums, but at who put them there. By not coming with me, Jean-Jacques, you were saved the pain of hearing such opinions, from which I'm afraid I don't entirely dissent.

Going eastwards, I traversed the park of Vincennes and emerged in the suburb of Nogent-sur-Marne. At Les Yvris–Noisy-le-Grand, close to the end of my walk, where the suburbs gave way to parkland, I sat at the edge of a stream and typed Cyprien's name into my phone. In contravention of my own rule against using the internet during my walks, I spent over an hour sifting through dozens of pages related to his achievements – aimlessly at first, one link leading to another, but soon more resolutely in search of reviews of his recent prize-winning book on Sade. I came upon a forum, evidently unmoderated, featuring readers' reviews. For his book, eight in total. Four and five stars. Friends of his? Then near the bottom of the page, under a single star, this:

'Haven't read book but was a student of Professor Abreo's. He didn't try it on with me because he knew I'd have cut his dick off, but rumour had it that he had private sessions with female students whom he

forced to do all kinds of kinky shit. Didn't think it was true at time but do now. Believe women.'

I dropped the phone down on the grass. In the midst of my agitation, there came to mind a famous story about Sade during the Revolution. At that tumultuous time (which I've avoided mentioning to you; suffice to say, it happened, and it's better that you weren't around for it), Sade had the chance to take revenge on the people who had imprisoned him by keeping them on the execution list, but instead saved their lives by taking them off it. Would you, Jean-Jacques, have done the same? Would I?

Once, at the critical moment, rather than sending my tormentor to hell, I found it in my heart to spare him. But given the chance now, would I do it again?

SEVENTH WALK

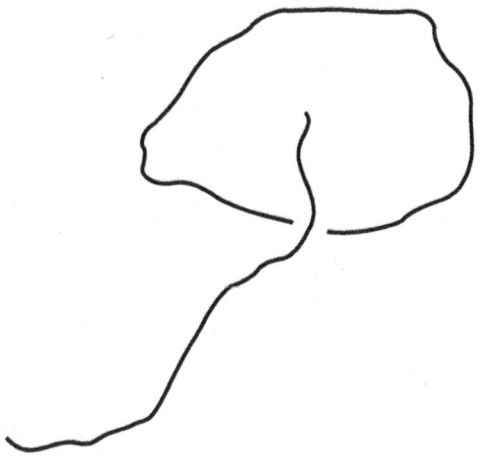

(To Vauhallan, walking southwest: rue J.-J. Rousseau –
Montparnasse – avenue du Maine – boulevard Périphérique –
Montrouge – Fontenay-aux-Roses – Sceaux –
Igny – Vauhallan; 21 km: 5 hours, 10 minutes)

Anger

Letter 55: GAVIN MULVANY to ZOÉ CHAUVIN

Paris, 15 August 2022
Resent: 19 August 2022
Resent: 23 August 2022

I'll cut to the chase. I'm back in town doing research for a book. Cyprien, don't ask me how, tracked me down. Call it lunacy, but I agreed to meet him. The faculty have suspended him until they finish their internal investigation, but he's positive his career is over. He told me that at first there was one complainant: you. Then there were two. Now, five. He asked me to convey a message to you. You'll appreciate the complicated position that puts me in. As you see, I'm keeping my word. But not as he intends me to. I have no desire to help save his skin. I'm not on his side. I just want to have a friendly chat with you. If nothing else, we could clear things up between us. I have no bad feelings for you personally, never did. I'd like to think that's mutual. We were both young and in deep water. In other circumstances we'd have been friends.

Letter 56: GAVIN MULVANY to ZOÉ CHAUVIN

Paris, 24 August 2022

Maybe I wasn't clear enough about my intentions. All I want is for the truth of what went on to come out. For better or worse, a complete picture will only be possible with me in it. I possess – I *am* – a key piece of the puzzle. An intervention from me will determine if Cyprien hangs or walks free. Think about it. Your case won't get off the ground without me. I can do mornings.

Letter 57: GAVIN MULVANY to JEAN-JACQUES ROUSSEAU

Paris, 24 August 2022

Zoé Chauvin: everything I wasn't. Black eyes. Sallow skin. Thick eyebrows. Long thin nose. Persian-looking, though with a cross on the gold necklace she wore. I first saw her in person when I visited the Sorbonne on a Tuesday in October to attend one of Cyprien's lectures. I arrived a good ten minutes before the start to find the amphithéâtre Descartes already full. Sitting on the stairs wasn't allowed, but the people in the back row kindly compressed themselves to free some space for me at the end of the bench. Among the tiers of heads sloping down, Zoé was a high accumulation of curly dark brown hair at the very front, though as yet I hadn't made the connection. I didn't think to pick her out until halfway into Cyprien's address, when I noticed that his gesticulations were veering in her direction, and that he seemed to smirk at her whenever he quoted anything exceptionally outré.

Since the start of the new term, I'd been badgering Cyprien to give me his timetable so that I could sit in on one of his Enlightenment classes. He'd always demurred, saying I should hold off until he'd dealt with the boring stuff and got to Sade, which, he said, was when things got spicy. In this jaded internet age, do Cyprien's Sade lectures still have the mythical status they had then? I doubt it. The lecture hall was buzzing. It was the place to be. Students who weren't even enrolled in French literature had turned up. The numbers were such that there was an overflow, not everyone could fit in, causing tension as students jostled at the doors and as accusations of unfair seat-reserving were launched and parried.

Cyprien spoke without notes. Onto the screen he projected engravings from Rousseau's novel, *The New Héloïse*, featuring modestly dressed figures in respectable arrangements, and from Sade's *Philosophy in the Boudoir*, of explicit orgies. These images he alternated – no fucking, then fucking – to create a visual match for the conceptual juxtapositions he was making in his arguments. The Sade images, however, he was careful to leave up for longer, so as to make of them a kind of scenery in front of which he paced, and as an amusement for us, a distraction from how dusty, how dry, the information he was feeding us actually was.

Before long the excitement in the room had settled into a familiar mix of attentiveness, bewilderment and boredom, momentarily elevating for a shared laugh or groan, then weakly discharging at the end as a smattering of claps. Because he'd run over time, Cyprien didn't open the session up for questions. Rather he quickly gathered up his books and papers and exited stage left in the company of Zoé.

The flash of envy arrived shockingly late. During the applause I'd watched, barely conceiving it as real, as Zoé came out of her seat, went to the top table and engaged Cyprien in a dialogue. (No fussing with her hair. No fiddling with her Nokia. No apologies. No nerves.) And then I'd continued to watch as they made their escape, he holding the door open for her.

I left the amphi and headed in the direction of Cyprien's office, all the while saying to myself that I shouldn't do this, that I had no reason to go there. Other, that is, than to give him my view of his lecture, which, now that I thought of it, had been pretty lacklustre. The office door was slightly ajar. I knocked, stepped back. Cyprien swung the door open with some energy. I was surprised to see how surprised he was to see me.

'I told you I was going to come today,' I said.

'Ah, sieve for a brain!'

Behind him, Zoé was on her feet – not sitting in the visitor's chair or on the little sofa by the bookshelf, but commanding the centre of the room – and peering at me over his shoulder.

'You've met Zoé, right?' he said.

'No,' I said.

He presented her to me as a PhD candidate working on Julia Kristeva and as a student rep in the faculty council. 'Your paths haven't crossed?'

'First time,' I said.

'What time did you used to come to the house, Zoé?' he said, twisting half-round.

'First thing,' she said.

'That explains it. Gavin was last in the day.'

'Anne-Laure is great, isn't she?' Zoé said.

She was addressing me across the threshold. Keeping me in a state of exclusion. It must be lovely to be able to do that, I thought.

Letter 58: GAVIN MULVANY to JEAN-JACQUES ROUSSEAU

Paris, 25 August 2022

Now that she was attending her new school, I gave lessons to Anne-Laure only once a week, on Saturday mornings. (The plan had been to stop all her private classes, but she'd chosen to keep mine up. Either that or Cyprien had had a moral compunction about making such a drastic cut to my earnings. I didn't know which.) Leading up to the next session, I was storing a great deal of anger that I didn't know what to do with, and was profoundly tired as a result. En route to the flat, I picked up an American *Rolling Stone* (cover: Keith Richards, topless, aged sixty) and gave it to Anne-Laure to read.

'Nice one,' she said, taking it to the armchair and putting her feet up on the little table that was supposed to be for a plant.

'I went to one of your father's lectures.' (The event was unsayable, yet I was saying it.)

'Lucky you.'

'Do you want to know what it was about?'

'Afraid philosophy ain't my bag.'

'It was about himself.'

Sighing, she rested the magazine on her lap. Scrunched up her features. 'Something going on, Gavin?'

'Like, that's what it was really about. Beneath the surface.'

I gave her a précis of the lecture's main argument, to which she listened, out of a concern for me that showed through a veneer of bored mockery.

'So you see,' I said, 'your father presented Rousseau and the Marquis de Sade as the two extremes of the matter.'

'Which matter?'

'Anger! The whole point he was making was about anger.'

'I'm lost.'

'His thesis was basically that there's an anger that approaches and there's an anger that withdraws. The first is a masculine type of anger. Loud, hot, quick to blame, confrontational. That's Sade, according to your father. The second is a feminine type that monitors and suppresses the feeling of anger, rather than letting it out, perhaps by ruminating, or crying, or even nodding and smiling. That's Rousseau.'

'Why are you telling me this?'

'I'm telling you because your father, in his lecture, was suggesting that Rousseau's version of anger, the suppressed kind, is unhealthy. That it's responsible for addiction, eating disorders, skin disorders, migraines –'

'Skin disorders?'

'– divorce, and general mayhem. A bit tongue in cheek, but that's what he said. By not allowing ourselves to get angry, we're making ourselves sick. And, while we're at it, we're giving free rein to the forces of authority that want us to be docile pawns.'

'I'm getting a migraine just listening to you.'

'Of course he was making a feminist point as well. Which was that, still today in the west, women aren't allowed to show anger, so they conceal it in tears. And men aren't allowed to show sadness, so instead of crying they have angry outbursts. Your father blamed Rousseau for this. He said the regime of emotional perversion that we live in is basically Rousseau's legacy. To smash it, all anger, male and female, must be released. And for this, Sade is the example to follow, because he was the first philosopher to express, fully and unashamedly, the true fury that we hold within us.'

Anne-Laure threw the magazine sideways, onto the couch.

'Do you want a yoghurt?' she said, getting up.

I nodded distractedly. 'Strawberry.'

'Don't you find it strange though?' I said when she came back and handed me the plastic pot and a teaspoon.

'I don't know,' she said, licking the lid of hers. 'My father says a lot of shit.'

'I'm not crazy then. You see it too. During our disagreements, I'm left marvelling at the fierce calm he achieves. It must come at the cost of a strain that's painful to imagine.'

'What do you disagree about?'

'Oh, abstract stuff. Work. The point is, he once shamed me for losing my temper over something on the news. In his best mellow voice, he called me "aggressive" and "scary", can you believe it? I told him, "It's going to bring me no pleasure to have to point out the obvious to you."'

'The obvious being . . .'

'That he's just as angry as me. If not angrier.'

'Right.'

'The only difference is, he's motivated to withdraw because he doesn't want to appear socially inappropriate. He fears being punished for his loss of control. He advocates for Sade's revolution of expression, while behind the scenes he belongs to Rousseau's tradition of suppression!'

'Finished?' Anne-Laure took my spoon and empty yoghurt pot to the kitchen. She came back with two loose cigarettes, taken from a stash somewhere. She put the one I refused behind her ear, lit the other one and started smoking it out of the open balcony door: her arm held into the breeze outside, her thumb flicking the ash over the railing, her body still in the room and half-turned to me.

'Mum calls him "passive aggressive",' she said.

'Is that the term?'

'A therapy thing. She's definitely the badass in the relationship. She doesn't hold back. I guess she knows Dad can take it.'

Cyprien in therapy? I couldn't see it. A man who won't show anger is a man who says he doesn't need it, right?

'Does your mother lose her temper?'

'Erm, yah!'

'How does your father react?'

'He tunes out.'

'And you? Does he allow you to get angry?'

'Not sure it's a permission thing. At least not any more.'

'How about as a child?'

'Hmm.' She sucked, inhaled and pondered. 'I don't remember getting angry so much. Waste of energy.'

Well before the white of the cigarette had burned down, she stubbed it out on the balcony floor and, without checking for people below, threw the butt over the edge.

'So, you do therapy?' I said.

'That' – she took up the magazine and plonked herself back down – 'is none of your fucking business, you freak.'

I went to the stereo and rifled through the stack of CDs sitting on top, without choosing any of them to play. 'Does Zoé still come to tutor you?'

'No.'

'What was she like? As a teacher, I mean.'

Like a horse she blew air hard through her lips. 'Way out of your league, mate.' Then, after leafing through a few more pages, she said, 'Look, I wouldn't if I were you. With her, you'd be talking about the price of a baguette and she'd bring it round to women's rights in Afghanistan. Unbearable, honestly.'

Letter 59: GAVIN MULVANY to JEAN-JACQUES ROUSSEAU

Paris, 26 August 2022

A fortnight later came Anne-Laure's birthday party, for which I didn't receive an invitation. Smarting at the thoughtlessness of this, I made plans that would take me far from the neighbourhood, in case I was tempted to gatecrash. Then a day in advance – his style – Cyprien texted me:

<<DO YOU HAVE A GOOD SHIRT? I'LL PAY YOU>>

When I arrived in the morning, Mathilde and Anne-Laure were out clothes shopping. I cleaned the bathroom sinks. Laid out the glasses and the bottles. Removed the pre-ordered food from its packaging and put the buffet table in order. Then I took Coco around the block. Picked up the cake and some extra lemons. Rearranged the chairs in the sitting room. Made Anne-Laure's bed, so that the guests could leave their coats on top. As I worked, quite independently, Cyprien came in and crouched down beside me – I was kneeling in front of the open freezer, packing it with bags of ice – and pressed first his nose, then his forehead against mine and let out a long sigh, and I for some reason told him I'd missed him.

'But I haven't gone anywhere,' he said. 'I've been right here. For whatever you need. Just a call away.'

The first arrivals, on the dot, were Cyprien's parents, whom Cyprien installed on the sofa with pastis and with whom he urged me to converse – not the easiest task in the world. Next to come, in quick succession, were several groups of Mathilde's associates from the art world, among whom was a thin, grey-haired man, immaculately turned out, whose voice must've reached Mathilde in the bedroom, for she came out saying his name: 'Gaspard!' She embraced him at the same time as putting an earring in her ear, and she apologised for running late at the same time as subtly blaming Anne-Laure for this. Then she took Gaspard through to the sitting room, joined to him as though he was her co-host, and made some introductions, at which point what had hitherto been mutterings became loud declarations and interjections – the party had started.

I handed out drinks on a tray. Gradually the gaps in the room, through which I was navigating, filled up with Cyprien's academic colleagues. 'Ah, you're still here, chipping away?' said one. 'I haven't forgotten,' said another. 'I'll make that call on your behalf. Remind me of your specialisation?'

Mathilde's father arrived with three generations of a family, not his own, in tow. He introduced the grandfather and the father as long-time friends and neighbours of his, and put special emphasis on the teenage son – flabby, a thick side parting, a hairless chin, the identical turtleneck jumper and navy blazer with gold buttons as the father – as a potential new friend for Anne-Laure. Anne-Laure was summoned from her room, from which she hadn't yet emerged, and was put standing next to this boy. The adults' attention shifted to her, to them, and there came a momentary cessation of speech as everyone took in the sheer incongruity of the match. Anne-Laure's face hardened and reddened. I felt protective of her. None of her friends were here. My impulse was to let her know – what was to stop me simply calling out? – that she didn't have to go along with this; that she could just go back to her room and stay there, if that's what she wanted to do.

The man standing next to me on the outer ring of spectators introduced himself to me as Cyprien's best friend. They had, he said, grown up together in Plaisir. I told him who I was: 'the tutor'. Information which, it turned out, he already possessed. Cyprien had spoken of me to him. With a look of surprise, I let it be known that

Cyprien had never mentioned an Arthur from Plaisir to me. 'When we were kids,' Arthur said, 'I was the more inventive one. He used to follow my lead. Now I'm the one who listens to him. It's amazing what I'm prepared to accept if it comes from him.'

I went into the kitchen, diminished. I washed some dirty glasses at the sink and in my mind demanded that everyone in the world, starting with Cyprien and his set, recognise my dignity and equal worth. While drying my hands, I noticed Mathilde on the balcony with Gaspard; the two of them shoulder to shoulder, listening to a second man tell what appeared to be an amusing story. In the city lights, next to these two attractive men, at a distance from her family, soaking up the in-talk, she looked uncharacteristically joyful. And why wouldn't she be? Despite lacking any traits that might make her worthy of it, she had it all.

Back in the sitting room, the guests had settled into an arrangement of sufficient cohesion – an uneven circle with the coffee table at its core – to allow a single discussion to be sustained. Audible above this exchange was a breathless voice coming from the hall, where Zoé was furnishing Cyprien with her jacket and, along with it, an intricate account of the altogether boring reasons for being late: '*I left the house on time but –*' What had possessed him to invite her? How could being among his family and friends be considered a privilege, if she got to be here too? Sensing them approach, and fearing that he was about to offload her on me, I went in search of Anne-Laure, who had disappeared from the main crowd.

Circling out to the hall, I collected some glasses and left them on the sideboard by the entrance to pick up on my way back. I passed down the corridor and pushed open Anne-Laure's bedroom door, which had been left ajar. Inside, by the open window, Anne-Laure was pulling on a cigarette, maybe even a joint, that Arthur was holding. For an instant my frame of perception was reduced to his two fingertips pressed against her lips. Gasping (sort of), I stepped back out and slammed the door unintentionally behind me.

In the bathroom, I rubbed some water into my eyes, wiped some more through my hair and studied my reflection in the mirror. Shut into this flat, we, all the people, seemed to form a total society, endowed with its own economy, morality, language. The game was imagining the number of combinations that could be created: him with her, her with her, him with him, to infinity. Lines could be drawn connecting Cyprien to any number of others, and them to others again, until the single stroke that joined him to me appeared weak and insignificant. Imagining this, I was undoubtedly in pain and saw no quick path back to composure. My only possible ploy was to turn the suffering to my advantage. To put myself completely at Cyprien's disposal. To be ready at every moment to be tyrannised by him. To put myself forward for the worst of his tortures. And to ensure, when under his scourge, that my contortions and my cries afforded him the most happiness. That, for better or worse, was my plan.

Cyprien was standing with a small group by the kitchen door. Zoé – who in her white shirt and black skirt to the knee looked every bit the hired help, but who also appeared to have no intention of doing any work – was beside him, holding a tumbler of vodka or gin, into which Cyprien was dropping an extra cube of ice from his bare hand. I entered with sangfroid into this scene. The representation of the erotic was, I knew, more interesting to Cyprien than the lived experience. What he was doing with Zoé was nothing but the image of what he'd like to do with her. Passing into the kitchen, I put the glasses I'd collected into the machine, then returned to join their clique. Choosing a moment in which Zoé was distracted by an increasingly loud disputation emanating from the other side of the room, I turned my face to Cyprien's ear and almost whispered, *Are you trying to make this as hard as possible for me? You should know I'm able for it. I can take whatever you throw at me*, and in fact whispered, 'She's beautiful, I see what you see in her.'

Anne-Laure and Arthur returned from the bedroom and split off, she to sit close to her grandfather in the centre, he to melt back into a corner. Talk in the room had turned to the recent vote in the United States Senate giving power to Bush to invade Iraq. Anger, Mathilde's father was saying, deserved to be met with anger. Having been attacked, the Americans had a right to seek vengeance, and not only that, to choose freely, as the 9/11 hijackers themselves had done, the place where this vengeance should be directed. This created ripples of disapproval in the room. His interlocutors objected in a predictably polite fashion. Being wronged didn't earn either a person or a nation the right to wrong others, they said. Feeling anger wasn't in itself justification for behaving any old way. Not once in history has vengeance ever solved anything.

Mathilde was doing the rounds, filling up glasses, trying her best to ignore the ins and outs of the ongoing debate and the strained ambience it had created. Feigning to do something useful at the coffee table – she folded up the used wrapping paper, as though to take it away, then set it down again – she leaned towards her father and mumbled, 'All right, Dad, you've had your say now.'

To which he exploded in mock rage: 'Daughter of mine, you disappoint me. What have I said to you since you were little? If you have something to say, say it! Don't bottle it up!'

'Let's keep the focus on the right place today, shall we?' said Mathilde.

'We're all of us just expressing our views. When did that become such a frightening prospect?'

'Please just tone it down a bit.'

'Come on now! Anne-Laure, you're with me on this, aren't you? I'll tell you the same thing I used to tell your mother: if you feel passionately about something, if you're angry, don't run away from it, embrace it. Anger is nature's way of calling you to arms. A man who never gets angry when he's slighted or belittled is stupid. A woman who doesn't is servile. A nation, weak. Instead of finding fault with America's anger, we should be emulating it. In this day and age, anger is nothing less than our patriotic duty. France is great, the west is great, because it doesn't hesitate to use its anger for good.'

'You're speaking exactly like a jihadist.'

Were those the exact words? By now Mathilde had left her father's side and was making for the kitchen with an empty wine bottle and an ashtray. She didn't flinch when the pronouncement was made, so my presumption was she didn't hear it, or didn't want to. I was standing right next to Zoé, so I didn't have the same luxury. I'd been keeping a close eye on her, out of curiosity about how she was coping with the problem of Mathilde's father, my presumption being that her scholarly ego – the part of her that believed that the authority to speak on matters of consequence was slowly and expensively acquired, and therefore unavailable to most – would override any etiquette forbidding her from meddling in the workings of other people's families.

'Virtuous anger,' she went on, 'of the kind you're describing, is really just an excuse to make others pay for one's own moral failings.'

In my memory it was Anne-Laure who smiled at this first, then her grandfather. The two of them glanced at each other, caught their own reflections coming back, then turned to Zoé and shot them straight at her, the full two barrels. With a sideways glare, Zoé pleaded with Cyprien for back-up, but he just shook his head: ignore them.

'Ladies and gentlemen,' said Mathilde's father, 'the waitress has an opinion! And has got herself worked up about it too! Are you all watching how it's done? Apparently I've found my match.'

Murmurs of encouragement from Mathilde's father's guests. Otherwise, grumbles. Uncomfortable bodies shifting. Behind me, through the kitchen door, I could hear Mathilde already clearing things away, even though it was still early.

'I'll concede one thing,' your father said, addressing only Zoé now. 'War isn't the only or even the best method for triumphing over our enemies. It's one part of a much larger project. If the west is to come out on top, once and for all, western women, French women, Christian women like you, need to have babies. More babies. Three, four times as many. Are you a mother, miss? Do you intend to be one day?'

Scoffing, outraged, Zoé turned her back to him and pointedly engaged a woman nearby, a scholar from Cyprien's crew, on another subject.

'Ah,' said Mathilde's father. 'She has turned her back on us, Anne-Laure. We've lost her. A hit-and-run. The coward's tactic. Fling an insult, then shut down. My dear, I want you to take a good look at that woman over there. Examine her from head to toe. Forget what your teachers say. That there is what a real bully looks like.'

Letter 60: GAVIN MULVANY to
JEAN-JACQUES ROUSSEAU

Paris, 27 August 2022

Soon after this, the party dissolved. Zoé was one of the first to slip away. She and Cyprien exchanged rasping whispers while the latter helped her back on with her jacket. Together Cyprien's parents thanked me personally for my help and passed me a crumpled five-euro note (which, in fairness, was worth much more in 2002 than it is now). At the door, Mathilde's father, who brought the flashiest and most expensive gift, exhorted Anne-Laure to take it back to the shop if it wasn't to her liking. She embraced him with warm affection, waved him into the lift, then went straight to her room, leaving Arthur, who'd been hovering nearby, to depart without a goodbye.

I put the leftover food into the fridge. Emptied the dishwasher and put on a fresh load. When I came back out, Mathilde and Gaspard were at one end of the semi-cleared table, smoking, drinking, listening to a Danyèl Waro CD: subdued but not in any apparent distress.

'Should I check in on Anne-Laure?' I said.

'Cyprien's with her.'

I sat a little further down the table and topped up my glass. We listened to the music together, in silence except to acknowledge now and then a particularly powerful phrase. After a while Cyprien came in and sat opposite us. 'She'll be all right.' I got him a fresh glass and poured him a drink. He pulled out the neighbouring chair for me to sit on. We talked until dusk. At which point Anne-Laure emerged, looking as though she'd just woken up. We retrieved the leftovers for an impromptu dinner. You produced the uneaten cake, and we sang happy birthday and had a toast. Over coffee, Gaspard gave a long and riveting report of a trip he had taken across North Africa. As she listened, Anne-Laure passed her index finger – left to right, right to left, over and over – through the candle flame.

MS Extract: from *Rousseau's Lost Children* by GAVIN MULVANY

Last edited: 28 August 2022

Rousseau took his epigram for *Émile* from Seneca's essay 'On Anger': 'We are sick with evils that can be cured; and nature having brought us forth sound, itself helps us if we wish to be improved.' The aim of the education that Rousseau describes in *Émile* is, first and foremost, to cure mankind of the sickness of anger. The boy is educated at a distance from the family unit in large part to spare him from the angry tyranny of the father. The tutor teaches the boy to honour his father but demands that the boy obey him only. In gaining and sustaining the boy's obedience, the tutor avoids using anger. He is not interested in instilling fear in the boy. He understands that, while it might succeed in cowing him, fear cannot lead the boy to freedom and happiness.

For Rousseau, fear and anger are two sides of the same coin: both imply human bondage. The angry person, like the fearful one, is dependent on others and therefore unhappy. A man becomes angry when he desires something he cannot obtain; he wishes to instil fear in, and to hurt if needs be, whomever he perceives as preventing him from getting what he wants. The boy in *Émile* is not disposed to anger because he does not have desires that can be frustrated by others. Rather he 'wants only what he can do and does what he pleases'. He is happy because he knows how to suppress excessive or unnecessary desires and refuses to want things simply because others do. Which is to say, he can perceive the difference between what is necessary and what is not. He rebels only against those things that he knows could be otherwise; he resigns himself to those things that must be so. Any anger he feels is simply a signal that he has not understood all the factors lying behind what he initially perceived as unjust.

Rousseau's fascination with anger, and his yearning to describe a style of life in which anger would not be needed or used, also underpins the plot of *The New Héloïse*. Julie and Saint-Preux express their love for each other privately in letters, but they hold back from getting engaged or expressing their feelings openly, out of fear of Julie's father's inevitable anger. And it turns out their fears are well founded. When Julie's father finds out about their relationship, he beats Julie mercilessly. Curiously, the novel, while claiming to be 'a great example to imitate' in the quest to make oneself 'good and happy', is at pains to justify this violence. It does so on the basis that the father's intention in becoming violent, that of preserving his daughter's virtue, is honourable. His violence is unfortunate yet comprehensible. After his righteous rage has passed, the father is seen to suffer too. He feels anxiety to begin with, then sheepishness, then regret. Seeking release from these distressing feelings, he sits Julie on his lap, as though to soothe a baby by bouncing it, before finding that he is uncomfortable in this position (she is a grown woman after all) and unable out of embarrassment to apologise to her either in words or with caresses. This leaves it up to Julie, quite literally the injured party, to take the initiative and bring about reconciliation. She claims that this opportunity to forgive her father his violence, and thereby free him from his shame and guilt, is 'the most delightful moment in my life'. More than that, she is willing, she looks forward to, being treated in the same way by him in the future, for the pleasure of absolution and rapprochement will be as certain as the pain that preceded it: 'I am only too happy to be beaten every day at the same price, and no treatment could be so harsh that a single one of his caresses wouldn't efface it from the depths of my heart.'

Julie's attitude to this paternal oppression is one of abidance, deference. Her father's despotism is, for her, a pure and natural force, like gravity. As long as she expects to be its victim, and does not presume to try to escape it or fight against it, she will, she believes, be able to manage it. When the blows end, so too will her pain. Their memory will not travel with her into the future. The wounds on her body will heal, and she will remain, almost miraculously, trauma-free. Of this outcome she seems secure.

What is happening here exactly? Rousseau is quite simply taking the blame away from the father and in the process turning the daughter into a masochist. Yet even granting her this perversion, it is hard not to be suspicious of Julie's apparent ability to sweep instantly under the rug the abuse she has suffered. That she lacks autonomy is not surprising; that she is empty of the spirit of rebellion is. What superhuman powers does Julie possess that would prevent her father's cruel treatment of her from causing lasting damage to her emotional or mental well-being?

Then again, perhaps she has no such powers. Perhaps what Rousseau presents positively as resilience, submissiveness, saintly forgiveness on her part, is in fact the conduct of a traumatised child. After being beaten, Julie breaks off relations with Saint-Preux and accepts the match that her father has arranged for her. She marries, and professes to love, a man, Wolmar, who is completely devoid of anger. A man who is so even-tempered that he observes the world with perfect impartiality. Whose capacity for total emotional self-control makes him immune to conflict. Who is in fact nothing if not an anti-father, chosen for her by her father.

As commanded, Julie swaps a home life of violence for a married life of absolute restraint. Wolmar asserts his authority over Julie, not by force but through a system of surveillance – a bit like the tutor in *Émile*. Wolmar forbids Julie from having any secrets from him. He requires her to be honest and open at all times. 'A single precept of morality can do for all the others,' he says. 'Never do or say anything that you don't wish everyone to see and hear.' He encourages her to be reasonable like him, to express her feelings by crying, if she must, but to reject heightened emotion of any other kind, be it anger or 'the blind transport of passionate hearts'. Julie refuses to rebel against this prohibition, with the result that she turns her strong emotions on herself, employs them as a tool of self-punishment. Wolmar, in exercising his power over her, never has to get angry, because she has already done the internal work of being angry with herself for feeling as fervently as she does.

Rousseau's preoccupation with relations of authority and obedience, and the anger on which they seem to rely, did not end with *Émile* and *The New Héloïse*. While still living under the protection of Louise d'Épinay, he wrote a third major work, a treatise called *The Social Contract*, in which he widened the scope of his inquiry from power relations between individuals (tutor and pupil, father and daughter, husband and wife) to those between national populations and their rulers. How might people in society live in liberty while also being required to obey rules that restrict their freedom?

Is it inevitable that curbs on personal freedom will provoke angry resistance? Or is there a way to be happy while also being less free?

The solution that Rousseau proposes to these questions is characteristically paradoxical. Most people, he says, understand that being constrained in society is, to some extent, inescapable. Problems arise when people feel subjected to arbitrary rules not of their making, when they feel forced to do things, or not to do things, for no good reason. To avoid this, he argues, people must pool their resources to form a civil society that places itself under the guidance of its own 'general will'. In such a set-up, society would rule over itself. The laws emanating from the general will would apply to everyone equally, no one would be outside or above them. Nor would these laws be unnecessarily burdensome or restrictive. Self-imposed rule would in fact be liberty: 'Obedience to the law one has prescribed to oneself is freedom.'

Rousseau does not provide a precise statement of what the general will is. He is, however, adamant about what it is not. The general will is not the will of all, which is merely the sum of private and thus necessarily conflicting interests. Rather it is a kind of invisible influence – something like love or trust – that cancels out differences of opinion and binds everyone together in the name of the common good. There is something mystical in the way in which Rousseau passes from the notion of a group of individuals, each pursuing his own aims, to the notion of a *moi commun*, a 'common me', which submits to something that is itself and yet greater than itself. 'Each individual,' he writes, 'uniting himself to the rest, still obeys himself and remains as free as before.' In other words, the individual puts aside his own selfish pursuit of an absolute good in favour of membership of a community in which everyone can attain the greatest good possible. Authority and liberty no longer conflict; they coincide. A person no longer needs to be angry with authority, for, as part of the general will, he is at one with authority; any such anger would be self-defeating.

In Rousseau's vision, the freer you are, the more authority you have, and also the more you obey. The more liberty, the more control. Naturally there will be occasions when an individual's personal wishes run counter to the general will. What matters is that the general will takes precedence, and that he accepts this. And if he does not? Rousseau makes no bones about what will happen to anyone who threatens the unity and unanimity of the general will: 'Whoever refuses to obey the general will shall be constrained to do so by the entire body: which means nothing other than that he shall be forced to be free.' The general will, because it is an expression of the people's collective sovereignty, cannot be mistaken. It always wills what is best for the community as a whole. It is 'the rational will everyone ought to have'.

From this, it is plain to see that Rousseau is not in favour of unbridled feeling. On the contrary, he believes that sentiments divide people, whereas reason unites them. Sentiments are subjective, individual, vary from person to person, culture to culture. Reason alone is one in all people, and alone is always right. When faced with laws based on sentiment, a person's reaction is bound to be anger. But it is absurd to be angry with rational laws. If you are feeling angry with the common good, you have a duty to suppress it, sublimate it or, failing that, direct it elsewhere – such as inside, at yourself. Self-control implies a form of self-surveillance that keeps anger at bay, and this is freedom. Act, freedom demands, as if you are being watched over at all times by a tutor, as if you are being threatened constantly by a violent father, both of whom only want the best for you.

Letter 61: JEAN-JACQUES ROUSSEAU to GAVIN MULVANY

Paris, 29 August 1777

This morning I received a fat bundle of letters from you that seemed endless. In truth, you must have an enormous amount of time on your hands, and you must also assume I have all the time in the world to reply – an assumption that occasioned such a fit of ill temper in me that I found myself stamping around the house trying to formulate a riposte, until my housemaid ordered me out of the house: 'Go to the café and find yourself a game of chess!'

At Café de la Régence I particularly noticed a man whose simplicity pleased me. I attached myself to him, and he to me, such that we found ourselves playing several games in a row in almost complete silence. Unfortunately in due course I attracted a multitude of spectators. This explains both the scene you walked in on and my desire to get away from it. As irked as I was that Thérèse would disclose my whereabouts to you, I was grateful for your intercession: 'My friend, let's go,' you said with a sort of authority, and steered me out.

To detach us from the admirers who followed us, you took us on a lap of the Palais-Royal, which brought us back down rue des Bons-Enfants. A thick crowd had gathered at the junction with rue Saint-Honoré, where the royal carriages would presently be passing by on their journey back to Versailles (or so the voices said). Our way was blocked, I had no intention of trying to get through, so we loitered about fifty paces away in the hope of catching a glimpse over the people's heads. Needless to say, this was your hope, not mine, as I lack the height. My only relief from having to study the oil stains on men's collars was to count the clouds in the sky directly above us, or to hunt for fallen *liards* on the ground directly beneath us.

I was undeniably restless. Agitated by the clamour. But, more than that, bored and would happily have abandoned this pointless wait in favour of spending the hour or two that remained of the morning studying botany. 'I shall leave you to it,' I said more than once. But you would not let me go. You were in an obvious state of irritation, ruminating about something, and, in the same aggressive tone you had used with the men in the café, you let me know that any premature departure of mine would be a personal insult against you. 'It's a bit rich,' I said, 'that you show up in this mood. By rights I'm the one who should have the pout on his face, after the stunt you pulled last time, walking me straight into that prisoners' snare in Vincennes. Sometimes I think you forget who I am. Do you know how many copies of *The New Héloïse* have been sold across Europe? I durst not tell you, lest your knees buckle from under you.'

Were you even listening to me? Nearby a cluster of pedlars were speculating jokingly about why the queen, after seven years of marriage and three years on the throne, had not yet borne any children. She was frigid, they were saying. A lesbian. Too busy with her other lovers. And should not the king take his share of the blame? For was the royal foreskin not too long to permit proper erections? 'He should be whipped like a donkey,' one of them whispered, 'to make him ejaculate out of anger.' You seemed more preoccupied with this than anything that came from me.

I was almost glad then when a hush descended and the men took off their hats and everyone bowed their heads. Even then, coming up onto my toes, I was unable to make out anything in front. So I just joined the others in lowering my gaze and in listening. Emerging from the silence: the horses' hoofs, the turn of wheels, the sprinkling of hired cheers that did not fool anyone. You were able to confirm the passing of two carriages, a berlin and a coupé, though you could not say which vehicle, if any, had contained our monarchy, as the shutters in all the windows had been closed.

As soon as the end of the procession had gone by, the squeeze of bodies loosened, then dispersed. We resumed our walk. You steered us towards the quays, saying you wanted to keep going south, deep into the countryside beyond Sceaux, as far as Vauhallan. I offered to accompany you across the river and no further. Although I am in the fullness of my mental powers, my physical body has entered decline; I saw no gain from putting it to the test. You suggested we hire a hackney to the city limits, from where you could continue your walk and I could take the ride back home. Needless to say, the only carriage willing to take us that far was of the mean variety, barely adequate for two. As soon as you mounted and wedged yourself into the space beside me, so that the entirety of your left side was pasted to my right, I regretted my acquiescence.

'In *The Social Contract*,' you said, once I was trapped, 'you speak of a general will. A community in which each individual is united with the common good. Does such a community exist anywhere in the world? Can it exist? Answer me!'

'I wouldn't have written about it if I didn't believe it could exist.'

'Is it true that in this ideal community of yours, a father is justified in beating his daughter if he succeeds in preserving her virtue, as required by the general will?'

'There are a thousand cases where it's an act of justice to hurt someone we love.'

'And a tutor is right to lie to his pupil, to manipulate him, if the result is a grown man who adheres to the common good, whether or not it's personally beneficial for him to do so?'

'Total freedom in society is impossible. The goal is as much freedom as possible for as many as possible, so there is bound to be some push and pull. In some unfortunate circumstances, one man can preserve his own freedom only at the expense of someone else's.'

We had passed Luxembourg Palace and reached the point on rue du Faubourg Saint-Jacques where the road becomes uneven. It was hard not to fall into your lap or hit our heads together. As we approached the chemin de Bourg-la-Reine and the houses turned to hovels, groups of children ran alongside the carriage and tapped on the windows, begging for money. The sight of them clearly unsettled you. You were at a loss as to how to behave. But not me. I waved at them and laughed, and, in order to respond to their calls, pulled down the window so that there was nothing separating us. Did you see?

'My friend, Cyprien, had a lover,' you said, obviously not seeing. 'A young woman called Zoé. At a certain point their affair soured. Zoé accused Cyprien of a crime against her person. She went to the police and filed a complaint. Cyprien asked for my help, which I willingly gave to him.'

'What did you do?'

'I lied. To the police. Without knowing if there was any truth in Zoé's accusation, I acted to discredit it.'

'You did this to save your friend from trouble?'

'And to save our friendship. I couldn't just stand by and watch the onslaught. Would Cyprien have forgiven me if I'd refused to come to his aid?'

You injured this Zoé woman, who was possibly telling the truth, in order to protect your friend Cyprien, who might have been guilty – this, I gathered, was the situation. Your dilemma was whether or not you had any authority to act as you did. Whether or not your actions conformed to the general will.

'I believed,' you said, 'that the accusations, even if true, didn't merit Cyprien's going to prison, or his career being ruined. Zoé's relationship with him was never going to last. She would recover if she lost her case. But Cyprien would be destroyed if she won it. At the time, I thought that what I did was right, in the larger balance of things.'

'But now you're not so sure?'

'I haven't been sure for years. As soon as Cyprien dumped me as a friend, and I stopped being angry with Zoé, doubts appeared, and I began to feel remorse about what I'd done.'

I rapped on the ceiling and the driver stopped the carriage. I tried to open the door for you, but it was less awkward for you to do it yourself. Once you were outside, I slammed the door shut (a little vigorously, I admit), for I had gone off the idea of gathering some flowers before heading back into town.

'You ask,' I said through the open window, 'if I think what you did was reasonable. The final judgement on that must be yours. But I will say this. Even now in my old age, I sometimes imagine that I'm dreaming a bad dream, from which I'll wake with my pain gone to find myself again in the company of a friend. Were such a miracle to occur, I would have to believe that it had been willed. That, in being given this exceptional gift, I was being asked to build a model that others might follow, for the greater good. In that case, would I tolerate outside attacks either on my friend or on my bond with him? Would I hesitate to ensure that at all times my friend is safe and free to be with me?'

It took the driver a while to turn the carriage around on the bad road.

'In my life,' I said, sticking my head out, 'the actions of mine that have caused the greatest harm to others, and that have aroused the fiercest self-reproach in me, I carried out believing that I was acting as a true citizen. My heartfelt regrets have told me that I was mistaken. But my reason has offered me different advice. At the end of the day, I thank heaven that I was forced to wound the people that I did, for in doing so I preserved them from the far graver injuries that threatened to be their lot.'

Out of the back window I watched you crossing the meadow towards the two windmills. The breeze had lifted your hair and made your shirt cling to the contours of your back. You did not turn around to see whether you were alone yet, whether you had reached the state of being unobserved. With resoluteness you ploughed straight on. To me, it seemed as if I had been granted a privileged perspective on myself, in my middle age, succumbing to the fear that in making friendship the idol of my heart I had sacrificed my whole life to an illusion.

EIGHTH WALK

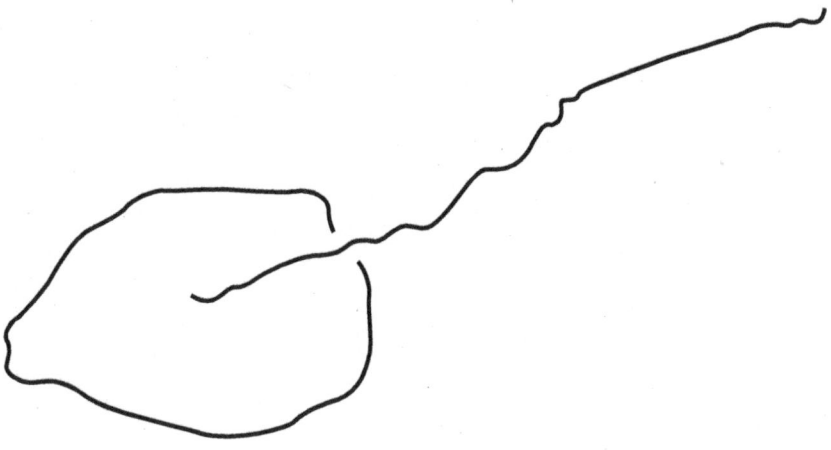

(To Sevran, walking northeast: rue J.-J. Rousseau – rue Tiquetonne – rue de Turbigo – rue du Faubourg du Temple – rue de Belleville – boulevard Périphérique – les Lilas – Romainville – Noisy-le-Sec – Bondy – le Raincy – Clichy-sous-Bois – Sevran; 24 km: 6 hours, 40 minutes)

Guilt

Letter 62: GAVIN MULVANY to PEDRO SOUZA

Paris, 2 September 2022

I'm writing this from a Lebanese restaurant up the road from the seminary. The food here is only all right, and the prices are indefensibly high. But I come anyway because there's white linen on the tables, which, when I run my hand across it, reminds me of Nana: how, when she moved in with us after Dad left, she insisted on a fresh tablecloth at every meal. While we ate, she'd unconsciously rub the linen and smooth it down, scooping up crumbs, real and imaginary. And afterwards, as soon as the plates were cleared, she'd check the cloth for any spots or stains and if necessary wash it with baking soda and vinegar, and then iron it and store it with the others in the special cabinet. The sensation of the linen resting on her thighs, its evenness under her fingertips, its cleanliness, seemed like the last thing separating her from the fracturing marriages and the dissolving families and the drug dealing and the joyriding that she deemed to be taking place in the streets all around us. Today, in my core, I understand her.

I'm at my usual corner table by the window. The view outside isn't bad. The passers-by are mostly undergraduates from the nearby faculties. Ambitious French kids strenuously trained in the elite lycées to be envied and resented in equal measure for their entire lives. After endless rounds of tests, and extra private lessons, and dialogues over dinner, and the Complete Works of Racine and Molière and Voltaire, they have now come to take their places at the École Normale or at the Sorbonne. The thousands of hours of instruction on the multiform structures of nature and society shows in their gaits, almost, as they head for the cheap ramen restaurants around l'Odéon, where only some will be able to manage chopsticks and the others will ask for forks, which will be okay with everyone.

But they'll tolerate as subjects of conversation politics and philosophy only. No trivialities or small talk allowed.

Their outlooks and demeanours I can't help contrasting to mine when I was their age. While it's true that as a student in Dublin I was part of a distinct beau monde, one that lived in isolation from large swathes of the local population; and while it's equally true that I had an ironclad conviction that accolade was coming fast down the line to me, I was, at one and the same time, wholly incapable of funnelling my immature feelings into expressions of deep conviction or gestures of earnestness of the kind that come so naturally to these *sorbonnards* and *normaliens*. Unlike them, I entered adulthood having developed no realistic gauge of the power of my own feelings, bad or good, nor any capacity for fashioning them, when they inevitably arose, into something useful: into logic or polemic or even just an articulate plea for understanding.

And how could it have been otherwise, when my mother had forced me throughout my upbringing to apologise continually for my very presence? 'Say excuse me.' 'Say sorry.' 'Move out of the way.' 'Let the man through first.' 'Shh, be quiet, they're looking at you.' And when she sucked the glory out of every honour and award I won by the sweat of my brow, by urging me to consider how lucky I'd been, how on another day the jury's decision might've gone another way. And by compelling me to shake hands with the losers and to tell them I was truly, mortally embarrassed by my triumph, that in fact they were worthier of the prize than me – all because she believed this false modesty made me even better than them, an even more deserving winner.

The restaurant owners, meanwhile: get a load of them. A pretty fifty-something with a skirt that reaches only halfway down her bronzed, hairless thighs. And her equally pretty son, simultaneously muscular and effeminate, immaculately dressed in light-coloured fabrics on which I've never seen a splash of anything. What a pair. I must admit to being quite fascinated by them. I'm itching to ask them about their lives. How they ended up in this little square of prime real estate. And what it's like working together as mother and son. They must've noticed my attentiveness, for they don't hold back from sending over big smiles every time they catch my eye. And they seem to enjoy fussing over me. Encouraging me to order their specialities, bringing me little tasting plates, and giving me free top-ups of their homemade lemonade.

Perhaps even more than the Sorbonne students passing by outside, I envy this mother and son. They seem to have so much that I don't have and would like to have – I mean in my relationship with my mother. An apparent naturalness in the public performance of their bond. An ability to give orders to one another with grace and to receive them with ease. An embracing of the light-hearted and the inconsequential in their dialogues. A mutual agreement to remain at a level at which it's possible to enjoy together the surface of life. A shared aversion to extending further down, where there might be pain. I want to ask the mother whether, when she was raising him, she informed her son that only by entering the family business would he make her happy. And I want to ask the son whether he ever resisted the pressure to do what his mother wanted him to. Did he ever dream of becoming an architect, a designer, a hairdresser, a drop-out – anything but assuming the role that she'd prepared for him in advance without his consultation? Do they ever think about what else they could be doing, and with whom, if they weren't tied to one another in this place? My malicious side suspects they've faked their way to contentment. That after years of putting on a happy front for each other's benefit, they've become properly happy within themselves. Maybe that's their secret. Maybe that's what my mother and I never learned to do.

I must admit, though, that the main reason I'm here is to avoid the other artists and writers in the seminary. I want to feel warmth for them, but I can't. I'm on the stairs, looking through the window, watching them mill around the courtyard, and there's nothing. Or to be frank, less than nothing. The sight of them drops me head first into the dumps. I come upon them microwaving their cartons of soup in the communal kitchen, and it affects my senses. They see me hesitate, they see me turn away, and then they hate me, or pity me. They accuse me of wanting to be original – with their looks, they do this – and of trying to be different from others, when in fact I've no thought of doing as others do or doing something different. I simply want to pass by, go my own way, apart from their agitating entanglements, allurements, expectations.

When did I get so diffident? At what point did the promise of connection with others become the threat of entombment, of a fall into terrifying obscurity? My first impulse is to blame Cyprien for this, but you don't let me get away with that. Lazy thinking, you call it. My problems, you say, began way before meeting him. Cyprien is merely an object to which my insecure state of mind, formed long ago, attached. 'Don't you have memories of a pre-Cyprien universe?'

If you must know, I do. For instance, I remember my Nana taking me to the Canaries to give my mother a break, because she was depressed after her separation from Dad and couldn't handle me very well. How old was I? Around eight or nine. At first I despised being away. I understood that I was being swindled by one more adult scheme intended to keep me ignorant of the true order of things. I raised a storm whenever Nana enjoined me to take my head out of my comics and get out for some fresh air: 'Look at all the other kids playing in the swimming pool. Don't you want to be having fun like them?' On one such outing, in the queue for the waterslide, which I'd agreed to join so that Nana could take a photograph, in return for which she'd promised me an ice cream, a boy several places behind noticed my scowling and skipped the queue specifically to show me the eczema on his elbows and knees, and to explain to me in perfect English what a pain it was, and how itchy, and that the sun was really the only cure for it, which was a pity because for most of the year Sweden, where he was from, didn't have much of that – all of which he presumably thought might cheer me up, given that I myself hadn't to contend with this affliction.

I felt myself drawn instantly to this boy, Per, by the force of courtship. From then on at the pool, to which I rushed as soon as Nana would let me out of the door, Per became the cynosure of my gaze. I paid attention to his every move. I did this not merely as a mental exercise. His mode of being, both his advantages and his difficulties, mattered to me, just as I desperately wanted mine to matter to him. My sudden transformation from loner to boon companion delighted Nana. She had only rarely seen me play with a friend, and certainly never so intensely, and had come to believe that my aversion to social intercourse, whether it was an innate fault of mine or damage that my warring parents had inflicted on me, was permanent and unfixable. In her wisdom, however, she foresaw how aggrieved I'd feel when it came time to say goodbye to my new pal. In the evenings, among her orders to me to brush my teeth and get into my pyjamas, she slipped me subtle warnings that I should expect some sad feelings when we'd have to leave at the end of the week. I'd be able to write to Per from Ireland, she said, and perhaps one day he could visit me there, but before that could happen, there was going to be a separation, which wasn't going to be easy for me.

Her words, much as I could recognise their logical sense, did little to mitigate the devastation I experienced as I watched Nana pack our bags the night before our flight home, nor the fury I felt towards Per as I observed him the following morning from across the breakfast hall, eating with his family. Nana encouraged me to go over and give him a final hug, but I refused – for how dare he have his own parents, his own sister, his own country, his own life, and how dare he put all that before me. I put on a brave face for the journey home so as not to make a scene, which was what Nana most forcefully demanded of me. But as soon as I was back in my bedroom, which was cold and lacking a telephone with a free line to Per's room, I threw myself onto the bed and wept inconsolably. I never wanted to go on holiday again. Never wanted to see the sun or the sea, or to have the smell of chlorine on my skin. And as long as I lived, since no one could possibly be a match for Per, I never wanted another friend.

MS Extract: from *Rousseau's Lost Children* by GAVIN MULVANY

Last edited: 5 September 2022

In 1745 – that is, a decade before the appearance of the *First Discourse*, while he was still an obscure drudge on the make – Rousseau met and formed an alliance with a laundress ten years his junior, Thérèse Levasseur. Rousseau's new Enlightenment friends in Paris looked down on Thérèse, whom they regarded as stupid and narrow. Defending himself against such condescension, Rousseau liked to imply that the relationship was merely one of convenience. Thérèse was, he said, 'the supplement I needed'. Since his relationship with Françoise-Louise de Warens had ended a few years before, he was in the market for 'a successor for Mummy'. Thérèse, although she had an unspoiled freshness, a modest demeanour, 'the heart of an angel', was less attractive and far less educated than Warens, and never came to command Rousseau's affections in the same way. Nevertheless, she was to remain his companion until his death.

Unlike Rousseau's relationships with other women, that with Thérèse was properly carnal. That is to say, Rousseau did not content himself with adoring Thérèse from a distance; he had sex with her. Often enough, at least, to get her pregnant and make her a mother five times in quick succession. Directly after each of these births, Rousseau took his newborn infant from Thérèse and deposited it in the foundling hospital, Hôpital des Enfants-Trouvés. To his mind at the time, there was no question that this was the right thing to do. In order to make his name in the world, he needed to be free from the responsibilities of fatherhood. Until such a time as fortune came his way, he was going to be broke. By abandoning them, he was saving his children from the even bigger calamity of having a father who was unable to feed them. The disposal of the infants thus struck him, not as a moral, but as a practical problem. He sought advice from friends, who agreed that this was the best way to extricate him from his embarrassment. To be sure, convincing Thérèse was a challenge: 'I had the greatest difficulty in the world in persuading her to accept this sole means of saving her honour.' But he managed, and after that, once the deed was done, 'I reflected no more deeply on the matter.'

Until, that is, Voltaire published an anonymous pamphlet in 1764 entitled *The People's Feelings*, in which he announced to the world, most contemptuously, what Rousseau had done: 'We avow with grief and shame that Rousseau is a man who drags with him, from village to village, from mountain to mountain, the wretched woman whose children he exposed at the gates of an asylum.' After this public unmasking, yes, Rousseau did indeed start to reflect on his past actions, and discovered that in fact they did not sit entirely well with him. Any justifications that hitherto he had kept to himself, he now felt compelled to express to others, at gatherings, in letters and, when that failed to win him the vindication he sought, in his autobiographical writings.

Against his prior excuses, Rousseau took to claiming that for several years his peace of mind had indeed been disturbed by feelings of self-reproach. It was true he had deposited his children at the Hôpital, knowing that in its wards they would be crammed together in grossly unhygienic conditions and would have only a tiny chance of seeing their first birthdays. But he refused to entertain the idea that he had sent them to their inevitable deaths. On the contrary, he imagined them all still alive and leading a more dignified life, as labourers and peasants, than the one he himself had had to pursue as a 'fortune seeker'. 'I chose for my children what was best for them, or what I believed to be so. I would have liked, I still would like, to have been brought up and provided for as they have been.' To the broader accusation that he hated children, he used his philosophical work as a shield. 'It would certainly be the most amazing thing in the world,' he said, 'for *The New Héloïse* and *Émile* to be the work of a man who did not like children.'

These attempts at self-defence are not convincing so much as they are revealing of a specific structure of guilt. The guilt that Rousseau belatedly admits to comes tightly bound to a sense of righteousness. And vice versa, his expressions of righteousness are driven by an underlying guilt. His guilt and his righteousness are mutually reliant; one cannot function without the other. The presence of guilt is, for Rousseau, necessary in order to be able to justify himself, while the act of justifying himself opens him up to accusations of guilt. He will be vindicated once and for all, as soon as he feels enough guilt. And he will be guilty for as long as he has the will to defend himself against it.

This contrasts markedly with the way in which Rousseau articulates his feelings of guilt about other aspects of his past – in particular about his mother, who died soon after giving birth to him. 'I cost my mother her life,' he believed, 'and my birth was the first of my misfortunes.' As a young boy, unable to fathom the full meaning of this event, he shifted the focus of his concern to his father: 'I never knew how my father bore his loss; but I do know that he never got over it.' Rousseau had no memory of the loss he had suffered. Innocently, he filled this void with his father's grief, to which he was forced to bear witness, and for which he assumed culpability. In his imagination, he transformed himself into his mother and entered a surrogate relationship with his father. He behaved as if his mother, through him, was a living witness to his father's anguish. 'My father thought he could see my mother in me, without being able to forget that I had deprived him of her; he never caressed me without my sensing, from his size, from his urgent embraces, that a bitter regret was mingled with them, for which, however, they were the more tender. "Ah!" he would sigh, "bring her back to me, comfort me for losing her; fill the emptiness she has left in my soul. Would I love you so much if you were only my son?"'

Thus Rousseau took upon himself a weighty burden of guilt for an act – being born – over which he had no control. When his father obliquely blamed him for taking his wife away from him, Rousseau put up no defences. Still a child, knowing no better, he heard his father's charge and instantly admitted the wrongdoing. His was the word of absolute authority, to which there was no counterargument: Rousseau was guilty, pure and simple. Issuing from this unadulterated guilt, then, was a lifelong anxiety about how much he was valued. And this anxiety in turn left him unequipped to put a true value on his own children when they came along. He would be better off without them, he judged, and they without him – 'a misfortune of which I must complain, and not a crime to reproach myself for'.

Letter 63: GAVIN MULVANY to CYPRIEN ABREO

Paris, 7 September 2022

Today Jean-Jacques and I set off from his flat and went in a north-easterly direction, across rue Saint-Martin and up rue du Temple towards the Faubourg du Temple, where Jean-Jacques hoped to find some Geneva bugleweed for his collection of dried flowers. We progressed by fits and starts. Of his various ailments, the most pressing is a urinary complaint that painfully retains his water then suddenly has him needing to release it. When nature calls, he abruptly draws us to a halt and, regardless of where he is or who's looking on, and pointedly ignoring any walls that might be close at hand, he relieves himself, like a horse in a dead stand, onto the path between his feet.

Ours is a delicate attachment. I must refrain from being too keen to bond, lest I call up his defences. But today, during one of our longer stretches of uninterrupted striding, I allowed myself for the first time to talk about my past, that is, the part that pre-dates you. A bit about Dad's desertion of us. And my mother having to raise my sister and me alone. And Nana moving in to help. And Per. Enough to wet our feet. None of which he objected to or seemed bored by. After I'd finished, I let some silence grow between us. Then: 'Have I been oversharing?'

'Oversharing?' he said.

'Saying too much about myself.'

'Don't you want to be a writer? A writer needs to tell people everything, to make them understand him.'

'No holds barred?'

'If in a man's life the good outweighs the evil, it's in his interest to tell the whole truth.'

I put it to him that writing about oneself implies a measure of self-defence. The writer feels guilty about something. Perhaps something he can't even call to his waking mind. But something his conscience is alive to nonetheless, something he fears others can see in him. Which impels him to justify himself to the watching world.

'Do you feel guilty about something you once did?' he said.

'For years, I thought no. My self-justifications drowned out everything else in my mind. But that's no longer the case. Now the guilt gets through.'

'Is this resurgent guilt what's fuelling your desire to write?'

We were wading through the grasses in search of the violet-blue flowers of the Geneva bugleweed. I thought about Jean-Jacques's question for some time before answering.

'I'm thinking about Montaigne,' I said, 'who uses the image of the Spanish blister-fly to illustrate how guilt works. Do you recall?'

'Vaguely.'

'On stinging, the blister-fly secretes an antidote to its own poison. Its nature, it seems, is to take pleasure in doing harm and, at the same time, to harbour antipathy to the harm it does.'

'It does seem a waste, to infect and heal all at once.'

'The point Montaigne is making, I think, is that when a man intentionally does harm, he's acting on the belief that the harm he does will give him something, make his life better. He inevitably feels, or expects to feel, some measure of pleasure as a result. But on carrying out the act of harm, there's also born in his conscience an opposite displeasure, which tortures him with painful thoughts. For Montaigne, finding release from these thoughts is an agonising matter. The guilty man must perform the excruciating task of denying the rightness of what he formerly saw fit to do. For this, he must see himself completely, search every part of his inner world, as with the eyes of God. Which – correct me if I'm wrong – is an accurate description of what the writer does, or tries to do. The writer, in uncovering what's hidden within, enters the state of being repentant, whether he likes it or not. When he reveals something about himself for the first time, tacitly, inescapably he admits its disgracefulness. He asks to be forgiven as much for the act of revealing as for the act being revealed.'

Jean-Jacques seemed to contemplate my words as he bent over and straightened up, over and up, over and up, snapping stalks and dropping blossoms into his sack. After a while he said, 'The drawing rooms of Paris are infested with blister-flies.'

I laughed at this, while he remained quite serious.

'Your example from Montaigne,' he said, 'presumes that guilt requires an object. That it can't rightly exist on its own, unconnected to any past sin.'

'Isn't that the point of guilt? That it is about something?'

'I'm not certain that someone has to have done harm in order to feel guilt. I can imagine guilt residing in an innocent man.'

'I can't see how that makes sense. How could an innocent man, one who knows he's innocent, feel guilt? And anyway, is there such a thing as a wholly innocent man? Surely even the best of us, the kindest, the most gentle, the walking saints, have caused enough harm to generate at least some guilt in their system?'

Jean-Jacques reached his arms around to place his palms on his lower back, then arched his spine. Sighing out, he went to sit on a nearby mound. Took off his boots to give his feet to the air. Closed his eyes and gave his face to the sun. I joined him and did the same. In this position, then, we spoke about the mythical figure of Oedipus, whom Jean-Jacques introduced as an example of an innocent man who feels guilt.

'Oedipus kills his father,' he said, 'not knowing who he is, and marries his mother, not knowing who she is. His intention is never to commit patricide or incest. He's innocent of these crimes. Yet on discovering that he has inadvertently committed them, he feels such terrible guilt that he gouges out his eyes.'

'But is it guilt that causes him to do this?' I said. 'As opposed to disgust? Or grief? And how innocent is Oedipus really? The Delphic oracle has told him that he's fated to kill his father and marry his mother. In this way, the oracle equips Oedipus with the knowledge he needs to avoid his terrible fate. All Oedipus has to do is make two unbreakable rules for himself: never to kill an older man, and never to marry an older woman. But that's precisely what he does. The chances are slim that, out of all the people in Greece, the man he kills will turn out to be his father, and that the woman he marries will turn out to be his mother. But they aren't zero. He knows when performing these acts that he's taking a risk, however small. Therefore his conscience can't be entirely clear. He's capable of guilt on that basis.'

I could hear Jean-Jacques shifting round beside me, though I resisted opening my eyes to check on him. 'It's amusing to hear Oedipus explained in this novel way,' he said, sounding closer than he was before. 'Whenever I've heard the play spoken about, the consensus has always been that the tragedy of Oedipus's predicament is that he's innocent.'

'What makes the play tragic,' I said, 'is surely the guilt that Oedipus feels for his failure to make use of the small amount of autonomy that the gods have permitted him to save himself and his family from disaster.'

'You seem to be saying,' he said, calmly handing me my boots, 'that in moving through the world, we're bound to cause some hurt, therefore we're obliged to live with guilt. That it's inevitable.'

I tied my laces and put my rucksack back on. 'Is that what I'm saying? Probably.'

We resumed our walk, my left elbow brushing against his right shoulder.

'Isn't it possible,' he said, 'for a person to do harm intentionally and feel no guilt for it?'

'Murderers? Madmen? I can accept that such people don't appear on the outside to feel guilt. But I'm sceptical about the claim that they don't feel guilt inwardly. Perhaps they override their guilt with other feelings. Or saturate themselves with guilt until they become insensitive to it. But I think guilt must continue to form part of the constellation of feelings they're experiencing, even if they don't recognise it as such.'

'So your opinion is that guilt is integral to the human experience? Passed down from father to son, as with the colour of one's eyes or the shape of one's nose?'

'I was raised a Catholic. All my adult life, I've fought against the idea of inherent guilt. Yet now I find myself thinking that it might well be that we're born with the potential for all classes of guilt, which enables us to absorb our parents' guilt into ourselves over time. I can see how effortless it'd be for a child to begin to blame himself for the same range of things that he sees his parents blaming themselves for.'

We left one field and crossed into another. Here we separated for a few minutes, arcing away from each other, before slowly merging once more. I put the flowers I'd picked into his sack.

'Do you know what this is?' he said then, holding his hand out daintily, as though waiting for me to kiss it. He wiggled his middle finger to draw my attention to the ring that adorned it: an engraved signet that I'd noticed at our first meeting and often wondered about. 'It's my mother's name in Persian characters. My father, God rest his soul, was an engraver. He once worked in Constantinople and brought this back as a gift for me.'

'It's unusual,' I said.

The ring pressed into the flesh of his finger; it appeared too tight to take off. He crooked and lifted his elbow so that he could turn his hand around, with his fingers pointing towards his chest, and view the engraving the right way up.

'Suzanne,' he said. 'She was beautiful. And good. Wealthier than my father. He didn't win her easily.' He let his hand drop to his side, as though to say we'd looked long enough, though I could see him continuing to play with the ring with his thumb. Deep in thought, he lowered his gaze to his feet, then after a few moments lifted it to a spot just above my eyes. 'I killed her.' He spoke matter-of-factly. 'I killed my mother.'

'I don't think the death that your birth caused is the same as killing. As a newborn baby, you're incapable of intending to do harm.'

'I think you've just been arguing the opposite case. Does the blister-fly intend to do harm? As it releases its poison, even if it feels an instinctual pleasure, is it conscious of its intentions?'

'Probably not.'

'In the moment in which I was being born, getting to live was all I cared about. It's not merely that I had the desire to live. Rather the entirety of my being was nothing more and nothing less than this desire. Nothing could stand in my way.'

I had objections to this. But I held back. With his ringed hand, he took me by the arm and we began walking again. The grass crunched under our step. Flowers aplenty, but we didn't pick them. I think the botanising was over for today.

'You weren't to blame,' I said.

'Wasn't I? I can't recall a time that I didn't know I was guilty. My father only had to say to me, "Let's talk about your mother," and I to reply, "Then we'll weep together," for him to be moved to tears. "Ah!" he'd say, groaning, "give her back to me, console me for her, fill up the emptiness she has left in my soul."'

We'd come to the edge of a field. Ahead of us, there was a hill. Without pausing, Jean-Jacques took a right, away from the incline, onto a rough path that would take him back to Faubourg du Temple, from where he'd follow the road back to Paris. I stayed at the field's edge, watching him move away. I was touched, for some reason, by the sight of the grass stains on his yellow cotton coat, and his round wig that was coming down a bit on one side.

'I'm going to keep going,' I called after him. 'I want to explore the forests beyond Clichy.'

As a goodbye, he flashed his ringed hand over his shoulder without turning round. And I waved back, despite knowing he wouldn't see the gesture. I continued to observe him for the minute or two that it took for him to disappear behind a hedge and for the modern-day Paris cityscape to return.

Letter 64: GAVIN MULVANY to PEDRO SOUZA

Paris, 7 September 2022

On a walk today, I found myself climbing rue de Belleville. I had the impression that I was fighting against the general flow. I was going up while everyone else was coming down, aggressively indisposed to making way for me. At the cemetery at the top of the hill, which is surrounded by high stone walls, a prostitute asked me if I wanted something.

'Only a little information,' I replied. 'Do you know how to get into the graveyard? I can't see a door.'

'I don't know anything about that,' she said.

'The Belleville cemetery,' I insisted. 'It's right behind you. Weren't you aware?'

She blinked at me, feigning incomprehension, before locking her gaze firmly onto the screen of her phone.

Crossing over *le périph* into the suburb of Les Lilas, I soon reached Bondy. Under an intersection of eight overpasses a population of impoverished people was gathered. Mostly Roma families, along with several cliques of Arab men. Perhaps residents of the adjacent tower blocks, perhaps inhabitants of an unseen camp nearby, perhaps occupants of these uninhabitable streets, perhaps just passing through, they were scattered into separate, dislocated huddles, forming a chaotic assemblage with no apparent centre. Connecting them were their voices and their gestures, which they employed loudly and freely to engage with one another, both as individuals and as groups, calling out and calling back, across the busy streets, over the traffic. What was at stake in their communications, I couldn't be sure; I presumed it was money. On the pavement at one of the busier street crossings sat a little boy who was poking holes into a piece of cardboard.

Once clear of the intersection, I came off the busy main road and steered a course through the suburban maze of Le Raincy to Clichy-sous-Bois. The sight of a complex of enormous blocks of flats built perpendicular to the road was simultaneously underwhelming and awesome. To my eyes, it looked as though someone had stripped

Versailles of its ornamentation, broken it up into pieces, spread it out into isolated parcels and left it here to rot. The distances between the various blocks, and between the blocks and the road, varied maddeningly. The paths and the roads that connected the blocks were convoluted. No doubt the plan, underwritten by foolproof sociological reasoning, had been to establish pleasing variation; the result, however, was a testament to carelessness, to bureaucratic inhumanity. Just walking past made my head hurt. Out of nine blocks that I counted, one had been through a process of regeneration, which had left it with a panelled exterior in bright crimson, cream and turquoise (not quite liberty, not quite equality, not quite fraternity). The rest of the blocks had a brown-and-yellow surface that was peeling away, and boarded doors, and windows fixed with parcel tape, and plastic folding shutters that from a distance looked like corrugated iron. On the north-facing façades, satellite dishes sprouted like warts. *Bienvenue au château de la privation.*

In an open space near the end of the road, less than a kilometre from the forest that was my destination, a fairground had been set up. With an open-air cinema. A stage for plays and story nights and dance shows. And a circus tent. The gates to the grounds were open, people were milling about inside; I could have joined them, entry was free – a government initiative, I conjectured, to make up for the lack of cultural amenities in the area – but, looking through the railings, I felt apprehensive. What I saw was familiar, but this didn't make it welcoming to me.

My mother was raised in a working-class suburb similar to this one. On Sunday morning once a fortnight, we, my family, made the journey there from our basement flat in the city, about a thirty-minute drive, to visit Nana. My father, being an alternative type and therefore not in ownership of a car, borrowed a neighbour's for the occasion: a Renault 4 that he never quite got the knack of driving. Once we'd got clear of the city proper, the route to my grandparents' house took us along long, straight roads bordered with rows of identical grey suburban houses, which at a certain point abruptly gave way to an extravagant conglomeration of warehouses and car dealerships and purveyors of tiles and carpets. A landscape of spectacular mundanity. To which the only modification, itself predictable, took place in the winter. In the lead-up to Christmas. Right around my birthday on the tenth of December. When, at a junction between two identical roads, on a patch of mud-land sandwiched between a fast-food outlet and a wholesalers, a double-peaked tent in red and white appeared. This was Circus Castelli.

Normally the day of my birthday didn't vary greatly from any other. There was a card and a gift in the morning, and an extra kiss. And on the following weekend, we, just the family again, would go to a film or a show and have a pizza in a restaurant afterwards. The idea of breaking this convention and going to the circus instead, which I proposed a week before my eleventh birthday, was, for my parents, a bolt out of the blue.

'Get out of that garden,' my mother said, believing me to be making fun of where she came from.

'Count me out,' my father said, for he was a vegetarian and against cruelty to animals and didn't want his money financing it.

My parents, on our drives to visit Nana, had never taken it upon themselves to point the circus out as we drove past it. It was true they were often busy fighting or giving each other the silent treatment. But it wasn't always so. Plenty of times they were just sitting there, listening to the radio. The sign saying 'Castelli' that sat on top of the tent was lit up. Flashing. Impossible to ignore. And still they never slowed down and said: 'Look!'

'I want to go,' I insisted. 'And I want to invite some friends from school.'

After much wrangling, a compromise was reached. I could bring two classmates, and my father would stay at home with my sister. In the event, none of the boys or girls I picked out to ask along agreed to come, so my mother roped in a pair of the neighbour's kids, to whom I had a longstanding aversion. Their parents were the owners of the Renault 4, however, and my mother felt obliged to give a quid pro quo.

Our tickets were for the Friday evening show. Our seats were ringside, but right at the end of the row, so we were looking at the backs of the performers as they entered. We sat on long benches with nothing dividing one spectator from another, so, as the place filled up, our bodies slid closer and closer, until everyone was fairly crushed. I took my mother's hand and found her eyes. She winked at me and smiled.

'Happy?' she said.

'Yeah,' I said.

But the exact truth was that I was not. And then when it started, and right to the end, I was even worse: as miserable as I'd ever been.

Which goes some way to explain why, twenty-five years later, I was sympathetic to your nephews when we took them to Circus Castelli (unbelievably still in business and pulling in the crowds) and they were unimpressed. I'd suggested going to the Christmas pantomime, but you said the kids, whose English wasn't perfect, would more easily understand the circus. Your brother's wife, if you recall, mounted a whole scene about leaving her sons alone with us: 'Please no adult talk in front of them!' My own concern was of a different, more cultural order: who on earth travelled all the way from São Paulo to sit in a tent in a desolate field in west county Dublin?

Do you still deny that they had a rotten time? From the driver's seat of the rented car on the way back, you excitedly went over everything we'd seen. Listening to you, I thought, Who is this alien? Who in their right mind would have enjoyed that? First freezing cold, then boiling hot. A suffocating mist of smoke and dry ice and burning oil and manure. Sawdust caught in the throat. Ears ringing from the drums and the trumpets and the motorbike engines that got louder and louder the faster they went around the spherical cage. And what about the horses trotting circles around camels, and monkeys riding on Shetland ponies – how could anyone sleep after being subjected to them? Was that still legal? Had I really been the only one who'd wanted to put the ringmaster onto his knees and crack the whip at *him*?

'And you, João,' you said when we were stopped at a traffic light, permitting you to twist round and check on your younger nephew in the back, 'what did you think of it?'

'Full of *favelados*,' Bruno, the older one, said before João could open his mouth.

By then, I'd picked up enough Brazilian Portuguese to know what he meant. In fact, I recalled a conversation between you and me, soon after we met, during which we tried to land on the precise equivalent in your language for the Irish term 'knacker'. We concluded that it had to be '*favelado*'. That is to say, 'someone from the favelas'. A slum dweller.

You examined Bruno for a few seconds. Returning your gaze, Bruno didn't dare to breathe. I could almost see the blood pulsating in his head, his chest. The light went green, and still you looked. The cars behind started beeping, and your lips parted, ever so slightly, as though to emit a sigh. Then you were driving again, in silence now. And the rain was hitting the windscreen. And the wipers were beating out their furious rhythm.

When dropping the kids back to your brother at the hotel, we had to delay for a chat you plainly didn't want to take part in. After that you refused to get back into the car, saying you weren't in a fit state to drive, so we left it in the hotel car park and returned to the flat on foot. You walked ahead of me the whole way. Then let us in. Put the keys on the counter. Took off your jacket. Your scarf. Your shoes. Your jumper. Stalked down the hall with your trousers open, then into the bedroom. Closed the door behind you.

'What's wrong with you?' I said, coming into the darkness.

You were lying on your back on the bed, under the duvet, your head cupped in your hands. You didn't answer.

'It's just a word,' I said. 'He'd have picked it up at school.'

'Don't blame the school. It's his parents. My brother. His wife. Their attitudes. Their jokes. Turning those kids into the absolute worst of the country.'

'What can you do about it? It's their business.'

You turned onto your side.

I sat next to your feet. Put a hand on your thigh. 'Why are you taking this so personally?'

'Because it is personal! Doesn't it bother you that there's no test that people have to pass before having children? No training? That men like my brother, without any natural aptitude, get to be fathers, while we can't even make an adoption application?'

'You think you'd do a better job than your brother?'

'Of course I would.'

'What makes you so sure?'

You sat up and put your back against the wall. 'What's that supposed to mean?'

'Sorry, Pedro. I'm sure you'd be a great father. I'm just not sure I would. That's what I meant.'

'That's your internalised homophobia speaking. Obviously there's still a part of you that believes there's something wrong with you. Something that means you'd fail at raising children.'

'But I don't have any such ambition.'

'Nonsense. You've just convinced yourself that it's useless to want it. And on top of that, you're afraid to repeat your father's mistakes. You think that, like him, you'd lack the staying power. But I know you better than that. You'd bend yourself backwards to be different from him.'

It seems that any time you bring up my father, it's to criticise him. This is my fault. The picture you have of him is the one I've painted for you. All the same, I couldn't help feeling gripped by an urge to defend him. To say that in fact he was a man of integrity. A good father, especially to me, even if other attachments tempered his affection for me.

Pushing this away, I said, 'In the unlikely event that adoption for us becomes legal any time soon, do you think the authorities would even consider us, with my medical history? Have you forgotten how hard it was to get bloody home insurance?'

'Don't bring up your hospitalisation again. That was a one-off. You broke down, then you picked yourself up. What you learned from the experience would make you a better dad than most.'

'Not sure that view would hold water at the government offices. And to be quite honest, it's not my hospital record that I'm most worried about. It's knowing what I've done, what I'm capable of, that's the problem.'

'You mean attempting suicide?'

'No, I mean hurting others. Choices I made that caused real harm to people.'

'Who? What harm? Am I going to hear at last the whole story about Cyprien and those scars?'

'I'm not getting into that now. It's a general point I'm making. I did someone an injustice, that's all you need to know.'

'With your own children it'd be different.'

'Where's the guarantee? What I do to one person, I can do just as easily to another. And to my children, who knows, maybe do even worse.'

Letter 65: PEDRO SOUZA to GAVIN MULVANY

Dublin, 10 September 2022

Is that how that conversation went? I recall you being just as appalled as me about what Bruno said. Either way I know where you're going with all of this. The trip to the Canaries with your mother. Which for the 100th time wasn't my idea. Though that doesn't stop you blaming me for it. It wasn't fun for anyone. But personally I don't regret it. Things finally got cleared up. You talked. And that was your choice. You have to admit that no one forced you to open your mouth.

Letter 66: GAVIN MULVANY to PEDRO SOUZA

Paris, 11 September 2022

The Canaries was the last place I'd pick. And my mother only agreed to it to please you, which has been her primary aim for twenty years. The two of you trapped me. I went to the restaurant early to make sure they'd given us the table I'd reserved and to organise the cake. You arrived together very late, your eyes puffy from your respective siestas.

'We're the first ones here,' Mum said. 'No Spanish people eat at this time.'

'It's the end of civilisation,' I said. 'And also the only way to get this spot, on this terrace, with this view.'

(Are we on the same page so far?)

Sitting down at the empty place in front of me, the first thing you did, before saying hello even, was to tilt your head and cast a piercing glance over my shoulder: it was unbelievable. Thirty paces down the road was the façade of a popular gay bar, with wooden casks used as tables outside, and the usual types gathered around them having cocktails. My back was turned to it, I couldn't see it, but I knew it was there. A man can choose not to look.

'On the walk here,' Mum said, 'Pedro was telling me that you want to move to Brazil. First I've heard of this.'

'A change of scenery,' I said. 'And it's none of your business.'

'What's going on?' she said. 'Are you in trouble at the university? Is your job secure?'

'It's just an idea, Mum, that Pedro shouldn't be sharing with you. And, no, I'm not losing my job. I just feel we're treading water a bit here. It'd be nice to shake things up a bit.'

'What would you do there?'

'I really haven't thought that far ahead.'

'How often would you be back?'

The waiter was leaning on the bar inside, with his back turned to us. 'If we go,' I said, waving uselessly through the restaurant window, 'it'd be a clean break.'

'What does that mean?'

'It means you wouldn't see us for a while.'

'You're resolved to break my heart.'

'Oh, Mum, I was joking. But the fact is, it's a huge distance. If we went, we wouldn't be able to pop forward and back.'

'Not even for Christmas?'

'I don't know, Mum.'

'You worry me. I'd hate to see you running away like your father.'

'Well, the idea would be for Pedro to come with me.'

'Is there anything there for you, Pedro? Work-wise?'

Half-concealed behind the menu, studying its lower portion with strenuous focus, you pretended to be only half in our world: 'I'd find something, I suppose. Gavin has given the whole thing much more thought than me.'

'I always knew he was special,' said Mum, addressing you while referring to me, 'I knew he'd outgrow Dublin one day. From the day he came home with his first school report, I prepared myself for his goodbye. All I heard from him as a teenager was London-this and Berlin-that, which confirmed it.' (And? Don't most people want to walk out of the sad fucking lives they've been handed?) 'Of course, then he decided on Paris. You should have seen how mighty he was, sitting there, telling me he was going for good and not coming back. "I deserve a new start," he said.'

You closed the menu with the look of a man who'd picked his dinner and was so immensely pleased with his choice that everything else existed on a lower plane of significance. 'Gavin can be on the melodramatic side.'

'Where do you think I got that?' I said.

'What tore me apart,' Mum said, 'was to see him turn "goodbye" into "I don't know you", just as his father did.'

'Oh God,' I said.

'Oh God, is right,' she said. 'You've tried to live elsewhere before. To say it was a disaster is putting it mildly. You're better off at home, where you have support.'

Separation from what I'd inherited at birth. The liberty to become the man I'd chosen to be. The freedom, yes, the freedom to struggle for an alternative destiny. To actually get that from life, instead of settling for the first throw of the dice. Suddenly on that terrace facing the town hall, with the orange light of the setting sun on our skin, this became the question again. 'I realise that the way I handle things isn't the way you do, Mum. And that's okay.'

'Oh, your way. Right.' She held back for as long as it took the waiter to figure out our order, which you insisted on making in your weird semi-Spanish. Then: 'I hate to bring him up, Pedro, the man in Paris. I don't like to talk about him in your company.'

'I don't mind,' you said. 'We all have our histories. But look, today is your birthday. Why don't we leave that stuff aside, and drink this wine, and have a nice meal.'

For a moment she appeared to agree with this sentiment. 'It's a miracle,' she said then, 'that you came along when you did, Pedro. Before you, he had no head for choosing company.'

'Cyprien wasn't that kind of company,' I said. 'He had a wife. A kid.'

'That doesn't mean anything,' she said.

'So we're going there after all?' you said.

'Not all men are the same, Mum,' I said.

'You're the expert all of a sudden?' she said.

'He was a mentor to me. He helped me set myself up.'

'You didn't know him from Adam, and you went to live with him.'

'He was a major academic figure in my field. Still is. And I didn't live with him.'

'Why are you defending him?' she said. 'After what he did to you? The marks on your body, Jesus. The man should be locked up. Why you refused to go straight to the police, I'll never understand.'

'You don't know what you're talking about, Mum. I wasn't the victim of anything. If you must know, I was a perpetrator. Along with Cyprien. I'm not excusing him. But the truth is, what I did caused the real damage.'

Morality says you can't do this to your mother. You can't inflict this pain on her and then think you can find forgiveness for it later. Once you've done this much violence it can never be undone. It's unpardonable. All you can do is live with it.

When I'd finished explaining – out loud, at last – what I'd done to Zoé Chauvin, you just stared at me with a fist pressed against your lips, and left the utterances to her: 'Do you want to kill me, is that it? Kill me dead?'

Letter 67: PEDRO SOUZA to GAVIN MULVANY

Dublin, 12 September 2022

How did your mother and I end up alone in the restaurant? She wanted to leave after that, but you said you'd go instead. She took off anyway. Then you went after her. There was an argument somewhere. Then she came back on her own. Some scene like that. In any case, as soon as she sat down again she started: You can't stay with him. You'll have to leave. No one in their right mind would blame you. Me on the other hand, I'm blood. I've no choice but to stand by the little prick, God help me.

It's not as though dumping you didn't cross my mind. I gave it plenty of thought. I felt the pressure. Then and later. But in my heart I knew I wasn't going to follow through. By choosing to be with you in the first place I'd broken a professional taboo. I'd read your file. Witnessed your outbursts. Monitored your highs and lows. I couldn't claim not to be aware of the layers and layers of reality in you. I was taking you on as you were. For who you were. And against everyone's advice. In such circumstances I had to believe I was signing up for the long haul.

As I said to your mother in so many words, the world is full of people who go around believing they've got everything figured out. People who'll never end up in the psych unit despite putting themselves and their loved ones through hell with their endless certainty. I'm better off with a partner that only partly understands. And that

I myself only partly understand. That's what I told her. I've seen what's comprehensible and have concluded that only the incomprehensible sheds any light. Total clarity in a person is false to me. The vulnerable and/or fragile can be cruel, but they have endurance. They stick around long enough to reveal their secrets. Which are never any darker than I imagined them to be. They spare me from the truth so that when it comes out I can see it better.

NINTH WALK

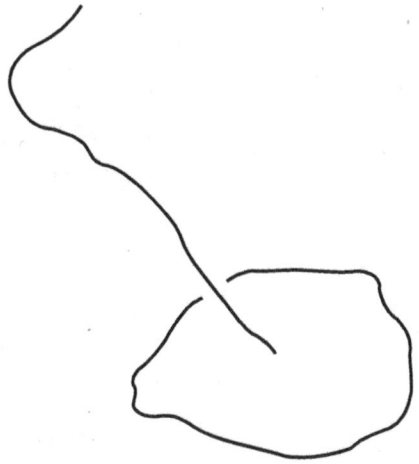

(*To Taverny, walking northwest: rue J.-J. Rousseau – gare Saint-Lazare – rue de Rome – la Petite Ceinture – boulevard Périphérique – Levallois-Perret – Bois-Colombes – Gennevilliers – Cormeilles-en-Parisis – Montigny-lès-Cormeilles – Taverny; 27 km: 7 hours, 40 minutes*)

Sorrow

Open Letter A
Signed by PROFESSOR JEANNE
CLOUTIER and 237 others
[published in *French Journal of Eighteenth-Century Studies*]

Paris, 19 September 2022

We, the undersigned, call upon the eighteenth-century studies community in France to take meaningful action to reduce the incidents of sexual harassment, inappropriate behaviour, abuse, assault and rape in the university departments, libraries, research centres, conferences, workshops, summer schools, events, etc., in which it operates.

We are writing in the context of the much-publicised suspension from teaching duties of Professor Cyprien Abreo, a leading figure in eighteenth-century studies at the Sorbonne. But our experience tells us that the problem goes beyond the actions of a single academic in one institution. We too are survivors of sexual harassment, assault, abuse and rape in academia, or we know others who are. The evidence shows that the problem is widespread and deeply rooted, and that it has been going on for some time. Our hope is to elicit immediate and meaningful action to eliminate from the eighteenth-century studies community this longstanding culture of mistreatment and impunity.

Our demands are fair, reasonable and proportionate. We ask for clear indications that this behaviour is unacceptable, in the form of official statements published on faculty websites and in academic journals, conference materials, etc. We ask for an implementation of a code of conduct, including a clear explanation of how complaints are to be processed. We ask for multiple clear, confidential channels for the reporting of abuse without fear of retribution. And we ask for punitive measures for academics who have amassed more than one complaint about harassment and/or assault (or who have been found guilty of any other sexual offence).

Eighteenth-century studies is our chosen field. We have a great respect for you, the wonderful people who work within it. We invite you to participate actively in this movement to put an end to harassment, exploitation, assault and rape in our community. We request that you help us make a better work environment for all.

Open Letter B
Signed by PROFESSOR ELIZABETH
WAWRZYCKA and 304 others
[published online at *www.openletter.com*]

Paris, 28 September 2022

On 19 September 2022, the *French Journal of Eighteenth-Century Studies* published an open letter about 'inappropriate behaviour' and 'a culture of mistreatment and impunity' in the eighteenth-century studies community. This letter paints a thoroughly distorted picture of the crisis currently gripping our field. Among its authors are the originators of a 'safety' campaign broadly inspired by the #MeToo movement. This campaign has knowingly encouraged and facilitated the vilification of several fellow scholars for offences vaguely whispered about but never openly declared. The result has been to rive apart what has traditionally been an exceptionally welcoming, convivial and nurturing international community.

An atmosphere of suspicion and insinuation, fostered by the authors of the open letter, has culminated in the indefinite suspension of Professor Cyprien Abreo from the Sorbonne. To our knowledge, five women have made complaints against Professor Abreo, all of which he has denied. Although he has not been formally charged with a single crime, Professor Abreo has been barred from entering the university buildings and from making contact with any registered students. The disciplinary hearing that came to this decision was improvised, expedited and procedurally flawed. The sanction applied contravenes the principle of 'innocent until proven guilty' and is directly responsible for the public blackening of Professor Abreo's name, without evidence, on several online forums. All in all, this is an attempt to malign a central and much-loved figure of the eighteenth-century studies community.

Without disputing their good intentions, we call on those acting in the name of 'safety' to urgently reconsider their conduct. It is time for our community to come together again around its core purpose: the study and celebration of that great philosophical movement, the Enlightenment, that sought to clear away the false beliefs that have blinded people to their own interests and thereby increase the well-being of all humanity.

Letter 68: ALAN KEOGH to GAVIN MULVANY

Bristol, 2 October 2022

1) Zoé Chauvin.
2) Caroline Fresneau.
3) Giorgia di Michele.
4) Agata Bartosz.
5) Louise Veuillot.

He told me he didn't recognise 2) at all. He claimed to have met 5) only once, when he was a member of the jury for her final thesis. 1), 3) and 4), he did admit to having physical affairs with, but swore that it was they who approached him, they who proceeded to pursue him, they who wouldn't leave him alone, until he relented. Which he did with extreme trepidation, he said. In the knowledge that he, unlike them, had something to lose (professional stature, marriage) should their dealings turn sour. Obvs you didn't hear any of this from me.

Note by GAVIN MULVANY

Paris, 2 October 2022

Put list down in front of him. Demanded he go through names one by one and tell me everything he remembered. No angry preliminaries. C. paused to take in information. Then pressed fingertips against face. Fingers on forehead. Thumbs on jaw. And turned on waterworks.

'You piece of shit, pull yourself together.' Couldn't stand to see eyes filled with tears. 'You think you can afford to sit here and drivel? They're coming for you. Suspension from your job is just the beginning. Prison is on the horizon, do you understand? A criminal record. I got you out of this mess once before. If you want my help again, then wipe your eyes, be a man and tell me what the hell you did.'

'Let them come for me. I don't care any more.'

Countenance: man in midst of greatest calamity of unhappy life. But then rapid shift. From distress to amusement. Crying blended into laughter. No trace of agonies just tearing him apart. Caused me to think we judge sadness too much on basis of appearances. Suppose it to be where it's least present. Crying, an equivocal sign. A crying man more often than not a fortunate one who seeks to mislead others. This crying man? Got what was coming: clean slap across the face.

This in his attic room. Arrived to find him on sofa, looking like a jilted lover in an old T-shirt. Loose boxer shorts. Brown towelling bathrobe open at front. Its panels spilling over cushions on either side. Hands resting on bare thighs. Eyes squinting against the natural light now streaming in because I'd just opened shutter. Skin appeared paler than at our last rendezvous. Lines on his face deeper. In pain. Quite right.

Me: 'You look like crap.' My jacket still on. Began to clear away wine bottles and takeaway cartons strewn around. Automatically. Picking up where I'd left off 20 yrs ago. Receipts stapled to Deliveroo bags: 'Nearly a hundred on sushi? Really?' Put what could be saved into fridge. Threw rest out. Changed bins. Left full rubbish bags by door to take out. Washed hands at the sink using washing-up liquid. Watched water run through fingers onto the dirty dishes underneath. Fought against a voice telling me to deal with them too.

Him: 'You nutjob, what are you doing?'

Brought him glass of water. Stood over him while he drank.

Me: 'Louis XVI and Marie Antoinette in the Temple. Imprisoned, their days numbered, and lunching daily on two main courses and dessert, with champagne.'

Him: 'You think this is imprisonment? I wish to God I was in prison. The obscurity would be good for something. I'd cut my hair short like a monk's. I'd devote myself to the study of some abstract branch of learning. But this isn't that. It's something far worse. It's exile. I've been excommunicated. Banished from the one place in the world I belong, and to which I gave my heart and soul for over thirty years.'

Objects in room. Small number of transfers from old flat. Stark reminder. Extent to which Mathilde sustained old life. One thing I recognised: print on wall. Used to hang above desk in study. Crooked. Went. Inexplicably. To straighten it.

Me: 'I take it you've been looking online.'

Him: 'My God, my God. What a nightmare we're all living in. I understand that lots of people are making lots of money from it, but is anyone actually enjoying it?'

'Stay away from the internet, Cyprien. It won't help.'

'You know, they're using my book to attack me personally, did you see? Bigots of every sort, people who have no taste for literature, who for the most part haven't read my work, are working themselves into a fury about it. I ask you, are we still in France? Have I gone to sleep and woken up in Iran? Should I expect stones to start raining on my windows at night?'

Open cardboard box on table. Inside fresh samples of prize-winner. Paperback ed. Fresh from printers. Took copy out. *The Ecstasy of Pain*. Oil painting on cover: man peeping through door as two women get undressed. Turned it around a couple of times.

Him: 'I'm confident of the utility and the beauty of that book. Everything about it is in order.'

Me: 'It's a fine piece of work. But more talked about now than I'd wish for it.'

'The fucking mob. You've got to hand it to them – they've realised there's nothing to be gained from burning books, so they've turned to burning their authors instead.'

'Be that as it may, Cyprien, you mustn't focus too much on the reaction to your book. It's a distraction from the real and serious problem you're facing.'

'Can I tell you what bothers me most? It's seeing people who don't know me from fucking Sartre, who've never set foot inside the Sorbonne, or any other university for that matter, upbraid the faculty authorities for treating me too leniently. Actually there's something that bothers me even more than that. The silence of my colleagues in the face of this upbraiding. People, close friends, who should have spoken out in my favour, have said nothing.'

Sofa: no-go area. Made room at table. Removed box to floor. Took list from pocket. Unfolded. Smoothed on tabletop.

Zoé
Caroline
Giorgia
Agata
Louise

'I beg you, please, take a breath, gather your thoughts, and come and look at this.'

Stalled. Took a while. But eventually. Pulled himself up. Staggered across. Sat down opposite me. Scanned names once. Then brushed paper onto floor. I retrieved it. Replaced it in front of him. He swiped it off again. That's when crying started. Lost my temper. Didn't stop at slapping either. Also seized hair at back of head. Thicker there. Tightened grip. Till pulling at roots.

Him: 'There it is. Your secret envy that was only waiting for an occasion to vent itself.'

Brought face close. Two beautiful eyes. Best feature. Merged into single monstrous blob. 'You understand, don't you, that I don't have to help you? That I'm not obliged to you in any way? That in fact, if I was so inclined, I could make things much worse for you and still sleep fine at night?'

Shook his head to escape grip: 'I don't need your help. Or anyone's. I'm innocent.'

Took two paces back. Made some space. Threw off jacket.

Jumper. Opened shirt. Pointed at mark. 'Have you ceased to remember this?'

'What? I can't see anything.'

'Look closely. There.'

'You're imagining it.' In his features no crying left. But not hard to discern deep torment. Burning slow. Like green wood. 'Now get the hell out of here. Go and wank yourself to sleep, and have some lovely dreams about me.'

Letter 69: ZOÉ CHAUVIN to GAVIN MULVANY

Paris, 14 October 2022

I've often thought about what I'd say if I ever got the chance to speak to you. For a long time I was extremely angry and wanted to give you hell. But more recently, after a lot of analysis, I've opened my mind to the possibility that you too were a victim of sorts. That in protecting Professor Abreo you were acting under coercion. Then again, I can't be sure of this either. And I wouldn't say I've found forgiveness. I need to be persuaded that Professor Abreo's treatment of you, as a man, can justly be compared to his treatment of me and the other women. And I'm in no doubt that what you did to discredit me and undermine my attempt to bring him to justice was a crime, for which it's your duty to make reparations.

For this reason, since receiving your email, I've been in two minds about responding. If I'm reaching out now, it's in the hope that I can persuade you to come forward and set the record straight. Tell the police you lied. Give new evidence. And in so doing, help me and my co-accusers to get a conviction at last.

Mr Mulvany, let me be blunt. It's time you made amends. Not only to me, but to all the others who've been victims of Professor Abreo, yourself included.

I can state categorically that we, my co-accusers and I, aren't the authors of the open letter published in *Eighteenth-Century Studies*. Nor are we responsible for any posts that have appeared online in relation to Professor Abreo. The pillory isn't our tactic. Our goal is an old-fashioned judgement in a court of law. To this end we're gathering as much material evidence, and as many corroborating witnesses, as we can. Nothing is so trivial that it might not make the difference between success and failure. This is new territory for us, we are prepared to make mistakes – and we expect to win.

Because we exist in a culture where power still belongs to men, and where women remain alienated from the system of legal and political decision-making, we're adamant that our endeavour be spearheaded by women. That said, we wouldn't object to your presence at our meeting next Saturday (22 October, venue in link below). In extending this invitation, we are not making any commitments to you. You'll find us receptive, but we'll also remain vigilant until such time as your integrity has been established and ongoing engagement with you is unanimously deemed to be of benefit.

Letter 69a: ZOÉ CHAUVIN to GAVIN MULVANY
[Marked 'Postscript']

According to your own admission, you're currently in contact with Professor Abreo. We don't claim to know your motivations in maintaining relations with him at this time, but please understand that we'd expect you, in advance of our meeting, to break them off unequivocally and permanently.

Letter 70: GAVIN MULVANY to CYPRIEN ABREO

Paris, 22 October 2022

At the meeting with Zoé and the others today, I put it to them:
  'I find it hard to see him in this state.'
  To which Agata said, 'I knew this was a bad idea.'
  'As hatefully as he has behaved sometimes,' I said, 'I don't hate him.'
  'Don't worry,' Zoé said. 'We won't take you to task for your feelings.'
  We were in the nineteenth arrondissement, in a ground-floor nursery school run by Zoé's sister, who gives the group permission

to hold their meetings there after hours. The main classroom is also used for adult classes in the evenings. When I arrived, a hypnobirthing session was just finishing up, and Zoé and the others were waiting on the street for the participants to leave.

The process of sharing testimonies was tense, efficient. The essential points were made. No one went into unnecessary detail. My own contribution was largely emotionless. I found some degree of composure by riveting my attention on the children's artwork Blu-Tacked to the walls. Afterwards, questions. Had my relationship with you been sexual? Had I been in love with you? What had been your methods of control? Before the night you scarred my skin, had you ever been violent or physically threatening to me? Had it been my idea to destroy Zoé's credibility? Who invented the story I gave to the police?

'You've left it twenty years,' said Caroline. 'Far, far, far, far too long. The onus is on you now to withdraw your false statement and tell the police the truth. Can you commit to doing this as soon as possible?'

'I know it's the right thing to do,' I said. 'I want to.'

'What's so hard? Just go and do it. We'll help you with the admin side.'

'I need a little more time. To think it through.'

'It sounds like you're more worried about implicating yourself than doing what's morally correct.'

'That's not it. The problem is, I don't know how to explain why I did what I did. To myself, never mind to the police. If I say I was under Cyprien's sway, it'll seem like a cop-out. If I say I acted freely, I'd be taking the rap for something I could never have conceived of alone.'

We were sitting in an uneven semicircle around Zoé, the unofficial convenor, who was cross-legged on a low windowsill in front of the window. Her red ballroom shoes from back in the day had been replaced by white trainers with a sparkly designer logo, and the chain with the gold cross had disappeared. Now she wore a wedding band, and was, as a middle-aged woman, even more alarmingly beautiful than she'd been in her twenties.

'It's hard for us to get our heads around too,' she said. 'How and why does a supposedly intelligent person surrender his or her own sense of autonomy to someone else? We've had to ask ourselves the same question.'

'It's a drawn-out process,' Giorgia said. 'A man like Cyprien isn't going to barge in to your life and assume control over you overnight. He's going to be sneakier than that. He's going to try to define you first. Then start to break you down.'

'In my case,' said Louise, 'it started with the mind. He made me feel that I was being tested the whole time. That I had to prove myself as a thinker. Subtly he'd make it known what he thought my outlook should be, and I conformed as best I could, because I respected him. He fed me opinions, which I rearticulated, or adjusted slightly, then sent back to him. Everything I said, he took with the utmost seriousness. He treated my ideas as though they really had originated in me and were completely novel to him.'

'He does that,' Caroline said, 'so that he can then present himself as someone completely compatible with you. He sets it up to look as if you're the one choosing him. As if you're the one who's really in the driver's seat.'

'At the same time,' Zoé said, 'he understands that you fancy him. That you're keen on more than friendship. That you're flattered by his interest and therefore persuadable. I, for one, didn't hide my feelings from him. He used this openness of mine to lead me on. He switched from hot to cold. Flirted with me, encouraged me to express my emotions, and then shamed me for it. Made promises, some of which he kept, others not, to keep me on my toes. Was it the same for you, Gavin?'

'Yes and no,' I said. 'He wanted me to be in love with him. But I think homosexuality frightened him, actually. He could only deal with the concept abstractly, as it appeared in books. The physical act of sex between men, the reality of it, he found embarrassing, off-limits.'

'As far as I could tell, women's bodies terrified him also.'

'Women's bodies and women's minds, both,' said Caroline. 'He's a classic misogynist.'

My face was hot, as though I were facing into a row of big lamps, when in fact the room was chilly. We all had our coats on. With the blind drawn, the passers-by were visible as shadows moving across a wet and blurry streetscape.

'He liked to gossip,' said Zoé. 'Part of his method of seduction was to be charming with me in his unkindness to other people. Especially other women.'

'It was a technique he used with me too,' said Caroline. 'He bad-mouthed other women to me, so as to define them in contrast to me. He'd say that they, those other women, were the mainstream. They were the establishment. They were pampered little wives. They weren't proper feminists. They were stupid. They were ugly.'

'With me it was the other way around,' I said. 'He'd praise women to put me in competition with them. He'd say, "These days all my best students are women. They're the future. Are you going to be able to keep up?" Or he'd say, "Look how gorgeous that woman is. How can it be that you don't desire even a specimen like that?" Like this, he'd make a point of telling me how much he admired women. But then he'd change tack and say they weren't to be trusted. That I was lucky to have relationships with men, because it meant I could take my partners at face value and didn't have to suspect them of artfulness, of cunning, or to subject them to constant assessments as regards their intentions or their integrity.'

'He played with you as a homosexual,' Zoé said, 'but accepted you as a man.'

'The deal seemed to be,' I said, 'that if I could induce him to desire me as though I were a woman, while swearing never to be duplicitous like a woman, I'd have a shot at being for him something even better than a wife.'

Speaking these words, I had in mind the evening you and I went to the cinema to see the newly released Almodóvar film, *Talk to Her*. If you recall, a woman directly in front of us sobbed through most of the last quarter. More than irritating, I found this incomprehensible. The message of the film seemed to be that a man's crimes, including rape, were justified as long as it could be proved, first, that he'd been overpowered by feelings, second, that he experienced these feelings as genuine, and, third, that he understood these feelings to be love. Far from seeing anything sad in this, I was outraged, and imagined that as a woman I'd be doubly so. In the foyer on the way out, I expressed this view to you. You dismissed it.

'You're a man, Gavin,' you said, 'who has relationships with men, and you think you know what true sadness feels like?'

'I think I do, yes.'

'Let me see. It's Sunday and it's raining, and you have the right music on, and you peer out of the window and notice that the world is carrying on without any intervention on your part, and you wonder, "If I were to die, if I vanished out of existence, would anyone notice? Would anyone feel the loss?" Isn't that it, more or less? Well, don't kid yourself. Your puny male melancholy doesn't even scratch the surface of the female variety. For them, sadness is everything you feel it to be plus hundreds of other feelings that you've been spared.'

You pulled open the foyer door and stood back to let me pass, then remained in that position, the chivalrous one, to allow a line of people that was following close behind me, mostly women, to go out also, each of them thanking you in turn. Standing out on the street, looking in at you, I caught a glimpse of what it was like to see you for the first time. With innocent eyes. Having never been on the receiving end of your dark professions of faith.

'A woman's aim,' you continued as we walked, 'is to become necessary to someone. Who? A man, of course. But not just any man. One who will, in their presence and eternally, regret them. This is the core of women's belief system. Scratch the surface of the nearest feminist, and you'll find a conviction that she's destined to encounter the man who's such a giant that he'll stand in for God. Conversations with this man won't just be conversations, they'll be illuminations. Sex won't be sex, it'll be ecstasy. Pain will be agony. Sadness, uncontrollable floods of tears. On an average day: hallucinations, fits, convulsions, levitation – there's nothing they won't expect him to induce in them.'

'So you're the saviour that women have been looking for?'

'Ha ha, good one. I'd have to be a master illusionist to trick any woman into thinking I was divine. There's only one thing I can do to help them. And that's to look with a cold eye into their hearts and see the false images of men they're keeping there. My unenviable job is to exorcise these holy images. To tear them out. Not an easy assignment. But those who reach me tend to be desperate. I do whatever it takes.'

'Which I suspect is usually the maximum.'

I shared this memory with the group, who shook their heads in response.

'He was using misogyny as a hook to pull you in,' said Agata.

'Were you game? Would you call yourself a misogynist also? Some homosexuals are.'

'Back then, I would've been offended at the suggestion. But the reality was, I didn't shoot down his arguments, or put up any solid resistance to his expectation of assent. I wanted him as he was, regardless of what he thought about women, or about anything else. What he thought about me was all that mattered.'

'That's how misogyny works,' Louise said. 'It wills one man to acquiesce to another, and then that man to acquiesce to another again. This way other men's approval is always put before the well-being of women.'

'I'll give Cyprien one thing,' said Giorgia. 'I think women do possess a type of sadness that men don't. Not the sadness of power. Not the sadness of conquest. But the sadness of wanting to understand, which has no equal.'

After the meeting, I walked Zoé to the metro. She hadn't got an umbrella and there was room under mine for two.

'Is it really true you haven't decided?' she said.

'Zoé, I –'

'Don't. The only worthwhile apology you can make is in a statement to the police.'

'I feel resolute one minute, then get cold feet the next.'

'It's not a trivial matter. What you did wasn't trivial.'

'Is it loyalty to him? I don't know.'

The water rolling off the edge of the umbrella was creating a transparent barrier between us and the city.

'I'll be honest with you,' she said. 'My impression is that you're not convinced that what Cyprien did to me, to you or to the others was really a crime.'

'He's at fault and deserves all the bad press he's getting.'

'You're conflicted, though, about whether he should be prosecuted.'

'I wouldn't object to seeing him in the dock. I just don't have a clear idea about what I, or any of us, would get out of it.'

'Isn't justice important to you? Or even just having a sense of closure?'

'I'm not sure what that's supposed to mean. What, and where, are these doors that I'm supposed to be able to close on major parts of my life? How would my life be better?'

The tips of my shoes were drenched. As was my left shoulder, which was poking out beyond the umbrella's circumference. I was allowing myself to get wet so as not to huddle closer to Zoé.

'You know,' she said, 'things didn't have to go this far. Before going to the police, we contacted Cyprien privately and invited him to admit culpability and apologise. In all honesty, we'd have been content with that, but he didn't answer us. More recently, we made it known to the officer in charge of our case that, in the event of him being arrested, we'd be open to court-supervised mediation, if he wanted to make amends to us face to face.'

'To show remorse, you mean?'

'It's unlikely, we know.'

'Mission impossible.'

'Some men need to be pushed to the cliff edge before they'll relent. According to our lawyer, many men who forcefully deny the allegations end up pleading guilty and showing remorse in court.'

'Is shedding a few crocodile tears to obtain a lighter sentence remorse? How sincere can sorrow be when it has a motive?'

'Frankly we'd prefer insincere remorse to none at all. We want to hear the words come out of his mouth. Once on the public record, an apology is an apology. As long as it isn't a substitute for punishment, it'd be a victory for us.'

We'd arrived at the station some minutes before, and I'd accompanied Zoé down the steps to the shelter of a harshly lit passage, through which the hot air from the tunnels below was being funnelled up and out. Zoé held her flying hair back in order to look me in the face for a moment, before parting.

'Hold on,' I said.

A couple of metres away, she stopped and turned, becoming an obstacle around which the oncoming people flowed.

'Can I ask,' I said, 'did he ever talk about me?'

'Back then? That might be hard for you to hear.'

'What did he say?'

'Not much.'

I went forward to be near her again: 'Tell me.'

'Let me think,' she said. 'I remember he liked to refer to you in that American mode, as someone suffering from trauma.'

'He must've meant my father.'

'Your father?'

'Nothing like that. He just left when I was young.'

'That explains why Cyprien called you "faggot" sometimes. You were the typical faggot, he'd say, who lacked a male role model at home, and who was confused and insecure as a result, constantly in search of an authority to follow.'

The gusts of wind were driving into my face and drying out my eyes. I felt outside of things, only then to be immersed. The world appeared unbearably full without me, while being empty with me inside.

'He thought he had me figured out,' I said.

'He claimed,' she said, 'that he'd taken you under his wing because he was afraid of what would happen to you if another, unscrupulous man were to take advantage of your neediness. He advised me to see you as a negative example. If I wanted a career in academia, do everything that you weren't, and don't do anything you were.' She jerked her head to restore some errant strands of hair. 'You did ask.'

Unable to meet her eyes, I looked between the white tiles and an advertisement for €3.49 sausages at Carrefour.

'Look,' she said, 'it's not the end of the world if you don't make a new statement. We're confident we'll get an arrest with the evidence we already have.' I sensed she was going to embrace me, then decided against it. 'I just hope you understand how compelling it'd be for a jury to see that the crimes that you, I and the others were victims of took place in the same room.'

Letter 71: GAVIN MULVANY to CYPRIEN ABREO

Paris, 23 October 2022

It used to happen that when I returned to the flatshare after tutoring Anne-Laure, I'd find things in my room had been moved around. The order of the CDs in my stack, altered. A disc – almost always Pergolesi's *Stabat Mater* – left in the stereo with the power still on. The cushions on my bed rearranged. On the duvet cover, the definite outlines of recent activity. The smell of perfume and pot. With good reason, I blamed my flatmates. And, after it had happened a few times, I went at them: 'Which one of you thugs has been entertaining sluts in my sanctuary?'

Then, on All Saints' Day, I got the truth. The holiday landed on a Friday. You notified me in advance that we wouldn't be able to have our usual walk as you'd be tied up with a family function. You explained the tradition. A morning visit to Mathilde's mother's grave in Passy cemetery (€10k per square metre). After that a catered lunch at Mathilde's father's house (Lenôtre, starting at €100 per person). At 11.30 a.m. on that day, I was in the kitchen switching between a *MacGyver* rerun and the ongoing analysis of the Moscow theatre siege, when the doorbell rang. As I wasn't expecting anyone, I allowed my flatmate, off work for the bank holiday, to answer. A minute later I heard him in dialogue with you in the corridor: light chit-chat, how-are-you-I'm-fine-and-you, during which you used the familiar form of address, as did my flatmate in return. So far during my stint as a tenant, I'd never known you to enter the flat. To my knowledge this was the first occasion, and I anticipated something adverse. Coming out to the corridor, I found you standing on the threshold of my room. At the time I didn't clock that you knew which one it was.

'Are you busy?' he said. 'Can we talk?'

In my room you refused my offers of the desk chair, the bed, a cushion on the floor to sit on. Instead you put yourself in the light of the window and wrung your hands and distorted your face in a manner altogether frantic.

'What's eating you?' I said.

With a rough pull of the cord, you dropped the window blind down, casting darkness on everything, and told me to lock the door. Without any light to guide you – and with, to me, surprising foresight – you found the switch for the lamp by the bed. Located the Pergolesi CD in the stack. Operated the stereo without instruction from me. And retrieved from the desk drawer the lighter, with which you lit a large candle. Still I somehow didn't put two and two together.

'What in God's name are you doing?' I said. 'Shouldn't you be at the cemetery?'

From a flattened cigarette packet that had been in your trouser pocket, you took a joint, lit it and took several heavy drags from it. Then you said, 'Did I ever tell you my father-in-law is a member of

Opus Dei? That's what I'm dealing with there. I'll give the man Christmas. Easter at a push. All Saints' Day? He can fuck off.'

You passed me the joint, from which I took a comparatively moderate hit. Holding the smoke in my lungs, I held it out to give it back. From two paces away, you looked with indifference at my offering. Then you plumped suddenly on your knees. My perception was that, intending to sit on the bed, you'd missed the edge and fallen. I went forward to aid you. But, before I reached you, a whimper came out of you, so high-pitched and harsh that I became alarmed and retreated.

'You're scaring me now, Cyprien,' I said, depositing the joint in the ashtray. 'What do you want here? Why aren't you with your family? Can't you just swallow your pride and give your wife's father one day?'

The truth was that you'd excused yourself from the gathering on the grounds that you were an atheist – something you did every year, part of the tradition, apparently. Thus liberated, you'd made a rendezvous with Zoé at her flat, which had ended with her breaking off your affair, forbidding you to contact her again and threatening to call the police if ever you showed up at her home or came near her at the university. You'd come directly to me after this.

'That bitch is out to get me.'

'Stop catastrophising. She's just angry about something. What did you do? When she calms down, apologise for whatever it is. She'll change her mind.'

You lay back on the bed. I helped you put a pillow under your head. Once in position, you rested an arm across your face and wept into the crook of your elbow. I was at a loss. Who was this broken-down man? I knelt on the mattress next to you and rubbed your chest, your belly. When that felt no longer useful, I rested a hand on your thigh and just watched you.

'Sorry,' you said when the upheaval had subsided.

'You don't have to apologise.'

You didn't merely wipe your eyes but ground your wrists into your sockets: 'One of those days.'

'Do you want to tell me . . . ?'

'Let's just listen for a minute.'

You got up, roughly, very nearly pushing me off the bed to get past me, and put the Pergolesi CD back to the start. Turned the volume up, two notches past respectful. You then reclaimed the extinguished joint, carefully smoothed out what remained of it, relit it and powered through most of it.

'*The grieving Mother stood weeping beside the cross where her Son was hanging.*'

'Turn it down,' I said, accepting the leftovers of the joint from you. 'My flatmate is here. The neighbours will complain.'

'Shh! Can't you shut up for a single minute?'

Visibly overheated, you tore off your jacket, your jumper. Unbuttoned your shirt, then jerked and swung your arms to get them free of the sleeves. Threw everything on the chair. Flung off your shoes. Now down to your vest and trousers, you paced back and forth.

'*Through her weeping soul, compassionate and grieving, a sword passed.*'

'Cyprien, you're worrying me.'

'Press charges against me?' Laughter came whistling through your teeth, then blew down your nose in a succession of short bursts. 'She says, "I need to defend my freedom against your infringements." And in the same breath says she's gone to the police to get me arrested.'

Then I realised it was serious. And at the same time the penny dropped about the room.

'Have you been meeting her here?'

Mathilde, it turned out, was the owner of the flatshare. My landlady. A spare key for the property hung among the others in your entrance cupboard, not even hidden away, but right there, dangling from a rainbow-coloured lanyard, for you to grab as you dashed out of the door.

'That's fucking trespassing.'

'Oh please. You barely pay any rent. People like you don't live in the eighth arrondissement! Count your lucky stars you're not in some godforsaken suburb beyond the ring.'

'Only Zoé? Or other women as well?'

Ignoring this, you came to me and grasped me by the shoulders: 'Listen to me. You have to help me.'

Zoé had taken photos of herself. In her bra. Showing fresh wounds on her skin. And was taking these photos to the police.

'What kind of wounds?'

'It was a game. We were playing.'

'That's what you're into?' Already I'd made the judgement that what interested you, more than pain, was the quietness that followed it. 'You hit her?'

'No. There was no hitting.'

You rummaged in my bedside drawer. Produced the wax stamp that I'd had made to match yours. Began heating its metal face, the ornate 'G', over the candle flame.

I shifted along the mattress to be further away from you: 'What the fuck, Cyprien?'

When you judged it to be hot enough, you pressed the stamp onto the bare skin of your upper arm, but not for long, only a short second, before letting it drop to the floor. You hissed out the pain. 'This isn't going to work. You're going to have to do it.' You took off your belt and, without needing to search around for a suitable place, fixed your wrist to the radiator valve. 'Put it right here on my arm.'

I didn't move. 'Have you done this before? Did Zoé . . . ?'

'You're catching up.'

'I don't see any wounds on your skin.'

'I wanted her to do it to me too, but that's not her thing. She's into receiving, you know?'

'So it was a consensual thing?'

'It started out as a childish game. Playing around. It'd be easy to say things got out of hand. But that'd be bullshit. She orchestrated everything. She wanted me to go further. I was the one who put on the brakes.'

I picked the stamp off the floor. Examined it. 'This all happened here? With this?'

'I'll make it worth your while. I'll pull some strings. An interview. A job. You name it.'

I made three marks. Two on your arm and one on your back. Each time you screamed a terrible scream into a pillow. And writhed around. Then, afterwards, you were still, tears running down your face.

'Now you.'

At the police station that week I was brought into a small room, where I took off my shirt and peeled the bandages off the wounds, to show the officers.

'How did these get here?'

'Professor Cyprien Abreo put them there.'

'Professor Abreo assaulted you?'

'Absolutely not. I asked him to do it. And I did the same to him, with his consent. There are rules, limits, which Cyprien is always careful to respect, as am I.'

'Where did this happen?'

'In my room. Using a utensil I had made specifically for the purpose.'

'You like the sensation of burning? It pleases you?'

'I would say so, yes.'

'Is Professor Abreo your, what do you say, boyfriend?'

'We believe in personal liberty. We don't put a title on it.'

'You like to burn each other though?'

'With the utensil. As part of our lovemaking.'

'Is Professor Abreo a homosexual?'

'Admittedly he likes women too. But he has, what would you call it, a dysfunction. Penetration for him isn't a simple matter, you understand? He must find other ways.'

'Do you also have the same dysfunction?'

'Similar.'

'So you are a passive homosexual?'

'That's right.'

'Are you here under duress? Has Professor Abreo bribed or threatened you?'

'Professor Abreo, I call him Cyprien, is dear to me, and I to him. We feel only affection for one another.'

'Were you and Professor Abreo alone while . . . ?'

'Often we prefer one-to-one. But on this occasion we had a guest.'

'One guest?'

'Yes, one other person.'

'Male or female?'

'A woman named Zoé Chauvin. It's a little game we play from time to time, the three of us together.'

MS Extract: from *Rousseau's Lost Children* by GAVIN MULVANY

Last edited: 25 October 2022

By the height of the Enlightenment in the mid-eighteenth century, French had been the lingua franca of polite discourse across Europe for over a hundred years. At the same time, men with ambitions to be philosophers began to turn their back on the established academies in France, which they considered to be too restrictive and inefficient as vehicles for the dissemination of knowledge. Emerging out of this historical development was the 'Republic of Letters': a virtual network of intellectual exchange, with Paris at its centre, comprising any individual of wit, intelligence and cultural accomplishment who could speak and read in good French. In this network, the ideal of the intellectual was no longer the churchman in his cloister studying divine texts; rather it was the autonomous individual, loyal to empirical science, who entered into discursive exchanges, often publicly, with other autonomous individuals, in accordance with a model of mutual respect and friendship.

In the Republic of Letters, the dominant form of writing was the letter. Private letters were sent through the postal service, on which the king had a monopoly. The daily structure of those who sent and received private letters was marked by the public time of arrivals and departures: a letter writer could read a reply to his previous missives only after the letter carrier had come, and impatience often compelled him to write follow-ups before the original letter had reached its destination. Missing or lost letters were a source of great anxiety, not least because of the risk of their falling into the wrong hands. Maintaining a correspondence was not a casual activity but a formal engagement implying reciprocal responsibilities. If one of the correspondents failed to carry out those responsibilities, the other ended the relationship, in most instances by asking that all previous letters be either returned or burned.

The letter was far from an exclusively private medium, however. Writers increasingly, and creatively, used letters to bridge the gap between the closed circles in which they gathered and the public arena in which they sought to shape and make their name. In this sense, writers did not simply write letters; they employed and deployed the epistolary genre in the public sphere, transforming ostensibly private correspondences into a variety of media aimed for general consumption. Their letters ranged from short notes and letters of introduction to lengthy newsletters and scientific reports; in them, they evaluated new books, announced discoveries, reported scholarly debates, requested information, provided obituaries of deceased scholars, dealt with publishers and sought and offered patronage. Sometimes letters were transformed into newsletters and then into journals. Pamphlet wars constituted letter exchanges initiated by men of letters and continued by the broader public. The 'gazette' was largely a collection of correspondences.

In the early 1760s, talk of two inflammatory new works by Rousseau diffused quickly through the Republic of Letters. In April 1762 copies of *The Social Contract* began to arrive in France, having been printed in Amsterdam. Among the many radical propositions contained in this text was one that represented an open challenge to prevailing, sanctioned ideas on religion: the lawgiver, Rousseau argued, should reinforce belief in the body politic by fabricating a civil religion while making people believe he has received it from on high. A month later, his novel on education, *Émile*, left the presses in Paris (with a title page that included the conventional precaution of claiming that the work had been published outside the king's jurisdiction, in The Hague). In *Émile*, the boy is taught, among other provocative lessons, that the Bible and church authority were not the sole source of knowledge about God, whose goodness could be amply deduced from the visible universe. A being of some kind must have made the world, but not necessarily a personal God who cares about individual humans and rewards or punishes their actions.

Despite efforts by the Paris authorities to suppress these blasphemous and seditious ideas, clandestine copies of the book, official and pirated, spread far and wide. On 9 June 1762 the authorities published a formal *arrêt*, or judgement, which stated that copies of the works were to be 'lacerated and burned at the foot of the great staircase in the courtyard of the Palais de Justice', and issued a warrant for Rousseau's arrest. Behind the scenes, however, they were writing letters of a different sort. Not eager to create a martyr out of Rousseau, they sent letters of warning to his aristocratic protectors, which gave him time to get away.

Once again Rousseau was forced onto the road. Thérèse stayed in Paris to protect their property against likely confiscation. Rousseau promised to send for her as soon as he had a safe place of refuge. His prior decision to abandon their children, who would at this time have been aged between nine and sixteen, suddenly seemed prescient. In this time of crisis it was better not to be slowed down by dependants of his own, nor impelled to turn them into refugees.

First he fled to Geneva, only to find his works outlawed and burned there too. Far from welcoming him back, his homeland wanted nothing to do with him and pushed him out. He tried some of the nearby villages but was chased out of those as well. Onwards, then, to Môtiers in the foothills of the Jura Mountains, where a banker's widow gave him use of an unoccupied house. He summoned Thérèse to join him there. On his daily walks in the surrounding hills he abandoned himself to his feelings of disgust about his treatment at the hands of his fellow Swiss, and to his suspicions of human society more generally. In 1763, he went so far as to publish a letter responding to a pastoral letter in which the archbishop of Paris had prohibited the reading of *Émile*. In his rebuttal, Rousseau defiantly reiterated the points that had caused the book to be banned, creating a sensation in Paris. As though to prove his indifference to the scandals he was causing, he began to take a serious interest in botany, memorising the names and attributes of hundreds of plants.

The following year, Voltaire – the acknowledged patriarch of the Republic of Letters, and himself in exile in the countryside just outside Geneva – published his pseudonymous pamphlet *The People's Feelings*, condemning Rousseau's decision to abandon his children. Oddly, despite having a history of vicious disputes with Voltaire, Rousseau never realised who the real author of this pamphlet was. In his public reply, he denied having abandoned his children, for indeed he had registered them in the Hôpital with all due formality. But this economy with the truth was not going to put the matter to rest. Since the appearance of *Émile*, Enlightened parents all over Europe had regarded Rousseau as their guide, and the thing he feared most was a public perception that he did not practise what he preached. It was high time to explain to the world just who he was and what he stood for. That is, to make a confession in writing, in the name of self-defence. To put on the public record his sorrow, not about his actions themselves, which were supported by reason, but about their having been misunderstood.

Letter 72: GAVIN MULVANY to THÉRÈSE LEVASSEUR

Paris, 28 October 2022

Having steered your husband from our meeting point outside your flat to the parvis of Notre-Dame cathedral, I marched him straight to the gate of the foundling hospital opposite, fully expecting him to take offence at my unsubtle manoeuvre and to make a break for it. But, no, he stayed, and waited in silence beside me for an answer after I'd rung the bell. To the right of the gate was a kind of cylindrical box, a foundling wheel, that opened onto the street, into which babies could be deposited, like a letter or a parcel, though today a rusty padlock puts it out of use.

'I imagine that's because they're finding too many dead ones in the morning,' said Jean-Jacques. 'I went in, like a civilised person, and put a name in the book.'

A nun, a Sister of Charity wearing a cornette, received us in the vestibule. Overlooked by a bust of Vincent de Paul, I told her our business. After we made the advised donation, she summoned a colleague, older and whose cornette's wings didn't quite stay up, who led us to the main building, where she ushered us into a large room with six windows and very white curtains, named 'the Crib'. Running down the length of the room were four rows of cots in which unweaned infants – tightly swaddled and therefore absolutely still – wailed in unison for their wet nurses. In the next room, a much smaller group of weaned infants, around one year old, survivors of the Crib, fought against their wrappings and cried out for their pap while they waited to be sent to nannies in the provinces. In the next room, three-year-olds, returned from the countryside, a smaller cohort again, were crawling around in pens, on standby for transfer to one of the city's hospitals; those who weren't comatose, or near starvation, whimpered and shrilled like beasts in captivity.

Enfeebled by these sights, feeling faint, and needing urgently to escape the smell, I told the nun that we'd seen enough. But your husband, Thérèse – I suspect as an exhortation to me to check my desire to enlighten others on matters about which I myself know nothing – insisted that we finish the tour. More than that, he requested, nay, demanded that we be given access to the place where the dead babies are put. Without blinking – the policy seemed to be that we, the public, shouldn't be shielded from the mess we've created – the nun brought us up a flight of stairs and around a bend, and, after covering her mouth and nose with her ample sleeve, opened an inconspicuous door: we could look in, she mumbled, but not enter. Across the threshold, in gloom, white and green caskets were ranged against the walls of a small chamber, and on the floor, laid out on lengths of white linen, were the latest corpses – I glimpsed four or five before I shut my eyes – awaiting burial, with crucifixes and crowns of white daisies and immortelles placed on top.

'Where will they be buried?' said Jean-Jacques.

'Don't fret about that,' the nun said vaguely. 'They all receive extreme unction and have good deaths.'

Promptly she led us up another staircase to a corridor on a separate wing, containing two large dormitories and four classrooms. Here, she explained, fifty older children, chosen from among the most beautiful, were being educated. She opened a classroom door to reveal twenty or so young boys sitting at desks, studying sheets of music. No noise, no smell, yet, to my eyes, the saddest room of all.

'What future do they have?' Jean-Jacques asked their teacher.

'They'll sing in the cathedral choir,' she said. 'And on special occasions they'll follow the parade of benefactors through the streets.'

Downstairs once more, the nun dropped us off at the registrar's bureau, outside which we sat for a long time, before a corpulent nun, wearing a different uniform that bore testimony to her authority, showed us in. We wouldn't be allowed to consult the register ourselves, she said. But if we gave her the relevant information, she could have a look on our behalf. Jean-Jacques relayed the babies' given names and their dates of birth as best he could remember them, as well as the false moniker he'd used for himself, and she took it all down on a piece of paper.

'Sometimes,' she said, 'a father might mark the newborn by hanging around its neck or hiding in its clothes a ribbon, or a medal, or similar, as proof of a desire to take the child back later . . . ?'

'With the eldest, the firstborn, I did so,' Jean-Jacques said. 'Into his lace shirt I put a letter with my cipher stamped on the seal.'

Knowing from my research that this was the case, I'd had the foresight to bring one of your husband's letters with me, which I presented now to the registrar: placing it on the desk in front of her, I closed the flaps over to reunite the broken wax disc that displayed the distinctive brand 'JJR'. She used a pin to attach this letter to her written note, then disappeared through a door.

She was gone for around an hour, though it felt much longer, for we could hear the cries of the babies through the walls, and while every minute I'd think they were about to stop – I'd beg them to – they wouldn't.

The registrar finally came back, returned the letter to me and gave a sheet of notes to Rousseau, which he read.

'Any questions?' she said.

He shook his head. Tore the page into small pieces. Left them on the desk for the nun to dispose of.

Back on the street, the bells of Notre-Dame were announcing the civil hour of eleven o'clock. On pont Notre-Dame, we paused at a gap where a house had been demolished and looked onto the river. A strong breeze was coming against us.

'Are you going to tell me what became of them?'

'Never.'

'Will you tell Thérèse?'

'Neither. I don't bring the subject up with her.'

'Do you feel any remorse for what you did?'

'I don't repudiate what I chose to do. It was the right choice. This is what's meant when it's said that remorse is a product of free conscience.'

'If you could go back, would you do the same thing again?'

'The situation was such that, whatever I did, someone was going to suffer. If I kept them, I'd have lived a frustrated life, a poor life, which would have been their life too. We all would have died years ago.'

'Instead you had them suffer so that you could be free.'

'Truly, I feel great sorrow about that suffering. But the other option would simply have produced suffering of another sort, for which I'd also have felt remorse.'

We cut through the narrow streets of Les Halles towards the Corn Exchange. Jean-Jacques stopped to buy a bouquet of violets and some young peas. As soon as we stopped we were harassed by sellers of clothes and fruit, and by prostitutes, with whom Jean-Jacques was firm but not haughty or scornful. He paid a street urchin to carry his purchases home.

'It isn't breaking my moral principles that I feel remorseful about,' Jean-Jacques said as we walked. 'That is the arena of guilt. Rather I feel remorse when I remember the harm caused by my positive actions, the deeds I undertook in good faith, which I wouldn't change if given the chance today. Remorse is true sorrow. It comes from knowing that when I did harm, I did what I should have done.'

At the flat, once he'd opened the door and sent the urchin up to you with the items he'd bought, he bowed, lower than usual, and disappeared inside. Disappointed not to have been invited in to talk further, and resistant to the idea of the long, solitary walk ahead of me, nevertheless I headed off.

1) In a launderette near gare Saint-Lazare, sitting on top of a washing machine and taking immense pleasure from its vibrations: let's call her Zoé.

2) In the seventeenth arrondissement, on a disused railway, now a park, running along the track with a little dog on a lead: Agata.

3) On rue de Saussure, in the balcony of a block of social housing whose façade looked like folded cardboard, waving and calling to me: Giorgia.

4) In Levallois, riding on pink micro-scooters through a park built on old railway bridges, complete with wild grasses and a swampland with bulrushes: Louise and Caroline.

5) On rue Jean-Jacques Rousseau in Bois-Colombes, no children, but in a church, Coptic Orthodox, whose makeshift construction consisted of a wooden tunnel leading to a

low-ceilinged shed filled with icons and pews, I sat and rested alone – until the patriarch came in, took one look at me and said, 'Tears, my son, are one of the ways to purify the heart': Gavin.

Note by GAVIN MULVANY

Paris, 29 October 2022

Facetime with P. 'Do me a favour, root out the photo album: PARIS 2002.' Reluctant. 'Flip through them slowly. Stop, that one there. Take a photo of it, can you, and send it to me?'

Went straight to C. Buzzed me in. Upstairs door ajar. Inside dark. Wi-Fi box in corner flashing red. Laptop on the floor. Plugged in to charge. Big lump under duvet.

'It's the middle of the afternoon, get up. We're going for a walk. I'll drag you out if I have to.'

Père Lachaise. 750 m. 10 mins at most. Took three times that. Shuffling like old man.

'The pigs called me in again. Same fucking questions.'

'Trying to catch you out.'

'They say they have enough evidence to press charges. My lawyer thinks they're just trying to spook me.'

'What do you think?'

'Every day I expect them to kick down my door.'

Tomb of H. and A. Brushes fallen leaves off nearby slab. Pauses to read gold inscription. 'Best buddies with Zoé and the crew now, eh?'

'They said you brought them here too. Have you really such a lack of imagination? The same places. The same words.'

And the same tricks. Checking map at entrance. As if he didn't know route.

'If you're going to betray me, I wish you'd just fuck off and get on with it. You're not going to make me believe you're a victim of anything.'

Pulled up picture on my phone.

'What am I supposed to be looking at?'

'My old room in the flatshare.'

'Right, right, the torture chamber. What do you want from me? Tell me, I'll give it to you, if it'll put a stop to this.'

'Cyprien, if you only showed a modicum of regret –'

'You want regret? Don't you already have enough of that to last a lifetime? I mean, isn't your own regret what this is all about? Of your free will, you, and Zoé, and all those other whores perform certain acts in an adult, mutually consensual situation. Then, after the fact, you regret your actions and decide, ever so conveniently, that you haven't been acting freely after all. You'd been assaulted by me. Raped. Which is to say, you want me to take the fall for the remorse that you feel for your own decisions. And you have the gall to call this justice?'

Strode away. I stayed put. At 10 m he turned back. Called out, 'From now on, I want you to stay away from me. And enough of these emails. An innocent man has his good conscience as company, and it's plenty.' At 20 m: 'And what should this regret you want look like anyway?'

'I've only ever seen you sad for yourself, your own misfortunes. Never for another human being.'

'You're asking too much. No one in history has ever cried for anyone but number one.'

TENTH WALK

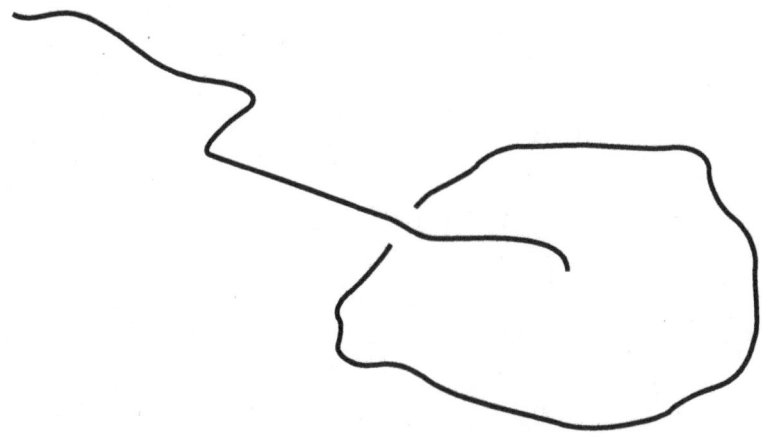

(*To Maisons-Laffitte, walking northwest: rue J.-J. Rousseau – Champs-Élysées – avenue de la Grande Armée – boulevard Périphérique – Neuilly-sur-Seine – La Défense – La Garenne-Colombes – Argenteuil – Les Bruyères – Sartrouville – Maisons-Laffitte; 20 km: 5 hours, 50 minutes*)

Love

Letter 73: GAVIN MULVANY to CYPRIEN ABREO

Paris, 10 November 2022

Before long, remuneration for work done. Your reward to me. 'An interview. At the university in Arras, in the north. Not a permanent position. The teaching pool. Paid by the hour. But it'd be a foot in the door.'

The interview was in the first week of December, a fortnight hence. A thirty-minute presentation of an undergraduate survey course in eighteenth-century French literature, followed by a panel interview. You more or less cleared your diary, and we met every second evening in your study to compose my presentation and talk through my interview answers. My instinct was to keep the presentation simple: an overview of the key novels of the era, focusing on the epistolary form and its importance in the Republic of Letters. But you were having none of that. 'We' (your word) needed to pull out all the stops. Do something bold that would make me stand out. Make such a dazzling impression that they, the big minds of Arras, couldn't in good conscience overlook me.

The approach we settled on, after some forward and back – i.e. after too little resistance from me – was to take eighteenth-century literature in its broadest sense, as encompassing philosophy and natural science as well as fiction in France and across Europe, and to tell the story of its development through the lens of love. The main thrust of my argument would be that the Enlightenment's concern with producing correct, valid reasoning, was at base an attempt to learn, or relearn, how to love ourselves and others, after centuries of brutal religious wars. Likewise, the Enlightenment's quest to bring emotions under the control of reason implied comprehending our feelings rather than suppressing them, with the aim of distinguishing true love from false passion.

The presentation took place in a large classroom with the desks arranged in a square formation, around which thirteen members of staff were seated. To break the ice, I joked that Beckett's French accent had been nearly as incomprehensible as his Irish one, and that I hoped mine wouldn't similarly confuse them. Smiles all round and, a minute in, I was already congratulating myself on my fluid command of PowerPoint XP and on my equally fluid transitions between textual and visual analysis. My spectators were open-faced, benign. The overweight middle-aged woman in the floral dress and the orthopaedic shoe, whom I'd picked out at the beginning as a possible antagonist, was nodding encouragingly. I had it in the bag.

The mood quickly shifted, however. I noticed that a young flame-haired woman, a recent hire, was gathering her colleagues' eyes and smirking. The head of the department was leafing through the printed lesson plans I'd passed around, seemingly in search of something that might resemble the task I'd been set. All at once I became nightmarishly conscious of the frequency with which I was pronouncing the word 'love': 'in love . . . out of love . . . for love . . . against love . . . love match . . . love triangle . . . love lost . . . love found . . . labour of love . . . love and leave . . .' My tongue felt too large for my mouth. Sweat pricked through the extra layer of moisturiser on my face. And, as I continued to deliver, at an ever-increasing pace, the presentation that you'd conceived, I began to visualise the one I'd have written if I'd been left to my own devices, which caused in me a drastic dip in confidence and a longing to flee. I began to bungle my lines. To skip chunks of essential information. To lose track of my slides, so that the image I was referring to frequently bore no relation to the point I was making. And, after each mishap, to apologise and say, 'I'm not usually this ditzy, really.'

The interview was cursory. The expected questions were asked, which I answered correctly, as drilled. No curveballs. No follow-ups. The outcome had already been decided; we were all just going through the motions. The splendour of academic protocol. On the train back, you called but I didn't answer. I was physically unable to speak. At home, the 'please fuck off' had already arrived, so I forwarded that to you instead. When, a couple of hours later, you called again, I looked at your name flashing on my screen, heartbroken that I wasn't more worthy of you.

'What did you do to botch it?'

'I did everything exactly as we planned. All the love shit.'

'Don't get pissy with me. You've no idea of the favours I had to call in to get you this.'

'Look, they just didn't take to your idea. It wasn't to be. Let's file it as a learning experience and move on.'

'You've embarrassed me.'

'I was the one who had to stand in front of all those arseholes and give a presentation I didn't believe in.'

'So you sabotaged it?'

'The decision had obviously been taken before I got into the room. They knew I was your protégé. They were anticipating something left field and were ready to hate it. When I spoke, they weren't fooled. They understood I wasn't speaking for myself. Ultimately they didn't reject me at all; they rejected you.'

Hearing silence on the line, in that instant I had the feeling, which came far in advance of the thought, that you were separating from me for good.

That Friday, just as I was leaving the house, I got this:

<<NO WALK TODAY>>

Accordingly, during the lesson the following morning, the atmosphere in the flat was tense. Anne-Laure showed me in. Everything was still. Although it was a dull day, all the lights were off. I could hear Coco scratching on your bedroom door. While taking my coat off, I peered around for signs of your presence: your coat was there, as were your boots. Old newspapers lay on the sofa in the living room. On the way to get some water for us in the kitchen, Anne-Laure opened a balcony door to admit some fresh air, causing the leaves of an adjacent plant to rustle.

In the study, she wittered on in a state of high nerves about whether it was okay to like the Flaming Lips, given that the band had once appeared in an episode of *Beverly Hills 90210*. Were they cringe-cool or sell-outs, did I think?

At the end of the hour, she saw me to the door.

'Is your father here?' I said.

'Breakfast in bed today, I think.'

'Can you tell him to come for a second?'

She went into your bedroom, there were murmurings, then she came back out and lingered at the corridor entrance. An overlong minute later, you appeared in your pyjamas and dressing gown.

'Hi, Gavin,' you said. 'We're having a lie-in. Late night last night.'

'I thought we might talk,' I said.

'We actually have to make a move,' you said. 'We're off to Plaisir to visit my parents.'

'You've had no word, then? About that official business I helped you with?'

'Which . . . ? Ah, no. None. It seems the people in charge are no longer interested in me.'

'Wow, is that right? They've dropped it?'

'Looks like it. Not enough in the file. But, listen, I'll be in touch mid-week, okay?'

Precisely as promised, an email arrived on Wednesday: 'Anne-Laure's teachers have advised us to end her private lessons. They judge her English conversation to be above par and believe she would be better served by some exam preparation courses. They also said the examiners in the entrance interviews for the Big Schools might be thrown by the Irish dialect.'

Feeling abandoned was a little like falling in love, in the way it flamed up and charged me with a kind of incandescence. All the things in my environment become closer and more vivid, as though my gaze rested on them with the same intensity it had once reserved for the beloved. The material world, which barely concerned me before, transformed into a single great obstacle in my path, something that I needed to climb over or roll aside in order to get back to the place I'd been, to retrieve what I'd lost. Without checking what I was wearing, or even changing out of my house slippers, I stormed out of the flat – door after door after door – and through the neighbourhood – body after body, flesh and metal, glowing under the Christmas lights – to your building. I buzzed for several minutes, in the belief that my finger, by pushing this specific button, had the power to collapse the façade of the entire street. When I got no answer, I crossed the road and shouted up at the windows:

'Dialect? Dialect?! Come down here and say the word "dialect" to my face, you motherfucking son of a bitch!'

The waiters from the Chinese restaurant gathered outside to look. A neighbour came onto her balcony and told me to shut up or she'd call the police. 'Call whoever you like!' I said, for I was fully loaded and wasn't going to stop. A minute later, however, the shutters on the windows of your flat – ever so slowly, one by one – came down. I was wasting my energy. It was over.

The next day I went to the faculty and loitered outside your office until you returned from your master's class: 'Sexualities, Gender and Knowledge in Literature and the Arts'. You arrived with a female colleague and two female postgrads, neither of them Zoé.

'A nice surprise, Gavin.' You dropped your bag inside the door, then locked up again. 'We have a lunch meeting now, internal business. Are you on campus all day? Maybe we could grab a coffee later?'

'How long will you be? I'll wait for you. We've a lot to catch up on.'

'Hard to tell with these things. I'll text. Don't hang around, if you've somewhere else to be.'

The following Monday, having failed to get hold of you, I went at lunchtime to Anne-Laure's school. It was the last week of term before Christmas. At the entrance, I asked a group of pupils in Santa hats to do me the favour of finding Anne-Laure and sending her out. A family matter, I said.

When she came – displaying fear and confidence in equal balance – she didn't greet me but immediately started down the street.

'I don't think you should be here,' she said when I caught up with her.

'Do you know what's going on?' I said.

'You're acting like a nutjob.'

'Do you want the lessons to stop?'

'I never wanted them to start in the first place, you dork. They were a punishment that my parents devised for me.'

'Don't you want to be totally fluent? What about your dream of moving to America?'

'What's your problem? Why is this so important to you? Just get another pupil. Better, get a proper job.'

'I thought we were sort of friends.'

'Stop it now, you're creeping me out.'

We'd rounded the corner and entered gare Saint-Lazare, which hadn't yet been upgraded to a shopping centre and was still grubby and ill-smelling. Anne-Laure bought an apple pie at McDonald's.

'Make that two,' I said, and paid for both.

'You don't have to buy me anything,' she said.

'Can't you talk to your dad on my behalf?'

'And tell him what?'

'Tell him he still owes me.'

'Owes you?'

'Tell me, from me, that he has a debt outstanding, for which I'd appreciate repayment.'

She nibbled the top off the pie, then blew into the hot filling. She was having trouble looking at me. 'A question,' she said. 'Have you ever given any thought to what all this might be like for me?'

That evening, a phone call: 'You've really done it now. You thought you'd get away with harassing my daughter? She was scared. You scared her, do you understand? I said a while ago that you could spend Christmas with us, but you can forget about that, it's off the table. Not going to happen, no way. Go home to your own family.'

To which I said, 'Don't do this,' hurriedly, as though trying to get the words on the record before the tape ran out. Then: 'I love you' – my first avowal, irresponsibly uttered at a moment when it could have no meaning other than fear.

Letter to the Editor A: CÉLINE LABILLE in *Libération*

Rennes, 13 November 2022

Is there anywhere that women can truly feel safe? Where they will not run the risk of being bothered, harassed, assaulted, raped? The latest man to be charged with crimes of harassment and assault against women is a professor at the Sorbonne, confirming what many women – not least those of us who have been through the elite education system ourselves – have long known: that the universities, those bastions of freedom and enlightenment, are no more immune to abuse of power than the spheres of business or entertainment.

The man in question has denied the charges. The principle of 'innocent until proven guilty' applies in this case as much as in any other. However, it was right of the Sorbonne to suspend him (on full pay) while he is being investigated. Often institutions are genuinely unaware of individual misconduct and cannot be held responsible for it. Yet they, as do we all, still need to learn the most important lesson: that men are not gods and should never be treated as such.

Letter to the Editor B: ESMÉ OZANNE in *Le Figaro*

Lyon, 19 November 2022

The crime of rape ought always to be punished to the full extent of the law. We are still a long way off a criminal justice system in which women are confident of being taken seriously and hardened perpetrators are genuinely afraid of getting caught. The #MeToo movement constitutes a legitimate awakening to the sexual violence that women are subjected to, particularly in their professional lives, where some men abuse their power. This is necessary.

But the movement that was supposed to liberate voices has descended into a witch hunt. From being a campaign aimed at legal redress for serious crime, it has transformed into a frenzy of public accusations and indictments, in the press and on social media, against individuals who, without being given a chance to respond or defend themselves, are put in the same category as sex offenders. Let us be clear about one thing: it is not a crime to try to pick someone up, however persistently or clumsily. Just as the freedom to offend is essential to artistic creation, the freedom to bother is indispensable to sexual freedom. The freedom to say 'no' to a sexual proposition can't exist without the freedom to propose. As women, we must learn how to respond to this freedom to bother in ways other than by framing ourselves in the role of the victim.

Sexual impulses are, by nature, primitive. Reason tells us the difference between an awkward attempt to seduce someone and a sexual assault. As someone who decided to have children, I think it is wiser to raise my daughters to understand the importance of drawing their own boundaries and saying 'no' when something does not feel right for them, so that they live their lives without being intimidated or blamed. Incidents that affect a woman's body do not necessarily affect her dignity and must not make her a perpetual victim. We are not reducible to our bodies. Our inner freedom is inviolable, but this freedom is not without risks and responsibilities.

Letter 74: ALAN KEOGH to GAVIN MULVANY

Bristol, 22 November 2022

Presume you've seen. Eleven counts, including assault and rape. Facing lots of jail time.

Here the community is divided into rival factions. Scholars my age and older are refusing to attend conferences out of outrage at the way he's been treated. On the other hand, in the past week alone, ten postgraduates and early-career researchers have said they're leaving because they feel betrayed by those supporting him. I fear a schism. The future of the field is in the balance. If a solution isn't found, we'll be reduced to a few old fogeys drinking alone in a seedy bar.

As you can imagine, there's a lot of pressure to take sides, which I'm trying to resist. I'm worried about what he'll do to himself tbh. Made inquiries. Apparently he's gone to stay with his parents in Plaisir. Will text you address. Not suggesting you go there, but if you do, send me a report – in strictest confidence.

Note by GAVIN MULVANY

Paris, 23 November 2022

First time in Plaisir. No advance warning. Mother in front garden. Remarkably good shape. Raking leaves. Didn't remember ever meeting me. Told her who I was. Why I'd come. Bent over to inspect a shrub: 'You're the first. Everyone else has run to ground.'

Took me inside, depositing rake on front step. Hung my coat on end of banister. Father: Alzheimer's? Sunk into the large armchair on far side of living room. In front of TV. At full volume. In response to my greeting blinked vacantly: 'Cyprien?' 'Cyprien's friend,' mother said. Then called into kitchen: 'I'm bringing this man upstairs!' Father's helper at the sink. Came out. Wiping apron. 'This is Holy.' Holy nodded solemnly: 'I'll put some coffee on.'

On landing. Mother knocked lightly. 'His old bedroom.' Entered without invitation. 'You have a visitor.' Crossed narrow strip of blue carpet. Opened curtains a little. Creating single bar of light that sliced diagonally across tumble of blankets on bed. Cyprien sitting up against wall with laptop on lap. Papers spread round. Jug on bedside table. Mother poured water into glass. Removed still-full cup. Plate of untouched toast. Repaired to landing. 'I'll leave you to it.'

Where to be? Chose spot at end of bed. Said his name several times.

Finally looked up from screen. 'Here he is, my favourite correspondent.'

'You're looking better.'

'Have you come to slap me around again? Does the violence of your emails not satiate you?'

Came round bed to look at screen. Word doc. Lots of black on white. 'Back working?'

'Had enough of doing nothing. I'm taking a leaf out of your book and writing everything down.'

'For the trial?'

'For the future. For after I'm acquitted. My side of the story. When they wake up from this delirium, people will want to know the truth. They'll be ready to listen to reason then.'

'Like a memoir?' Fear confirmed. Trial won't be end of calamity. Even verdict of not guilty won't satisfy him. New front will open. 'No one will publish it.'

'We'll see about that.'

'Will I be in it?'

Laughs.

'What about Mathilde? Anne-Laure? Pause and think about what you're doing. The impact it'd have.'

Slaps computer closed: 'You think I don't think? All I do, all day long, is fucking think!'

'So this is your new identity? Victim of the feminist conspiracy? The little guy who stands up for all the other little guys being oppressed by the new order?'

'Your words reveal the shallowness of your feelings. And, frankly, the paltriness of your imagination.'

'What's next, macho podcasts and trolling?'

'Get out! I won't listen to your moaning voice one second longer!'

Made for door. But couldn't leave: 'Why the hell are you doing this?'

Computer open again. Face illuminated. Deep lines around mouth. Troughs under eyes. 'I said, get out.'

'Why are you putting yourself through a trial you can't win? You should've pleaded guilty to the lesser charges and cut a deal. I can't know if you've done everything you've been accused of. But I don't believe you're entirely innocent, and a jury won't believe it either.'

Closed eyes. Swallowed. Waiting for me to disappear. 'Finished?'

'The trial doesn't start for months. The end of March next year, I read. Are you going to stay here till then, stressing your mother out? Hasn't she enough on her plate already, without having to deal with you too?'

Pulled covers up as far as chest. Eyes pinned shut. Locked out.

'I want you to know something, Cyprien. I didn't retract my earlier statement. I thought about it. Several times I was on the brink. But then the news broke about the charges, and it was too late. So this is the end of it for me.'

Out. Closing door behind me. His voice following after: 'You don't have to worry. I forgive you all the wrong you've done me.'

Downstairs. Table set for coffee. Lingered on my feet. Itching to make exit.

Mother: 'That was quick.'

'I have to get back to Paris. I'll drop in again soon.'

Holy helping father to eat biscuit. Holding plate under chin while he bites. Then tipping over-milked coffee past lips. Washed around mouth. Noisily gulped down. 'He shouldn't be having either. But he won't appreciate seeing you get some, if he doesn't get any himself.'

Coffee and biscuits right now: headache or even vomit. Out of politeness sat down, accepted both. TV beyond enormous. Tuned into consumer-protection programme *It Could Happen to You*.

Me: 'Perhaps we might turn it down a bit?'

Holy: 'Oh, he won't like that.'

Mother: 'We could move to the garden, but it's cold there.'

Put our coats back on. Went out back. Holy brushed off bench. Brought out second helpings of coffee. Then went back inside. Stayed there. Sharing seat with mother. Spoke about garden. What had recently disappeared. What would reappear in spring. Told her I'd known nothing about plants till I read Rousseau. For a book I was writing.

'My son has published ten books.'

'Closer to fifteen.'

'A life's work. What will become of it now?'

From living room sound of father calling out in distress. Mother rushed to back door. Opened it. Paused there. Looking in while Holy tackled situation taking place inside.

'He might just be hungry for his lunch.'

Things settled down. Closed door. Came back to bench. This time chose not to settle. But to perch on edge. In readiness for another trip inside.

'I'm glad my husband is unable to comprehend what's going on. It would've killed him.'

'He'll recover.'

'Oh no, he has –'

'I meant your son. Cyprien will get better. It's best to stay positive. The process isn't a foregone conclusion. It might go his way. That happens too.'

'That we're putting men on trial for nothing more than gallantry. What kind of society are we living in? Somewhere along the line, we took a wrong turn. We've lost all sense of perspective.'

'I'm most concerned about what will happen after the trial. Even if he gets off, he's going to need a lot of support. They might not give him his job back. A change of career could be on the cards. He may need to go into something unrelated to writing and books. In any case, he's lucky to have you.'

Heavy evergreen foliage by garden walls. Doesn't allow eye to penetrate. In Plaisir people don't worry about opening perspectives. They want to be separate from everything that might trouble or afflict them: '*Perish if you will, but I'm safe.*' Sound of crunching pebbles. Car pulling into driveway.

Me: 'Sounds like you have another visitor.'

Mother: 'Cyprien's daughter visits us from time to time. She likes to check in and see how we're doing.'

'Is that her now?'

'Oh no. She hasn't come since Cyprien has been here. She phones but won't speak to him. I wish she would.'

Doorbell. Extra-loud. Holy shouted out: hands full. Mother went. Checked on my phone for trains back to city. Wondered nervously about how I'd play it if caller did turn out to be Anne-Laure.

Mother returned accompanied by Cyprien's old schoolfriend Arthur. Shook hands. Unthinkingly checked for wedding ring: none.

'We met twenty years ago, at a party in Cyprien's flat.'

Face of not remembering: 'Where are all his party friends now?'

Here to drive Cyprien to police station. Part of bail conditions. Must report twice a week. Mother went to get him out of bed.

Me: 'I should make tracks.'

Arthur: 'They had to remortgage the house to post bail.'

Looked at phone: 'My train leaves in a few minutes. I'm sorry.'

'We can drop you off en route.'

'That's all right, I can walk.'

Cut through living room. Grinned goodbye at Holy, who was sitting on armrest of armchair. Holding father's hand. Arthur followed me to hallway. Awkward. Didn't have knack with door. Nor did he leave me enough room to get past.

Paused on doorstep to zip up coat against cold.

Arthur: 'Mathilde is evil. She lit this fire.'

From upstairs, mother's voice goading Cyprien into bathroom to wash face.

Me: 'I'm in a rush.'

Arthur: 'I warned Cy not to marry her. But he had the scent of money in his nose. I don't blame him, it's tempting, but he's paying dear for it now.'

'I think Anne-Laure is the real victim in this.'

Spat on ground. Right there. In space between our feet. Glistening glob: 'Do me a favour. None of this would have happened without that little slut's say-so.'

Letter 75: GAVIN MULVANY to CYPRIEN ABREO

Paris, 25 November 2022

It just occurred to me that in fact I met Arthur a second time in 2002. One evening during that terrible period when you were blocking me out of your life, I was having dinner in the Chinese restaurant opposite your building – at a table by the window, so that I could keep an eye on your front door, with the hope of catching up with you and resolving our misunderstanding – and I noticed an old, cheap car, of which there were few in this area, drive past slowly, then pause for a moment at your address, before moving on down the road and turning the corner. I only noticed the car because I'd seen it pass by, in the same scoping manner, just a minute before. When it came round again, I made sure to get a good look at the driver, and, although in the dark I only had a general shape to go on, I could have sworn it was your childhood friend.

This time the car stopped before the junction and switched on its hazard lights. I paid my bill and got out in time to see Anne-Laure emerging from your door, apparently in a rush, one arm in her jacket, the other searching behind her for the errant sleeve. She reached the car half running, then fairly dived into the passenger seat. I remember thinking to myself, As long as the lights are flashing, I still have time.

I knocked on the window on the driver's side, expecting it to be rolled down. Instead I had to make do with a play of shadows through the glass. Then Anne-Laure's voice, muffled but quite comprehensible, telling Arthur to put his foot on it. To get her out of here. To run 'that wacko' over if need be.

Letter 76: GAVIN MULVANY to
ANNE-LAURE ABREO-GOUDICHAUD

Paris, 25 November 2022

I found a work address for you online. I hope it's still valid. What am I to say? I went to visit your father in Plaisir this morning, which drew into memory the happier times he and I shared as friends, and of which you were so often part. In particular that day – I doubt you ever think about it – when we, the three of us, met by chance at the Jardin des Plantes. You were there to complete an assignment for your biology tutor while I happened to be passing through on one of my regular walks, and we bumped into each other outside the hothouses. Then your father, whom I texted to tell of the coincidence, came to join us. After viewing the exotic plants, we took a break from the humidity, and from the hot sun outside, in the Mineralogy Gallery. We ended up spending most of the afternoon there, in the dark, peering at the spotlit specimens of crystals, gems and other stones, and, animated by your father's prompts, contemplating the duration of non-human things. Following that, we decided to get some couscous at the nearby mosque. At the table next to ours an extended family was celebrating the birthday of a boy no older than four or five. I was struck by the fuss the adults were making of this lad. There seemed to be no moment in which he wasn't being beamed at or showered with praise. When I commented upon this, in order to contrast it to my own parents' approach to me, which had been marked by a dread of being seen to spoil me, your father shook his head sadly.

'That's such a pity,' he said. 'Those early years are so –'

He broke off then and turned to address you. What he said next came back to me today in Plaisir, and has prompted me to write to you.

'I like to think, Anne-Laure, that at the very centre of your psyche, surrounded by the clouds of changing pictures and moods, there's a tiny core, an exquisite stone, completely indestructible, structurally unique, which I planted there when I was raising you. And that no matter what happens between us, if we're separated, or if I disappoint you, or if I die, you can look in and see this stone, even reach in and touch it, and remember who and what it represents.'

I'm reminding you of his words in the hope that they have the same effect on you as they had on me. That is, that they help you see that your father's strategy of revenge – I'm referring to his plan to publish his version of events – is really a search for someone to keep him from causing further destruction. And there's no one this 'someone' could be, other than you.

MS Extract: from *Rousseau's Lost Children* by GAVIN MULVANY

Last edited: 27 November 2022

In exile in Môtiers, Switzerland, in 1763, feeling utterly rejected by his countrymen, Rousseau renounced his Genevan citizenship. The following year he penned what would be the last published work of his lifetime: a trenchant critique of Genevan politics entitled *Letters from the Mountain*. In 1765, after a campaign against him organised by the local Protestant clergy, which resulted in his house being stoned, he moved from Môtiers to lac de Bienne. Before long, however, an idyllic stay on île Saint-Pierre was abruptly terminated by an official order to vacate.

At this point, in desperation, Rousseau accepted an offer of refuge in Britain from Scottish philosopher David Hume. In England, Rousseau and Thérèse stayed as guests of a wealthy widower in his mansion at Wootton, Staffordshire. Initially ecstatic with their new home – 'Here I am as if born through a new baptism' – Rousseau hiked in the hills collecting plants and tried his best to learn English. But he quickly began to feel cut-off and lonely, and in a matter of weeks was overtaken by paranoid obsessions. In a long letter to Hume, which the latter subsequently made public, Rousseau accused his host, without evidence, of conducting a monstrous plot against him. Unable to bear his fantasies of persecution, Rousseau fled the safety of England in a state of panic, and returned to France – where his arrest warrant was still in force and the danger real.

First he lodged at Trye, seventy kilometres northwest of Paris, under the protection of a prince. Then he moved to Lyon, then Grenoble, then between the two to Bourgoin, where Thérèse joined him, and where they went through a form of marriage, not legally valid, after twenty-three years as a couple. As they journeyed together, he used an assumed name, Jean-Joseph Renou, while Thérèse pretended to be his sister.

It was now 1768. Rousseau would live ten more years. Throughout this final phase of his life, he was convinced that his former companions in the vanguard of the Enlightenment, assisted by Voltaire, who had always loathed him, were in league with his political enemies in a vast network of conspiracy against him: a republic of hostility. Probably as a result of this stress, Rousseau's health worsened. He complained of a swollen stomach, headaches, heart palpitations, a feeling of suffocation, ringing in the ears and insomnia. While staying at a farmhouse near Bourgoin, he resumed his country rambles, but these expeditions seemed only to aggravate his various complaints. As he walked, he ruminated, which caused him to become ever more enslaved to his fantasies of victimhood. He had come to believe, however, that instead of fleeing France again to escape his enemies – whose allies, in any case, were in place all over Europe – he had to confront them directly in their Paris stronghold.

Rousseau and Thérèse arrived in the capital in June 1770 and installed themselves in a small flat on their old street, rue Plâtrière, where they waited for an arrest that never came. In fact, it quickly became clear that Rousseau could move around the city with impunity. So long as he stayed out of trouble, the government had no wish to disturb him. Nevertheless – his paranoia by now too deeply rooted to relinquish – he remained wary of public attention and resumed a life of seclusion.

Rue Plâtrière, being right in the city centre, was noisy, but the woods and fields – and all the other elements of nature that he believed were sensitive to him and with which he claimed to converse – were close enough to be reached easily on foot. Rousseau took day-long excursions, often though not always alone, collecting leaves and plants, which on his return home he pressed for beautifully arranged herbariums. His health improved. He ate good fruit, vegetables and fowl, obtained cheaply in an unfashionable neighbourhood. For money, he copied music. And, tirelessly, resolutely, he continued to write.

At this time, Rousseau's intellectual work took a decidedly inward turn. In exile, beginning in England, he had embarked on a major work of autobiography; now, in Paris, he completed it: his *Confessions*. In 1771, in an effort to rehabilitate his reputation, he gave readings from the manuscript of *Confessions* at sympathetic aristocratic salons. The listeners' responses ranged from shock, to bewilderment, to worry, to amusement, for, unlike the great memoirs in history, such as those of Saint Augustine and Saint Teresa, which stuck strictly to the writer's mystical experiences and relationship with God, Rousseau's *Confessions* included, alongside strenuous defences of his own character, extremely intimate details about his upbringing, his sexuality, his faults, his petty crimes, his abandonment of his children, all of which were shown through the prism of the author's unvarnished feelings: the first modern autobiography. The responses to his readings left him feeling that he had not been listened to – or worse, that, despite his monumental effort in the service of self-revelation, he had once again been misunderstood. For a long time he had been judged by his enemies without an opportunity to present his side of the case, and now that he had finally done so, his motives were misconstrued or disregarded, his appeal for justice dismissed. To avoid further indignity, he decided not to publish the autobiography in his lifetime.

His project of self-reflection was not over, however. In response to the reception of his first effort, he doubled down and wrote a follow-up. In 1776, after four years of work, he completed *Dialogues: Rousseau Judges Jean-Jacques*, which once again revolutionised the genre, this time by employing an innovative structure that bifurcated the author's identity into two characters, 'Jean-Jacques' and 'Rousseau', and showed one commenting on the other. Equal parts searing self-criticism and vociferous self-defence, the work evinces a craving on Rousseau's part for understanding and approval from the public, and a simultaneous impulse to avoid further victimisation by others by rehearsing an even more powerful kind of torture, that of the self by the self. Resigned to being ignored in his lifetime, consoled by the conviction that to be great is to be misunderstood, Rousseau did not attempt to have *Dialogues* published either.

Later the same year, Rousseau was knocked down on a narrow street by a large dog that had been running alongside its master's carriage. From this point on, his health began to decline. Sensing his own mortality, and resigned at last to his obscurity, he embarked on what would be his final, unfinished, and in many people's eyes his best, book: *Reveries of the Solitary Walker*. In this work, he presented each chapter as a walk ('First Walk', 'Second Walk', etc.), though, in most cases, he gave little or no attention to the location, or the time of day, or indeed the sights and sounds of the walks he purported to be on. Painting an accurate picture of his surroundings was not really the point. What he wanted to do, rather, was transmit a copy of his thoughts, as they came to him, and in the random order of their appearance, while he walked. His aim was to leave behind after his death a self-portrait so wholly accurate that it would obliterate, once and for all, the false pictures of him painted by his enemies, and – never too late – would lead to him being universally loved.

Letter 77: GAVIN MULVANY to THÉRÈSE LEVASSEUR

Paris, 29 November 2022

Yesterday afternoon I intended to pay a call on Mr Rousseau unannounced. I thought if I came in person, I'd be able to twist his arm into joining me for one last walk to the countryside. My research is nearly complete, you see, I'll be quitting Paris before long, and I don't want to leave things on a stormy note. Which explains why I happened to be going up rue Plâtrière at the precise moment that the man himself appeared with a packet of papers under his arm.

I pursued him to the river, then across to île de la Cité. On seeing him turn left onto rue des Marmousets, then cut south through the lanes towards the parvis of Notre-Dame, I feared that he was heading back to the foundling hospital, with the intention of causing an unnecessary additional scene. In the event, however, he made directly for the cathedral. Powered through the central door. Went hell for leather up the nave to the choir. There he found his destination, the altar, blocked by a metal grille. Infuriated, he banged on this obstruction with his fist. Called out for someone, anyone, to come and remove it. When no one did, he turned to me, as though I were an assistant whom he expected to be present but to be of no help at all, and said, 'I thought that on a Saturday afternoon, when the choir is deserted, I'd have an easy time reaching the altar and placing my deposit there.'

'Is that your deposit,' I said, 'in the envelope?'

He folded back the flap and pulled out a stack of pages: the manuscript of *Dialogues*.

'The only fair copy?' I said.

'What does it matter?' he said, roughly pushing the pages back into their covering. 'I've abandoned hope of witnessing its publication.'

He struck the metal barrier with the manuscript, once, twice, and I suspect he'd have kept going, until either he'd drained himself of his strength or the papers were ruined, had I not constrained him.

'Now even God's own table has been closed off to me,' he said, shaking himself free of my grip. 'The Almighty has become complicit in man's conspiracy against me.'

Mr Rousseau's idea, which I grasped only after a long and jumbled interrogation, was to leave the manuscript on the altar, where his enemies wouldn't find it, and where God, or failing that a kindly priest, would keep it safe and perhaps even bring it to the attention of the king.

'The ceiling above my head has eyes,' he said, 'the walls have ears. The holy statues subject me to malevolent surveillance.'

'Don't go overboard,' I said. 'Breathe.'

'The plot against me, which I previously saw as nothing but the fruit of human malevolence, I now can't help regarding as a divine secret. From being the horror of the human race, the laughing stock of the rabble, I pass to being persecuted by God Himself.'

'Come and sit down, we can talk it through. I'm inclined to think you're getting worked up over nothing.'

'The Lord is just, He knows my innocence. Yet His will, ever mysterious, seems to be that the world should take pleasure in spitting on me and burying me alive. Let men and fate do their worst!'

With that, he was overcome by a dizziness, like a man with apoplexy, followed by an upheaval, a spasm, during which he released foul curses that were, to my ears, distinctly out of character. I tried to calm him, to embrace him, to shepherd him to a pew, but he threw off my advances.

'At least give me the manuscript to hold,' I begged. 'I don't want the pages to fall or get scattered.'

'Get your grimy hands off!' he said.

Breaking away from me, he left the cathedral rapidly, resolving aloud never to go back in his life and surrendering completely to his agitation, which took the form of wild gesticulations and exclamations. I dashed after him, and for the entire remainder of the day followed everywhere he wandered, without any idea where we were going and without a firm grasp on the drift of our conversation, until, in the Tuileries after dark, he ran out of steam at last and had to lean against a tree.

'Let me get you home,' I said. 'You should be lying down.'

I was glad that you were there to take him in. Did he sleep through? I had an unsettled night, out of worry for him. Knowing that he's had similar episodes before didn't make observing his throes any less disquieting. This morning, wanting to see how he was, I passed by the flat several times, but didn't get an answer. Troubled by this, I scoured the vicinity and eventually found him in the arcades of the Palais-Royal, where he was, of all things, passing out leaflets to passers-by: 'TO ANY FRENCHMAN WHO STILL LOVES JUSTICE AND TRUTH. TELL ME AT LAST WHAT MY CRIMES ARE, HOW AND BY WHOM I HAVE BEEN JUDGED.'

'You're out of control,' I said.

'Help!' He whirled round in search of the very favour that, according to his leaflet, he no longer expected from the general populace. 'This foreigner is accosting me!'

'Enough for today, I'm taking you home.'

You weren't there when we got back, so I helped him climb the stairs. Undressed him. Put him to bed. Went down again and brought some water up. Prepared him an infusion. Lay a cold cloth across his forehead, which was burning.

'This can't go on,' I said. 'They'll take you for a lunatic and put you in Bicêtre.'

Now that he was lying down, he claimed to be too feeble to sit up, so I gave him to drink with a spoon. He rested, but when he felt himself fall asleep, his eyes shot open and he said, 'What am I doing wrong?'

'Shh, go easy.'

He turned on to his side and coughed some liquid into the pan that you keep there for that purpose, then he fell back onto the pillow. 'Do you know when I was most happy?' he said. 'When I was most free? Have I ever told you?'

'Hush,' I said. 'You've exhausted yourself. Tell me tomorrow. Sleep, now. Dream.'

Letter 78: GAVIN MULVANY to CYPRIEN ABREO

Paris, 5 December 2022

Of the violence that occurred in our relationship, the most detrimental was your ending of it. Ten days before Christmas, my flatmates told me – of course, I didn't hear it from you directly – that we, all of us, had to move out before the new year. I spent Christmas day alone in the flat, eating pasta and tomato purée and going for long walks through the subdued streets, though in the spirit of truce I avoided yours. My mother and my sister phoned from Dublin, and my father from Alicante; to everyone I lied that I was having lunch with your family and couldn't talk long. I received no word from you.

While still in bed the following morning, St Stephen's Day, I received an extremely unexpected call from an anxious postgrad of yours called Giorgia. She had agreed to stay in your flat for the whole week after Christmas to mind Coco while you were away, but something had come up that would take her out of Paris on the twenty-eighth and the twenty-ninth. She knew it was a lot to ask, but could I cover for her on those two days? Although she must have got my contact details from you, she didn't tell me if this request had come from you, or even if it had been passed by you, and I didn't ask. 'Of course. What are colleagues for?'

In the flat on the twenty-eighth, the changeover was fast. She was in a rush to leave.

'Just one thing,' I said, 'where did they go? Are they on the island?'

When she'd left, I took your family albums down from the shelves in the study, and removed a selection from the pages marked 'île d'Oléron'. The three of you, in various configurations, on a sandy beach (1992), on top of the old lighthouse (1993), at the breakfast table in the father-in-law's holiday house (1993), on a boardwalk in a fishing village (1995), at a restaurant called *Le Jour du Poisson* (1999), in front of the saltwater marshes (2001). Over the next forty-eight hours I made the arrangements: a train ticket, a coach ticket, a hotel room, an overnight bag, a map of local walks. When Giorgia got back on the morning of the thirtieth, I handed her back the key to the flat – 'All yours!' – and went straight to the station.

The hotel, at which I arrived in the dark after a full day's travel, was a white two-storey house with green shutters in the town of Saint-Pierre-d'Oléron, in the centre of the island. My room, which I had got thanks to a late cancellation – 'You were very fortunate,' I was repeatedly told – was the smallest and cheapest, tucked away behind a staircase, with a single small window looking onto the swimming pool, now covered for the winter. The five others were occupied by members of a large family from Bordeaux who were much amused by me and my solitude.

The next day, New Year's Eve, I got up before light and walked for two hours through the marshes to the eastern coast, then three hours north along the sands from Boyardville beach to La-Brée-les-Bains. The sky was clear and bright, the breeze almost warm. The lapping of the waves, a continuous yet undulating noise. It was dark by the time I returned.

The following morning, I cut through the island interior to the lighthouse at the northern tip. Then I came back down the western coast as far as La Menounière. A nine-hour round trip. I was surprised to see so much Mediterranean vegetation this far north: oleanders, eucalyptus, agaves and mimosas already in flower, not to mention palms, figs, oranges, even olives. Gradually succumbing to the impressions of my surroundings, I forgot about you and the question of your whereabouts and sat on the crest of a dune and looked out at the empty surface of the sea.

On the second of January, my last day, I followed the western coast down to Gatseau beach, at the southern extreme, then came back up through the wooded marshlands: ten hours, dawn to a little after dusk, during which nature seemed to embed your absence in its own magnificence. The gold of the sand, the bright green of the duckweed on the marsh water, the myriad shade and shape of trees moving in the breeze, the variety of herbs and flowers that I trampled underfoot, held my mind in a continual alternation of seeing you and not seeing you.

Stopping to rest on the bank of a marsh, my mind strayed to the period immediately after my father's departure for Spain with his new girlfriend, which my mother spent cursing his name and declaring what a bad father he was and how much she hated him, and calling him to tell him so. When this succeeded neither in bringing him back nor in expunging him from her mind, she sat me down one day with a pen and a piece of paper and ordered me to write him a letter.

'What should I write?' I asked.

'Do you miss him?' she said.

'Yes.'

'Tell him.'

So I wrote, 'I miss you.'

'Do you want him to come home?' she said.

I did, so I wrote, 'Please come home.'

'Do you want him to be with another woman, or with me?'

I wanted him to be with her, so I wrote, 'Please be with Mum again.'

'Do you want him to raise another boy, or raise you?'

I wanted him to raise me, so I wrote, 'Please be my Dad.'

I don't know if she sent it. If she did, my intervention didn't work. My father's love didn't return to either of us.

I arrived back at the hotel as night was falling. Conversing with the other guests at dinner, I savoured a feeling of deep calm, troubled only by the anxiety that it mightn't go away. Spontaneously, I booked an extra night's stay without knowing how I was going to pay for it. The pleasure I felt about this outcome was inseparable from the pain of feeling forced to take such a decision. During my walks, I had sometimes thought about how nice it would be to come back to this island every year, with you, for the rest of my life. Now I realised how gladly I would exchange such a life, which was of no interest to me, for the freedom of being able to leave, of being able to walk away without restraint.

The next morning I borrowed a bike and did a tour of the nearby towns and hamlets. In each pharmacy I found open, I bought a carton of Doliprane 1000mg, and in a supermarket on the road back, using the final bit of cash in my wallet, a bottle of Armagnac.

FREEDOM

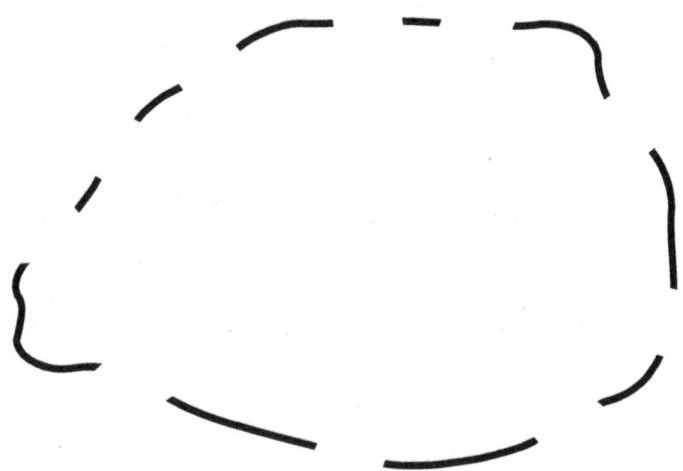

(*Le périphérique de Paris, walking anticlockwise: porte d'Orléans – porte d'Italie – porte de Charenton – porte de Vincennes – porte de Bagnolet – porte de la Villette – porte de Saint-Ouen – porte de Clichy – porte Maillot – porte de la Muette – porte de Sèvres – porte d'Orléans; 35 km: 8 hours, 55 minutes*)

Gratitude (II)

Letter 79: JEAN-JACQUES ROUSSEAU to GAVIN MULVANY

Paris, 23 March 1778

You are still here? Having had nothing from you in months, I thought you had left Paris without saying goodbye. My first impulse was to regret having befriended you. I could not reconcile this inattentive conduct with the signs of intimacy that you had given me on our previous meetings. I wanted to write to you to complain; I did not have the strength to do so.

The crocus you sent, with its long stem and corm intact, reminded me of how much of us remains underground, how little of us is seen, how surface change can both captivate and deceive. I have replanted it in a pot rather than pressing it for my collection, conscious that the troubles that rise up in me now are nothing as beautiful, nothing as purple as sorrow.

Letter 80: GAVIN MULVANY to JEAN-JACQUES ROUSSEAU

Paris, 24 March 2023

At the last minute, I decided to extend my stay in Paris. I should've written sooner to tell you. Will you accept an explanation now? I spent the Christmas period, when the seminary was closed, alone on île d'Oléron, retracing walks that I took there twenty years ago. Directly from there, I should have caught a cheap flight home from La Rochelle. My teaching at the university in Dublin was supposed to resume in January. And my loved ones were waiting for me and deserved explanations of their own for my recent neglect of them.

But on the island I realised that I needed a little more solitary time, and that I needed to spend that time in Paris. There was a chance that, if I left before completing a full draft of my book, I'd never finish it. And – my other, less fathomable motivation – I didn't want to desert Cyprien in the weeks before his trial. In all sincerity I hoped never to see him again, yet I felt obliged to be on hand, close by, ready, if for whatever reason he needed me. On the off chance he reached out, I wouldn't deny him aid.

My department manager in Dublin refused to extend my leave, even unpaid, so – the first expression of the full terror of liberty – I left my job. Pedro, for his part, said it was the last straw, he was out. 'I'm not going to try to justify myself,' I said to him. 'You're a free man. But when the time comes, when I've done what I need to do here, I intend to make it up to you.'

On my return to Paris, I booked myself into the seminary for a further four months and immersed myself in my writing. For the first time in my life I found real pleasure in the process, its monotonous, repetitive daily rhythm, and quickly made headway. I now have a completed manuscript and can say, with no pretence, that it's mine.

What comes next, however, I can't say. I can't construct my own story beyond the book. I have a ticket for a flight back to Dublin at the end of April. Unless I die beforehand, I'll be on that plane. I refuse to be in Paris when the trial begins.

Letter 81: JEAN-JACQUES ROUSSEAU
to GAVIN MULVANY

Paris, 25 March 1778

After a wicked winter, during which Thérèse was sick for a long time, unable to do any housekeeping and depending on me for her every need, we too have resolved to leave. Farewell, Paris, celebrated city. Farewell, city of noise, smoke and mud, where the women no longer believe in honour and the men no longer believe in virtue. We are seeking innocence again. We shall never be far enough away from you.

What we lack, as yet, is a refuge. Any place outside the city where we can survive on our means, without my having to do any copying, which by now is beyond my capacity. However I am treated, whether I am kept in a formal enclosure or in apparent liberty, I consent to it, provided that my wife receives the care that her state requires, and that we are given the simplest clothes and blankets, and the most sober food, until the end of our days. For this we will give everything we can in money, effects, and rent.

Pray, foreigner, do you know of any such haven, and could you, with all urgency, recommend us to its owner? Have you any influence in society that you could exercise in my favour?

Letter 82: GAVIN MULVANY to JEAN-JACQUES ROUSSEAU

Paris, 25 March 2023

You're asking the wrong man, Jean-Jacques. When it comes to sway in the social world, I'm as destitute as you. But I have an idea. As you might have heard, Voltaire has returned to Paris. The Comédie-Française is putting on his latest play, and it's rumoured that, one of these nights, the man himself is going to attend. Why don't we go together? Lend our eyes and ears to the tumult? Before we bow out of Paris, let's take one final look at the epitome of its decrepitude and be confident that we're truly not fitted for it. And, while we're at it, we can put word out about your hunt for a retreat. No doubt there'll be a sea of great thinkers and wits, lawyers, men of letters and women who can be relied upon to give us a hearing.

Letter 83: GAVIN MULVANY to THÉRÈSE LEVASSEUR

Paris, 29 March 2023

I've suggested to your husband that we go to this Voltaire play that everyone's talking about. His pride, I suspect, has prevented him from getting back to me. I do understand why he mightn't want to appear at the theatre himself. But I'm also inclined to think that he'd welcome an accurate eyewitness account, transmitted to him by two people he trusts, of what's happening there, both on stage and off. Moreover, without him there to sabotage our approaches, you and I are more likely to evoke sympathy for your cause. If you were well enough, I could pick you up tomorrow at four.

MS Extract: from Rousseau's Lost Children by GAVIN MULVANY

Last edited: 30 March 2023

Like Rousseau, Voltaire was forced into exile for publishing irreligious and politically incendiary material. In every other aspect, however, Voltaire's experience of banishment was radically different from Rousseau's. Thanks to his great wealth, Voltaire spent most of his twenty-seven years abroad in splendid isolation in a country residence near Geneva. There he was assisted by his niece, who acted as his helpmeet, four gardeners, twelve servants and twenty artisans. He received so many visitors from all over Europe that he had to extend the already spacious house and convert barns and outhouses into guestrooms.

In this kingdom of his own, Voltaire lived as free from outside interference as it was possible to be in eighteenth-century Europe. He exploited this autonomy to undertake ceaseless literary activity, by which he steadily increased his renown. He wrote his most famous work, the novella *Candide*. He bombarded the church with condemnatory pamphlets, and waged long, expensive battles on behalf of ordinary people facing religious persecution. He amused himself by antagonising the Calvinistic fathers of Geneva. And all the while he was writing plays, producing plays and acting in plays. Thanks to this prodigious output, his name remained in the public mind in France, despite his absence. At the same time, the complex reality of the man was gradually superseded by the figure of an idol. To his countrymen, he became a distant, almost mythical figure, even more remote than the king.

At last, in his eighties, over a quarter of a century since he last set foot there, Voltaire decided to return to Paris. He was determined that his life should end with a bang, and the only proper stage for this was the city of his birth. In January 1778, the Comédie-Française agreed to perform his latest dramatic work, *Irène*, more out of gratitude towards its author than out of any enthusiasm for the play itself. Voltaire expressed a desire to supervise the production; he envisaged sitting in triumph at its first night. The young Louis XVI, despite his reactionary opposition to change, made no objection to this. The world had moved on, and many influential people supported the idea of Voltaire's rehabilitation.

Voltaire arrived in the capital on 10 February, planning to be there for six weeks; he would end up staying for three and a half months, until his death on 30 May (just two months before Rousseau's). On his first walk, on the quai d'Orsay, it was carnival time; passers-by laughed and street urchins jeered at this clown in his thick fur coat, old-fashioned wig and extraordinary red bonnet. In society, however, his fame guaranteed him a rapturous welcome. All of polite Paris – which did not include Rousseau – sought his company. In salons, coffeehouses and taverns, he was the centre of attention. On a carriage ride through the city, he was surrounded by a throng all straining to catch a glimpse of him through the window. Unfortunately no invitation to Versailles came, but a rumour circulated that the queen was going to attend the opening night of *Irène*, which indeed she did, on 16 March 1778.

Voltaire could not be there himself, for he was in a perilous physical state. He was passing and excreting pus and spitting blood: the advanced stages of bladder and prostate cancer (as the post-mortem would soon reveal). Aware that he was close to the end, he worried about the consequences of dying in Paris, fearing being refused a Christian burial. His doctor forbade him from speaking or having visitors, and bled him several times. Eventually, on 30 March, he rallied. He would, he said, attend his play that evening.

Letter 84: GAVIN MULVANY to JEAN-JACQUES ROUSSEAU

Paris, 31 March 2023

In the hall, which was a kind of private theatre, an auditorium in miniature, the stalls were full. Thérèse and I were obliged to remain in an alcove by the door, the only available space. On seeing her lean against the wall and struggle for breath, an attendant brought a stool for Thérèse to sit on. And indeed it was awfully hot and noisy, even for me. I used a fan borrowed from a passing lady to beat some air into your wife's face, and thought perhaps it was a bad idea to have come, that I should take her straight back home to bed. Right then, however, it became clear that Voltaire had entered the hall, for a huge roar rose up, and everyone strained for a view of him as he took a position on the second tier. Leaving Thérèse where she was, I pushed into the throng to catch a glimpse: in a box to the left of the stage, an emaciated figure in voluminous fur, occupying a seat in the shadows behind two elaborately dressed women. On cue, d'Alembert entered the empty stage and read out a eulogy in which he stretched our credulity by comparing Voltaire's poetic skills with those of Boileau and Racine. After this, there was an ovation, which went on and on and threatened not to stop, obliging Voltaire to remove his fur – he was wearing a black coat with crimson velvet underneath – and join his female companions in the front seats of the box. There he waved at the crowd, who added whoops of delight to their applause now that they could finally see him in the full light. He did not look well.

Then he was crowned. A member of the Comédie-Française entered his box holding a laurel wreath and invited one of the ladies – the voices around me identified her as the marquise de Villette – to place it on his head. A few raucous minutes later, the play began, which I watched by your wife's side, at the rear. It wasn't easy to make out the story. The actors did their best.

When it was over, the public applauded with unheard-of transports, and Voltaire rose to acknowledge their enthusiasm. Again I waded in to see: he was pale, exhausted, his eyes wet with tears. The laurel was no longer on his head, having slipped off perhaps, or been removed out of modesty or for fear of looking ridiculous. Then came a general gasp: the stage curtain was rising once more to reveal Voltaire's bust, brought in from the foyer and set on a pedestal, where it was now surrounded by the entire cast holding garlands and wreaths. An actress recited some lines, and then each player came forward and crowned the bust with green. By now even Voltaire himself had had his fill, and left.

I bundled Thérèse out in time to catch a glimpse of him being helped into his carriage. A throng of people – merchants, vagrants, stallholders, flower girls, mothers, who themselves couldn't have read a word of Voltaire's, who would have known him only by his reputation – had gathered round. They called for torches, the better to see this stranger whom they presumed to be acquainted with, and they shouted their approval of him: 'Long live the defender of the persecuted!'

Thérèse and I travelled home in a two-seater diligence. She leaned her head against the panel.

'Defender of the persecuted?' she said. 'That man, by his persecutions, blackened my husband's name and broke his heart while he was at it.'

Then she dozed. As she drifted in and out of consciousness, the city outside flickered between your century and mine.

Letter 85: JEAN-JACQUES ROUSSEAU to GAVIN MULVANY

Paris, 1 April 1778

Every artist loves applause. What does he do to obtain it? He lowers his genius to the level of the age. He submits to compose mediocre works that will be admired during his lifetime, rather than labour at sublime achievements that will not be admired till long after he is dead. If by chance there is found amongst men of average ability an individual with the strength of mind to refuse to debase himself by puerile productions, his lot will be hard. He will die in indigence and oblivion. This is not so much a prediction as a fact, already confirmed by experience.

As for Voltaire, I do not presume to condemn the honours paid to him in a temple of which he is the God, and by priests who, for fifty years past, have lived by his masterpieces. Who else would we have crowned there?

Note by GAVIN MULVANY

Paris, 28 April 2023

Concierge knocked on door. 'You have a visitor.' Downstairs in courtyard. Sitting at table under balustrade. Slow approach. Time to take in nondescript navy business suit. Blow-dried bob. Round-toed leather shoes with small square heels. Sheer tights at ankle. Flesh of foot bulging slightly. Stood up: heavier and plainer than teenage girl I remember.

Her: 'I got your email.'
Me: 'I wasn't sure you would.'
'I had a meeting in the area.'
'You haven't changed. How are you?'
'My grandmother told me you'd visited and that you were staying here. I wasn't sure if you'd already be gone. Am I disturbing you?'
'No, I'm just packing. Let's find a more private spot.'

Led her across the courtyard to secret kitchen. Observed by concierge. Put kettle on. Gave surfaces quick wipe. She sat. Put her handbag on table. Rested hands on top. Manicured nails. Clear varnish. Moved her gaze in criss-crossing fashion around room: 'Through my parents, I got to see a few of these retreat places in my time. Why are they all so, what's the word?'

'Dirty? Creepy?' Put her mint tea down. Spoon. Saucer to put used bag on. 'Careful, it's hot.'

Told me she was manager at multinational bank in La Défense. Lived near workplace. Neuilly-sur-Seine.

Me: 'Fancy.'
Her: 'I can afford it.'

'Partner?'
'Divorced. You?'
'Husband. Pedro. Admittedly we're at a crossroads at the moment.'
Steam rising from cups. Neither of us drinking.
'Have you talked to your father?'
'Not recently.'
'Will you?'
Free hand rummaged loudly in bag. Emerged with phone. Top of range. Jabbed with thumb. Passed it to me. YouTube video. Views: 761. Zoé Chauvin accepting 2022 Prix Médicis essai.
Handed phone back: 'I've seen it.'
'Have you read her book?'
Work of non-fiction entitled *The Veiled Act*. Personal narrative about experience of sexual assault. Interwoven with historical accounts of feminist politics. Plus literary analyses. Camille Kouchner. Christine Angot. Annie Ernaux. 'No.'
'I'm not a big reader, but I did buy that one because I remembered Zoé as one of my father's girlfriends or whatever.'
'Any good?'
Didn't respond to that. Instead: 'My father put another girl into that flat when you moved out. She had the whole place to herself. And there were others before you too. All shapes and sizes.'
Wanted to lean against wall. With head in arms. Turn my back on everything. Close my eyes.
Must have shown.
'What do you have to complain about? You were out for what you could get too.'
Got up. Brought my cup to sink. Hadn't touched tea: 'Maybe this wasn't a good idea.'
Watched me. Dark-faced. For time it took me to return to table.
Her: 'My fear was one of them would get pregnant.'
Me: 'So you knew what was going on?'
'I understood far less than I do today. But I understood enough.'
'Maybe it's weird to say, but whatever your father did, however he behaved with others, he loved you. That was certain.'
'Hmm. Jury's out on that. What I do know is, he helped me out when I really needed it. And I'm grateful to him for that at least.'

Phone lying face-up on the table. On mute. Recording of Zoé's speech still rolling. 'My way of saying thanks to him was not kicking up a fuss about her.' Glanced at screen. 'And the others.'

'I don't follow. How did he help you? Are you talking about the trouble in school?'

'I don't count the years or mark the anniversaries. I'm not sentimental like that. I don't regret ending the pregnancy.'

'Pregnancy?'

'I suspected you didn't know. I was pregnant while you were tutoring me. The first couple of weeks anyway. Then Dad helped me get an abortion.'

'That boy in your class? Was he . . . ?'

'Poor Milo. Really he was just a boy I admired. We kissed a few times. But it was more of a friendship, honestly. His parents were fuck-ups too, so we used to hang out and share war stories. He was beautiful, maybe gay, I don't know. I certainly never slept with him. He just took the bullet.'

'He didn't deny the charge against him when it was made?'

'Oh, he did. But no one believed him. Not even his own parents. There was too much evidence, however false, stacked against him.'

'He was expelled as well, wasn't he?'

Nodded: 'Don't know what happened to him after that. I heard something about a boarding school in Reims.'

Zoé's speech over. Now playing: ad for same phone that video playing on. Tapped pause. Still unsatisfied. Dropped phone back into bag.

Me: 'Arthur?'

Her: 'That obvious? How fucking stupid was I?'

'I can't believe it. He was your father's friend. Did Cyprien know?'

'He says he didn't, but I'm sceptical. How could he have missed it? I can forgive a lot, but this part is difficult for me to get past.'

'So they remained friends, even after that?'

'They had a blow-out and went cold on each other for a long time. But they never completely lost touch, no.'

Shaking my head in outrage: 'My God, Arthur was, what, late thirties, early forties at the time? You were fifteen. The man raped you.'

'I was a few months over the legal age.'

'Doesn't matter. With that age difference, you could've gone to the police, made a case.'

'He didn't force anything.'

'People, especially girls of fifteen, aren't always free and able to consent to sex even if no physical force was used.'

'I went with him freely.'

'You were still a kid. The man took advantage of you. You should've made a complaint.'

'That would have involved telling Arthur about the pregnancy.'

'Not necessarily.'

'Look, I just didn't, all right? Sometimes people don't do things, and it isn't a choice. You understand that, don't you?'

Hot-faced: 'I do. I'm sorry.'

Shifted round in chair. Removed vape from pocket. Then returned it without taking hit. 'My mother's upbringing was very right-wing. I wasn't sure how she'd react. I was worried she'd tell my grandfather and he'd start sticking his oar in. It was easier to go to Dad. He sorted it out. Brought me to the clinic and all the rest. I genuinely think he was happy to have this secret between us.'

'You kept your mother in the dark?'

'We told her we were spending the day shopping or something. Then afterwards we agreed to keep the whole thing from her. A promise I kept until June of last year.'

'What happened in June?'

'I bought Zoé's book. Right when it came out. Zoé doesn't use my father's real name, but it's obvious she's writing about him. After I'd finished it, I gave it to my mother. She didn't want to read it. But I kept pushing.'

'Why?'

'I don't think my mother is as faultless as she claims to be. She knew more about Dad's actions than she's willing to admit. I mean, she owned the flat where everything happened. I felt it was important that she read about the events from Zoé's perspective. Anyway, we ended up having a big argument about it. During which I told her about my abortion. Not something I'd planned to do.'

'How did she react?'

'How?' Phone out again. Click of nails on screen. Then suspended in front of me: screenshot of Mathilde's social media post accusing Cyprien of sexual misconduct. 'That's how.'

Transcript: Prize Acceptance Speech by ZOÉ CHAUVIN

Downloaded: 28 April 2023

In accepting this prize, I am one. An individual writer simply doing her lonely job.

And, at the same time, I am five. Zoé-Agata-Giorgia-Caroline-Louise. What links us? We are scholars of one stripe or another. We have jobs, though not all of us remain in academia or earn salaries for our work. Some of us live in family units, some alone. Against how some of the media prefers to paint us, we are not all petits bourgeois. Rather – call it chance, call it getting on – we, from our different starting points, found refuge in literature.

Officially we are intellectuals; to ourselves we are simply persons of judgement. And nonetheless we, as younger women, found ourselves trapped, used, disliked, disdained, assaulted by men. Notably by one man, the same man, operating in a system designed by men to enable and protect men like him.

We cannot say that we were not forewarned. When we were starting out, the 'whisper network' told us who to steer clear of, or, if that was not possible, to tolerate at arm's length. As astute as we were, as geared up, we were also young and ambitious, keenly aware of how difficult it was to advance in the academic sphere and eager to show ourselves to be above gossip and hearsay. Regrettably, as a result, we were slow to become cognisant of, and subsequently reluctant to condemn, the manipulation, control and abuse that we suffered. Advanced degrees, it transpires, do nothing to reverse a repression so perfect that it is not felt by the woman who endures it, that is unconsciously accepted by her, thanks to a sexist upbringing spanning many long years, followed by a chauvinistic priming in the so-called institutions of enlightenment.

Since we formed this alliance, we have been meeting regularly, always the five of us together, to discuss what happened to us and how we ought to deal with its legacy. Do you think we do this because we care more about our abuser than about each other? Wrong. Society sells confusion and fear that discourages women from joining forces in the way we have done. At our meetings, each of us becomes the pupil of whichever one of us can best teach her what she needs to learn. What wounds are we afraid to bring out into the open? What are we holding back, out of shame?

Our first task was to admit the harm we did to ourselves – innocently – in going against the advice proffered to us and allowing our abuser into our lives. We shared our grievances with each other, before asking each other what we should and could have done differently. In the heat of this exchange, we found ourselves revealed in a common anger, and we discovered the courage to suspect and criticise each other, going on from accusing our perpetrator to accusing each other to our faces, and realising that we could tolerate this. It was possible, we saw, to take responsibility for the mistakes we made without having to let our abuser off the hook.

After that, the time of discipline began. The rooting out of what terrifies us. We owed it to ourselves to weigh up what we risked or what we stood to lose by seeking redress. What weapon might we use, and what weapon might we scorn to use? In our fire, our will was forged. Revenge: no. Just reward: yes.

Letter 86: GAVIN MULVANY to CYPRIEN ABREO

Paris, 28 April 2023

My last week in Paris, and Anne-Laure came to visit. When I got back to my room after our meeting, I took one look at the open, half-filled suitcases on the floor, and my clothes strewn across the bed, and realised that I couldn't stay cooped up here, folding and rolling; that I needed to walk. I grabbed my backpack and left again, this time heading for the metro, which I took as far as porte d'Orléans.

Staying within the city bounds, keeping as close to the inner edge of *le périph* as I could, I set off in an anticlockwise direction. To make up for my late start – it was already past noon, and I wanted to complete as much of the circle as I could in daylight – I maintained a fast pace, pausing only briefly at each gate to survey the scene, the incoming and the outgoing, and take a photo.

By the halfway mark, it was dusk, and the street lamps and the car beams on *le périph* had begun to take over. The transition was quick. By the time I reached porte d'Asnières, night had already fallen. Suited workers trickled out of the newly built headquarters of an electronics company. Directly across the road, hugging the ring-road wall, was a gypsy camp composed of ten or twelve makeshift huts. Spread out on the path was a rug, on which four men sat, one on each corner, shooting craps. As I passed, a throw had just come up snake eyes, aces up, double one, causing the men to laugh and squabble and throw banknotes down. Further along, in a semi-hidden place behind a hut, where huge rats scuttled around, a woman was wiping an outdoor table clean, and a man was sitting with his arms resting on his belly, waiting for his dinner to be served.

Is there a country, a tribe, that guarantees to every man the exact degree of freedom of which he believes he's capable? If you were the inhabitant of such a place, what sort of freedom, and how much of it, would you take? I ask because, when I picture you in prison, what I see is a man who keeps his habits. You make the bed as soon you rise. Stretch on the floor, first thing. Skip breakfast in favour of a strong coffee. Maintain an even, alternating pattern of reading and writing throughout the morning: an hour of one, an hour of the other, and so on. Take a siesta after lunch. Delve into more intellectual work till dinner. Write letters till lights out.

Would you agree that a man is free who gets what he wants? An independent life, outside the universities. An outlaw from the mainstream. Time to write the book you've always wanted to write. A novel, perhaps. A radical departure in style. No more restraining the impulse to speak. Or taking account of convention. Or feeling the need for acceptance by others.

If your inner, better self, your free self, were allowed to speak, wouldn't it want all this for you, and more? The only thing you'd lack that you haven't already lost is the ability to walk. To wander, as I'm doing, through the wilds. But this – I understand now – isn't real freedom. You can go to a mountaintop that you might feel your liberty, and not feel a thing. Equally, you can be stuck inside four walls and say no like the storm clouds say no, and you can say yes like the open skies say yes, and be so grateful for how free you feel that it's impossible not to live.

Letter 87: GAVIN MULVANY to OLIVIA HAYES
[Copied to BARBARA DIGBY]
[Attached: *Rousseau's Lost Children*]

Paris, 28 April 2023

Here it is. I should warn you, it's a departure from the plan. I did all the research, expecting to stay within the agreed lines, but as soon as I put pen to paper, I knew I'd veered off on a different track; I didn't seem to be in control. Which was exciting, but at the same time I was aware that I was creating headaches for you. Do you have any appetite for what you see?

Voice note: PEDRO SOUZA to GAVIN MULVANY

Dublin, 29 April 2023

Finn, are we going to be nice to each other? Sorry, I'm babysitting your sister's kids, trying to get them into the car. We need to wait a minute and be patient, okay, Uncle Pedro? So I'm sending you one of these. I'm coming to pick you up at the airport. Your mum has insisted on coming too – bit of a committee, sorry. Can you use your inside voice, please, Eli? Eli, Uncle Pedro is talking. We'll have lunch and then she'll leave, she promised. We need to talk. Did you finish the book? Fuck, I hope so. You're right, Eli, Uncle Pedro is sorry. I said I'm sorry, Eli. Kind hands – no hitting. Are they going to give you back your job? Strap yourself in. No, Finn, you sit in the black chair – you can sit in the grey chair on the way back. About all these emails, what should I be thinking exactly? You said a lot of things. Just let Uncle Pedro finish this sentence and then we'll sort it out. Oh, look, I have to go. Text if you're delayed.

Letter 88: GAVIN MULVANY to PEDRO SOUZA

Paris, 29 April 2023

My mother was at her most level-headed when she came to île d'Oléron to accompany me back to Dublin. Speaking to the medical staff and the police, she was moderate and sensible. Entirely free of emotional extravagance. She went in person to the hotel and, discreet and businesslike, paid what I owed, along with the extortionate and unjust soiling charge, without disputing a cent.

On regaining consciousness after the overdose, and understanding I was in a French hospital ward – on realising, that is, that I'd been expelled from the sleep that had been so pleasurable to fall into – I'd had a violent outburst: I'd thrashed about and pulled at wires and screamed 'No!', and had had to be sedated. The next day, when I woke up to see my mother beside the bed, holding my hand, I'd had the same reaction; not because I didn't want to see her, I don't think, but because I didn't want her to see me. After my discharge, in the rental car on the way to the airport, I watched her drive and wondered when her composure would slip and the fierceness would show itself again. As a kind of repudiation of her equanimity and all that it had so quickly and so effectively achieved, I was assailed with memories of her flipping out, losing her temper, being agitated, being unreasonable, being violent. Most vividly, I remembered the scene of my father leaving the house to move to Spain, and my mother kneeling in the hallway, begging: 'So you're going to leave me here with those kids? I was fine with it being just two of us. It was you who wouldn't take no for an answer.'

Back in Dublin, she put me to bed and cared for me around the clock for the entire week that it took to get me a place in a clinic. Once I was installed in the clinic ward, and she became a daily visitor, she remained unperturbed, dispassionate, practical. How was I feeling? Who had I seen? What had they said? What should she bring tomorrow?

'Your mum's classy,' you said to me after she left one evening. 'She has the right attitude.'

After a month or two – I can't say precisely when, though it was certainly long before anyone was talking about seeing measurable improvements in my condition – my father came to visit and brought with him my three half-brothers, whom at that point I'd never met. In they swaggered: the boys, ranging in age from five to eleven, wearing the same red-and-blue striped jerseys – the fucking absurdity of it – and my father in a V-neck jumper with nothing underneath so that the world could fully appreciate the deep lines that the Spanish sun had carved into his neck.

'I'm so sorry to see you here,' he said while bending over the bed to hug me.

Then he introduced me to his sons, who managed to look remarkably like him without looking in any way like me. They were awkward and didn't speak unless addressed, which I refused to do, obliging my father to rehearse two sides of a dialogue in our names: Gavin is like this, my sons are like that. Gavin likes this, my sons like that.

'Does Mum know you're here?'

'She knows we're in the country.'

'I mean here, in the hospital.'

'The boys and I wanted to come personally and invite you to Spain. Isn't that right, lads? My wife too would love to meet you. It's not right that you've never visited. It upsets me that you-know-who turned you off the idea. Probably forbade you to come. But we're all grown-ups now, right? The solution is in reconnecting and starting over.'

During all of this, you were passing up and down the corridor, hovering at the door, pretending to check on things. When they left, you succeeded in stalling less than five minutes before coming over.

'I've never met them before,' I said.

'That's bizarre,' you said.

'Oh, it's a whole drama.'

'No, I mean, it's bizarre that he chose to introduce you to your half-brothers here. If I'd known, I wouldn't have allowed them access. You don't need that kind of unexpected stress.'

'I'm glad that you see it too.'

'See what?'

'That I'm not the crazy one.'

If anything had the capacity to make my mother lose her cool at last, it would be learning that my father had come here with his other children. Had it been equally in my power to be silent and to speak, I'd have told her. But experience shows that there's nothing which I've less power over than my tongue: I didn't breathe a word. To this day she believes I've never met my half-brothers. Or, more probably, she knows I have and refuses to speak about it with me. With the result that there's a brute in her that for twenty years has lived in a box. Nothing or no one has ever driven her to open that box. Even in her worst frenzies, of which I've witnessed many, she hasn't dared to let the brute out, for half an hour, for two hours, to do its worst. I'd say it's about time that changed. I should help her free herself of that force.

I keep hoping, Pedro, that things aren't over for us. That, after veering off, we can come together again. I can imagine several routes that we could take. But you must understand that having children isn't one of them. You say that we're running out of time, that soon it'll be too late. I won't know what love is – these are your words – until I have kids of my own. Please: you mustn't speak to me of this sort of love any more, because I refuse it. For there to be suffering, good people, acting in the name of love, must do harm. And it seems to me that I'd be doing the greatest harm in the world to the feelings in my heart if I were ever to harm a child.

I don't need to try suicide again. I abandoned that tactic on meeting you. By your side, I set out again, trying to repeat an encounter with the world whose clarity, whose brightness, remained within me from childhood. Which isn't to say I don't still count on the future. As ever, I throw my dreams far ahead of me. But today I'd like to propose for us a duet: how beautiful life would be for you and me, as a pair, if we didn't expect children to complete us. How intact our bond would be if we weren't dying of loneliness because there aren't more people in the world who depend on us. Every day I experience for at least a few moments the feeling of having no one or of lacking someone to hold me by the hand and nonetheless going on. And just as often I picture walking beside you, being sustained by your hand, and feeling the gratitude that comes from knowing that all memory of us will disappear along with us.

Letter 89: JEAN-JACQUES ROUSSEAU to GAVIN MULVANY

Paris, 30 April 1778

A family, the Girardins, has offered us lodgings in Ermenonville. I – this man here so jealous of his liberty – have accepted, and I now reproach myself bitterly for my weakness. There is, however, no going back. Already I have told Thérèse to pack her things and have booked two men to transport the furniture. In three weeks' time we will be out of Paris, and I dare say we shan't be back.

It was good of you to drop in this morning to say goodbye to Thérèse, who seems to look on you as a friend to me. It is back to the island for you, so? I won't deny the presence of some envious feelings. Do you want to know where I was most happy? The answer is, on an island. One called île Saint-Pierre, in the middle of lac de Bienne in Switzerland, where I lived when banished from France. In all, only about half a league in circumference. But within this small space, all the principal commodities necessary to life. Fields, meadows, orchards, woods, vines. The house I inhabited, the only one on the island, was spacious and comfortable and lay in a hollow that sheltered it from the wind. On arrival, it seemed to me that here I would be more isolated from other men than ever before, more shielded from their insults, more forgotten, more abandoned, in a word, to the joys of idleness and the contemplative life – and so it turned out to be. I bade farewell to the world and took the decision to confine myself to this sanctuary for the rest of my days.

After living on the island for a while, I set out to describe every single plant on its surface, in enough detail to keep me busy until I died. They say a German once wrote a book about a lemon skin; I would have written one about every grass in the meadows, every moss in the woods, every lichen covering the rocks; I did not want to leave one atom of vegetation without a full and detailed exposition. In accordance with this noble plan, every morning after breakfast I'd set out with a magnifying glass in my hand and my *Systema Naturae* under my arm to study one particular section of the island, which I had divided for this purpose into small squares, intending to visit them all one after the other in every season. Nothing could be more extraordinary than the raptures I felt at every discovery I made about the structure and organisation of plants, and the operation of their sexual parts in the process of reproduction.

Once, I remember, as evening approached, I came down from the heights of the island and went to sit on the shingle in a secluded spot by the edge of the lake. There the plash of the waves and the movement of the water, taking hold of my senses and driving all agitation from my body, plunged me into a delicious reverie in which night stole upon me unawares. I was conscious of nothing else than what I beheld. In every instant I was being born again, and it seemed as if all I perceived was filled with my frail existence. Entirely taken up by the present, I could remember nothing. I had no distinct notion of myself as a person, I did not know who I was, nor where I was. I felt through my whole being such a wonderful calm that whenever I recall this feeling I can find no pleasure to compare with it. In a state of blissful self-abandonment I lost myself in the immensity of the beautiful order, with which I felt myself at one. All individual objects escaped me; I saw and felt nothing but the unity of all things. And it occurred to me then that I had come upon true gratitude, for I could be happy only in a happiness that was universal in scope; I could be happy only in the happiness of all.

Acknowledgements

Rousseau's Lost Children was born out of an article I wrote in 2020. My thanks to Nadja Spiegelman for publishing this article in the *Paris Review*.

The idea to turn the article into a book was Sarah Caro's. I am grateful to Sarah for seeing potential in my work and giving me her backing.

I am also grateful to Alexey Kokhanov, Iñaki Moraza and Ursula Carlin for their love and succour; to my agent, Rebecca Carter, for her continued guidance and many insights; to Rebecca's assistant, Tilda Butterworth, for making everything easier; to my editor, Nicholas Pearson, for his enthusiasm from the beginning; and to the entire John Murray team – Caroline Westmore, Katharine Morris, Talya Baker, Howard Davies, Sara Marafini, Kelly Llewellyn and Alice Herbert – for their work in refining, designing, producing and promoting this book.

A portion of the research – including the walks – was done during my stay at the Centre Culturel Irlandais in Paris. My thanks to Nora Hickey M'Sichili and Yann Le Cadre for helping to make my time at the CCI so productive.

Thanks to Owen Feeney and Juan-Carlos Cordovez for their hospitality during subsequent research trips.

Back home, a bursary from An Chomhairle Ealaíon (Irish Arts Council) funded a year of uninterrupted writing. My sincere thanks to Sarah Bannan, Audrey Keane and the entire literature team at the Council for this support.

Finally, *obrigado* to Guilherme and Caique for their help with Brazilian Portuguese.

When quoting from Rousseau's work in this novel, I have referred to the Flammarion critical editions in French, as well as Peter France's translation of *Reveries of the Solitary Walker* (Penguin, 1979) and Allan Bloom's translation of *Émile* (Penguin, 1979).

Lyrics from 'Ne Me Quitte Pas' by Jacques Brel are reproduced with permission from Warner Music and Fondation Brel. The translation is mine.